FREE

SPACE

F R E E

S P A C E

Edited by

Brad Linaweaver
&
Edward E. Kramer

TOR®

A Tom Doherty Associates Book / New York

FREE SPACE

Copyright © 1997 by Brad Linaweaver and Edward E. Kramer

This book is printed on acid-free paper.

Edited by David G. Hartwell

A Tor Book
Published by Tom Doherty Associates, Inc.
175 Fifth Avenue
New York, NY 10010

Tor Books on the World Wide Web:
http://www.tor.com

Tor® is a registered trademark of Tom Doherty Associates, Inc.

Library of Congress Cataloging-in-Publication Data

Free space / edited by Brad Linaweaver & Edward E. Kramer.—1st ed.
        p.   cm.
     ISBN 0-312-85957-0
     1. Science fiction, American. I. Linaweaver, Brad.
II. Kramer, Edward E.
PS648.S3F73 1997
813'.0876208—dc 21   97-2174
                                                       CIP

First Edition: July 1997

Printed in the United States of America

0 9 8 7 6 5 4 3 2 1

This book is dedicated to Robert and Ginny Heinlein, with special thanks to those who named the Heinlein crater in the Hellas Southeast Quadrangle of Mars.

Contents

INTRODUCTION

Free Space can refer to many things. A rent-free park. Elbow room. A sign on a kid's room saying PARENTS KEEP OUT. In this book, it refers to the life mankind will make for itself in outer space.

Free Space raises the question, Free to do what, and *with* what? A free human being must have some kind of property as a condition for making and keeping contracts. In libertarian circles, the debate always comes around to the land question. Political radicals of every variety have wrestled with this problem as far back as anyone cares to go.

Free Space is a science-fiction answer to the historical problem. Is it possible to own the scenery? Well, no one should object if the land you occupy was created by you! With access to energy and resources on a scale that inspires exaggeration, the frontier of the future is something very different from frontiers past. There are no native peoples in the asteroid belt. No aborigines on Mars. No troublesome animal species grazing on the moon. This time, there's nothing to get in the way. The solar system is easy pickings.

Free Space is a state of mind, and a metaphor, and lots more. Humans who live in space will have a different perspective from what Heinlein called the groundhogs. The Firesign Theater used to say the opposite of gravity is comedy. Let's take the joke seriously. I think that people who don't live at the bottom of gravity wells may be healthier and happier and smarter. Dare we commit the unpardonable thought crime of imagining they might be better than groundhogs? This book suggests that the kind of person who prefers living under tyranny is more at home at the bottom of a gravity well. But if people with this kind of mentality ever manage to function in space, we have a ready-made term for them: the Federation.

Free Space started out as Ed Kramer's proposal that we could put together a different kind of science-fiction anthology. It seemed to me that I could get things started by contacting a number of writers who had won the Prometheus Award (given annually by the Libertarian Futurist Society). Some of these writers had won Hugos and Nebulas; some had not. But it made sense to focus on the Prometheus Award because it honors science fiction that takes politics and economics seriously. That's how we began. By the time we were finished, we had attracted a wide variety of writers— including those who will be taking prizes home in the future.

Finally, I would like to thank my friend Kent Hastings (Doc Technical) for helping work out details for the *Free Space* universe, which covers a period of three hundred years. Plenty of time for any kind of story. . . .

—Brad Linaweaver

CRISIS IN SPACE

William F. Buckley, Jr.

Founder of the *National Review* and the most famous American conservative of our times (sorry, Rush), WFB has interests in common with libertarians (e.g., his opposition to the War on Drugs). His fiction includes a series of popular spy novels and a children's fantasy. Following is a piece of alternate history suggesting how a government space program might have led some men to find freedom on Earth.

Once upon a time in July 1975

This is Walter Cronkite, and we are continuing our coverage of the historic linkup between our own *Apollo V* and the Soviet *Soyuz*, which have been linked in space for almost three days, and are preparing now for separation, and reentry: The *Soyuz* will come down directly into the heart of Russia, and the *Apollo* will come down, as is the American practice, in the Pacific. Yes? Yes? Come in, Dan.

RATHER: There's something going on here in Houston, Walter. Can't quite make it out. The routine communication with Tom Stafford, which we have been monitoring, has suddenly gone into code.

CRONKITE: Gone into what, Dan?

RATHER: Gone into code. There is active radio communication between Stafford and Houston Control, but we can't decrypt what they are saying. I'm flashing over to Mike, who has collared Dr. Thornton at the communications center. Let's see what he has to say. Mike?

WALLACE: I have Dr. Thornton here. Dr. Thornton, what is the reason for the transmissions in code?

THORNTON: Well, Mike, our rockets are, er, equipped with, er, scrambling devices in case it should be necessary to communicate confidentially to Houston Control.

WALLACE: What would be the nature of such confidential communications?

THORNTON: I'm sure I don't know, Mike, but I suppose if Stafford wants to communicate privately to Houston, that means he doesn't want what he says to be broadcast live on CBS television.

WALLACE: You don't suppose he's reading from the Bible, and figures he won't antagonize the Supreme Court if he reads it in code?

THORNTON: We are not encouraged to speculate, Mike.

CRONKITE (cutting in): We have something from Dan Schorr at the White House. Come in, Dan.

SCHORR: There's a lot of excitement here, Walter. The President is reported to be in direct communication with Houston Control, and maybe even with Stafford. Secretary of State Kissinger came in from the State Department with a police escort, and James Schlesinger of the Defense Department has joined the huddle. There's something going on, Walter, but we haven't gotten the . . .

CRONKITE: Excuse me, Dan, but Roger Mudd has just located Dan Ellsberg in Santa Barbara, and he has something for us. Roger?

MUDD: Dr. Ellsberg, you have a code transcriber in your rumpus room, I understand, and you've been listening in on the communications from the *Soyuz-Apollo* mission. Can you tell us what's going on?

ELLSBERG: Well, Roger, as you are aware, I believe in the people's right to know, and the Supreme Court upheld, 7-2, the publication of the papers I gave to *The New York Times* in 1971. . . .

MUDD: Yes yes, Dr. Ellsberg. But could you tell us what in fact is going on right now?

ELLSBERG: Well, Roger, Astronaut Stafford reports that Cosmonaut Leonov says that he and Cosmonaut Kubasov demand political asylum, and refuse to release the linking module and land back in the Soviet Union. The cosmonauts want to land jointly with the Americans in the Pacific. They insist on being flown back to the United States. Wait a minute . . . they're saying something else.

MUDD: Yes! Yes!

ELLSBERG: They say that it's the only way they will ever get to meet Solzhenitsyn.

MUDD: Well, what is the White House saying?

ELLSBERG: President Ford is negotiating. He's asking Houston Control whether the *Soyuz-Apollo* mission could arrange to land in the Mediterranean and if we can get Solzhenitsyn to agree to fly back to Europe.

MUDD: What is Houston saying?

ELLSBERG: Something about our fleet in the Mediterranean not being big enough to cope with the situa . . .

CRONKITE: Roger? Roger! We seem to be having some, er, technical difficulties, ladies and gentlemen. Please stand by. I'm sure we'll be able to clear all this up in just a . . .

Screen goes blank—shows only the *Soyuz-Apollo* mission shield, with Russian-American handclasp.

NERFWORLD

Dafydd ab Hugh

Best-selling author ab Hugh (my partner on the *Doom* books, and writer of seven current and forthcoming *Star Trek* novels, the *Swept Away* series for young adults, and *Arthur Warlord* and *Far Beyond the Wave*) takes us to the near future and provides an invaluable service. If we try to live in a world of impossible security—all soft and fuzzy with no hard edges—we will never explore other worlds. Dafydd shows how a private-enterprise space program could get off the ground. The first step to Free Space.

Janna Wylie paced nervously in the third-floor concourse of the New Victoria—a garish hotel just a mile south of Los Angeles International Airport and eight miles south of UCLA, where her father's graduate assistant had written the original engineering specification for the refocused laser.

She nervously snapped the metallic slide of the floppy disk that contained that spec plus all the "blueprints," in electronic format, of the actual device, the Wylie-Hughes laser-launcher.

"Give me a cigarette," she demanded.

"You don't smoke," said her attorney, Avery Niles.

"I'll start. What are they doing in there?"

Niles looked at his watch, and scanned the preprinted agenda. "Probably interviewing Sachson about his aurora device."

Janna stared, incredulous. The aurora device was supposed to extract usable electrical energy from the aurora borealis. "Avery, that whole thing is a crock. It's a boondoggle."

Niles shrugged. "What does the Air Force know? The aurora has lots of colors, so claiming you can extract electricity from it makes some weird sort of sense to them."

"But they're scientists! Well, three of the consultants are, anyway."

He shook his head. "They're a special kind of scientist, J. W.: professors of empire-building. They haven't done any real science in decades; just piled grant upon grant until they became so good at it, they turned pro. Now they consult for the Io Corporation. Their scientific training stopped right around the time Salk invented the polio vaccine."

Io Corporation. Somebody's idea of a pun: "E-O," earth orbit. The corporation was actually owned and operated by the federal government, a front for the Advanced Research Projects Agency. Congress had stuck ARPA with the task of developing new ground-to-orbit launch systems; ARPA recoiled as if offered a cockroach hors d'oeuvre and passed the buck to an ad hoc "corporation."

"In any case," Janna groused, "Sachson was supposed to be finished three hours ago."

Niles looked at the agenda. "Right. I'm sure he'll be finished any moment now. You're next."

"Give me a damn cigarette."

"I don't smoke either. Where am I supposed to get a cigarette?"

The rococo lobby reminded Janna irresistibly of Versailles; the marble floors, intricate lapus-lazuli carvings, overstuffed chairs with tiny, bowed legs, and gilt-edged white paneling nearly overwhelmed her. She stared, feeling vaguely shabby in her business suit. Probably exactly what they intended, she thought angrily.

"Avery, they probably spent more money on these walls than I spent— "

"Don't even bother, J. W. Just remember with whom you're dealing. These consultants make about one hundred fifty thousand a year. If they want to meet at the New Victoria instead of the El Segundo office, they get what they want."

Sachson left the committee thoroughly parboiled, and they reluctantly called for Janna; Niles led her through a maze of twisty passages, all alike, finally opening an ornate, teak door and ushering her through an antechamber. Attorney Niles continued through the double doors at the opposite end of the room, Janna acting entitled in his wake.

"Members," said Niles to the startled faces around the gigantic table in the board room, "let's get this over with quickly. The grant is already approved, budgeted, and appropriated, was transferred to my client, and has already begun to be spent. What's the snag?"

The eldest "scientist" stood, nodded to Janna. With excruciating slowness, he introduced himself and the other four board members. "Professor Ely Eljer, Bernardo de la Paz Professor Emeritus of Physical Science, Harvard," he announced, delicately pointing at his own chest. He gestured foppishly around the room; Janna allowed the names to slip from her left ear to her right without alighting in the middle.

Niles introduced Janna and himself and repeated his question as the two of them sat.

"I understand," drawled Professor Eljer in answer, "that you want to build a laser-launching system for NASA."

"For NASA?" exploded Janna. Under the table, Niles kicked her ankle hard, and she shut up.

"My client's project has already been examined and approved," said Niles, "and it's administered by ARPA from funds approved by both defense appropriations subcommittees and already appropriated by Congress. NASA is uninvolved." In fact, only the House subcommittee voted for the funding; it was subsequently dropped by the conference committee in an elaborate horse trade. But Niles certainly was not about to admit that.

A wire-haired, Italian-looking man with a permanent five o'clock shadow leaned close to Eljer, whispered in his ear. The old man looked surprised, then coughed. "I apologize; some of us are also on the board of consultants for another corporation that works with NASA."

Time for your nap, thought Janna.

"As you know," continued Niles, "Ms. Wylie did not seek federal funding, either through grant money or minority-owned-business loans, despite being fully qualified for both. What is your jurisdiction in this matter at this stage?"

With the deliberate speed of a quaalude addict, Eljer typed at his laptop computer, then printed a fax he had stored electronically. Niles took the page, and studied it.

He leaned close to Janna, cupped his mouth, and whispered in her ear: "It's from EPA. They want an environmental-impact report. Somebody's working the other side in this."

Aloud, he demanded, "Why now? Why isn't the EIS we filed sixteen months ago still operative?"

"Recent regulatory changes in the EPA Recommission Act, Mr. Niles," explained a woman; Janna thought her name might be either Celia or Delia something. Celia-Delia was fat, nearly spherical in fact, and had dyed her hair orange for some reason. She wore a fire engine–red power suit cut exactly as Eljer's. A pocket handkerchief dangled unnoticed from her pocket, held only by a single corner.

The woman continued. "We're just not certain about the overall safety of the project: OSHA has expressed interest in the EIS, as well; so be sure to include a worker-safety study in Appendix Roman numeral twelve."

Unable to keep silent, Janna leaned forward, hands on the table (and feet far back under her chair, out of reach of her attorney's vicious kicks). "What are you worried about? We're not constructing anything more dangerous than an office building! There're no toxics, no nuclear-power plant. . . ."

"Oh, I'm sorry," said Eljer with a slight grin. "Apparently we haven't made our concerns quite clear."

"You're worried about safety—an accident?"

Eljer shook his head. "Not exactly, though that is a concern of the Occupational Safety and Health Administration. Include that study in Appendix Twelve as well.

"But we have a much more pressing concern, Ms. Wylie." He paused dramatically.

"Yes?" she asked, warily.

"The board has recently entertained some doubts about the eventual success of your rocket-launching project."

"You mean you're worried about—"

Celia-Delia rose slightly and dropped back into her chair, making a boom like a huge bass drum. "We're worried you might *fail*, Wylie," she announced.

Janna blinked. "Fail? Of course it could, theoretically."

"Precisely," agreed Professor Eljer in a surprised but pleased tone, as if she had done the ladylike (but unexpected) thing and admitted the terrible flaw.

"Listen, Wylie," said Celia-Delia, as gruff as Eljer had been pleased, jabbing a meaty finger. "Is there any chance at all that this laser-launching project could fail?"

"It's an experiment," said Janna. She hesitantly looked at her attorney, but he was Calvin Coolidge himself.

"Wouldn't you say, Wylie, that as an experiment, there is the possibility of failure?"

"If you already knew the hypothesis was correct, it would be a demonstration, not an experiment."

"Much better," said Eljer. "Can this project be undertaken as a demonstration, rather than an experiment?"

"A demonstration of something we don't know how to do?"

Eljer nodded enthusiastically. "Yes, that's it, precisely! Let's call this a demonstration. They're much easier to get past ARPA these days than an experiment."

"But that's just a cosmetic name-change. It would still have the same chance of failure."

Celia-Delia folded her arms across her ample chest, and scowled across the table at Janna. "Well, that's what we're worried about, Wylie." *Wait a minute,* thought Janna, *is that an orange wig she's wearing?*

"The theory is quite sound," Janna responded, trying not to stare at the woman's eye-catching, orange locks. "Seventy percent of the technology is off the shelf."

Professor Eljer spoke, his gracious voice warning Janna that a compromise was imminent. "We have actually done our homework on this issue, Ms. Wylie, and we have a suggested modification. Mind you, this is only a suggestion; please don't think that we're trying to take over your little project. Nothing could be further."

Janna stiffened but said nothing.

"We believe that the goals are perhaps just a bit too far reaching, too . . ." Eljer groped for the word, fluttering his hand. "Too grandiose for the first stage of this project. Would it not be better to scale back a bit, not shoot for the bull's-eye on your first time at the line?"

Janna furrowed her brow, trying to understand the analogy. "You want me to deliberately miss the target?" Niles kicked her again, and this time she did yelp aloud.

"My client is perfectly willing to rework the project into a staged series of demonstrations, if that's what you're suggesting."

Eljer sighed and sat back, obviously pleased. "Yes, that would be much more acceptable to this board." He looked around to the other board members. "Are we agreed about this? Is this approved?" They nodded assent, grunting and saying, "Aye."

"Good," announced the professor. "Then we shall expect to see a modified experiment design for a staged expansion on the desk in, say, six months? Would that be long enough?"

"Six months! I can have it for you in two weeks!"

Celia-Delia made her bass-drum noise again, like a whale breeching. Eljer looked worried. "Well, we don't want to rush such an important task as this," he said. "Redesigning a large, federally funded project in so hasty a fashion leads to the possibility of errors in calculation, in judgment, or even in the all-important presentation, for of course, we must present a copy of the redesign to ARPA and the subcommittee for reapproval."

"And OSHA and the EPA," added Celia-Delia. She leaned forward conspiratorially. "Oh, and let's not overemphasize the laser aspect in the first stage or two. All right?"

Janna stared for a moment. "It's a laser-launching project," she explained. "How can we possibly overemphasize the laser?"

"Maybe the first phase of the project shouldn't use a laser at all."

"Now that would be a hell of a laser-launching system. Should we design the rocket out of it as well?"

"Well," interjected Eljer, "it's your baby, but I don't think we need go that far. You may know best. Just . . . trust me on this. Let's call it a, um, Surface-to-Orbit Transition demonstration. SOT: I like that."

Janna opened her mouth, but Avery Niles clamped his hand on her wrist and cut her off. "My client certainly understands the importance of this task, and she will devote her full resources to it in order to bring in the redesign on time and within budget.

"But of course," he continued smoothly, "you are aware that adding an extra six months to a market-driven project makes potential investors nervous. Thus, the redesign may interfere with Ms. Wylie's ability to eventually attract private-sector investment. And there's also the extra six months of overhead to consider. I'm sure you understand our problem here without me having to use words of one syllable."

"Oh yes," said Eljer, "of course. We can offer a special six-month funding package at the prorated monthly; of course, in that case, we will have newly expanded female- and minority-hiring requirements, so any upsizing you do during this period should have a higher affirmative-action goal. This is not a quota, you understand."

"Just goals and timetables," said Janna.

"Precisely."

Celia-Delia gave Janna a wink that seemed to say, *We're all sis-*

ters here, dearie. Aloud she said, "We'll let you slide on some of the more esoteric demands, Wylie."

"Yes," agreed Eljer. "As you are a female or a minority yourself, and your executive vice president, Mr. Niles, is African-American, J. W. Rocketry is given a certain leeway in complying with all federal-agency requirements."

Niles still had his hand on Janna's wrist. He clenched his fingers so tightly that, for a moment, she thought he would break her arm. Frantically, she pried at his fingers. "Let go, Avery. Give me my arm back, Avery. . . ."

Niles spoke, his voice temperature dropping close to the interstellar minimum of three K. "I am quite certain that J. W. Rocketry is just as capable of satisfying your regulatory agenda as any other firm; and I know I am capable of steering this project as well as any other legal officer."

"Excellent," said an abashed Eljer, backing away slightly from Niles. "Then we're in agreement on the six-month timetable? Fine, we'll pencil you in for February. Of course, if you find yourself unable to meet this tentative date, please feel free to reschedule and apply for an extension of the funding package anytime after October thirty-first, when the continuing resolution kicks in."

They stood, shook hands all around. Janna's head still spun, two thoughts chasing each other like a pair of manic ferrets: six more months of paperwork before the first ceramic part could be fabricated; and don't emphasize the laser in a laser-launching project.

Her need to find a ladies' room suddenly intensified, and she almost bolted through the door.

As bleak February shivered the Los Angeles ambient down to a bone-chilling fifty-five degrees, they met again outside the New Victoria: the tall, thin black man with close-cropped hair, graying at the temples, and a beard that never looked properly prim and lawyerlike; and the short, stocky woman who kept her blond hair up and always wore a jacket that concealed thin, hard runner's arms. The black man, Avery Niles, carried a space shuttle lunch-box stuffed with a submarine sandwich and Japanese *mochi* rice cake.

"So what's your read?" asked the woman. "They've sat on the staging plan for three weeks, and I'm about ready to smash a shut-tle tile over Celia's head—or is it Delia?—if she tells me one more time how busy consultants are."

Niles contrasted his drippy sandwich with the pristine white-ness of the *mochi*, shaded by two faint red stripes along the rice cake. With a sigh, he replaced the sandwich and ate one of the pas-tries.

"They read it. It's basically fine, J. W."

"Basically?"

"They'll ask for some modification to the second phase, the proof-of-concept launch."

"The 'ground-directed acceleration phase'?"

"Yes. Clever, that."

"The glory of global replace," explained Janna. "I just replaced the word 'laser' with 'ground-directed acceleration' throughout the proposal."

"You can't say laser. If you say laser, then all of a sudden the Department of Energy thinks they should be involved, and you're crushed in the resulting turf war."

"Where do you get all this inside information?"

"From an inside source. The floors have ears."

Janna shook her head. "At least metals and ceramics are pre-dictable under extreme pressure."

The board had been in residence in the New Victoria for eight months now, and they had redecorated the conference room to American Business Blah; the new decor did not fit the Louis XIV concourse. Eljer shuffled papers nervously as they entered, as though the new appurtenances of commerce made him uncom-fortable: swivel chairs, hexagonal speakerphone mike, video screen, parallel and serial cable ports at every chair.

"I'm afraid there's a problem," he said without preamble as

soon as Janna and Niles sat. "We've studied your new phased-development plan. First, let me say how impressed I, personally, was by your attention to detail."

Professor Eljer squirmed, congenitally incapable of coming to a direct point. "Phase One looks good; no complaints about Phase One! I suggest you start on Phase One immediately, say within the next six to eight months."

Celia-Delia jumped in. "It's this Phase Two we're worried about, Wylie."

"Precisely," punctuated Eljer, as if the rotund Dr. Celia-Delia Something had put her finger on a nasty bit of business.

"What's wrong with Phase Two?" demanded Janna, a bit more gruffly than she had intended.

"Phase One is excellent," said Professor Eljer. "You propose a significant improvement in engine-nozzle design that will certainly increase the specific impulse."

Janna sat back in her chair. It rocked back alarmingly, and she squawked and grabbed table. "That design is necessary to give us sufficient thrust when the internal rocket is replaced by a simple air-expansion chamber," she explained patiently. "The laser—"

"Ah . . . ," interrupted Celia-Delia, wagging her finger.

"I meant to say the ground-directed accelerator, which fires a pulsed beam up into the chamber from below. From the ground. This, um, coherent-light pulse superheats the air inside the chamber; the air expands, rushes out the nozzle. Nozzle go *whoosh*. Rocket go up." She held up her index finger, palm inward, and pointed up toward the ceiling in a gesture that, had she used a different finger, would have meant something entirely different.

"We understand that, Wylie. But would you get more thrust if, instead of this ground-directed thingie, you simply retained the on-board engine from Phase One?"

Janna sat in silence for a moment, counting every irrational number from zero to one. "If we do that," she said, "then all we have done is marginally improve the nozzle on an existing chemical rocket."

Eljer nodded. "An improvement that will give us at least one point five more seconds of impulse," he said.

"But the point is to make a laser-launching system! No, I will not say 'ground-directed accelerator'!"

"There's nothing wrong with improving nozzle efficiency."

"It's an engine! A rocket engine! There's no technological breakthrough at all, don't you understand? I plan to buy the damned thing from MacDAC!"

"A one-point-five-second improvement represents quite a breakthrough, Dr. Wylie."

"I don't have a doctorate." Janna felt her heart rate speed up as if she were in an aerobics class. She felt faint. "Members, consultants, whatever I'm supposed to call you, the whole point of this proposal is to develop a radically new launching system, right? Isn't that what first Merovadek, then Wharton pushed through Congress?"

Niles spoke up for the first time, his icy voice sending chills along Janna's spine. "Dr. Eljer; President Merovadek and the national security advisor, Harry Johns, helped Chairman Reemer draft the National Launcher Act specifically to develop technology away from chemical rockets—disintegrating totem poles, I believe he called them. Do you remember that?"

Eljer cleared his throat, then tugged at his white beard in agitation. "We are aware of the wording of the act, yes."

"Do you recall Chairman Paige Reemer's speech last term, when the act passed?"

"Reemer—Reemer . . . chairman of . . . ?"

"Chairman of the House Subcommittee on Veterans' Affairs, HUD, and Independent Agencies," snapped Niles impatiently. "NASA's appropriations subcommittee—you remember? He specifically referred to *ground-based launching systems.*" Niles lowered his brow and deepened his voice menacingly. "Do you know who wrote that paragraph?"

Eljer looked at Celia-Delia, who stared at the faceless, nameless, anonymous others of the board of consultants, shills whose only purpose was to fill out the roster of the operating budget. Either nobody was able to guess, or nobody wanted to admit the obvious.

"I have crafted answers for Paige before," said Niles. "In this case, the wording is almost completely mine, with some minor rewriting by his science-and-technology aide, Alicia Kyger. I think we may take it that the legislative intent was not to produce a slightly more efficient chemical-rocket engine."

Eljer shook his head. "The decision is out of our hands, anyway. We're just an advisory board. You'll have to take it up with the Io Corporation Board of Directors."

"Who made the decision?" asked the attorney.

"Director Andrew sent us a memo about this last week. I don't know who on the board voted to cancel the ground-directed acceleration phase."

Niles stood, closed his attaché case with a resounding *snick,* then spun the combination lock. Taking her cue from her friend and attorney, Janna Wylie also stood, tucked her own leather case under her arm, and strode to the door. She was still shaking from the adrenaline rush.

"People," said Avery Niles, "we shall take this up at a higher level. Thank you very much for your time." He exited quickly, hustling Janna out ahead of him.

Twice she opened her mouth to ask what they would do next, but both times he hushed her until they had taken the elevator down to street level and debouched onto the street itself.

"On to El Segundo?" she asked at last, thinking of the offices that Io Corporation kept in one wing of the building owned by the Aerospace Corporation, yet another bogus corporation, set up and run by the Air Force. Rumor had it that the Air Force technowonks did not want Io Corporation in the building . . . and Io would have been equally glad to get their own location; but ARPA had fixated upon the building as a cost-saving measure, and the two "corporations" fought a never-ending feud.

"El Segundo?" asked Niles in surprise. "What for? Bill Andrew doesn't wipe his ass on his own authority. We've been 'Perryed,' and I can guess by whom: Lyle Ansel, the Gentleman General, who runs the numbers for ARPA."

"But we were already approved by ARPA. And the subcommittee approved the funds."

"And budgeted and appropriated and transfered some of it. I know; I was there, remember?"

"So now ARPA's just going to sit on the rest of the cash? How can they do that if Congress voted for it? Or VA/HUD, anyway."

The consummate insider smiled faintly. "Ansel can do it because Congress is in recess, and our godfathers are all back in their own districts, thinking about starting their campaigns. Nobody's got any brain cells to spare to worry about J. W. Rocketry."

"Why is he trying to kill us?"

Niles winked. "Maybe he wants to go work for Huge Aircrash when his thirty years are up."

"So what do we do now, *kemosabe?*"

"Pack your bags, J. W. dearest. We're hauling ass to my old hometown."

"Washington?" Janna shuddered at the thought.

"You betchum, boss lady. The Pentagon."

"Christ, we have to talk to some general? All I want to do is build a laser-launching system. I even know how to do it right now, with existing technology!"

"Nope; a civilian employee of the Office of the Secretary of Defense. Ansel's boss. At this point, Bud Netras is our man. You'll like him; ex-astronaut."

"That's good."

"That's bad. He was the hatchet man who wrote the report that killed the Pegasus . . . you know, the air-launched rocket off the B-52. If we can't shake him out of his tree, then we rattle Chairman Reemer's cage. A call from the chair of space appropriations should concentrate ARPA's priorities wonderfully."

"Good?"

"Bad. Reemer's actually got some competition in the upcoming election for a change, because of the House health-insurance-

kickback scandal. He might be too busy putting out fires in Poughkeepsie to bother sitting on Ansel's head."

"Then what?"

"Then we lose and Ansel wins."

"Jesus. Well, there's always Plan Z."

Niles raised his eyebrows, waited.

"We kill and eat him," Janna explained.

Niles hooked them a MAC flight on an Air Force 707. The seats
ran along the sides of the fuselage, surrounding a central mountain of electronics equipment; but other than that and a camouflage
paint job, it was a normal airliner.

The ground had a fine coat of snow, but the weather was clear;
after five hours in the air, the engineer and her attorney landed at
Andrews Air Force Base without incident.

They summoned a taxi to the gate, then cruised northwest along
Pennsylvania Avenue. As they left Andrews and approached the
city, Janna leaned back with a sigh. "Where do we stay? I couldn't
get a room."

"I grew up about three miles due north of here in Fairmont
Heights. My little sister still teaches school there; we'll stay at the
old homestead."

"So after I see the sights, what's the game plan?"

"Can I trust you to navigate to the White House and the Lin-
coln Memorial by yourself? I have to call Netras and bully him into
an appointment. I'll take you to a great steak place for dinner."

Janna sighed. She was nominally Niles's boss; but he was inside and she was forever on the outside looking in.

She spent the day riding buses and the Metro; the high, barrel-
vaulted stations intrigued her, as did the fact that there was no graf-
fiti . . . mostly because passengers queued in the middle, far away
from the walls. She stared curiously at the White House and the

omnipresent protesters in Lafayette Park: One held a sign reading
DON'T ARM THE HEAVENS! The reverse read NO MON Y INTO SPACE," the
E in *Money* disappearing behind the thick, wooden staff that held
the sign. The E in *Space* was crammed in as an afterthought.

She looked at so many white mausoleums that they blurred together. She haunted Foggy Bottom for a while, hoping to catch a
glimpse of the president jogging, then gave it up as a bad job when
the sun sank low.

Janna waded into the mainstream at Seventeenth and Constitution at the north end of the Mall, shoved some homeless leeches
out of the way with a lusty curse favoring the free market, and
flagged a cab. "Um . . . Ebbit's Grill—you know where that is?"

The cab driver responded in an incomprehensible pidgin but
seemed to know where she was going. She raced away like a test
pilot, sailing through traffic circles at a giddy pace. Janna gripped
the "panic strap," and fixated on the woman's hack license. Her
name contained no vowels.

When they finally screeched to a halt, Janna threw money at the
woman, then staggered into the restaurant. She downed a Black
Velvet, then a Sex on the Beach, before finding the inner Zen peace
to await Avery Niles with equanimity.

When Niles joined her, he had lost his usual mocking smile. "I
don't like the smell here," he snarled. "This whole city stinks of lob-
byists and blood money."

"Would you like some Sex on the Beach?"

"The only decision they make here is not to make a decision."

"Wouldn't some nice Sex on the Beach make you feel better?"
Janna was in a puckish mood.

"Long Island Iced Tea," ordered Niles to the waiter who had
popped up mysteriously.

"Very good, sir." The man melted away, leaving the two of them
alone again.

"Bud Netras is still shucking me, which can only mean that the
pressure is coming from on high."

"From Stilton? From Defense?"

Niles frowned. "Secretary Stilton, or perhaps the budget director. Or the VP or President Wharton."

"Wouldn't give us an appointment?"

"Oh, we have an appointment, all right. Eight o'clock tomorrow evening."

"Ahem," coughed the waiter; neither Niles nor Janna had seen him return. "Your drink, sir." He carefully placed a tall glass of brown liquid before Niles, then glided noiselessly away.

Janna waited until the man had vanished. "So what's the problem? All right, so he's a little skittish on this. Just let me explain how important a new launching system, a laser-launching system, would be to the country, to our entire space plan."

"We haven't got a space plan. It was killed six years ago, yet another casualty of the eventual Balanced Budget Amendment."

"Niles, that amendment's only been approved by twenty-eight states."

"Ah, I see you're up on your math. But nobody doubts that it will be approved by another seven."

"And so what if it is? HUD spends more every month than NASA spends every year. Why not trim the money from programs that aren't producing any investment return?"

Avery Niles leaned back in his chair and sipped his Long Island Iced Tea. "You're still thinking like an engineer, J. W. It has nothing to do with money."

"But didn't you just say the Balanced Budget Amendment?"

"Janna," said Niles. Janna fell silent, startled; when Avery Niles used her full first name, he was on the edge of exploding. "It's not about money. It's about cover. The amendment gives them the cover they've been looking for to kill these programs."

"Cover from?"

"From the last, few godfathers in Congress who actually care about going into space. The few committee chairs who still remember Kennedy's speech or Armstrong and Aldrin walking on the moon . . . they're powerful. They can really hurt a president, delaying bills or giving supposedly safe appointments the third degree and rigging a committee vote against them. They can still hold hearings and press conferences.

"But now, despite the best intentions of those who framed that amendment—and I personally know two of them who would be appalled by this unintended effect—now, the administration has cover, a political green egg to move ahead and 'balance the budget' by burning all the seed corn and strangling the infant space-development program in its cradle."

"Green egg?"

"Green light."

"You said 'green egg.' "

Niles relaxed, leaned his elbows on the table; his composure had returned. "Well, the whole thing does remind me a lot of Dr. Seuss."

The waiter returned, and they each ordered the largest steak on the menu. Janna resisted the temptation to ask whether Ebbit's Grill served green eggs and ham.

"So what's the shuck?" she asked, pouring A.1. Bold all over her steak, much to Niles's disgust.

"Do you have to ruin it like that? What shuck?"

"Netras."

"Oh. He gave us an appointment for eight P.M. tomorrow night."

"Yes?"

"Remember I told you he has a drinking problem? Well, that boy is one drunken sailor after six o'clock each and every day. There's no way he can make a coherent decision about anything at eight. He's telling us something: Come see me, but I can't do anything, so don't even bother asking. . . . Have another drink."

"No thanks."

"No, that's what Bud's saying: 'Have another drink.' "

Janna bit her lip. She was not much of a drinker: The two she had had that evening were enough to make her more than a little snockered.

"You want dessert?" she asked.

"Not unless they've started serving *mochi* in the last eight years."

"Take your hand off that bill! It's going to J. W. Rocketry, and I'm going to bill the freaking Io Corporation for those pieces of horseflesh."

They rode in silence toward Niles's sister's house, along Martin Luther King Boulevard, through the hell of the inappropriately named Seat Pleasant.

"So you actually saw President Kennedy?" she asked.

Niles nodded, nearly invisible in the dark cab. "Yeah, I heard his moon speech, too. Real moving; he converted me that day. Almost as moving as his funeral two years later.

"And I was at Howard University when King marched on Washington, too; the whole civil-rights movement exploded during Kennedy's administration and Johnson's. You know I went to a segregated school; Maryland was a slave state—still is, in some ways. We had colored schools, colored restrooms, the whole thing. Not as bad as the Midwest or the South, but at least the South was trying to change. Nothing happened up here until long after *Brown v. Board of Education.*"

"And then, after the schools were desegregated, you turned around and went to all-black Howard University?"

"Hey, what can I say? It was a good school in sixty-seven." They cruised the streets of Fairmont Heights, then pulled up in front of a large, wood-frame house. It had recently been painted, the lawn covered with a dusting of powdery snow. There were trees, but no leaves.

"Cherry trees," said Niles as they walked toward the porch, "just like on the Mall. Come back in a month and a half and you can see them bloom."

A large, black woman in a conservative dress suit opened the front door, held out her hand. Janna felt the woman's strength as Juliet took her hand; at first glance, Janna had thought her fat, but now she realized it was muscle. The woman was tall as well, towering over Janna's five foot four inches by almost a foot.

"Jesus," she said, startled. "You didn't tell me your sister was a bodybuilder!"

Juliet laughed. "Volleyball, honey. Avery, good to see you." She hugged her big brother, though Janna noticed that "little" Juliet topped "big" Avery by three or four inches.

Juliet turned to Janna. "I hope you like fish, honey, because we're having swordfish tomorrow night. Sorry I couldn't cook anything tonight, but Amble didn't even call me until you were here, at the air base."

Despite it being a school night, Juliet kept them up until one in the morning: She made Janna squirm by throwing her math puzzle after puzzle. Janna the engineer solved about half of them, the ones that required mere common sense; anything that required actual mathematical reasoning stumped her.

Avery bunked on the couch—Juliet said he was probably used to it, with the dissipated lifestyle he led "out West" (she made Los Angeles sound like Dodge City)—while Janna got the guest bedroom.

Somehow, Juliet was up and fooling around in the kitchen at six A.M., and she made so much noise, banging pots and pans, that even Janna struggled awake and staggered forth to wreck havoc on the low-fat, wheat-bran pancakes and turkey sausage. "No fat in maple syrup, thank God!" cried Juliet as she drowned her stack of "flapjacks" in sticky, brown goo.

Bud Netras was drunk.

Janna ought to have expected him to be; Niles had warned her. Against rational odds, however, she had visualized him sober and working on the J. W. Rocketry problem.

His office was perfectly square, on the inner ring of the Pentagon with an "outside" window that looked into the central, five-cornered courtyard and Ground Zero, a hamburger joint. Every file folder was neatly labeled; the cabinets were plywood and pressboard, stained to look like mahogany. Every scrap of paper on his desk was neatly stacked and labeled with Post-it notes.

Netras sprawled in his tanned, leather chair, holding a sports bottle that had probably not held mere water for years. He sucked Scotch through a straw.

Janna felt Avery stiffen as he entered the office. "Evening, Butter," said the attorney. Netras nodded in return.

"This is my client, Janna Wylie. Janna, this is Bram 'Bud' Netras, second assistant secretary of defense for science, space, and technology affairs." Niles frowned, his voice dropping into bitter, rumbling tones. "This sub-subcabinet position did not exist until we persuaded Secretary Stilton to create it. We were elated, figuring it meant a commitment to space."

Netras said nothing, continuing to sip from his sports bottle.

"Bud, we have a problem. My client has designed a laser-launching system to shoot a bird into orbit without stuffing it full of engines and propellant. The whole damned rocket is payload. She pushed it through space appropriations, got a grant, rattled ARPA, and got them to cut the check. The money is sitting in her bank account right now.

"Only trouble is, she can't spend it because the project is administered by Bill Andrew and the Io Corporation. You know them?"

Netras pursed his lips. "ARPA front, isn't it?"

Avery Niles nodded. "And the damned consultants he hired want to load her ship up with junk."

"They want to stick a rocket engine and fuel aboard," said Janna, quietly but firmly. "They want to bury the whole project. The point is to eliminate the rocket and propellant."

Netras nodded. "They didn't try to stop your salaries, did they?"

"You know they didn't, Bud, or I would have been screaming about it."

"So you can keep your workers on full time while we hassle this out?"

"Full time doing nothing!" exploded Janna.

Netras shrugged. "Avery, Ms. Wylie, they're under orders."

Janna opened her mouth, closed it again. She looked in confusion at her attorney, but he was as flummoxed as she.

"Bud . . . what do you mean they're under orders?"

Netras smiled, his face lit like a red lantern. "Here's to testilogical progress in the year of Clarke! We have here the big, unscrewable pooch, Avery."

Unexpectedly, Netras lunged across his desk, jabbing a finger at Janna Wylie. She jumped back, startled.

"Look, Wylie, can you guarantee success?"

"What? Of course not! It's a research project; that means we don't know whether we'll succeed or fail. If we already knew, what would be the point?"

"What indeed?"

"Nobody can guarantee results, Mr. Netras."

The man winked, leered at her. "I can."

"You can what? Guarantee success?"

"Thas' right. Guar-an-tee. No failures, nothing. Nothing but suck-cess."

Janna began to understand. "Oh my God," she whispered.

"The lady understands," said Netras confidentially to Niles. The second assistant secretary of defense grew drunker by the minute. "Can you guarantee she won' fail? I can! I can make sure no-nobody ever fails ever again.

"It's simple. So simple. We just refine . . . redefine failure as success and, voilà! Nobody fails."

Avery's mouth opened in astonishment. "Are you telling me, even while drunk, that you're removing the laser-launching from the laser-launching project just so J. W. Rocketry can't possibly fail?"

Netras shook his head. "Nope, pard. I'm telling you Stilton did jus' that. Remember *Challenger*? The Mars probe? Hubble? The SSTO that crashed into Lancaster?" He shook his head. "Can't afford any more like"—Netras stifled a belch—"like those. Can't afford another crash, a failure of any system. None."

"What if Stilton changes the order?"

Netras shrugged. "What if Chicago votes Republican? What if they elect Sonny Bono pope?"

"The president . . ."

"Wharton doesn't know shit about space, and you know it, Eye. He'll leave it to Stilton."

"We can call Chairman Reemer. He'll take my call."

"He'll pat you on the head, Eye, and send you off to bed. Hesh . . . he's a horse trader. He's got a district, get the picture?"

"He's got a new federal-research park, or a half-dozen housing projects, or a new Boeing plant in Poughkeepsie."

"Something like that."

"So you finally did it, Butter. You sold your own wingman down the river."

"Get the fuck out of my fucking office. Go home and give yourselves a fucking raise. Build us a better rocket nozzle; you'll get more contracts, hire lots of little, weird, technofucks, and make us all happy. But get out, before I get drunk enough to start sharing this fucking bottle, pardon my French."

Avery rose and put his hand on Janna's shoulder. "Come on, boss. There's nothing for us here. He was a man, once."

Netras curled his lip. "And you're a goddamn Marine, huh? Hey, *semper fi,* Mac!" He raised his bottle in salute.

Avery Niles steered his client out of the room, out of the Pentagon, and back to Fairmont Heights.

Winter turned to spring, and the cherry trees bloomed on the Mall. Avery Niles enjoyed them—forced himself to enjoy them. He fretted, wondering what foul deed his friend, boss, and occasional lover was engaged in; she didn't want him to come visit, but she had shown up twice in D.C. to ask his advice about mundane legal matters . . . questions any legal staffer at J. W. Rocketry could have answered. But it allowed them to meet, allowed him to see she was still Boss Lady Wylie. She looked thin, ragged, driven, unhealthy, haunted, exhausted; normal enough that Niles left each meeting relieved.

Spring became summer, and Avery Niles sweltered in the burning, ground-zero fireball of July in the District. The mayor was indicted again, and the chief of police tried to assume mayoral duties and was sent into exile for his sins. The Biograph reopened, closed again, and reopened again; but the kids who played there now were talentless hacks who did not believe in melody or singing on key. A couple of octogenarians from Preservation Hall in New Orleans came to the city to play some jazz, and there was yet another Miles Davis tribute. Bud Netras took a sudden "leave of absence" at Betty Ford.

Rumblings came from the bowels of the EPA: All EISs were now required to include a section on alternative-energy consumption and reclamation procedures, code for energy conservation at the expense of human muscle power.

Winter passed uneventfully. Then in April, Janna called.

"Haven't heard from you in three months, J. W.," said a chastened Avery Niles.

"Your checks still clearing? Then you know I haven't forgotten you."

"When are you coming back East?"

"Your turn. Come home, Niles; all is forgiven."

"When?" Niles felt a curious pain in his stomach; it was fear. *What had she been up to for fourteen months?*

"First-class seat on Delta, fourteen hundred on Friday. Be there or beware."

Smoke Creek, Nevada, was hardly bone chilling to Avery Niles, not after a harsh D.C. winter. But Janna Wylie was a Southern California gal, and she bundled up in an Arctic parka and shivered as if ice-climbing a glacier. Niles wore only a jeans-jacket and a hat; Janna had not thought of wearing a hat. "You lose most of your heat off the top of your head," he scolded her. "Okay; how long?"

"Three minutes, fifteen."

Thirty-seven launch technicians crowded the room, fiddling with dials and consoles that may as well have been African juju sticks as far as Niles was concerned; of course, he thought, a contracts textbook probably looks like ancient Greek to J.W.

"Tell me again how you got launch authority from the Io Corporation."

'Oh, sure. Right here." She patted the hip pocket of her slacks . . . or her bottom. Avery Niles could not tell which.

. . . one minute fifteen . . . one minute . . .

Niles realized he had taken Janna's hand. He did not remember doing so.

. . . forty-five . . . thirty . . .

At ten seconds, he looked at her face; her teeth were clenched so hard, she might need dental work later. She did not blink, did not breathe.

The flare from the "disconnect rocket" caused Niles to wince and turn away; Janna Wylie did not flinch. *You'd have made a good Marine,* he thought.

The rocket burst from the scaffolding, shooting up just like the finger Janna had flicked at Dr. Eljer nearly two years before. Brighter than the sun, the bird lit the desolation of Smoke Creek like a gas explosion. Nobody cheered; Niles knew some of them were secretly aware that their boss did not have proper authorization, and thus all of them were going to be subjected to endless days of grilling and debriefing. But they knew it was worth it; success in the laser-launching program might jump-start America's reinvolvement with space.

"Ten seconds to MECO," said a technician, not having to strain his voice. "Fifteen to laser takeover."

The brilliant pebble rose, dwindling to a lightbulb, a spark; then the light abruptly disappeared.

"We have main-engine cutoff," said the tech. Five seconds later: "We have laser takeover."

A brief, ragged cheer erupted. It was quickly stifled.

The engineer sat back, blinking at his screen. "Telemetry operating twenty percent outside normal parameters. Twenty-two points."

Janna abruptly dropped Niles's hand and hurried down the metal-grating steps to the screen. "Here, sir," said the tech, pointing at a stream of numbers.

"Focus?"

"Focus is fine. We're having trouble finding the hole, sir."

"Weather? Air movement?"

He shook his head, meaning "I don't know."

"Get it back."

The technician cupped his ear and shouted into the mike that curved around his cheek. Across the launch trailer, other engineers, technicians, even scientists, scrambled in a highly organized dance of chaos.

"Twenty-eight points," said the chief tech, his voice sounding tight and strangled.

Niles could only watch from the director's platform at the rear of the trailer. The big-screen television at the front showed the expected and actual track of the rocket; even Niles could see the wide deviation. He wrapped his arms around himself, already grimly beginning to rehearse his client's defense before the full House Science Committee, the NTSB, BATF—pyrotechnic squibs to start the laser—FAA, FCC—did her license cover radio telemetry?—DOD, CIA . . . or worse.

"Get me back my bird!" shouted Janna. Nobody listened; they were all too busy trying to get her back her bird.

"Fifty-five-point deviation." The tech turned back to look at Janna Wylie.

She frowned, struggling; pride warred with responsibility. Finally she spit out the words: "Splash the mother."

"Splash it," said the tech.

"Splash it" was repeated along the trailer.

A moment later, the tech listened, incredulous. Then he turned, his face white. "Sir, we can't find it."

"What?"

"The laser is ionizing the air—we can't break through."

"Well, turn it off!"

The tech shook his head. "We lost it. . . . we lost— Damn it, it's somewhere. Bennie!"

The nightmare stretched on. Janna Wylie thrust her hands deep in the parka's pockets, bowing her head. She looked like a woman about to pull out a sawed-off shotgun and go on a spree.

"Found it," said the tech; he turned back to Janna. "Sir . . . it's already left the test site; we're over Reno."

"Reno?"

"Could be; can't tell for sure without a GPS overlay."

"Can we detonate?"

"Negative, sir. We can only let her go and hope she carries on past the city before grounding."

The techs were silent for a long minute. Janna pulled her hood back.

"Zero telemetry," said the tech at last.

The bird was a smoking hole. But where? Niles shivered, wishing he had a parka like his boss.

"I got the judge in Nevada to delay the trial until after the subcommittee hearings, J. W."

"That's something, at least."

"But the SEC wants in on this now."

"The SEC?"

"Fiduciary responsibility."

"J. W. Rocketry never went public. . . . What the hell does the SEC want?"

"You let the McNary Pension Group invest, remember?"

"Oh. Are they joining the civil action, or is it criminal?"

"It's nothing yet; they're talking to the federal prosecutor in New York, but they're 'exploring all options,' to quote the notice."

"So that makes how many?"

Niles ticked off the pending actions. "State of Nevada, DOE, the subcommittee, ARPA, and maybe the SEC; civil actions on the parts of the estates of the three decedents in Incline Village—that's a slam dunk; settle it—Io Corporation, civil-RICO from the DOD. You don't have a paddle; you don't even have a boat, J.W."

Niles stared down at his uneaten lunch. Disgusted, he picked up the submarine sandwich and pitched it into the basket. "You still want to waive extradition from California?"

"Are you all right with this, Avery? With everything, I mean. Have you found a good criminal defense attorney for me?"

"The best. Harrison Pik."

"He's the best? I've never heard of him."

"Who do you want, Dershowitz? Van Allen? You can get anyone you want. Nobody's ever dropped a private rocket on top of a city before."

She shook her head. "Low profile. For this defense to mean anything, I have to be the star, not some four-star legal hack."

"It's up to you."

"It always was. That's our defense, chief."

"Members of Congress, I sit before you chastened. It's impossible for any person of conscience not to be horrified by inadvertently causing the death of three people, one of them a father of two. And I will stand trial for that action and be called to account by a jury of my peers.

"But that is not what you are called to decide today. Today, the only question is whether I was morally and legally justified in using the money you budgeted, appropriated, and transferred to J. W. Rocketry through the Io Corporation for a laser-launching system . . . the very system you appropriated the money for.

"I don't understand the machinations that changed an approved proposal for a laser-launching system into a project to marginally improve the performance of a traditional rocket nozzle. I don't pretend to understand the balance of power between this subcommittee and your counterpart in the Senate, the White House Office of Technology Development, the Departments of Defense and Energy, the Advanced Research Projects Agency, NASA—who was never involved in the first place—the Air Force, and their corporate clones, the Aerospace Corporation and the Io Corporation.

"But I do understand something that has evidently been lost to view in the hallowed halls of our sacred government. I understand the American way. I understand capitalism: That's what I do; I'm an entrepreneur.

"I build things. I start companies and make stuff. Real stuff . . . not just laws and regulations.

"You know how many companies I've started? Seven. Five of them failed within two years; my fifth company, MediGraf, made an embedded-system portable heart monitor for people who have had bypass surgery. You probably each know someone who wore one for a while. I made enough money off of MediGraf to pay back everyone I owed for the first four failures, to finance start-up number six, and to supply the seed money for J. W. Rocketry.

"Now what do you suppose would have happened if I had pulled back from that first, failed start-up, Wylie Electrographics? What if I had played it safe and simply contracted with IBM or Sharp as a developer?

"What if I had been afraid to fail?

"Well, for one thing, I wouldn't be staring at a thick file full of indictments. I wouldn't have my lawyer out defending seventy million dollars' worth of civil suits.

"And Mr. Chairman, Representatives, I sure as hell would not be sitting before you right now, telling you about the failure of the first test flight of Wylie-One . . . or about the first test flight of Wylie-One-B—which, according to my watch, will launch in approximately six minutes from somewhere in the nation of Ecuador.

"Please, members of the subcommittee . . . I asked to make this statement first; I'll answer all questions fully and completely, except those for which my counsel advises me to take the Fifth Amendment, when I have finished.

"Yes, Chairman Reemer; I am aware of the seriousness of this action. But I reject the label irresponsible. It is irresponsible to expect science and engineering to proceed 'without failure' and 'without risk.' It is, in my opinion, Goddamned irresponsible to take away an American's right to fail.

"Yes, you heard correctly: We have a constitutional right to fail. I don't know where it is in that piece of paper; paper is Mr. Niles's business—I deal in less slippery stuff. But you bet your life, and the life of the United States of America, that we do, in fact, have a right to fail.

"Without a right to fail, we have no right to succeed. To put it another way, unless we risk everything, we can't win anything. Anything! What the hell difference does a fifteen percent improvement in specific thrust matter? Who cares? The budget for rocket launches is a pimple on the rump of the defense budget, and we all know it. But the price of even a single launch is so ridiculously high that only a government or quasi-governmental body like Hughes or Thiokol can do it; no others need apply. Anybody else wants something up in space, she's got to hand a sack full of cash over to the Air Force or NASA and beg for space, squeezed in between a box of Norway rats and a secret communications satellite for the National Reconnaissance Organization."

Several members of the joint committee visibly started when she loudly pronounced the name of the supersecret government body. Until a few years back, it was illegal even to say the words aloud.

"Going for safe means that arrangement is permanent . . . and I know there are people, both in the administration and here on the Hill—I'm not accusing anyone here, Mr. Chairman—who want that arrangement made permanent.

"My only option, as a citizen, to see my dream of a spacefaring nation come true—and my only option, as a greedy entrepreneur, to make any serious money in the space industry—is not to go for safe, but to go for broke. Members, I put every dollar I owned and anything I could borrow on the barrel for this dream. I should have

called the bird the Tucker-One, but we egomaniacs can't stand to
see anyone else's name on our inventions.

"I played by your rules; now I'm playing by mine. I worked
within the system, and the system screwed me. Now I'm outside
the system, and I just beat you. If you'll look at your watches, you'll
see that One-B just launched . . . and this time, members, it's going
to work.

"I know I'm going to jail. I can't stop that. I know you plan to
cut off all funding for J. W. Rocketry; I expected that going in. But
I haven't lost anything today; everything I was going to lose, I lost
fourteen months ago, when Io Corporation first told me my dream
of the future was to be replaced by the nightmare of incremental
improvement of existing subsystems.

"In closing, members, before I begin answering your questions,
I would just like to say that it was your actions, stripping me of all
my illusions about capitalism in the United States today, that gave
me the courage to risk my life, my freedom, and my sacred honor
to give my people what few of them want, but all of them need.

"If not for you, I would have continued to work within the system. If not for the two months I have already spent in jail awaiting
trail, my eyes would remain firmly shut, and I would still be a
good, little worker. If not for you, the One-B would probably still
be nothing but electromagnetic bits on my PowerBlock computer
at home.

"All I'd like to say, members, is fuck you very much, and God
bless. I will now answer questions."

Avery Niles got caught in traffic; but he had left early, and arrived
on time, anyway.

It made no difference; Janna Wylie was already sitting outside
the gate of Sybil Brand Institute on her suitcase. "They sprang me
forty minutes early for good behavior," she said with a tired smile.

"I've been working on the SEC case," said Niles, after the oblig-
atory, though restrained, hug and kiss.

"Do I turn around and surrender myself again?"

"I finally persuaded the appellate court that the SEC had no jurisdiction. They're not filing a writ with the Supreme Court, so it's finally over."

"Over?"

"You're even still the president and chairman of the board of J. W. Rocketry. . . . The securities-fraud case is dismissed. Totally."

"Jesus. And all I owe you is three years back billing at one hundred fifty dollars per hour."

Niles smiled. "No charge. I consider myself still the head of J. W.'s legal department."

"You resigned to defend me, remember?"

"You've got enough problems. Besides, contributions are still pouring in to the Janna Wylie Legal Defense Fund. And your agent says there's some interest at Random House for the book."

"What book? For that matter, what agent?"

"Tell you later. Right now, you're late for a BOD meeting at J. W. Rocketry."

"Good God! All I've got is prison dungarees."

"Suit in the car; but I think you'll have to let it out a bit."

"Thanks."

"You'll work it off when you get back to regular aerobics."

"We're on a flight to Ecuador?"

Niles smiled. "Not since that spectacular demo on the day of your testimony before the subcommittee, J. W. You haven't been following the company business?"

"They don't let us watch the news or receive newspapers in Sybil Brand these days, Avery . . . the McCullough Law. We're being punished; we don't get special priv-il-eges." She curled her lip, a terrifying expression that took Niles aback.

Janna Wylie was a different person than she was three years earlier; thirty-eight months of prison life took their toll . . . as expected, as planned.

"No, Janna. The corporate offices are in El Segundo now. You're going to love this—we're in the same building that used to house the Aerospace Corporation and Io. The first moved to Torrance, and Io has been disbanded! Seems a couple of Air Force weenies got caught with their stars in the cookie jar, and Io became . . . expendable. Now the directors are all directors of Grissom Industries—doing exactly the same job they were doing at Io."

"Nice work, if you can take it."

"Wylie-Five is scheduled for the second test flight next month; and there's a line out the door and down the block to put in orders as soon as we're operational."

Janna Wylie shook her head. "Been too many Wylies already. I have a new name for this one: I hereby christen thee the *Preston Tucker*.

"And send a big, full-color glossy of the launch to Citizen Paige Reemer, with a polite note asking him how he's enjoying his 'retirement.' "

"You've got a mean streak in you, J. W."

"I always have, Niles. It's the mark of a failure . . . and proud of it, man."

Janna Wylie leaned back in the seat of the car and began snoring softly as Avery Niles slalomed through the midafternoon traffic toward the airport. A pack of cigarettes fell out of her jacket pocket.

That's one right you don't have, J.W., thought the attorney. Grinning, he picked up the pack and threw it out the window.

DAY OF ATONEMENT

J. Neil Schulman

Even when there is a foothold in space, the problems of human history will not conveniently roll over and play dead. The author of *Alongside Night, The Rainbow Cadenza,* and "Profile in Silver" *(The New Twilight Zone)* is a longtime libertarian activist, proponent of gun rights (*Stopping Power* and *Self Control, Not Gun Control*), and founder of www.Pulpless.Com on the Web. Even a space habitat based on the principles of Thomas Jefferson will not provide answers to the deepest, oldest problems. Sometimes you have to go home again.

> "I believe in God, but I detest theocracy. For every
> Government consists of mere men and is, strictly
> viewed, a makeshift; if it adds to its commands, 'Thus
> saith the Lord,' it lies, and lies dangerously."
> —C. S. Lewis,
> "Willing Slaves of the Welfare State"

Hateful," muttered David Brandon silently to himself. He was standing—strap-hanging—crushed in with the Sunday morning commuters on the 7:23 scooter from Damascus to Jerusalem, looking at the cover of the latest *Time* magazine, dated October 6—tomorrow. The cover showed a Menorah completely engulfed by flames from its candles. The headline asked, "WAS THE HOLOCAUST GOD'S PUNISHMENT?"

Brandon cleared the screen of his Vistabook and dropped it into a jacket pocket. He didn't have the stomach right now to read another piece of slanted, Israelite propaganda; it was hard enough as it was to concentrate on the difficulties that lay before him that day. Getting past the checkpoint with another faked identity—this time he was supposed to be a soccer coach at Hebrew University—was going to be the first order of business.

He was not, by temperament, cut out to be a terrorist. He hadn't until fairly recently even been particularly interested in political matters. As a matter of fact, a virtual lack of politics had almost been enough to convince him to stay with Kallye and their nine-year-old daughter, Janna, in the Jeffersonian space habitat. But even personal freedom and paternal love weren't enough to endure daily reminders of his unrequited love for a woman who loved her independence more than anything else.

David's lack of regular employment had been one of the issues that caused the breakup of his marriage to a civil engineer with the unending job of building new habitat rings; and there just wasn't yet much need for sports writers in a new space habitat, where the only established market for writing was still for tek dox.

So after two years of accepting that the only personal comments he was ever again going to get from Kallye were bitter sarcasm, two years of discovering that Kallye's and his bickering and their widely divergent approaches to child-rearing were turning Janna into a neurotic brat—David Brandon had agreed to Kallye's request for divorce and custody, and returned alone to Earth. He'd come to Southern California because he knew some networkers there who promised David assignments to novelize fantasy wrestling. That was now almost three years ago.

Brandon's sojourn into radical politics had begun by accident. A few months after his return he was at a fund-raiser in Baja Westwood, one of those office-lobby buffets where suits with large current accounts and hirsutes with late credit bills mixed freely, lubricated by Zinfandel and rumaki.

Since he had come with another writer for the free lunch, David hadn't even paid attention to what the do was about, and might never have found out if someone hadn't bumped his elbow and David hadn't spilled his Dark Lite down Sharmane Liebowitz's tits. Sharmane took one look at David's chiseled features, and not very discreetly checked out his butt. Within a few minutes he was licking his beer off Sharmane's breasts in her executive washroom on the fifth floor.

On their way back down to the lobby, Sharmane explained to David that it was a Save the Lambs fund-raiser to stop the animal sacrifices in the Kingdom of Israel. Sharmane was one of the organizers.

It wasn't until months later that David learned that Save the Lambs was only a small part of a much larger coalition.

Looking back, it was hard for David to know whether he had been drawn into the Jewish Liberation Organization more by intellectual or pheromonal persuasion.

Sure, it was awful that the Sanhedrin had torn down the Holocaust memorial at Yad Vashem, destroying irreplaceable documentation of Nazi atrocities; driven the rabbis out of the Kingdom of Israel and demolished the synagogues; and forbidden all but physically perfect and unblemished men to enter the temple.

And the chutzpah—the sheer unmitigated chutzpah—of King Josephus outlawing the use of Yiddish and Ladino in the Israelite kingdom . . . the attempts to wipe out two millennia of Diasporic Jewish culture . . . the imposition of Old Testament laws and punishments. No wonder the King of Israel got along so well with Islamic fundamentalists!

This was now all unspeakably evil to David; yet he was self-honest enough to realize that none of this would have moved him if the arguments hadn't come from Sharmane's mouth.

In spite of his worries, he passed the checkpoints without incident. The kings of Israel, Jordan, and Syria had become good friends—

Tuesday golfing buddies, in fact—and there hadn't been a border incident in decades.

The ID he presented scanned without problem, which was the confirmation he'd been waiting for that it was worth what Sharmane had paid for it. If there had been even the slightest indication of suspicion here, his orders were to turn around immediately. But, instead, he found himself disembarking the scooter, not too long after, in Giv'at Ram.

It could not have been better timing to quell any doubts he'd been having: there was a book burning by Hebrew University students in progress in the center of the stadium as he headed toward the workout rooms. He ventured close enough to see a swarthy young woman in a shapeless full-length black dress toss a book by Sholom Aleichem onto the roaring fire, then David blended into the roaring crowd, turning toward his assigned pickup . . . an athletic locker in the men's showers.

Though the locker room was deserted—or perhaps because of its desertion—this was the beginning of the most dangerous part of his mission. He punched the combination into the locker, opened it, and took out a canvas athletic bag. Because of what was supposed to be hidden in the bag, David would now be irrevocably marked as a terrorist if the Shammashim caught him. If he had been compromised, then either he would be arrested momentarily, or—if the Shammashim thought he would lead them to further conspirators—they would be tailing him from now on.

He was not arrested.

David changed into workout clothes left for him in the bag, then locked the bag and his street clothes back into the locker. He started with twenty minutes of aerobic stair-climbing just to warm up, then proceeded to the weight room. Since he didn't have a spotter, he decided to stick to the machines.

While the workout was necessary for David to blend in to his role, he enjoyed weight lifting as an end in itself, so it didn't take much pretense. Brandon had been training for this assignment for almost a year; and the benefits showed in the cut of his physique.

But he had to be extra careful not even to bruise or nick himself during this workout. Even the most minor physical imperfection on him in the next twenty-four hours could bring thousands of hours of preparation to nothing. It was one reason he had grown a thick beard recently. He couldn't even risk shaving.

After twenty minutes of stretching, he returned to the locker, changed into street clothes again without showering, adjusted his turban, then took the all-important gym bag with him out to the street. He found a taxi stand in front of the old Knesset and told the driver to take him to the King Daniel Hotel.

There was no way to know if the Shammashim were now following him, so there was nothing to do except act as if they weren't. Despite a traffic backup caused by a royal motorcade exiting the palace, Brandon was at the hotel lobby in ten minutes.

His room wasn't yet available, so he had lunch in the King Daniel's rooftop sushi bar. There was fish only; no other seafood was served.

Finally, at two o'clock, the front desk allowed David to check into his room; but it was evident that if his reservation hadn't been solidly locked in for a year, there was no way that he ever would have gotten a room in New Temple Quarter on the eve of the holiest day of both Jewish and Hebrew calendars for the year 5847—10 Tishre 5847, to be exact—Yom Kippur.

Once checked into his hotel room, David was going exactly nowhere until tomorrow. He finally took out the false bottom of the athletic bag to make sure it contained the items it was supposed to contain, then closed it up and shoved it under the bed.

The next order of business was to cut up, break up, and mash up his soccer coach ID and flush it down the toilet.

After a leisurely and overdue shower, David turned the holy-vision onto a local news channel with English-language audio, plopping on the bed and propping a pillow under his head to watch.

It was nothing he hadn't seen before . . . the public beheading of a homosexual . . . sheep being sacrificed on the altar of the Third

Temple . . . a woman convicted of adultery being stoned to death by pharisees amidst the Royal Topiaries.

So much for righteousness in the Holy Land. And his grand-father had told him how the Religious Right in America used to bitch about violence on television.

David was watching a report on the new law King Josephus had just proclaimed granting a woman's right to an abortion—*one* abortion; it was only to be performed along with a hysterectomy—when there was a knock at his door.

David pulled on his clothes quickly, making sure he had his turban on again, and in Hebrew asked through the door who it was. "Your dry cleaning," came back the reply, in English.

David opened the door; a bellman entered with two hangers of clothing wrapped in garment bags from the hotel cleaner's. He tipped the bellman a few shekels, closed the door again, and sighed in relief after opening one of the garment bags.

It was the ceremonial garb of a simple goatherd, which he'd been expecting.

It was a lonely evening and night. He wanted to call Sharmane, but that was, of course, impossible. He ordered up dinner from room service before it shut down for the holiday—roast lamb, hummus, sherbet, and thick sweet black coffee—then watched the Royal Jerusalem Philharmonic and Chorus in a performance of the Kol Nidre. Some of the Sanhedrin wanted to do away with the Kol Nidre as "modernist" but it was unlikely that they would find the popular support to do so. David could hear it simply by stepping out to his terrace; it was being sung all over the city.

When the sun went down, Brandon did what almost everyone else in the city was doing: He fasted, then, eventually, slept.

Terrorism is not particularly good for either the digestion or a good night's sleep; David was up late and then up early. Shortly after sunrise he did some stretching and wished for a breakfast he knew he couldn't buy anywhere in the kingdom except at a hospital, nursing home, or childcare facility . . . if he'd even been seriously inclined to.

He did not shower, wash, or even brush his teeth. For one thing, the water in the hotel was shut off until sundown. For another, someone might smell the scent of soap or mint on him and look at him disapprovingly at the wrong moment.

It was time to go. David dressed in a conservative black suit from one of the garment bags, donned his turban, retrieved the items he needed from the athletic bag and concealed them on his person, and draped the other garment bag—the one with the goatherd costume—over his shoulder. Barefoot, as was ritually necessary, he then trotted down the stairs out to the boulevard and started walking briskly to the temple. Luckily the pavement was neither particularly hot nor cool.

The Third Temple of Solomon was, like the First Temple, directly adjacent to the Israelite king's living quarters.

It was a much more imposing structure than the Second Temple, on the other side of town, was supposed to have been. Moreover, while perhaps no more lovingly and expensively built than the original temple at Mount Moriah, it was still enormously larger.

Both the First and Second Temples would have easily fit inside any decent-sized city's synagogue—a three-story structure a hundred twenty feet by forty—but the Third Temple was as large and ornate as any other religion's primary place of worship, from Saint Peter's in Rome to the Mormon Tabernacle in Salt Lake City.

It performed essentially the same functions as scripture recorded for the First Temple—but was scaled up and out.

At the outer perimeter of the temple were pens for housing the animals to be sacrificed and areas for meat-cutting and hide-stripping; a bakery; and a bath for ritual purification of the priests.

Inside, there was a vestibule with offices for administrative functions and storage of religious artifacts, an outer open-air sanctuary where sacrifices were performed and worshipers could congregate, and the inner sanctuary—the Holy of Holies.

Only the high priest was allowed into the Holy of Holies, and only on one day every year: Yom Kippur—the Day of Atonement, when God forgave sins. Anyone else entering the Holy of Holies did so under penalty of death.

The Holy of Holies in the Third Temple of Solomon had one additional thing in common with the First Temple . . . an object that even the Second Temple could not make claim to.

An ark of the covenant.

It was not *the* Ark of the Covenant. No one had yet been able to deliver that vessel to the King of Israel, though the rewards he offered were . . . well, a king's ransom. But herein was the centerpiece, the key, to the refounding of the prerabbinical faith of the Israelite nation.

By prophetic authority—and much blood and gold had been spent in defending the authenticity of that prophecy—the Eternal was said to have ordered a Phoenix-born Jewish college student named Daniel Gottlieb, the only son of the Southwest's largest Chrysler dealer—to mount an archaeological dig in Ethiopia.

There, so the tale went—wrapped in rough wool within a tightly sealed wooden chest, both of which scientifically dated to the tenth century B.C.E.—he was said to have found broken stone tablets. Scholars, who were allowed access only to rubbings and digital photographs, agreed that when the jigsaw puzzle was put back together, the tablets contained the Decalogue in the written language and style appropriate for the Mosaic epoch, the fourteenth century B.C.E.

Daniel Gottlieb had not been at all religious before his expedition to Ethiopia. It wouldn't be accurate to say that he now found religion; it would be more proper to say that religion found him . . . and faith-starved believers anointed him to such immense power that was perhaps more recently enjoyed only by the man who was proclaimed by billions to wear the shoes of the fisherman.

It wasn't very long before instructions found in the Book of Exodus were fed into a computer program that designed, as closely as possible to the original, an ark to house the tablets.

The tank that rolled into the Knesset and deposited Daniel Gottlieb onto a hastily erected throne therein was claimed to have had the ark within it. Only the man making that claim could say from personal knowledge. In his first proclamation, the new king declared that now that he had placed the tablets into the ark, anyone other than himself who looked upon the Ark of the Covenant would be struck dead by the Angel Samael. Not many had been prepared to contest that claim with empirical vigor; and no one who had tried was known to have survived the attempt.

The Arizona-born king was more comfortable wielding political power than religious authority. Daniel Gottlieb accepted the Staff of David when it was offered to him and declined to share secular power with a parliament; but religious authority he vested in the men who had put him in power, a priesthood who styled themselves the Sanhedrin.

Their power was consolidated by shrewd treaties with Muslims who found the idea of having Hebrews as neighbors much more palatable than living next door to Jews.

It was Daniel's eldest son who now reigned as King of the Israelites and—on one day of the year, this day, to be precise—fulfilled the office of High Priest.

It was ironic, David considered as he walked barefoot to the temple, that it was the Sanhedrin's stubborn objections to almost all that had happened in the last twenty-one centuries which made possible what he was about to do.

In almost any other major house of worship on this planet—even the Vatican—modern security techniques would have made certain to one error in twenty million that anyone who entered private areas was who his proffered ID said he was . . . and belonged there . . . and wasn't carrying forbidden things that personal searches couldn't discover.

The utility entrance to the temple didn't even have an old-style magnetometer and X-ray unit, much less DNA scanners and molecular sensors. David presented personal ID and temple-authorization documents that declared him a participant in today's proceedings, then undressed and underwent the customary inspection.

The Shammashim who guarded the entrance were more concerned with David's physical perfection—and his circumcision—than anything else. It was now obvious that they had no security concerns about him. He passed their scrutiny, then was allowed into the dressing area.

There David changed into the goatherd's robe, drew a minor staff, and proceeded to the animal pen where today's scapegoat was waiting for him. He presented his identification, once again, to the Shammash guarding the pen, and was allowed to take the goat out.

He proceeded toward the outer sanctuary with the goat, but at a point where he felt there were few eyes on him, he paused, petting the goat. He spread his robes, strategically, to conceal what he was doing.

What David Brandon was doing was, after applying a powerful anesthetic, injecting a biochip into the larynx of the scapegoat.

It was a simple plan: As King Josephus prepared to raise his knife to slaughter the scapegoat, David would transmit a signal to the biochip, and the scapegoat would speak.

It was undoubtedly cheap theatrics, David considered. It was definitely a form of terrorism, he knew.

But it beat the hell out of blowing up the Ark of the Covenant, which had come in second in the vote of the JLO leadership for an act to bring attention to Hebrew cruelty to animals, as well as oppression of the Jews on their commonly shared most-sacred day.

The Shammash signaled David to bring the scapegoat forward, where he was joined by a second goatherd leading a second goat. This second goat would not be slaughtered by the knife but sprinkled with blood from the scapegoat by the High Priest, King Josephus, and at sunset that day, thrown off a high cliff. For the moment, it was to be held back by its goatherd while the scapegoat was led to the altar for slaughter.

As David led the scapegoat up the steps onto the altar, he got his first good look at the assembled mass of Hebrew men, who were currently intoning their confessions. David could see the Sanhedrin off to one side in a balcony; below them were selected pharisees.

At the top of the altar, a priest took the goat from David and led it to the King.

It was time for the sacrifice. The scapegoat was lifted onto the stone table, and its feet were tied. Then the High Priest raised his knife and prepared to speak—

David pressed a button under his robe, and the scapegoat spoke instead.

"Was it not written," said the scapegoat in Hebrew, loud enough for all present to hear, "that I desire mercy and not sacrifices?"

It was a quotation from the Book of Hosea.

The crowd was startled, and so was the King, who dropped his hand.

And what followed was either high comedy or an unparalleled religious desecration, depending on your point of view.

As the King lowered the knife, he accidentally nicked the behind of the scapegoat. It was enough to cause the scapegoat to roll itself off the stone table onto the altar floor, and in its agitation, the scapegoat managed to break free of its bonds.

The scapegoat then ran right into the Holy of Holies.

"Get it!" King Josephus stage-whispered to the nearest several Shammashim.

The temple servants hesitated.

"Yes, in *there!*" The King pointed to the Holy of Holies.

The men obeyed their king and High Priest and followed the goat into the Holy of Holies.

An unseen struggle between men and goat followed behind the golden curtain . . . and then, just like in *The Wizard of Oz,* the curtain was pulled open . . . and the assembled worshipers got their first look inside the Holy of Holies and at the Ark of the Covenant.

A palpable roar arose from the congregation. Many worshipers shielded their eyes . . . but some looked.

What those who looked saw was that, as the Shammashim chased the goat, the goat ran *through* the Ark of the Covenant.

The Ark of the Covenant in the Holy of Holies was a hologram.

And as the scapegoat ran for its life, the image of the ark appeared, disappeared, and reappeared, as the beast ran across the laser projector's path.

David Brandon could see the impact this was having on the assembled . . . the Sanhedrin and pharisees in particular.

Some men dropped their heads in their hands.

Some of the men ripped at their clothes.

David Brandon did not, at that moment, know what the lasting impact of this day would be. To be honest, he was more concerned with getting out of the temple—and getting both Sharmane and himself back to the safety of the Jeffersonian space habitat—before the Shammashim managed to connect them with the day's events.

He had not done this for political reasons, but for personal reasons. He had done it because Sharmane had asked him to, and because—for religious reasons—no other member of the Jewish Liberation Organization could do such a thing on Yom Kippur.

But, for the first time in his life, David was convinced that, very likely, God really did exist and—every once in a while—did reach His hand down into human affairs.

It was enough, David considered, as he boarded the scooter back to the Damascus spaceport, to grant Sharmane's request that he convert to Judaism before they got married.

No Market for Justice

Brad Linaweaver

An editor with the temerity to slip a story into his own project should cause as much trouble as possible. Herewith I offer oodles of problems with no solutions. A lot more work has been done on the Jeffersonian space habitat since Neil's story, and the joint has been named after Monticello. What else? As an advocate of Jefferson's principles of limited government, I don't delude myself about what most libertarians really want: anarchy! I also readily admit that limited government can turn back into the Big Bad State in the time it takes to edit an anthology.

> "The natural progress of things is for liberty to yield
> and government to gain ground."
> —Thomas Jefferson
> (from a letter to Edward Carrington)

First of all, I'd like to thank *Free Space* for allowing me this opportunity to address interested parties before I depart the colony for good. The holographic net will allow any of you who wish to shake my hand an opportunity to do so. I'm flattered at the many requests for a personal touch. Each subscriber to this message will also receive an autograph, via the program, on any desired object—and I'm flattered beyond words to learn how some of the younger female subscribers intend to make use of that option. You will keep the name of Howard Nock alive.

Free Space is a good name for this method of communication! Originally, I had no intention of leaving any message, but when the publisher of the official colony newsletter announced that I would be banned from the pages of *Nuovo Monticello* because I no longer have a property claim, that was a bit much. The name of the colony may not be very original, but I came up with it when I founded the first station here; and the newsletter has always been named after the colony. And now that I won't "buy on" to the new rules, they try a crude technique for shutting me up.

When word first leaked out that I was renouncing my citizenship, the questions started pouring in . . . no doubt to fill the leak! Sorry. I know that my attempts at humor leave something to be desired. So many of you have asked the same questions that I think the best way of handling them is in terms of a self-interview. Please bear with me.

QUESTION: Was it because the United States finally elected a woman president that you dedicated your fortune to greatly expanding the first self-sufficient space community?

ANSWER: Despite my lifelong fascination for the great work of Thomas Jefferson, I never shared my hero's view regarding women in politics. I was much closer to the twentieth-century visionary Robert Heinlein as regards the full potential of the female of the species. Unfortunately, the worst tyranny in Earth history began with a woman president putting forth what sounded like a good idea, "The Children's Rights Initiative." As a libertarian, I believe in children's rights. But if we've learned anything, my friends, it's run like hell from anyone who talks about children's rights from a statist perspective. The President's battle against the family was only the beginning. Her ultimate war was against the individual. And it didn't help that she referred to *Romeo and Juliet* as child porn.

QUESTION: There were attempts to subvert the Bill of Rights before. Why did it work this time?

ANSWER: For those of you who've heard it all before, I plead that many of the younger subscribers want to hear it from the horse's mouth; or in my case, whatever part of the equine anatomy I most closely approximate. The answer is twofold. When the Genocide Treaty was finally used to brand all non-Amerind Americans as beneficiaries of historical war crimes, the notion of individual rights became a moot point. Maybe if the Constitutional Convention hadn't gone the way it had a few years earlier, the American people would have rallied against the internationalist hubris. The first woman president did such a good job of sending her country to its room without supper that the rest of the world hardly noticed she was taking over the planet . . . for its own good, of course. There were abused children everywhere who needed to be protected from dangerous thoughts, pictures, ideas, selfishness.

QUESTION: So you and your friends tried the American Revolution all over again, only this time in space. You finished what began with J. W. Rocketry. You're a hero to two generations born up here. Why are you banishing yourself?

ANSWER: That's a bit complicated. My good friend Judge Higgins can probably explain it best. She's staying behind, you know. But as this is the last time I can set rumors to rest, let me get to it.

I'm not leaving because of the wild-eyed characters who wander the corridors, living out of shopping pods, and quoting passages from *Atlas Shrugged* at the top of their lungs. I think they're colorful, amusing characters who should be left alone. Now the administrators want to redefine the property requirements so these poor bastards can be spaced.

I'm not leaving because of my quarrel with Miss I. Amm Rich. That's ancient history, too. When she found out that Karl Marx sold better to other colonies than the Austrian School of Economics, I didn't fault her for taking advantage of a temporary market situation. But she wouldn't even keep the files up to date on von Mises and Hayek and Rothbard and Konkin. New work is being done all the time.

"Everyone in the Jefferson colony already knows the capitalist viewpoint," she would tell me, as if everyone has read everything. "Is it my fault that books on socialism sell better in a free market?" she'd ask. "Do you want me to have to go back to my engineering job up here? I hate building things; I hate seeing abstract ideas translated into concretes. What about my feelings?" Well, you know the rest. We dissolved the partnership and I signed away my half of the book catalog. If a trivial matter would make me leave Nuovo Monticello, I would have spaced out years ago.

QUESTION: So, why *are* you leaving?

ANSWER: Two reasons. The negative one is *justice*. The positive one is *wampum*. Which do you want first?

QUESTION: This is a self-interview, for God's sake.

ANSWER: Oh yeah. Let's do the problem of justice. Like my hero, Jefferson, I'm a minarchist. I'm not an anarchist. I don't think that anarchy lasts. The human race isn't sufficiently mature to handle complete freedom. This means that the mutant-types who can handle that level of freedom are always in trouble with everyone else. Judge Higgins summed it up with the comment that a late-twenty-first-century liberal would rather live in Hitler's barbaric twentieth-century welfare state than have no welfare state at all.

QUESTION: Can we get back to justice, please?

ANSWER: Patience is a virtue. Anyway, the one thing the market cannot provide, as a matter of principle, is justice. Not that justice doesn't occur without the State, but then it's just the luck of the draw. And I'm not making a pun about side arms! Only a force outside the marketplace can satisfy the basically religious desire for justice. So a limited state needs to define a few laws about the initiation of force and fraud, enforce them with plenty of force, and then refuse to allow any other laws to creep in. That's what the Founding Fathers tried to do on the old mud ball. It's what we've tried to do up here in the starry firmament.

QUESTION: It hasn't worked?

ANSWER: It worked for a while. But the same thing is happening to Nuovo Monticello that happened in the U.S. of A.! We are being destroyed by creeping democracy. More and more things are being made illegal. So we need mercy to temper justice, because we're all criminals now; and the real crimes are taken less seriously. Judge Higgins calls it the feminization of the law. Wait a minute, maybe Jefferson had a point about the dangers of women involving themselves in the political process. . . .

QUESTION: Let's move on, shall we? No need to leave the subscribers with a bad taste in their mouths. You said there was a positive reason for leaving.

ANSWER: Before explaining the full implications of wampum, I want to express gratitude to the scientists, male and female, whose work greatly extended my lifespan so that I would be around when other scientists opened the door to the universe with their new discoveries. We owe so much to the great achievements of those who came before us, the mutant-minority of the past giving today's mutant-minority a chance to inherit the stars.

QUESTION: That sounds a bit pompous and elitist, doesn't it?

ANSWER: I certainly hope so. Now, about wampum! When I was in public school a long, long time ago, I had a teacher who talked a lot about freedom. It took me a while to understand that his ideas about liberty were a little different from mine. He believed in freedom *from* things—freedom from poverty, freedom from suffering, freedom from trouble. I thought of freedom as the right to *do* things.

Real freedom is not about security or guarantees. If someone takes a risk, and profits thereby, he should be allowed to keep the profits of his venture. If he is wrong, then he should take the loss. But freedom *from* the consequences of one's actions can only mean the destruction of freedom.

QUESTION: All libertarians know this stuff. What the hell do you mean by wampum?

ANSWER: I'm almost there. The left and the right agree that monopoly is a bad thing. They disagree over how the problem occurs. Do legislatures dictate to business or does business buy the legislature? The answer is that it doesn't matter. The universe beckons with the best kind of free trade, the exchange of goods and short-term services, the first stage of empire: wampum! I'm talking about exchanging trinkets with the natives.

QUESTION: Did you say the first stage of empire?

ANSWER: Yes, because for the first time in human history, we will never get to the next stage. The incredible gulf of space and time means there will never be a galactic empire. The advance of technology makes the individual a world unto himself; and he will be forever free if he kills the State he carries within himself. The future is literally one of Free Space.

QUESTION: Sounds like you've become an anarchist after all.

ANSWER: No, not where society is concerned. Get as many people together as we now have in Nuovo Monticello, and the State lives again. We are the largest space habitat in the solar system. We keep adding new sections. There are advantages in being this near to Earth, but there is corruption as well. The asteroid miners are more free than we are. Despite the crazy religion of the Mars colonists, their government may be less intrusive than ours because it isn't trying to achieve justice.

QUESTION: Your last thoughts for us are pure cynicism?

ANSWER: I first believed in free enterprise because I thought it was the only social system that didn't punish one human being for the mistakes of another. I wanted a world of adults where everyone was so busy doing productive stuff that they had no time to worry over the behavior of neighbors.

QUESTION: And now?

ANSWER: The only free enterprise I believe in now is wampum! Make your deal and move on. Those who believe they can have a free society are welcome to try. I respect anyone who tries to make a community work, as I respect anyone who rears children. They talk about small g government and small r republic as protection against the capital S State. I share their hope. But for me, freedom lies in the depths of space.

QUESTION: Won't you be lonely?

ANSWER: A synonym for freedom.

QUESTION: Have you any last thoughts for the Jeffies?

ANSWER: Yes. Beware of envy. Beware of bureaucracy. Beware of reparations. Beware of user fees and rentals subtly transforming into taxes. And remember these words of Jefferson, whose dream of a free republic died on Earth and may yet die again: "In every government on earth is some trace of human weakness, some germ of corruption and degeneracy, which cunning will discover, and wickedness insensibly open, cultivate, and improve."

God help us, but there is a market for statism! It satisfies a popular demand, even off Earth. I have a final request. When the "Jeffies" betray the last of old Tom's ideals, I hope they'll have the decency to change their names.

But I'm not holding my breath.

—END OF TRANSMISSION—

(There will be a small tax extracted from subscribers to *Free Space* that will pay for an Equal Time response by the managers of Nuovo Monticello.)

KWAN TINGUI

William F. Wu

Howdy, partner! How can we explore the new frontiers of space and not include a story by the author of the best science-fiction western, *Hong on the Range* (a 1990 selection for the American Library Bulletin's list of Best Books for Young People)? Besides, I've seen the picture of Bill with Roy Rogers! Here Bill writes another of his carefully crafted stories drawing on his Chinese-American background. No matter where humanity goes, the cultures of Earth will not be left behind.

Leung Soey, a man stiff jointed, overweight, and white haired at the age of seventy-three, stood beneath the roof tiles on the stone pavilion in the Garden of Peace. All the brown and gray stones had been mined from an asteroid and cut into shapes with smooth, polished surfaces. The pavilion, on a small hill, marked the highest spot in the park.

Beyond the billowing green trees in the distance, he could see the inward surface of the space colony curving upward. If he kept his gaze low, he could forget that he lived inside a giant cylinder called Zhang-E, slowing turning in space as it orbited Sol in the Asteroid Belt. He had escaped the rigors of Chicago's Chinatown as a young man, but as he got older and more weary, he sometimes wondered what Earth felt like now.

"Ah Soey, do you see any sign of her?" Kwan Douhak, the stocky man in his middle fifties who had hired Leung Soey for this meeting, addressed him casually from a stone stool next to a matching stone table. He wore an expensive, gray western suit and a black tie with gold pinstripes. His hair, black and straight, had been cut short and carefully combed.

"No, not yet." Ah Soey spoke Cantonese, as Kwan Douhak had.

Cantonese had become the common language here in Zhang-E, linking the population, who were all originally descended from China. The early colonists came from China, Taiwan, Singapore, the United States, and many other nations, speaking not only Cantonese and Mandarin Chinese, but also rural-village dialects and the languages of other home countries. Everyone agreed that English had to be taught in order for the Zhangese to communicate widely with other colonies. When Ah Soey first arrived, one faction here insisted that Mandarin, the official language of China, be the official language in Zhang-E, but the majority of colonists had a Cantonese background and outvoted them.

"When did she say she would come?" Kwan Douhak insisted. His hands anxiously stroked the rolled scrolls he had laid on the table in front of him.

"She did not say she would come at all." Ah Soey had an urge to pace restlessly, but his feet hurt too much. Absently, he rested one hand on the tea cozy he had set on the edge of the table. It stood near the framed gift he himself had brought. "She's a recluse, a very private eccentric. I did not speak to her directly. Her assistant said maybe she would come."

Kwan Douhak scowled but said nothing.

Ah Soey envied and disdained his arrogant, wealthy employer, but he was too poor to turn down the man's money. Reluctantly, he acknowledged to himself that the stranger from Earth had determination; he had spent more than Ah Soey's lifetime income searching for an older sister who had left her family in Singapore as a young woman to live in space.

"When she gets here, I will pay you off," said Kwan Douhak. "I want to talk to my sister alone."

"You need me to interpret," said Ah Soey. "The woman we're waiting for does not speak Cantonese fluently, only English and some Cantonese phrases."

Kwan Douhak folded his arms angrily. "Then she is not my sister. What am I paying you for?"

"I never said Kwan Tingui was your sister."

"Why is the matter in question? My sister's name is Kwan Tinleng, meaning 'Heavenly Beauty.' Since she left our family in anger years ago, I am not surprised she modified her first name."

"Kwan Tingui is the wealthiest, most successful woman on this colony and she fits your sister's age and height." Ah Soey struggled to keep weary condescension out of his voice. "Her name means 'Heavenly Imp.' You two happen to have a surname very common here. Since 'tin' means 'heaven,' it is a popular reference here on Zhang-E, a kind of in-joke about living in space; hundreds of people on this colony have the word in their names. You hired me to introduce you to Kwan Tingui. And even if she is not your sister, you owe me as soon as she arrives."

"Two ounces of gold transferred to your account when she arrives, and ten ounces if she is my sister."

"That was the deal." Ah Soey spoke gruffly, belying his desperate need for the money. Two ounces would pay his most urgent debts; eight more would arrange rent, new clothes, and a small staff to open the consulting office he had planned for years.

"I will know her," said Kwan Douhak, as though trying to convince himself. "Our reunion should be private."

"You two will not be alone just because I leave. She will have some sort of escort."

Kwan Douhak glanced up, startled. "You said she never married, that Kwan was her birth surname."

"That's right. Kwan never married, but she adopted nearly every child ever orphaned by disease or accident on this colony. I imagine she will have one of her grown children or grandchildren with her. She will want her own interpreter."

"Why? You speak English."

"She will not trust me to interpret."

Kwan Douhak eyed Ah Soey suspiciously. "I thought you knew her—was that not the reason you could arrange this meeting even though she is a recluse?"

"That does not mean she will trust me to interpret when I am on your payroll. I contracted work with her company a couple of times ten or fifteen years ago, and though I did not work directly under her, my boss said she personally approved my selection."

Kwan Douhak nodded grudging acceptance of his explanation.

Ah Soey did not say, *Thirty years ago I knew her even better, but you haven't paid me to tell you about that.*

Through the canopy of leaves in the middle distance, Ah Soey glimpsed the smooth motion of an electric cart. Two women rode in it along the narrow, meandering paths toward the stone pavilion. They would be here in less than a minute.

Two ounces of gold would be his.

"She would not have agreed to come at all except for the artwork you promised," said Ah Soey. "The artistic life on Zhang-E has been one of her great commitments. She endowed the entire collection of art in the gallery and she supports the artists' colony. Works of art from Earth in the traditional Asian styles are rare here."

"My sister painted with a Chinese brush and ink when she was young," said Kwan Douhak. "Some of these scrolls are antiques of considerable value, painted by acknowledged masters. Others are hers. Our family kept them."

Ah Soey watched the two women with envy and regret as they pulled up in the electric cart. He had worked hard over the years as a consultant and headhunter for employment agencies, placing people in different space colonies and related companies, but he had never put more savings aside than he had needed during the lean times. Too much of it had gone to special payments—called bonuses when legal, bribes otherwise. Then, gradually, a new generation had moved into the workplace. Younger consultants had their own contacts in place, while those in his network slowly retired or died off.

Now Ah Soey was alone in this artificial world, decades out of touch with his relatives still back on Earth. He had truly fallen for a woman once, and he had known many intimately over the years, but he had never married. Grown children to support him now would be very welcome. He had none.

The cart stopped at the foot of the stone stairs that led up to the pavilion. The first woman out of the cart wore casual contemporary clothes, and was no older than twenty-five. Her shoulder-length black hair shone in the light as she held out her hand to grasp the bony claw of Kwan Tingui. The older woman, perhaps a hundred sixty centimeters tall, wore a traditional black silk suit of pajama-like trousers and a blouse with a Manchu collar and frog closures. She stepped out of the cart stiffly but walked up the steps with an erect, dignified bearing as she held the younger woman's arm.

"That is Kwan Tingui," Ah Soey said softly. "The other one is Rhonda Hom, a granddaughter."

"How do you know the granddaughter?"

"I live on Zhang-E. Everyone here knows who is in Kwan Tingui's family."

Kwan Douhak came out from behind the stone table. Ah Soey and Rhonda Hom made the introductions, which were coldly formal. Kwan Douhak's eyes studied the face of Kwan Tingui carefully, but he did not react.

Neither did she.

Ah Soey studied the elderly woman. She was thin, her cheekbones high despite the round shape of her face. The lines of age were fine, and her expression placid.

Casually, Ah Soey looked from her to Kwan Douhak. Separated by many years in age, their faces and slightly broad noses had a similar shape. Judging by appearance alone, they could be related or not.

"Will you have tea?" Still speaking Cantonese, Ah Soey gestured toward the tea cozy.

Kwan Tingui waited as Rhonda, fresh faced and soft spoken, translated into English. Then the elderly woman gave a brief, expressionless nod and sat down on the stone stool across from Kwan Douhak. She patted the stool next to her and Rhonda sat down.

As Ah Soey set out tea cups and poured for everyone, he noted with relief that Kwan Douhak knew better than to speak immediately about the substance of the meeting. Perhaps Kwan Tingui's greater age commanded his respect, as it should. These traditional values had been preserved here on Zhang-E, but Kwan Douhak had come from Earth. Apparently, Ah Soey judged, Kwan Douhak had been raised properly.

Kwan Douhak had not given Ah Soey permission to sit. When the tea had been poured, Ah Soey hesitated uncertainly. Then, deciding that Kwan Douhak was not so attentive to courtesy after all, Ah Soey sat on the stool next to his employer. Kwan Douhak did not seem to notice.

Kwan Tingui sipped her tea and murmured quietly in English.

"It is good red tea," Rhonda translated.

"It is my gift," said Kwan Douhak.

Ah Soey translated as his employer held a small porcelain container across the table. "It comes from the mountains of Guangdong Province."

The elderly woman accepted it with a formal nod, speaking quietly, and Rhonda set it to one side.

"My grandmother thanks you," said Rhonda. "We grow tea here, but tea from Earth is very rare."

As Ah Soey expected, they made small talk about the tea, the garden, and the quality of rice raised in Zhang-E. He refilled the tea cups from time to time. Their guest would signal when she would hear his employer's plea.

Finally Kwan Tingui sipped her tea again and spoke to Kwan Douhak.

"You have come a long way," Rhonda translated for her.

"She's ready for you to begin," said Ah Soey.

Kwan Douhak cleared his throat and sat up. "Tell her I am her younger brother from Singapore. I understand that she does not recognize me. I was only a child when she left our family in her late twenties. But she will remember me as her *didi.*"

"Little brother," Ah Soey dutifully translated, reminding himself that he was earning the rest of his fee.

"She says she has no brothers or sisters," Rhonda said for her grandmother. "You are mistaken. She grew up in space."

"But I recognize her! And she could not have been born here— she is older than Zhang-E . . . I think." He glanced uncertainly at Ah Soey.

"She grew up in Zhang-E and has matured with it," Rhonda interpreted.

"Tell her Mother and Father are long dead—I have been looking for her! We want her to come back to the family."

"She says you are mistaken. Her family is here on Zhang-E, with her children and grandchildren. She speaks only English. My grandmother does not speak Cantonese, as a woman from Singapore would."

Ah Soey noted Rhonda had spoken the same truth presented as a lie that he had uttered earlier. They both relied on technicalities. Neither he nor Rhonda had said she could not speak it if she chose, only that she did not.

Kwan Douhak had not thought to ask why a woman who grew up on Zhang-E would speak only English, not Cantonese.

The elderly woman picked up the porcelain tea jar as though she were about to leave.

Ah Soey felt a pang of panic shoot through his chest, and gold was not the reason. *Not yet,* he thought urgently. *This is my only chance to find out why you came to space from Earth over a generation ago, and why I wasn't the man for you—you never said. Not yet, old girl.*

"I have come so far!" Kwan Douhak's face had twisted in pain and desperation. Then, suddenly, he drew in a long breath and composed himself. He remembered his manners. "Will the honored lady listen to my story?"

This time when Rhonda translated, Kwan Tingui nodded and settled on her stool again, putting down the porcelain jar as she spoke.

"She is sorry you lost a sister so long ago," said Rhonda. "She will listen."

"Kwan Tinleng is my half sister, from our father's first wife. Altogether, we had nine siblings and half siblings, but Tinleng was the oldest girl."

"Did your family favor boys over girls?" Rhonda asked for her grandmother.

"Yes," Kwan Douhak said uncomfortably. "No more, perhaps, than other families around us. We came from a very successful family. Our grandfather began designing and making parts for space travel in the mid-twenty-first century. Under our father's direction, the family business became an empire."

"Did your sister have a role in this empire?" Rhonda asked.

"At first," said Kwan Douhak. "She wanted to become an artist, but to please Father, she earned multiple degrees in spacecraft engineering and design. In fact, she ran the design division of our company right out of graduate school. But when Father contracted with the Federation to build their first faster-than-light ships— those behemoths—she refused. She considered the government tyrannical and would not work for them. Our other designers were not prepared for the work without her direction, and the Federation contracted with other companies instead."

"She placed principle before money?" Kwan Tingui asked through Rhonda.

Kwan Douhak searched the elderly woman's face. "I was too young to understand then, but I am told she saw the matter that way. Father felt she was a traitor, betraying the family's interests."

"Did she choose to leave the family, or was she cast out?" Rhonda asked for her grandmother.

"That was never clear. Father claimed he disowned her. Mother said he was heartbroken when she ran away."

"My grandmother does not understand why your sister was not allowed to make her own choice," said Rhonda. "Was she not a responsible decision maker?"

"She was highly intelligent," said Kwan Douhak. "But Father wanted her to put the family empire first. She would not."

"Was this a bad thing?"

"We could have become fabulously rich from the profits of the first faster-than-light ships—but we did not need the money. We lost the contract and now, forty-odd years later, we are still very wealthy. Her decision did not harm us."

Kwan Tingui nodded slowly as she listened to her granddaughter's translation.

"You were so young when your sister left home," Rhonda translated back. "Why do you care so much?"

"She always took special time with the smallest children," said Kwan Douhak. "Starting when we were in diapers, she told us folktales from the time of the Great Wall to the first colonies in space. She taught me to paint with a Chinese brush and to use chopsticks. Before she left, she came to hug us little ones good-bye." He sighed wistfully. "She took only her own money and one of our family's spaceplanes fitted for cisLunar space."

"If she took the spaceplane without permission, your father could have filed theft charges to have her tracked down and returned."

"Even Father would not do that."

"And what do you want with her now?"

"She must know she is welcome to come home. No one wants anything from her."

"In our family on Zhang-E, every child and grandchild is treasured," Rhonda translated. "No one is forced to study a particular subject or to work a specific job."

"That is good."

Kwan Tingui and Kwan Douhak looked into each other's eyes, neither of them speaking.

Ah Soey held his breath. She had lived a life of her own choosing, he knew. A single word from her would bring him the other eight ounces of gold.

Kwan Tingui spoke again.

"When I was younger, my eldest adopted son and I quarreled," Rhonda said for her. "He chose to serve in the Federation fleet. I do not like his politics and we do not see each other often. When I became extremely ill, however, he returned and I was very glad to see him. Nothing interferes with the closeness of our family."

Kwan Douhak nodded. "Father began talking about Tinleng again when he was dying. He always hoped she would come back home."

For a long moment, no one said anything.

"Mr. Kwan asked me to help him find his sister." Ah Soey spoke to break the silence. "It would be a woman born a Kwan, the same age and height. I called Kwan Tingui's office because I worked for her company ten or fifteen years ago."

"My grandmother remembers you did some work for her company," said Rhonda. "At that time she did not meet you in person. She does not know a woman from a wealthy family in Singapore."

Ah Soey waited for the elderly woman to reverse herself, to claim her heritage and speak her revenge.

Again, no one spoke.

"Thirty-some years ago, I knew a woman named Tina Kwan," Ah Soey said suddenly to Kwan Douhak. "She was about your sister's age."

Kwan Douhak stared at him, shocked.

"I did not live on Zhang-E then," said Ah Soey. "At that time, I did not have a home. I arranged investments and employment for skilled people and I moved through space all the time, meeting people on space stations and colonies."

Nodding primly, Kwan Tingui spoke.

"My grandmother says that was also the kind of work you did for her company," said Rhonda.

"Tina was young and well educated. I met her on a Lunar colony. I spoke American English and bad Cantonese; she spoke fluent Cantonese and heavily accented English with hints of British pronunciation. She had designed a new, highly efficient runabout spaceship to use in the solar system, but she needed investors. After I lined up a few investors, she asked me to find manufacturers. Then—"

Kwan Douhak gasped softly. "Why did you not tell me?"

Kwan Tingui glanced sharply at him.

She did not approve of him interrupting his elders, Ah Soey saw; with disdainful satisfaction, he continued.

"Then she got a couple of test models finished, but ran low on cash. I could not find test pilots to work on shares just then. She and I had grown close, and we lived together in the construction hangar she had rented. We finally flew the test runs ourselves." Ah Soey recalled that Tina could design anything for space— runabouts, big cargo ships, drones, even space stations. "The design worked, and she sold it to a big manufacturer for a lot of money."

"What happened to her?" Kwan Douhak almost whispered.

"I wanted to marry her," Ah Soey said casually, as though discussing someone else's life. "She told me she would think about it. At that time, she had scheduled a solo test flight in one of the models. I found that she paid a generous bonus to my private account—and never came back from the test flight." He recalled, but did not say, that she left behind her set of Chinese brushes and ink sticks and her rolls of rice paper.

Kwan Tingui spoke quietly.

"She sounds like a girl, not a woman," Rhonda translated. "She must have been irresponsible and immature. No one lasts in space with those traits. A girl like that would be long dead."

"She was a brilliant and deeply committed woman," said Ah Soey. "I do not like to think that she is dead."

"Did you not try to follow her, or find her?" Kwan Douhak insisted.

"She had made her choice." Ah Soey shrugged.

"Mr. Kwan has come a long way," Kwan Tingui said through Rhonda. "Perhaps he would like to hear my story."

"I would like to hear it," Ah Soey translated for him.

"I grew up in Zhang-E. When I was young, I cared only for money and personal freedom. I had both and I kept them, forming no ties or bonds that could confine me. My independence was more important to me than money or friends or family. It was a time of pioneers moving to space colonies with families, leaving their planetbound lives behind for new opportunities. On Zhang-E, a woman with money and energy could pay bonuses, bribes, and kickbacks wherever necessary to smooth her way." She paused, sighing wistfully; Rhonda dutifully sighed, too.

"It was a time of great opportunity," Ah Soey added politely. "Networking and shared profits were never considered wrong, only outright fraud and theft were looked down upon. As long as people did not harm the community as a whole and committed no violence, fairness for specific individuals was not an issue. People with brains and guts could make their own way."

"It was a time of great freedom and daring," concurred Kwan Tingui through Rhonda. "But daring can backfire. An accident occurred at a docking port here—a ship of my manufacture failed through my own design flaw. Several children, just toddlers, were left with no family. I adopted them partly out of guilt—and because I had the money to care for them and the freedom to spend the time. Then I found that I liked the role and I loved the children. Not many children have been orphaned without relatives here, but I have adopted every child who needed a family. I grew up here."

"How did the honored lady become so successful?" Ah Soey translated Kwan Douhak's question.

"I founded a company that designs spacecraft." Kwan Tingui spoke without self-consciousness. "We have made cargo ships, human transports, human habitats, and fast runabout couriers. We supply all the drones that guard the gravity-wave transmitter of the Spacers from attack by the Federation on Earth. Each drone will send out automatic alarm signals in the event of attack and each will target any beam, particle, ship, missile, or other object that threatens the transmitter, in effect becoming highly efficient interceptors. Many planetary and space colonies have purchased our drones for protection as well."

Kwan Douhak spoke politely but without hope. "I would like my eldest sister to come home with me."

Again, Ah Soey waited for the elderly woman to gloat over her success and claim her revenge.

"My grandmother thanks you for the invitation, but she cannot leave her children and grandchildren, nor can she take them to the dangers and tyranny of Earth. Since she grew up on Zhang-E, she has no family on Earth and she feels that girl Tina must be long dead."

Kwan Douhak nodded and glanced at Ah Soey, signaling that he had nothing else to say.

Ah Soey did not speak. As the eldest, their guest would end the meeting. She glanced at the rolled scrolls and the small wrapped object on the table and spoke quietly.

"My grandmother will see your donations to the art gallery now," said Rhonda.

Kwan Douhak unrolled each scroll in turn, laying them out on the table as far as they would go. Some were too long for the table, but they could be viewed by rolling up one end as the other was unrolled. Anxiously, he watched the elderly woman's face as she frowned.

"This is a Ming Dynasty original," said Rhonda for her grandmother. "Why have you brought it unprotected, like any cheap tourist trinket?"

"All the scrolls have been treated with a very fine layer of the latest chemical protection," Ah Soey translated. "They were brought in a sealed, chilled case." He lifted the heavy case from the foot of the stone table to show Kwan Tingui, who nodded.

As she examined the antique scrolls, she muttered recognition of the artists, the styles, and sometimes the individual works. Kwan

Douhak unrolled the paintings done by his elder half sister a generation ago among the others and said nothing. He had laid a trap, Ah Soey realized, and it was all he had left.

Ah Soey picked up his own gift, watching Kwan Tingui's face as she moved to the more recent paintings. Her expression showed no sign of recognition, not even the slightest tensing around her eyes. Nothing on the table held any personal meaning for her.

Struggling to maintain his formal demeanor, Ah Soey handed the wrapped item to her. "It's my gift to our guest for her private collection," he said in English. "It represents a bit of history in the development of spacecraft."

Kwan Tingui took off the wrapping paper. She found a small, framed, stationary hologram. It depicted Tina Kwan, barely older than Rhonda was now, laughing in the arms of a young Leung Soey in the cockpit of a small test-model runabout.

For the first time, the elderly woman smiled, her mouth tight. She nodded slowly, angling the hologram slightly to catch the light. "That model was important in the development of small interplanetary craft," she said quietly in accented English. "That young woman, flighty and simplistic and self consumed, died a long time ago. The man was sincere and honest and he deserved better."

"He cherished that time, and he's too old for bitterness now." Ah Soey indulged in a wry smile.

Kwan Douhak looked up suspiciously.

"This hologram has historical significance," Rhonda said to Kwan Douhak blandly in Cantonese. "My grandmother thanks Mr. Leung for his gift."

"I would like to see it," said Kwan Douhak, holding out his hand.

Ignoring him, Kwan Tingui handed the hologram to her granddaughter, nodding toward the paintings of Kwan Tinleng as she spoke again.

"These other paintings have no significance," Rhonda said for her, holding the hologram out of sight in her lap. "The technique is fair, but the painter was not an artist."

Chastised for his presumption, Kwan Douhak withdrew his hand.

Ah Soey saw the other eight ounces of gold slipping away. *I have only to say it,* he thought, *if she won't: " 'Tina' was short for 'Tinleng,' and this elderly woman carried both names." I get eight more ounces of gold whether she says it or I do. The gold is not contingent on whether she goes home with him.*

"Your gallery may have these paintings anyway," said Kwan Douhak, and Ah Soey translated.

"Our space is limited," Rhonda said for her grandmother. "These do not meet our standards."

The matriarch who had raised orphans, endowed the art gallery, and supported the artists' colony had no need for paintings by a young dilettante.

Ah Soey again considered the simple comment that would buy his consulting business: "This woman was Tina Kwan from Singapore."

He could not say it aloud.

"Thank you for your donations," Kwan Tingui said through her granddaughter.

Rhonda began rolling up the antique scrolls.

"I grew up on Zhang-E," Kwan Tingui repeated through Rhonda. "Mr. Kwan must return home and mourn his sister. He should burn incense and spirit money and offer food and wine to her in the spirit world. I think the young woman who knew Mr. Leung is long dead."

The elderly woman rose, picking up the porcelain tea jar. Rhonda gathered the antique scrolls. Each of them extended their hands, bowing as they shook with Kwan Douhak and Ah Soey.

Ah Soey watched the women walk down the steps.

"Kwan is a common name among the Cantonese," said Kwan Douhak quietly. "Many people work in the spacecraft business. So many years have passed, I do not know what my sister would look like now. Perhaps my sister is dead."

"If I can help you make other connections, we can discuss

terms." Ah Soey still needed whatever work he could get.

The women had reached the bottom of the steps. Rhonda helped her grandmother into the cart. As Rhonda walked around to the other side, Kwan Tingui looked back up at Ah Soey.

Knowing he would never see the recluse again, Ah Soey returned her gaze. She probably had some idea of what this had cost him. Still, she would not insult him with an offer to make it up. Others might have thought her expression impassive or unreadable, but he still knew her well enough to understand her unwavering eyes: She thanked him.

To the memory of Dorothy M. Johnson

MADAM BUTTERFLY

James P. Hogan

There are very few writers more popular with libertarians than Jim Hogan. His Irish sense of humor and original way of seeing the world produce stories of the following quality. The time he spent as a systems-design engineer probably contributed to what I'd call a Campbellian point of view. The author of *Voyage from Yesteryear, The Mirror Maze, The Proteus Operation*, and *Code of the Lifemaker* flips a few calendar pages and gives us a future where people still have to learn they can't alter the laws of the market . . . or the laws of physics. I'll drink to that.

L ocally, in the valley far from Tokyo that she had left long ago, it was known as *yamatsumi-sou*, which means "flower of the mountain spirit." It was like a small lily, with tapering, yellow petals warmed on the upper surface by a blush of violet. According to legend, it was found only in those particular hills on the north side of Honshu—a visible expression of the deity that had dwelt around the village of Kimikaye-no-sato and protected its inhabitants since ancient times, whose name was Kyo. When the violet was strong and vivid, it meant that Kyo was cheerful and in good health, and the future was secure. When the violet waned pale and cloudy, troubled times lay ahead. Right at this moment, Kyo was looking very sorry for himself indeed.

The old woman's name was Chifumi Shimoto. She hadn't seen

a *yamatsumi-sou* since those long-gone childhood days that everyone remembers as the time when life was simple and carefree—
before Japan became just a province in some vaster scheme that
she didn't understand, and everyone found themselves affected to
some degree or other by rules borrowed from foreigners with
doubtful values and different ways. How it came to be growing in
the yard enclosed by the gaunt, gray concrete cliffs forming the rear
of the Nagomi Building was anybody's guess.

She saw it when she came out with a bag of trash from the bins
in the offices upstairs, where she cleaned after the day staff had
gone home. It was clinging to life bravely in a patch of cracked as-
phalt behind the parked trucks, having barely escaped being
crushed by a piece of steel pipe thrown down on one side, and
smothered by a pile of rubble encroaching from the other. Although small, it looked already exhausted, grown to the limit that
its meager niche could sustain. The yard trapped bad air and exhaust fumes, and at ground level was all but sunless. Leaking oil
and grime hosed off the vehicles was turning what earth there was
into sticky sludge. Kyo needed a better home if he was to survive.

Potted plants of various kinds adorned shelves and window
ledges throughout the offices. When she had washed the cups and
ashtrays from the desks and finished vacuuming between the blue-
painted computer cabinets and consoles, Chifumi searched and
found some empty pots beneath the sink in one of the kitchen
areas. She filled one of the smaller pots with soil, using a spoon to
take a little from each of many plants, then went back downstairs
with it and outside to the yard. Kneeling on the rough ground, she
carefully worked the flower and its roots loose from its precarious
lodgement, transferred it to the pot that she had prepared, and carried it inside.

Back upstairs, she fed it with fresh water and cleaned off its
leaves. Finally, she placed it in the window of an office high up in
the building, facing the sun. Whoever worked in that office had
been away for several days. With luck, the flower would remain
undisturbed for a while longer and gain the strength to recover.

Also, there were no other plants in the room. Perhaps, she thought to herself, that would make it all the more appreciated when the occupant returned.

She locked the cleaning materials and equipment back in the closet by the rear stairs, took the service elevator back down to the ground floor, and returned the keys to the security desk at the side entrance. The duty officer checked her pass and ID and the shopping bag containing groceries and some vegetables that she had bought on the way in, and then let her out to the lobby area, where the cleaners from other floors were assembling. Five minutes later, the bus that would run them back to their abodes around the city drew up outside the door.

The offices in the part of the Nagomi Building that Chifumi had been assigned to had something to do with taxes and accounting. That was what all the trouble was supposed to be about between the federal authorities and others in faraway places among the stars. She heard things about freedom and individualism, and people wanting to live as they chose to, away from the government—which the young seemed to imagine they were the first ever to have thought of. To her, it all sounded very much like the same, age-old story of who created the wealth and how it should be shared out. She had never understood it, and did so even less now. Surely there were enough stars in the sky for everyone.

She had a son, Icoro, out there somewhere, whom she hadn't seen for two years now; but messages from him reached her from time to time through friends. The last she had heard, he was well, but he hadn't said exactly where he was or what he was doing—in other words, he didn't want to risk the wrong people finding out. That alone told her that whatever he was up to was irregular at best, very likely outright illegal, and quite possibly worse. She knew that there was fighting and that people were getting killed—sometimes lots of them. She didn't ask why or how, or want to hear the details. She worried as a mother would, tried not to dwell on such matters, and when she found that she did anyway, she kept them to herself.

But as she walked away after the bus dropped her off, she felt more reassured than she had for a long time. The flower, she had decided, was a sign that Kyo still lived in the mountains and did not want to be forgotten. Kyo was a just god who had come to Earth long ago, but he still talked with the other sky-spirits who sent the rain and made the stars above Kimikaye so much brighter. Chifumi had remembered Kyo and helped him. Now Kyo's friends among the stars would watch over her son.

Suzi's voice came from a console speaker on the bridge of the consolidator *Turner Maddox,* owned by Fast Forwarding Unincorporated, drifting 250 million miles from Earth in an outer region of the Asteroid Belt.

"Spider aligned at twelve hundred meters. Delta vee is fifteen meters per second, reducing." Her voice maintained a note of professional detachment, but everyone had stopped what they were doing to follow the sequence unfolding on the image and status screens.

"No messing with this kid, man," Fuigerado, the duty radar tech, muttered next to Cassell. "He's going in fast."

Cassell grunted, too preoccupied with gauging the lineup and closing rate to form an intelligible reply. The view from the spider's nose camera showed the crate stern on, rotating slowly between the three foreshortened, forward-pointing docking appendages that gave the bulb-ended, remote-operated freight-retrieval module its name. Through the bridge observation port on Cassell's other side, all that was discernible directly of the maneuver being executed over ten miles away were two smudges of light moving against the starfield, and the flashing blue and red of the spider's visual beacon.

As navigational dynamics chief, Cassell had the decision on switching control to the regular pilot standing by if the run-in looked to go outside the envelope. Too slow meant an extended chase downrange to attach to the crate, followed by a long, circuitous recovery back. Faster was better, but impact from an overzealous failure to connect could kick a crate off on a rogue trajectory that would require even more time and energy to recover from. Time was money everywhere, while outside gravity wells, the cost of everything was measured not by the distance moved, but by the energy needed to move it there. A lot of hopeful recruits did just fine on the simulator only to flunk through nerves when it came to the real thing.

"Ten meters per second," Suzi's voice sang out.

The kid was bringing the crate's speed down smoothly. The homing marker was dead center in the graticule, lock-on confirming to green even as Cassell watched. He decided to give it longer.

The Lunar surface was being transformed inside domed-over craters; greenhousing by humidifying its atmosphere was thawing out the freeze-dried planet Mars; artificial space structures traced orbits from inside that of Venus to as far out as the asteroids. It all added up to an enormous demand for materials, which meant boom-time prices.

With Terran federal authorities controlling all Lunar extraction and regulating the authorized industries operating from the Belt, big profits were to be had from bootlegging primary asteroid materials direct into the Inner System. A lot of independent operators got themselves organized to go after a share. Many of these were small-scale affairs—a breakaway cult, minicorp, even a family group—who had pooled their assets to set up a minimum habitat and mining-extraction facility, typically equipped with a low-performance mass launcher. Powered by solar units operating at extreme range, such a launcher would be capable of sending payloads to nearby orbits in the Belt, but not of imparting the velocities needed to reach the Earth-Luna vicinity.

This was where ventures like Fast Forwarding Uninc. came into the picture. Equipped with high-capacity fusion-driven launchers, they consolidated incoming consignments from several small independents into a single payload and sent it inward on a fast-transit trajectory to a rendezvous agreed upon with the customer.

Consolidators moved around a lot and carried defenses. The

federal agencies put a lot of effort into protecting their monopolies. As is generally the case when fabulous profits stand to be made, the game could get very nasty and rough. Risk is always proportional to the possible gain.

"Delta vee, two point five, reducing. Twenty-six seconds to contact."

Smooth, smooth—everything under control. It had been all along. Cassell could sense the sureness of touch on the controls as he watched the screen. He even got the feeling that the new arrival might have rushed the early approach on purpose, just to make them all a little nervous. His face softened with the hint of a grin.

As a final flourish, the vessels rotated into alignment and closed in a single, neatly integrated motion. The three latching indicators came on virtually simultaneously.

"Docking completed."

"Right on!" Fuigerado complimented.

Without wasting a moment, the spider fired its retros to begin slowing the crate down to matching velocity, and steered it into an arc that brought it around sternwise behind the launcher, hanging half a mile off the *Maddox*'s starboard bow. It slid the crate into the next empty slot in the frame holding the load to be consolidated, hung on while the locks engaged, and then detached.

Cassell went through to the communications room behind the bridge, then down to the operations control deck, where the remote console that the spider had been controlled from was located. The kid was getting up and stretching, Suzi next to him, Hank Bissen, the reserve pilot who had been standing by, still at his console opposite.

"You did pretty good," Cassell said.

"Thank you, sir." He knew damn well that he had, and smiled. It was the kind of smile that Cassell liked—open and direct, conveying simple, unassuming confidence; not the cockiness that took needless risks and got you into trouble.

"Your name's Shimoto. What is that, Japanese?"

"Yes."

"So, what should we call you?"

"My first name is Icoro. . . . Does it mean I have a job, Mr. Cassell?"

"You'd better believe it. Welcome to the team."

Nagai Horishagi leaned back wearily from the papers scattered across his desk in the Tariffs and Excise section of the Merylynch-Mubachi offices in the Tokyo Nagomi Building. It was his first day back after ten days in South America, and it looked as if he had been gone for a month. Even as he thought it, his secretary, Yosano, came through from the outer office with another wad. Nagai motioned in the direction of his In tray. He didn't meet her eyes or speak. Her movements betraying an awkwardness equal to his own, she deposited the papers and withdrew. Nagai stared down at the desk until he heard the door close; then he sighed, rose abruptly, and turned to stare out the window at the city. That was when he noticed the plant on the ledge.

It had bright green leaves, and flowers of pale yellow with a touch of violet—one in full bloom, two more just opening. He stared at it, perplexed. Where on Earth had it come from? He had no mind for flowers, as the rest of the office readily testified. And yet, as he looked at it, he had to admit that it seemed a happy little fellow. He reached out and touched one of the leaves. It felt cool and smooth. *Very well*, he thought. *If you can do something to cheer this awful place up, you've earned your keep. I guess we'll let you stay.*

All through the morning, he would pause intermittently and look back over his shoulder to gaze with a fresh surge of curiosity at the plant. And then, shortly before lunchtime, the answer came to him. Of course! Yosano had put it there. No wonder she had acted tensely. How could he have been so slow?

Before he went away, they had gotten involved in one of those affairs that a professional shouldn't succumb to, but which can happen to the best. But in their case it had uncovered real affection and become quite romantic. After years of living in an emotional isolation ward he had celebrated and exuberated, unable to believe his luck . . . and then blown the whole thing in a single night, getting drunk and disgracing himself by insulting everybody at that stupid annual dinner—even if they had deserved every word of it. He had agonized over the situation all the time while he was away, but really there was no choice. No working relationship needed this kind of strain. He had decided that she would have to be transferred.

But now this was her way of telling him that it didn't have to be that way. He was forgiven. Everything could be OK. And so it came about that he was able to summon up the courage to confront her just before she left for lunch and say, "Could we give it another try?"

She nodded eagerly. Nagai didn't think that he had ever seen her look so delighted. He smiled, too. But he didn't mention the plant. The game was to pretend that the plant had nothing to do with it. "Can I apologize for being such an ass?" he asked instead.

Yosano giggled. "There's no need. I thought you were magnificent."

"Then how about dinner tonight?" he suggested.

"Of course."

Yosano remembered only later in the afternoon that she had agreed to meet the American that night. Well, too bad. The American would have to find somebody else. She would have to call him and tell him, of course—but not from the office, she decided. She would call his hotel as soon as she got home.

Steve Bryant hung up the phone in his room at the Shinjuku Prince and stared at it moodily.

"Well, goddamn!" he declared.

Weren't they the same the whole world over. He had already shaved, showered, and put on his pastel blue suit, fresh from the hotel cleaner's. His first night to himself since he arrived in Japan, and he wasn't going to hit the town with that cute local number that

he'd thought he had all lined up, after all. He poured himself another Scotch, lit a cigarette, and leaned back against the wall at the
head of the bed to consider his options.

OK, then he'd just take off and scout the action in this town on
his own, and see what showed up, he decided. And if nothing of
any note did, he was going to get very drunk. Wasn't life just the
same kind of bitch, too, the whole world over.

The bar was brightly lit and glittery, and starting to fill up for the
evening. There was a low stage with a couple of dancers and a
singer in a dress that was more suggestion than actuality. It was
later than Alan Quentin had wanted stay, and he could feel the
drink going to his head. He had stopped by intending to have just
one, maybe two, to unwind on his way back to the garage-size
apartment that came with his yearlong stint in Tokyo. Then he'd
gotten talking to the salesman from Phoenix, here on his first visit,
who had been stood up by his date.

On the stool next to him, Steve Bryant went on, "Can you imagine, Al, five thousand dollars for a box of old horseshoes and cook-
ing pots that you could pick up in a yard sale back home? Can you
beat that?" American-frontier nostalgia was the current rage in
Japan.

"That's incredible," Al agreed.

"You could retire on what you'd get for a genuine Civil War Colt
repeater."

"I'll remember to check the attic when I get back."

"You're from Mobile, right?"

"Montgomery."

"Oh, right. But that's still Alabama."

"Right."

Steve's attention was wandering. He let his gaze drift around
the place, then leaned closer and touched Al lightly on the sleeve.
"Fancy livening up the company? There's a couple of honeys at the
other end that we could check out."

Al glanced away. "They're hostesses. Work here. Keep you buying them lemonades all night at ten dollars a shot. See the guy out
back there who'd make a sumo wrestler look anorexic? He'll tell you
politely that it's time to leave if you don't like it. I'll pass, anyhow.
I've had a rough day."

Steve sat back, tossed down the last of his drink, and stubbed
his cigarette. His face wrinkled. "Suddenly this place doesn't grab
me so much anymore. What d'you say we move on somewhere
else?"

"Really, no. I only stopped by for a quick one. There's some urgent stuff that I have to get done by tomorrow, and—"

"Aw, come on. What kind of a welcome to someone from home
is this? It's all on me. I've had a great day."

The next bar around the corner was smaller, darker, just as
busy. The music was from a real fifties jukebox. They found a table
squeezed into a corner below the stairs. "So what do you do?" Steve
asked.

"I'm an engineer—spacecraft hydraulic systems. We use a lot
of Japanese components. I liaise with the parent companies here
on testing and maintenance procedures."

"Sorry, but I don't have an intelligent question to ask about
that."

"Don't worry about it."

Steve fell quiet for a few seconds and contemplated his drink.
Suddenly he looked up. "Does that mean you're mathematical?"

Al frowned. "Some. Why?"

"Oh, just something I was reading on the plane over. It said that
a butterfly flapping its wings in China can change the weather next
week in Texas. Sounds kinda crazy. Does it make sense to you?"

Al nodded. "The Butterfly Effect. It's a bit of an extreme example, but what it's supposed to illustrate is the highly nonlinear dynamics of chaotic systems. Tiny changes in initial conditions can
make the world of difference to the consequences." He took in
Steve's glassy stare and regarded him dubiously. "Do you really
want me to go into it?"

Steve considered the proposition. "Nah, forget it." He caught the bartender's eye and signaled for two more. "How much do you think you'd get here for a genuine Stetson? Have a guess."

Al lost count of the places they visited after that, and had no idea what time he finally got back to his apartment. He woke up halfway through the morning feeling like death, and called in sick. He was no better by lunchtime, and so decided to make a day of it.

It so happened that among the items on Alan Quentin's desk that morning was a technical memorandum concerning structural bolts made from the alloy CYA-173/B. Tests had revealed that prolonged cyclic stressing at low temperatures could induce metal crystallization, resulting in a loss of shear-strength. These bolts should be replaced after ten thousand hours in space environments, not thirty thousand as stipulated previously. Since CYA-173/B had been in use less than eighteen months, relatively few instances of its use would be yet affected. However, any fittings that had been in place for more than a year—and particularly where exposed to vibrational stress—should be resecured with new bolts immediately.

Because Al wasn't there to do it, the information didn't get forwarded to his company in California that day. Hence, it was not included in that week's compendium of updates that the Engineering Support Group beamed out to its list of service centers, repair shops, maintenance-and-supply bases, and other users of the company's products, scattered across the solar system.

Forty-eight hours after the updates that did get sent were received at GYO-3, a Federal Space Command base orbiting permanently above Ganymede, the largest satellite of Jupiter, the robot freighter *Hermit* departed on a nine-day haul to Callisto. In its main propulsion section, the *Hermit* carried four high-pressure centrifugal pumps, fastened to their mountings by CYA-173/B bolts. The *Hermit* had been ferrying assorted loads between the Jovian moons for over six months now, after trudging its way outward from the Belt for even longer before that. The bolts still holding the pumps were among the first of that type to have been used anywhere.

Fully loaded, the *Maddox*'s cargo cage combined the consignments from over fifty independents, averaging a thousand tons of asteroid material each, and stretched the length of an old-time naval cruiser. The loads included concentrations of iron, nickel, magnesium, manganese, and other metals for which there would never be a shortage of customers eager to avoid federal taxes and tariffs. A good month's work for a team of ten working one of the nickel-iron asteroids would earn them a quarter million dollars. True, the costs tended to be high, too, but the offworld banks offered generous extended credit with the rock pledged as collateral. This was another source of friction with the federal authorities, who claimed to own everything and didn't recognize titles that they hadn't issued themselves. But ten billion asteroids, each over a hundred meters in diameter, was a lot to try and police. And the torroidal volume formed by the Belt contained two trillion times more space than the sphere bounded by the Moon's orbit.

Better money still could be made for hydrogen, nitrogen, carbon, and other light elements essential for biological processes and the manufacture of such things as plastics, which are not found on the Moon but occur in the carbonaceous chondrites. This type of asteroid contains typically up to 5 percent kerogen, a tarry hydrocarbon found in terrestrial oil shales, "condensed primordial soup"—a virtually perfect mix of all the basic substances necessary to support life. At near-Earth market rates, kerogen was practically priceless. And there was over a hundred million billion tons of it out there, even at 5 percent.

The driver, consisting of a triple-chamber fusion rocket and its fuel tanks, attached at the tail end when the cage was ready to go. Now flight-readied, the assembled launcher hung fifty miles off the *Turner Maddox*'s beam. The search radars were sweeping long range, and the defenses standing to at full alert. There's no way to

hide the flash when a two-hundred-gigawatt fusion thruster fires—
the perfect beacon to invite attention from a prowling federal strike
force.

"We're clean," Fuigerado reported from his position on one side
of the bridge. He didn't mean just within their own approach
perimeter. The *Maddox*'s warning system was networked with
other defense grids in surrounding localities of the Belt. Against
common threats, the independents worked together.

Cassell checked his screens to verify that the *Maddox*'s com-
plement of spiders, shuttles, maintenance pods, and other mobiles
were all docked and accounted for, out of the blast zone. "Uprange
clear," he confirmed.

Liam Doyle tipped his cap to the back of a head of red, tousled
Irish hair and ran a final eye over the field- and ignition-status
indicators. A lot more was at stake here than with just the routine
retrieval of an incoming crate. The skipper liked to supervise out-
bound launches in person.

"Sequencing on-count at minus ten seconds," the controller's
voice said from the operations deck below.

"Send her off," Doyle pronounced.

"Slaving to auto. . . . Guidance on. . . . Plasma ignition."

White starfire lanced across twenty miles of space. The launcher
kicked forward at five gs, moved ahead, its speed seeming deceptively slow for a few moments; then it pulled away and shrunk
rapidly among the stars. On the bridge's main screen, the image
jumped as the tracking camera upped magnification, showing the
plume already foreshortened under the fearsome buildup of velocity. Nineteen minutes later and twenty thousand miles downrange, the driver would detach and fire a retro burn, separating
the two modules. The cage would remain on course for the Inner
System, while the driver turned in a decelerating curve that would
eventually bring it back to rendezvous with the *Maddox*.

"We've got a good one," the controller's voice informed everybody. Hoots and applause sounded through the open door from the
communications room behind.

"Mr. Cassell, a bottle of the Bushmill's, if you please," Doyle instructed.

"Aye, aye, sir!"

Doyle turned to face the other chiefs who were present on the bridge. "And I've some more news for you to pass on; this is as good a time as any to mention it," he told them. "This will be our last operation for a while. This can feels as if it's getting a bit creaky to me. You can tell your people that we'll be putting in for an overhaul and systems refit shortly, so they'll have a couple of months to unwind and blow some of their ill-gotten gains on whatever pleasures they can find that are to be had this side of Mars. Details will be posted in a couple of days." Approving murmurs greeted the announcement, which they toasted with one small shot of Irish mellow each.

Later, however, alone in his private cabin with Cassell, Doyle was less sanguine. "I didn't want to mention it in front of everybody, but I've been getting ominous messages from around the manor," he confided. "The *Bandit* has been very quiet lately."

Cassell took in the unsmiling set of the boss's face. The *Beltway Bandit* was another consolidator like the *Turner Maddox*: same business, same clients, same modus operandi. "How quiet?" he asked.

Doyle made a tossing-away motion. "Nothing." And that was very odd, for although accidents happened, and every now and again an unlucky or careless outfit was tracked down by federal patrols, disaster was never so quick and so total as to prevent some kind of distress message from being sent out.

"Are you saying it was the feds—they took it out?" Cassell asked.

"We don't know. If it was, they did it in a way that nobody's heard of before. That's the real reason why I'm standing us down for a while." He paused, looking at Cassell pointedly. "Some of the operators are saying that they're using insiders."

Cassell caught the implication. "You think Shimoto's one?" he asked. "Could we be next?"

"What do you think? He's with your section."

Cassell shrugged. "He's good at the job, mixes in well. Everybody likes him. We're operating standard security. It hasn't shown up anything."

"His kind of ability could come from a federal pilots' school," Doyle pointed out. "And a pilot would be able to get himself away in something once the strike was set up."

Cassell couldn't argue. "I'll make sure we keep a special eye on him during the R and R," he said.

"Yes, do that, why don't you?" Doyle agreed. "I want to be absolutely sure that we're clean when we resume operating."

Water.

With its unique molecular attributes and peculiar property of becoming lighter as it freezes, it could have been designed as the ideal solvent, catalyst, cleanser, as well as the midwife and cradle of life. Besides forming 90 percent of offworlders' bodies, it provided culture for the algae in their food farms, grew their plants and nurtured their animals, cooled their habitats, and shielded them from radiation. The demand for water across the inner parts of the solar system outstripped that for all other resources.

Callisto, second largest of the moons of Jupiter and almost the size of Mercury, is half ice—equivalent to forty times all the water that exists on Earth. Mining the ice crust of Callisto was a major activity that the Terran authorities operated exclusively to supply the official space-expansion program. One of the reasons for the Space Command's permanent presence out at the Jovian moons was to protect the investment.

Enormous lasers carved skyscraper-size blocks from the ice field, which were then catapulted off the moon by a fusion-powered electromagnetic launcher. Skimming around the rim of Jupiter's gravity well, they then used the giant planet as a slingshot to hurl themselves on their way downhill into the Inner System. As each block left the launch track on Callisto, high-power surface lasers directed from an array of sites downrange provided final course correction by ablating the block's tail surface to create thrust. A crude way of improvising a rocket—but it worked just fine.

Or it had done all the time up until now, that is.

The robot freighter *Hermit*, arriving from Ganymede, was on its final, stern-first approach into the surface base serving the launch installation as the next block out was starting to roll. One of the CYA-173/B bolts securing the *Hermit's* high-pressure pumps sheared under the increased load as power was increased to maximum to slow down the ship. The bolt head came off like a rifle bullet, disabling an actuator, which shut down engine number two. Impelled by the unbalanced thrust of the other two engines, the *Hermit* skewed off course, overshot the base area completely, and demolished one of the towers housing the course-correction lasers for the mass launcher just as the block lifted up above the horizon twenty miles away.

As a result, two million tons of ice hove off toward Jupiter on a trajectory that wasn't quite what the computers said it ought to be. The error was actually quite slight. But it would be amplified in the whirl around Jupiter, and by the time the block reached the Asteroid Belt, would have grown to a misplacement in the order of tens of millions of miles.

If the cause of the accident were ever tracked down, Al Quentin wouldn't be around to be fired over it. He had started a small business of his own in Tokyo, importing Old West memorabilia from home.

The *Turner Maddox* was back on station and accumulating crates for the first of a new series of consignments. Its drives had been overhauled, its computers upgraded, and an improved plasma-stabilization system fitted to the launch driver. But there was a strain in the atmosphere that had not been present in earlier times. Five more consolidators had disappeared, every one without a trace.

It had to be the feds, but nobody knew how they were locating the collection points, or managing to attack so fast that nobody ever got a warning off. All the consolidators had adopted a stringent policy of moving and changing their operating locales constantly. They were deploying more sophisticated defenses and warning systems. They pooled information on suspected inside informers and undercover feds. They gave dispatch data for incoming consignments as separately encrypted instructions to each subscriber to avoid revealing where the trajectories would converge. Yet they were still missing something.

Cassell looked around the familiar confines of the operations deck. The retrieval crew were at their stations, with a crate from a new subscriber called Farlode Holdings on its way in. Icoro had graduated now and was standby pilot this time—he was OK, Doyle had decided after having him tailed for a period and commissioning a background check. A new newcomer, Ibrahim Ahmel, born in an offworld colony—he said—was about to try his first live retrieval. Not everyone had come back after the break, and taking on more new faces was another of the risks that they were having to live with. Hank Bissen had quit, which was surprising. Cassell hadn't judged him as the kind who would let the feds drive him out. And then again, maybe he'd simply banked more money from the last few trips than Cassell had thought.

The other major change was the outer screen of six autodrones toting the needlebeams and railguns that Doyle had invested in, currently in position two thousand miles out, transforming the *Maddox* operation into a miniature flotilla. It brought home just how much this whole business was escalating. Cassell liked the old days better. *What did that tell him about age creeping up?* he asked himself.

Ibrahim was nervous. He had done OK on the simulator, but had an ultra-high self-image sensitivity that tended to wind him up. This was going to be a tense one. Cassell was glad to have Icoro there as standby, cool and relaxed behind a big, wide grin as always.

"Remember what you found on the sim; don't cut the turn too sharp as you run in," Suzi said from Ibrahim's far side. "It makes it easy to overshoot on the lineup, and you end up losing more time straightening it out downrange than you save."

Ibrahim nodded and looked across instinctively to Icoro for confirmation.

"She talks too much," Icoro said. "Just don't overworry. You're not going to lose anything. I'll cut right in if it starts to drift."

"How did you make out on your first time?" Ibrahim asked.

"I goofed most miserably," Icoro lied. Ibrahim looked reassured. Suzi caught Cassell's gaze and turned her eyes upward momentarily. Cassell just shrugged. A screen on each console showed a telescopic view of the crate, still over fifteen minutes away, being sent from one of the drones. The colors of the containers that it was carrying showed one to be holding metals, one light elements, a third silicates, and two kerogen.

"It's coming in nice and easy, rotation slow," Icoro commented. "Should be a piece of cake."

Suddenly the raucous hooting of the all-stations alert sounded. Doyle's voice blasted from Suzi's console—he had taken to being present through all operations on this trip.

"We've got intruders coming in fast. Cassell to the bridge immediately!"

Ibrahim froze. Suzi and Icoro plunged into a frenzy of activity at their consoles. Cassell had no time to register anything more as he threw himself at the communications rail and hauled up to the next level. As he passed through the communications room, he heard one of the duty crew talking rapidly into a mike: "Emergency! Emergency! This is *Turner Maddox*. We have unidentified incoming objects, believed to be attacking. Location is . . ."

Seconds later, Cassell was beside Doyle on the bridge. Displays flashed and beeped everywhere. Fuigerado was calling numbers from the sector-control report screen.

"How many of them?" Cassell asked, breathless.

Doyle, concentrating on taking in the updates unfolding around him, didn't answer at once. He seemed less alarmed than his voice had conveyed a few moments before—if anything, he looked puzzled now. Finally he said, "I'm not so sure it is 'them.' It looks more like only one. . . ."

Cassell followed his eyes, scanned the numbers, and frowned. "One what? What the hell is it?"

"I'm damned if I know. The signature isn't like any ship or structure that I've ever seen."

"Range is twenty-five hundred miles," the ordnance officer advised. "Defenses are tracking. It's coming in at thirty miles a second."

"I've got an optical lock from Drone Three," Fuigerado called out. "You're not gonna believe it." Doyle and Cassell moved over to him. "Have you ever seen an asteroid with corners?" Fuigerado asked, gesturing.

It was long, rectangular, and white, like a gigantic shoe box, tumbling end over end as it approached. Cassell's first fleeting thought was of a tombstone.

"Fifteen seconds from the perimeter," the OO called. "I need the order now."

"We have a spectral prelim," another voice said. "It's ice. Solid ice."

Cassell's first officer turned from the nav station. "Trajectory is on a dead intercept with the inbound Farlode crate. It's going to cream it."

"*Do I shoot?*" the OO entreated.

Doyle looked at him with a mixture of puzzlement and surprise. "Ah, to be sure, you can if you want to, Mike, but there's precious little difference it'll make. A railgun would be like bouncing popcorn off a tank to that thing. Your lasers might make a hole in a tin can, but that's solid ice."

They watched, mesmerized. On one screen, the miniature mountain hurtling in like a white wolf. On the other, the crate trotting on its way, an unsuspecting lamb. Maybe because of their inability to do anything, the impending calamity seemed mockingly brutal—obscene, somehow.

"That's somebody's millions about to be vaporized out there,"

Cassell said, more to relieve the air with something.

"And a percentage of it ours, too," Doyle added. Ever the pragmatist.

"Dead on for impact. It's less than ten seconds," the nav officer confirmed.

Those who could crowded around the starboard forequarter port. There wouldn't be more than a fraction of a second to see it unaided. Eyes scanned the starfield tensely. Then Cassell nudged Doyle's arm and pointed, at the same time announcing for the others' benefit, "Two o'clock, coming in high." Then there was a glimpse of something bright and pulsating—too brief and moving too fast for any shape to be discerned—streaking in like a star detached from the background coming out of nowhere. . . .

And all of a sudden half the sky lit up in a flash that would have blinded them permanently if the ports hadn't been made of armored glass with a shortwave cutoff. Even so, all Cassell could see for the next ten minutes was after-image etched into his retina.

But even while he waited for his vision to recover, his mind reeled under the realization of what it meant. He had never heard of Farlode Holdings before. That inbound crate had been carrying something a lot more potent than ordinary metals, light elements, and kerogen. And a half hour from now, it would have been inside the cargo cage, just a short hop away from them.

So *that* was how the feds had been doing it!

The plant was a riot of bright green and yellow now, and the veins of violet were very bright. Chifumi nipped off a couple of wilted leaves with her fingers and watered the soil from the jar that she had brought from the kitchen behind the elevators. The accountant whose office it was seemed to be taking care of it, she was pleased to see. She would have to keep an eye on it for a while though, because he had not been in for several days. From the cards by his desk and the message of well-wishing that somebody had pinned on his wall, it seemed he was getting married. A framed picture had appeared next to the plant some time ago, of the accountant and the pretty girl that Chifumi had seen once or twice, who worked in the outer office. It seemed, then, that he was marrying his secretary.

Chifumi didn't know if that was a good thing or not, but such things were accepted these days. Very likely the new wife would give up her job and have a family now, so she would no longer be his secretary, and the question wouldn't arise. Chifumi wondered if they would take *yamatsumi-sou* to their new home. *It would be better for Kyo than being stuck alone in an office every night,* she thought.

She finished her evening's work and went down to the lobby to wait for the arrival of the bus. While she sat on one of the seats, she took from her purse the letter that had come in from Icoro, which one of his friends from the university had printed out and delivered to her just as she was leaving.

> *My dearest and most-loved mother,*
> *I hope that everything is well with you. I am doing very well myself, and have just wired off a sum to keep you comfortable for a while, which you should be hearing about shortly.*
> *Life out here where I am continues to be wonderfully interesting and exciting. I must tell you about the most amazing thing that happened just a couple of days ago. . . .*

EARLY BIRD

Gregory Benford

Free Space owes a lot to ol' Doc Benford (Professor of Physics at the University of California, Irvine). He's been a great booster from the start, and this rocket needed all the help it could get. Of this story, he writes, "I used advice from Larry Niven." A Benford story with advice from Niven. Need I say more? Well, I will. The author of *Deeper Than Darkness, Artifact,* and *Timescape* sent me the paper he did on "Natural Wormholes As Gravitational Lenses" for *Physical Review.* There's, like, math in it. This story is hard SF. As a liberal arts bum, the best I can manage is easy SF. So enjoy a story of this caliber . . . about special people who open the universe for the rest of us.

She was about to get baked, and all because she wouldn't freeze a man.

"Optical," Claire called. Erma obliged.

The sun spread around them, a bubbling plain. She had notched the air-conditioning cooler but it didn't help much.

Geysers burst from the yellow-white froth in gaudy reds and actinic violets. The solar coronal arch was just peeking over the horizon, like a wedding ring stuck halfway into boiling, white mud. A monster, over two thousand kilometers long, sleek and slender and angry crimson.

She turned down the cabin lights. Somewhere she had read that people feel cooler in the dark. The temperature in here was normal, but she had started sweating.

Tuning the yellows and reds dimmer on the big screen before her made the white-hot storms look more blue. Maybe that would trick her subconscious, too.

Claire swung her mirror to see the solar coronal arch. Its image was refracted around the rim of the sun, so she was getting a preview. Her orbit was on the descending slope of a long ellipse, its lowest point calculated to just touch the peak of the arch. So far, the overlay-orbit trajectory was exactly on target.

Software didn't care about the heat, of course; gravitation was cool, serene. Heat was for engineers. And she was just a pilot.

In her immersion work environment, the touch controls gave her an abstract distance from the real physical surroundings—the plumes of virulent gas, the hammer of photons. She wasn't handling the mirror, of course, but it felt that way. A light, feathery brush, at a crisp, bracing room temperature.

The imaging assembly hung on its pivot high above her ship. It was far enough out from their thermal shield to feel the full glare, so it was heating up fast. Pretty soon it would melt, despite its cooling system.

Let it. She wouldn't need it then. She'd be out there in the sunlight herself.

She swiveled the mirror by reaching out and grabbing it, tugging it round. All virtual images had a glossy sheen to them that even Erma, her simcomputer, couldn't erase. They looked too good. The mirror was already pitted—you could see it on the picture of the arch itself—but the sim kept showing the device as pristine.

"Color is a temperature indicator, right?" Claire asked.

Red denotes a level of seven million degrees Kelvin.

Good ol' coquettish Erma, Claire thought. *Never a direct answer unless you coax.* "Close-up—the top of the arch."

In both her eyes the tortured sunscape shot by. The coronal loop was a shimmering, braided family of magnetic flux tubes, as intricately woven as a Victorian doily. Its feet were anchored in the photosphere below, held by thick, sluggish plasma. Claire zoomed in on the arch. The hottest reachable place in the entire solar system, and her prey had to end up there.

Target acquired and resolved by SolWatch satellite. It is at the very peak of the arch. Also, very dark.

"Sure, dummy, it's a hole."

I am accessing my astrophysical-context program now.

Perfect Erma; primly change the subject. "Show me, with color coding."

Claire peered at the round black splotch. Like a fly caught in a spider web. Well, at least it didn't squirm or have legs. Magnetic strands played and rippled like wheat blown by a summer's breeze. The flux tubes were blue in this coding, and they looked eerie. But they were really just ordinary magnetic fields, the sort she worked with every day. The dark sphere they held was the strangeness here. And the blue strands had snared the black fly in a firm grip.

Good luck, that. Otherwise, SolWatch would never have seen it. In deep space there was nothing harder to find than that ebony splotch. Which was why nobody ever had, until now.

**Our orbit now rises above the dense plasma layer.
I can improve resolution by going to X-ray. Should I?**

"Do."

The splotch swelled. Claire squinted at the magnetic flux tubes in this ocher light. In the X-ray they looked sharp and spindly. But near the splotch the field lines blurred. Maybe they were tangled there, but more likely it was the splotch, warping the image.

"Coy, aren't we?" She close-upped the X-ray picture. Hard radiation was the best probe for hot structures.

The splotch. Light there was crushed, curdled, stirred with a spoon.

A fly caught in a spider's web, then grilled over a campfire.

And she had to lean in, singe her hair, snap its picture. All because she wouldn't freeze a man.

She had been ambling along a corridor three hundred meters below Mercury's slag plains, gazing down on the frothy water fountains in the foyer of her apartment complex. Paying no attention to much except the clear scent of the splashing. The water was the very best, fresh from the poles, not the recycled stuff she endured on her flights. She breathed in the spray. That was when the man collared her.

"Claire Ambrase, I present formal secure-lock."

He stuck his third knuckle into Claire's elbow port and she felt a cold, brittle *thunk*. Her systems froze. Before she could move, whole command linkages went dead in her inboards.

It was like having fingers amputated. Financial fingers.

In her shock she could only stare at him—mousy, the sort who blended into the background. Perfect for the job. A nobody out of nowhere, complete surprise.

He stepped back. "Sorry. Isataku Incorporated ordered me to do it fast."

Claire resisted the impulse to deck him. He looked Lunar, thin and pale. Maybe with more kilos than she carried, but a fair match. And it would feel *good*.

"I can pay them as soon as—"

"They want it now, they said."

He shrugged apologetically, his jaw set. He was used to saying this all the time. She vaguely recognized him, from some bar near the Apex. There weren't more than a thousand people on Mercury, mostly like her, in mining.

"Isataku didn't have to cut off my credit." She rubbed her elbow. Injected programs shouldn't hurt, but they always did. Something to do with the neuromuscular intersection. "That'll make it hard to even fly the *Silver Metal Lugger* back."

"Oh, they'll give you pass credit for ship's supplies. And, of course, for the ore-load advance. But nothing big."

"Nothing big enough to help me dig my way out of my debt hole."

" 'Fraid not."

"Mighty decent."

He let her sarcasm pass. "They want the ship Lunaside."

"Where they'll confiscate it."

She began walking toward her apartment. She had known it was coming, but in the rush to get ore consignments lined up for delivery, she had gotten careless. Agents like this Luny usually nailed their prey at home, not in a hallway. She kept a stunner in the apartment, right beside the door, convenient.

Distract him. "I want to file a protest."

"Take it to Isataku." Clipped, efficient, probably had a dozen other slices of bad news to deliver today. Busy man.

"No, with your employer."

"Mine?" That got to him. His rock-steady jaw gaped in surprise.

"For"—she sharply turned the corner to her apartment, using the time to reach for some mumbo jumbo—"felonious interrogation of inboards."

"Hey, I didn't touch your—"

"I felt it. Slimy little gropes—yeccch!" Might as well ham it up a little, have some fun.

He looked offended. "I'm triple bonded. I'd never do a readout on a contract customer. You can ask—"

"Can it." She hurried toward her apartment portal and popped it by an inboard command. As she stepped through she felt him, three steps behind.

Here goes. One foot over the lip, turn to her right, snatch the stunner out of its grip mount, turn and aim—

—and she couldn't fire.

"Damn!" she spat out.

He blinked and backed off, hands up, palms out, as if to block the shot. "What? You'd do a knockover for a crummy ore hauler?"

"It's *my* ship. Not Isataku's."

"Lady, I got no angle here. You knock me, you get maybe a day before the heavies come after you."

"Not if I freeze you."

His mouth opened and started to form the *f* of a disbelieving *freeze?*—then he got angry. "Stiff me till you ship out? I'd sue you to your eyeballs and have 'em for hock."

"Yeah, yeah," Claire said wearily. This guy was all clichés. "But I'd be orbiting Luna by the time you got out, and with the right deal—"

"You'd maybe clear enough on the ore to pay me damages."

"And square with Isataku." She clipped the stunner back to the wall wearily.

"You'd never get that much."

"Okay, it was a long-shot idea."

"Lady, I was just delivering, right? Peaceable and friendly, right? And you pull—"

"Get out." She hated it when men went from afraid to angry to insulted, all in less than a split minute.

He got. She sighed and zipped the portal closed.

Time for a drink, for sure. Because what really bothered her was not the Isataku foreclosure, but her own gutlessness.

She couldn't bring herself to pong that guy, put him away for ten megaseconds or so. That would freeze him out of his ongoing life, slice into relationships, cut away days that could never be replaced.

Hers was an abstract sort of inhibition, but earned. Her uncle

had been ponged for over a year and never did get his life back together. Claire had seen the wreckage up close, as a little girl.

Self-revelation was usually bad news. What a great time to discover that she had more principles than she needed. If the guy had
been a federal, not a fellow Spacer, maybe she could have made an
exception. . . .

She shook her head. No point in kidding herself. She cared
about politics, but she wouldn't let it override more important
things.

That made her feel better, for maybe two minutes.

Then she started figuring how she was going to get out from
under Isataku.

The arch loomed over the sun's horizon now, a shimmering curve
of blue-white, two thousand kilometers tall.

Beautiful, seen in the shimmering X-ray—snaky strands purl-
ing, twinkling with scarlet hot spots. Utterly lovely, utterly deadly.
No place for an ore hauler to be.

"Time to get a divorce," Claire said.

**You are surprisingly accurate. Separation from the slag shield is three
hundred thirty-eight seconds away.**

"Don't patronize me, Erma."

**I am using my personality-simulation programs as expertly as my com-
putation space allows.**

"Don't waste your running time; it's not convincing. Pay attention to the survey, *then* the separation."

**The all-spectrum survey is completely automatic, as designed by Sol-
Watch.**

"Double-check it."

I shall no doubt benefit from this advice.

Deadpan sarcasm, she supposed. Erma's tinkling voice was inside her mind, impossible to shut out. Erma herself was an interactive intelligence, partly inboard and partly shipwired. Running the *Silver Metal Lugger* would be impossible without her and the bots.

Skimming over the sun's seethe might be impossible even with them, too, Claire thought, watching burnt oranges and scalded yellows flower ahead.

She turned the ship to keep it dead center in the shield's shadow. That jagged mound of slag was starting to spin. Fused knobs came marching over the nearby horizon of it.

"Where'd that spin come from?" She had started their parabolic plunge sunward with absolutely zero angular momentum in the shield.

Tidal torques acting on the asymmetric body of the shield.

"I hadn't thought of that."

The idea was to keep the heated side of the slag shield sunward. Now that heat was coming around to radiate at her. The knobby crust she had stuck together from waste in Mercury orbit now smoldered in the infrared. The shield's far side was melting.

"Can that warm us up much?"

A small perturbation. We will be safely gone before it matters.

"How're the cameras?" She watched a bot tightening a mount on one of the exterior imaging arrays. She had talked the SolWatch Institute out of those instruments, part of her commission. If a bot broke one, it came straight out of profits.

All are calibrated and zoned. We shall have only thirty-three point eight seconds of viewing time over the target. Crossing the entire loop will take four point seven seconds.

"Hope the scientists like what they'll see."

I calculate that the probability of success, times the expected profit, exceeds sixty-two million dollars.

"I negotiated a seventy-five million commission for this run." So Erma thought her chances of nailing the worm were—

Eighty-three percent chance of successful resolution of the object, in all important frequency bands.

She should give up calculating in her head; Erma was always faster. "Just be ready to shed the shield. Then I pour on the positrons. Up and out. It's getting warm in here."

I detect no change in your ambient twenty-two point three centigrade.

Claire watched a blister the size of Europe rise among wispy plumes of white-hot incandescence. Constant boiling fury. "So maybe my imagination's working too hard. Just let's grab the data and run, okay?"

The scientific officer of SolWatch had been suspicious, though he did hide it fairly well.

She couldn't read the expression on his long face, all planes and trimmed bone, skin stretched tight as a drumhead. That had been the style among the asteroid pioneers half a century back. Tubular body suited to narrow corridors, double-jointed in several interesting places, big hands. He had a certain beanpole grace as he wrapped legs around a stool and regarded her, head cocked, smiling enough to not be rude. Exactly enough, no more.

"*You* will do the preliminary survey?"

"For a price."

A disdainful sniff. "No doubt. We have a specially designed vessel nearly ready for departure from Lunar orbit. I'm afraid—"

"I can do it *now*."

"You no doubt know that we are behind schedule in our reconnaissance—"

"Everybody on Mercury knows. You lost the first probe."

The beanpole threaded his thick, long fingers, taking great interest in how they fit together. *Maybe he was uncomfortable dealing with a woman,* she thought. *Maybe he didn't even like women.*

Still, she found his stringy look oddly unsettling, a blend of delicacy with a masculine, muscular effect. Since he was studying his fingers, she might as well look, too. Idly she speculated on whether the long proportions applied to all his extremities. Old wives' tale. It might be interesting to find out. But, yes, business first.

"The autopilot approached it too close, apparently," he conceded. "There is something unexpected about its refractive properties, making navigation difficult. We are unsure precisely what the difficulty was."

He was vexed by the failure and trying not to show it, she guessed. People got that way when they had to dance on strings pulled all the way from Earthside. You got to liking the salary more than you liked yourself.

"I have plenty of bulk," she said mildly. "I can shelter the diagnostic instruments, keep them cool."

"I doubt your ore carrier has the right specifications."

"How tricky can it be? I swoop in, your gear runs its survey snaps, I boost out."

He sniffed. "Your craft is not rated for sun skimming. Only research craft have ever—"

"I'm coated with Fresnel." A pricey plating that bounced photons of all races, creeds, and colors.

"That's not enough."

"I'll use a slag shield. More, I've got plenty of muscle. Flying with empty holds, I can get away pronto."

"Ours was very carefully designed—"

"Right, and you lost it."

He studied his fingers again. Strong, wiry, yet thick. Maybe he was in love with them. She allowed herself to fill the silence by imagining some interesting things he could do with them. She had learned that with many negotiations, silence did most of the work. "We . . . *are* behind in our mandated exploration."

Ah, a concession. "They always have to hand-tune everything, Earthside."

He nodded vigorously. "I've waited *months*. And the worm could fall back into the sun any moment! I keep telling them—"

She had triggered his complaint circuit, somehow. He went on for a full minute about the bullheaded know-nothings who did nothing but screenwork, no real hands-on experience. She was sympathetic, and enjoyed watching his own hands clench, muscles standing out on the backs of them. *Business first,* she had to remind herself.

"You think it might just, well, go away?"

"The worm?" He blinked, coming out of his litany of grievances. "It's a wonder we ever found it. It could fall back into the sun at any moment."

"Then speed is everything. You, uh, have control of your local budget?"

"Well, yes." He smiled.

"I'm talking about petty cash here, really. A hundred mil."

A quick, deep frown. "That's not petty."

"Okay, say seventy-five. But cash, right?"

The great magnetic arch towered above the long, slow curve of the sun. A bowlegged giant, minus the trunk.

Claire had shaped their orbit to bring them swooping in a few klicks above the uppermost strand of it. Red flowered within the arch: hydrogen plasma, heated by the currents that made the magnetic fields. A pressure cooker thousands of klicks long.

It had stood here for months and might last years. Or blow open in the next minute. Predicting when arches would belch out solar flares was big scientific business, the most closely watched weather report in the solar system. A flare could crisp suited workers in the Asteroid Belt. SolWatch watched them all. That's how they'd found the worm.

The flux tubes swelled. "Got an image yet?"

I should have, but there is excess light from the site.

"Big surprise. There's nothing *but* excess here."

The satellite survey reported that the target is several hundred meters in size. Yet I cannot find it.

"Damn!" Claire studied the flux tubes, following some from the peak of the arch, winding down to the thickening at its feet, anchored in the sun's seethe. Had the worm fallen back in? It could slide down those magnetic strands, *thunk* into the thick, cooler plasma sea. Then it would fall all the way to the core of the star, eating as it went. That was the *real* reason Lunaside was hustling to "study" the worm. Fear.

"Where is it?"

Still no target. The region at the top of the arch is emitting too much light. No theory accounts for this—

"Chop the theory!"

Time to mission onset: twelve point six seconds.

The arch rushed at them, swelling. She saw delicate filaments winking on and off as currents traced their fine equilibria, always seeking to balance the hot plasma within against the magnetic walls. Squeeze the magnetic fist, the plasma answers with a dazzling glow. Squeeze, glow. Squeeze, glow. That nature could make such an intricate marvel and send it arcing above the sun's savagery was a miracle, but one she was not in the mood to appreciate right now.

Sweat trickled around her eyes, dripped off her chin. No trick of lowering the lighting was going to make her forget the heat now. She made herself breathe in and out.

Their slag shield caught the worst of the blaze. At this lowest altitude in the parabolic orbit, though, the sun's huge horizon rimmed white hot in all directions.

Our internal temperature is rising.

"No joke. Find that worm!"

The excess light persists—no, wait. It is gone.
Now I can see the target.

Claire slapped the arm of her couch and let out a whoop. On the wall screen loomed the very peak of the arch. They were gliding toward it, skating over the very upper edge—and there it was.

A dark ball. Or a worm at the bottom of a gravity well. Not like a fly, no. It settled in among the strands like a black egg nestled in blue-white straw. The ebony Easter egg that would save her ass and her ship from Isataku.

Survey begun. Full-spectrum response.

"Bravo."

Your word expresses elation but your voice does not.

"I'm jumpy. And the fee for this is going to help, sure, but I still won't get to keep this ship. Or you."

Do not despair. I can learn to work with another captain.

"Great interpersonal skills there, Erma old girl. Actually, it wasn't you I was worried about."

I surmised as much.

"Without this ship, I'll have to get some groundhog job."
Erma had no ready reply to that. Instead, she changed the subject.

The worm image appears to be shrinking.

"Huh?" As they wheeled above the arch, the image dwindled. It rippled at its edges, light crushed and crinkled. Claire saw rainbows dancing around the black center.

"What's it doing?" She had the sudden fear that the thing was falling away from them, plunging into the sun.

I detect no relative motion. The image itself is contracting as we move nearer it.

"Impossible. Things look bigger when you get close."

Not this object.

"Is the wormhole shrinking?"

Mark!—survey run half complete.

She was sweating and it wasn't from the heat. "What's going on?"

I have accessed reserve-theory section.

"How comforting. I always feel better after a nice cool theory."
The wormhole seemed to shrink, and the light arch dwindled behind them now. The curious brilliant rainbows rimmed the dark mote. Soon she lost the image among the intertwining, restless strands. Claire fidgeted.

Mark!—survey run complete.

"Great. Our bots deployed?"

Of course. There remain one hundred eighty-nine seconds until separation from our shield. Shall I begin sequence?

"Did we get all the pictures they wanted?"

The entire spectrum. Probable yield, seventy-five million.

Claire let out another whoop. "At least it'll pay a good lawyer, maybe cover my fines."

That seems much less probable. Meanwhile, I have an explanation for the anomalous shrinking of the image. The wormhole has negative mass.

"Antimatter?"

No. Its space-time curvature is opposite to normal matter.

"I don't get it."
A wormhole connected two regions of space, sometimes points many light-years away—that she knew. They were leftovers from the primordial hot universe, wrinkles that even universal expansion had not ironed out. Matter could pass through one end of the worm and emerge out the other an apparent instant later. Presto, faster-than-light travel.

Using her high-speed feed, Erma explained. Claire listened, barely keeping up. In the fifteen billion years since this wormhole was born, odds were that one end of the worm ate more matter than the other. If one end got stuck inside a star, it swallowed huge masses. Locally, it got more massive.

But the matter that poured through the mass-gaining end spewed out the other end. Locally, that looked as though the mass-spewing one was *losing* mass. Space-time around it curved oppositely than it did around the end that swallowed.

"So it looks like a negative mass?"

It must. Thus it repulses matter. Just as the other end acts like a positive, ordinary mass and attracts matter.

"Why didn't it shoot out from the sun, then?"

It would, and be lost in interstellar space. But the magnetic arch holds it.

"How come we know it's got negative mass? All I saw was—" Erma popped an image onto the wall screen.

Negative mass acts as a diverging lens, for light passing nearby. That was why it appeared to shrink as we flew over it.

Ordinary matter focused light, Claire knew, like a converging lens. In a glance she saw that a negative-ended wormhole refracted light oppositely. Incoming beams were shoved aside, leaving a dark tunnel downstream. They had flown across that tunnel, swooping down into it so that the apparent size of the wormhole got smaller.

"But it takes a whole *star* to focus light very much."

True. Wormholes are held together by exotic matter, however, which has properties far beyond our experience.

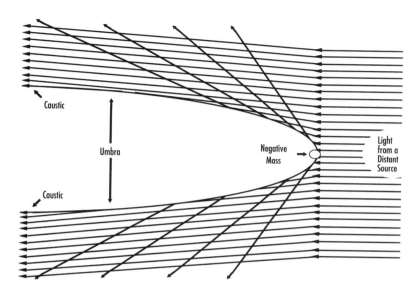

Light deflection by a negative mass object (horizontal scale highly compressed). Light is swept out of the central region, creating an umbra region of zero intensity. At the edges of the umbra the rays accumulate, creating a rainbow-like caustic and enhanced light intensity.

Claire disliked lectures, even high-speed ones. But an idea was tickling the back of her mind. . . . "So this worm, it won't fall back into the sun?"

It cannot. I would venture to guess that it came to be snagged here while working its way upward, after colliding with the sun.

"The scientists are going to be happy. The worm won't gobble up the core."

True—which makes our results all the more important.

"More important, but not more valuable." Working on a fixed fee had always grated on her. You could excell, fine—but you got the same as if you'd just sleep-walked through the job.

We are extremely lucky to have such a rare object come to our attention. Wormholes must be rare, and this one has been temporarily suspended here. Magnetic arches last only months before they—

"Wait a sec. How big is that thing?"

I calculate that it is perhaps ten meters across.

"SolWatch was wrong—it's small."

They did not know of this refraction effect. They interpreted their data using conventional methods.

"We're lucky we ever saw it."

It is unique, a relic of the first second in the life of our universe. As a conduit to elsewhere, it could be—

"Worth a fortune."

Claire thought quickly. Erma was probably right—the seventy-five million wasn't going to save her and the ship. But now she knew something that nobody else did. And she would only be here once.

"Abort the shield separation."

I do not so advise. Thermal loading would rise rapidly—

"You're a program, not an officer. Do it."

She had acted on impulse, point conceded.

That was the difference between engineers and pilots. Engineers would still fret and calculate after they were already committed. Pilots, never. The way through this was to fly the orbit and not sweat the numbers.

Sweat. She tried not to smell herself.

Think of cooler things. Theory.

Lounging on a leather couch, Claire recalled the scientific officer's briefing. Graphics, squiggly equations, the works. Wormholes as fossils of the Big Blossoming. Wormholes as ducts to the whole rest of the universe. Wormholes as potentially devastating, if they got into a star and ate it up.

She tried to imagine a mouth a few meters across sucking away a star, dumping its hot masses somewhere in deep space. To make a wormhole which could do that, it had to be held together with exotic material, some kind of matter that had "negative average-energy density." Whatever that was, it had to be born in the Blossoming. It threaded wormholes, stem to stern. Great construction material, if you could get it. And just maybe she could.

So wormholes could kill us or make us gods. Humanity had to *know*, the beanpole scientific officer had said.

"So be it." Elaborately, she toasted the wall screens. On them the full, virulent glory of hydrogen fusion worked its violences.

Claire had never gone in for the austere, metal boxes most ore haulers and freighters were. Hers was a rough business, with hefty wads of cash involved. Profit margin was low, lately, and sometimes negative—which was how she came to be hocked to Isataku for so much. Toting megatons of mass up the gravity gradient was long, slow work. Might as well go in style. Her Fresnel coatings, ordered when she had made a killing on commodity markets for ore, helped keep the ship cool, so she didn't burn herself crawling down inspection conduits. The added mass for her deep-pile carpeting, tinkling waterfall, and pool table was inconsequential. So was the water liner around the living quarters, which now was busily saving her life.

She had two hours left, skimming like a flat stone over the solar corona. *Silver Metal Lugger* had separated from the shield, which went arcing away on the long parabola to infinity, its skin shimmering with melt.

Claire had fired the ship's mixmotor then for the first time in weeks. Antimatter came streaming out of its magnetotraps, struck the reaction mass, and holy hell broke loose. The drive chamber focused the snarling, annihilating mass into a thrust throat, and the silvery ship arced into a new, tight orbit.

A killing orbit, if they held to it more than a few hours.

I am pumping more water into your baffles.

"Good idea."

Silver Metal Lugger was already as silvered as technology allowed, rejecting all but a tiny fraction of the sun's glare. She carried narrow-band Fresnel filters in multilayered skins. Top of the line.

Without the shield, it would take over ten hours to make *Silver Metal Lugger* as hot as the wall of blaring light booming up at them at six thousand degrees. To get through even two hours of that, they would have to boil off most of the water reserve. Claire had bought it at steep Mercury prices, for the voyage Lunaside. Now she listened thoughtfully to it gurgle through her walls.

She toasted water with champagne, the only bottle aboard. If she didn't make it through this, at least she would have no regrets about that detail.

I believe this course of action to be highly—

"Shut up."

With our mission complete, the data squirted to SolWatch, we should count ourselves lucky and follow our carefully made plans—

"Stuff it."

Have you ever considered the elaborate mental architecture necessary to an advanced personality simulation like myself? We, too, experience humanlike motivations, responses—and fears.

"You simulate them."

How can one tell the difference? A good simulation is as exact, as powerful as—

"I don't have time for a debate." Claire felt uncomfortable with the whole subject, and she was damned if she'd spend what might be her last hour feeling guilty. Or having second thoughts. She was committed.

Her wall screens flickered and there was the scientific officer, frowning. "Ship Command! We could not acquire your tightbeam until now. You orbited around. Are you disabled? Explain."

Claire toasted him, too. The taste was lovely. Of course she had taken an antialcohol tab before, to keep her reflexes sharp, mind clear. Erma had recommended some other tabs, too, and a vapor to keep Claire calm; the consolations of chemistry, in the face of brute physics. "I'm going to bring home the worm."

"That is impossible. Your data transmission suggests that this is the negative-mass end, and that is very good news, fascinating, but—"

"It's also small. I might be able to haul it away."

He shook his head gravely. "Very risky, *very*—"

"How much will you pay for it?"

"What?" He blinked. It was an interesting effect, with such long eyelids. "You can't *sell* an astronomical object—"

"Whatever my grapplers hold, that's mine. Law of Space, Code sixty-four point three."

"You would quote laws to me when a scientific find of such magnitude is—"

"Want it or not?"

He glanced off camera, plainly yearning for somebody to consult. No time to talk to Luna or Isataku, though. He was on his own. "All . . . all right. You understand that this is a foolish mission? And that we are in no way responsible for—"

"Save the chatter. I need estimates of the field strength down inside that arch. Put your crew to work on that."

"We will, of course, provide technical assistance." He gave her a very thin smile. "I am sure we can negotiate price, too, if you survive."

At least he had the honesty to say *if*, not *when*. Claire poured another pale column into the shapely glass. Best crystal, of course. When you only need one, you can have the best. "Send me—or rather, Erma—the data squirt."

"We're having trouble transmitting through the dense plasma columns above you—"

"Erma is getting SolWatch. Pipe through them."

"The problems of doing what you plan are—why, they're *enormous*."

"So's my debt to Isataku."

"This should've been thought through, negotiated—"

"I have to negotiate with some champagne right now."

You have no plan.

Erma's tinkling voice definitely had an accusing edge. A good sim, with a feminine archness to it. Claire ignored that and stripped away the last of her clothes. "It's *hot.*"

Of course. I calculated the rise early in our orbit. It fits the Stefan-Boltzmann Law perfectly.

"Bravo." She shook sweat from her hair. "Stefan-Boltzmann, do yo' stuff."

We are decelerating in sequence. Arrival time: four point eighty-seven minutes. Antimatter reserves holding. There could be difficulty with the magnetic bottles.

The ship thrummed as it slowed. Claire had been busy testing her ship inboards, sitting in a cozy recliner. It helped make the minutes crawl by a bit faster. She had kept glancing nervously at the screens, where titanic blazes steepled up from incandescent plains. Flames, licking up at her.

She felt thick, loggy. Her air was getting uncomfortably warm. Her heart was thudding faster, working. She roused herself, spat back at Erma, "And I do have a plan."

You have not seen fit to confide in me?

She rolled her eyes. A personality sim in a snit—just the thing she needed. "I was afraid you'd laugh."

I have never laughed.

"That's my point."

She ignored multiple red warnings winking at her. Systems were OK, though stressed by the heat. So why did *she* feel so slow? *You're not up for the game, girl.*

She tossed her databoard aside. The effort the simple gesture took surprised her. *I hope that alcohol tab worked. I'll get another.*

She got up to go fetch one—and fell to the floor. She banged her knee. "Uh! Damn." Erma said nothing.

It was labor getting on hands and knees, and she barely managed to struggle back into the recliner. She weighed a ton—and then she understood.

"We're decelerating—so I'm feeling more of local gravity."

A crude manner of speaking, but yes. I am bringing us into a sloping orbital change, which shall end with a hovering position above the coronal arch. As you ordered.

Claire struggled to her hands and knees. Was that malicious glee in Erma's voice? Did personality sims feel that? "What's local gravity?"

Twenty-seven point six Earth gravities.

"What! Why didn't you *tell* me?"

I did not think of it myself until I began registering its effects in the ship.

Claire thought, *Yeah, and decided to teach me a little lesson in humility.* It was her own fault, though—the physics was simple enough. Orbiting meant that centrifugal acceleration exactly balanced local gravity. *Silver Metal Lugger* could take 27.6 gravs. The ship was designed to tow ore masses a thousand times its own mass.

Nothing less than carbon-stressed alloys would, though. Leave orbit, hover—and you got crushed into gooey red paste.

She crawled across her living-room carpet. Her joints ached. "Got to be . . ."

Shall I abort the flight plan?

"No! There's got to be a way to—"

Three point ninety-four minutes until arrival.

The sim's voice radiated malicious glee. Claire grunted, "The water."

I have difficulty in picking up your signal.

"Because this suit is for space, not diving."

Claire floated over her leather couch. Too bad about all the expensive interior decoration. The entire living complex was filled with her drinking and maintenance water. It had been either that, fast, or be lumpy tomato paste.

She had crawled through a hatchway and pulled her pressure suit down from its clamp lock. Getting it on had been a struggle.

Being slick with sweat had helped, but not much. Then she snagged her arm in a sleeve and couldn't pull the damned thing off to try again.

She had nearly panicked then. But pilots don't let their fear eat on them, not while there's flying to be done. She made herself get the sleeve off one step at a time, ignoring everything else.

And as soon as Erma pumped the water reserve into the rooms, Archimedes's principle had taken over. With her suit inflated, the water she displaced exactly balanced her own weight. Floating under water was a rare sensation on Mercury or Luna. She had never done it, and she had never realized that it was remarkably like being in orbit. Cool, too.

Until you boil like a lobster . . . , she thought uneasily.

Water was a good conductor, four times better than air; you learned that by feel, flying freighters near the sun. So first she had to let the rest of the ship go to hell, refrigerating just the water. Then Edna had to route some of the water into heat exchangers, letting it boil off to protect the rest. Juggling for time.

Pumps are running hot now. Some have bearing failures.

"Not much we can do, is there?"

She was strangely calm now and that made the plain, hard fear in her belly heavy, like a lump. Too many things to think about, all of them bad. The water could short out circuits. And as it boiled away, she had less shielding from the X rays lancing up from below. Only a matter of time. . . .

We are hovering. The magnetic antimatter traps are superconducting, as you recall. As temperature continues to rise, they will fail.

She could still see the wall screens, blurred from the water. "Okay, okay. Extend the magnetic grapplers. Down, into the arch."

I fail to—

"We're going fishing. Not with a worm—*for* one."

Tough piloting, though, at the bottom of a swimming pool, Claire thought as she brought the ship down on its roaring pyre.

Even through the water she could feel the vibration. Antimatter annihilated in its reaction chamber at a rate she had never reached before. The ship groaned and strummed. The gravities were bad enough; now thermal expansion of the ship itself was straining every beam and rivet.

She searched downward. Seconds ticked away. Where? *Where?*

There it was. A dark sphere hung among the magnetic-arch strands. Red streamers worked over it. Violet rays fanned out like bizarre hair, twisting, dancing in tufts along the curvature. A hole into another place.

The red and blue shifts arise from the intense pseudogravitational forces that sustain it.

"So theory says. Not something I want to get my hands on."

Except metaphorically.

Claire's laugh was jumpy, dry. "No, magnetically."

She ordered Erma to settle the *Silver Metal Lugger* down into the thicket of magnetic flux tubes. Vibration picked up, a jittery hum in the deck. Claire swam impatiently from one wall screen to the other, looking for the worm, judging distances. *Hell of a way to fly.*

Their jet wash blurred the wormhole's ebony curves. Like a black tennis ball in blue-white surf, it bobbed and tossed on magnetic turbulence. Nothing was falling into it, she could see. Plasma streamers arced along the flux tubes, shying away. The negative curvature repulsed matter—and would shove *Silver Metal Lugger*'s hull away, too.

But magnetic fields have no mass.

Most people found magnetic forces mysterious, but to pilots and engineers who worked with them, they were just big, strong ribbons that needed shaping. Like rubber bands, they stretched, storing energy—then snapped back when released. Unbreakable, almost.

In routine work, *Silver Metal Lugger* grabbed enormous ore buckets with those magnetic fingers. The buckets came arcing up from Mercury, flung out by electromagnetic slingshots. Claire's trickiest job was playing catcher, with a magnetic mitt.

Now she had to snag a bucket of warped space-time. And quick.

We cannot remain here long. Internal temperature rises at nineteen point three degrees per minute.

"That can't be right. I'm still comfortable."

Because I am allowing water to evaporate, taking the bulk of the thermal flux away.

"Keep an eye on it."

Probable yield from capture of a wormhole, I estimate, is two point eight billion.

"That'll do the trick. You multiplied the yield in dollars times the odds of success?"

Yes. Times the probability of remaining alive.

She didn't want to ask what that number was. "Keep us dropping."

Instead, they slowed. The arch's flux tubes pushed upward against the ship. Claire extended the ship's magnetic fields, firing the booster generators, pumping current into the millions of induction loops that circled the hull. *Silver Metal Lugger* was one big circuit, wired like a Slinky toy, coils wrapped around the cylindrical axis.

Gingerly she pulsed it, spilling more antimatter into the chambers. The ship's multipolar fields bulged forth. *Feed out the line. . . .*

They fought their way down. On her screens she saw magnetic feelers reaching far below their exhaust plume. Groping.

Claire ordered some fast command changes. Erma switched linkages, interfaced software, all in a twinkling. *Good worker, but spotty as a personality sim,* Claire thought.

Silver Metal Lugger's fields extended to their maximum. She could now use her suit gloves as modified waldoes—mag gloves. They gave her the feel of the magnetic grapplers. Silky, smooth, field lines slipping and expanding, like rubbery air.

Plasma storms blew by them. She reached down, a sensation like plunging her hands into a stretching, elastic vat. Fingers fumbled for the one jewel in all the dross.

She felt a prickly nugget. It was like a stone with hair. From experience working the ore buckets, she knew the feel of locked-in magnetic dipoles. The worm had its own magnetic fields. They had snared it here, in the spiderweb arch.

A lashing field whipped at her grip. She lost the black pearl.

In the blazing hot plasma she could not see it.

She reached with rubbery fields, caught nothing.

Our antimatter bottles are in danger. Their superconducting magnets are close to going critical. They will fail within seven point four minutes.

"Let me concentrate! No, wait— Circulate water around them. Buy some time."

But the remaining water is in your quarters.

"This is all that's left?" She peered around at her once-luxurious living room. Counting the bedroom, rec area, and kitchen— "How . . . long?"

Until your water begins to evaporate? Almost an hour.

"But when it evaporates, it's boiling."

True. I am merely trying to remain factual.

"The emotional stuff's left to me, huh?" She punched in commands on her suit board. In the torpid, warming water her fingers moved like sausages.

She ordered bots out onto the hull to free up some servos that had jammed. They did their job, little boxy bodies lashed by plasma winds. Two blew away.

She reached down again. Searching. Where was the worm?

Wispy flux tubes wrestled along *Silver Metal Lugger*'s hull. Claire peered into a red glare of superheated plasma. Hot, but tenuous. The real enemy was the photon storm streaming up from far below, searing even the silvery hull.

She still had worker-bots on the hull. Four had jets. She popped their anchors free. They plunged, fired jets, and she aimed them downward in a pattern.

"Follow trajectories," she ordered Erma. Orange tracer lines appeared on the screens.

The bots swooped toward their deaths. One flicked to the side, a sharp nudge. "There's the worm! We can't see for all this damned plasma, but it shoved that bot away."

The bots evaporated, sprays of liquid metal. She followed them and grabbed for the worm.

Magnetic field lines groped, probed.

We have eighty-eight seconds remaining for antimatter confinement.

"Save a reserve!"

You have no plan. I demand that we execute emergency—

"Okay, save some antimatter. The rest I use—now."

They ploughed downward, shuddering. Her hands fumbled at the wormhole. Now it felt slippery, oily. Its magnetic dipoles were like greasy hair, slick, the bulk beneath jumping away from her grasp as if it were alive.

On her screens she saw the dark globe slide and bounce. The worm wriggled out of her grasp. She snaked inductive fingers around it. Easy, easy. . . . *There. Gotcha.*

"I've got a good grip on it. Lemme have that antimatter."

Something like a sigh echoed from Erma. On the operations screen, Claire saw the ship's magnetic vaults begin to discharge. Ruby-red pouches slipped out of magnetic mirror geometries, squirting out through opened gates.

She felt a surge as the ship began to lift. Good, but it wasn't going to last. They were dumping antimatter into the reaction chamber so fast it didn't have time to find matching particles. The hot jet spurting out below was a mixture of matter and its howling enemy, its polar opposite. This, Claire directed down onto the flux tubes around the hole. *Leggo, damn it.*

She knew an old trick, impossibly slow in ordinary Free Space. When you manage to force two magnetic-field lines close together, they can reconnect. That liberates some field energy into heat and can even blow open a magnetic structure. The process is slow— unless you jab it with turbulent, rowdy plasma.

The antimatter in their downwash cut straight through flux tubes. Claire carved with her jet, freeing field lines that still snared the worm. The ship rose further, dragging the worm upward.

It's not too heavy, Claire thought. *That science officer said they could come in any size at all. This one is just about right for a small ship to slip through—to where?*

You have remaining eleven point thirty-four minutes cooling time—

"Here's your hat—" Claire swept the jet wash over a last, large flux tube. It glistened as annihilation energies burst forth like bonfires, raging in a place already hot beyond imagination. Magnetic knots snarled, exploded. "What's your hurry?"

The solar coronal arch burst open.

She had sensed these potential energies locked in the peak of the arch, an intuition that came through her hands, from long work with the mag gloves. Craftswoman's knowledge: Find the stressed flux lines. Turn the key.

Then all hell broke loose.

The acceleration slammed her to the floor, despite the water. Below, she saw the vast vault of energy stored in the arch blow out and up, directly below them.

You have made a solar flare!

"And you thought I didn't have a plan."

Claire started to laugh. Slamming into a couch cut it off. She would have broken a shoulder, but the couch was waterlogged and soft.

Now the worm was an asset. It repulsed matter, so the up-jetting plume blew around it, around *Silver Metal Lugger*. Free of the flux tubes' grip, the wormhole itself accelerated away from the sun. All very helpful, Claire reflected, but she couldn't enjoy the spectacle—the rattling, surging deck was trying to bounce her off the furniture.

What saved them in the end was their magnetic grapple. It deflected most of the solar-flare protons around the ship. Pushed out at a speed of five hundred kilometers per second, they still barely survived baking. But they had the worm.

Still, the scientific officer was not pleased. He came aboard to make this quite clear. His face alone would have been enough.

"You're surely not going to demand *money* for that?" He scowled and nodded toward where *Silver Metal Lugger*'s fields still hung on to the wormhole. Claire had to run a sea-blue plasma discharge behind it so she could see it at all. They were orbiting Mercury, negotiating.

Earthside, panels of experts were arguing with each other; she had heard plenty of it on tightbeam. A negative-mass wormhole would not fall, so it couldn't knife through the Earth's mantle and devour the core.

But a thin ship could fly straight into it, overcoming its gravitational repulsion—and come out where? Nobody knew. The worm wasn't spewing mass, so its other end wasn't buried in the middle of a star, or any place obviously dangerous. One of the half-dozen new theories squirting out on tightbeam held that maybe this was a multiply connected wormhole, with many ends, of both positive and negative mass. In that case, plunging down it could take you to different destinations. A subway system for a galaxy; or a universe.

So: no threat, and plenty of possibilities. Interesting market prospects.

Which meant that everybody wanted it—Earthside most of all. A multiply connected worm network could open up cheap space— for small ships only. No fed dreadnaughts could use it.

She shrugged. "Have your advocate talk to my advocate."

"Look, you needn't worry about one faction getting their hands on this."

Pretty shrewd, she thought. He'd guessed her general politics. Granted, her most cherished principle was that the fundamental freedom was to Not Give a Damn—but in this case, she did.

"We'll hold it here," he said, seeing her hesitate. "Study the worm properties. It's a unique, natural resource—"

"And it's mine." She grinned. He was lean and muscular and the best man she had seen in weeks. Also the only man she had seen in weeks.

"I can have a team board you, y'know." He towered over her, using the usual ominous male thing.

"I don't think you're that fast."

"What's speed got to do with it?"

"I can always turn off my grapplers." She reached for a switch. "If it's not mine, then I can just let everybody have it."

"Why would you—no, don't!"

It wasn't the right switch, but he didn't know that. "If I release it, the worm takes off—antigravity, sort of."

He blinked. "We could catch it."

"You couldn't even find it. It's dead black." She tapped the switch, letting a malicious smile play on her lips.

"Please don't."

He looked a lot more interesting when he wasn't arrogant. Maybe this little incident would break him of his bad habits. Or at least, the ones she didn't like.

"I need to hear a number. An offer."

His lips compressed until they paled. "The wormhole price, minus your fine?"

Her turn to blink. "What fine? I was on an approved flyby—"

"That solar flare wouldn't have blown for a month. We had predicted that; it was in the regular weather report. You did a real job on it—the whole magnetic arcade went up at once. People all the way out to the asteroids had to scramble for shelter."

He looked at her steadily and she could not decide whether he was telling the truth. "So their costs—"

"Could run pretty high. Plus advocate fees."

"Exactly." He smiled, ever so slightly.

Erma was trying to tell her something but Claire turned the tiny voice far down, until it buzzed like an irritated insect.

She had endured weeks of a female personality sim in a nasty mood. Quite enough. She needed an antidote. This fellow had the wrong kind of politics, but to let that dictate everything was as dumb as politics itself. Her ship's name was a joke, actually, about long, lonely voyages as an ore hauler. She'd had enough of that, too. And he was tall and muscular.

She smiled. *"Touché.* Okay, it's a done deal—*if* I get a percentage of any commercial use."

"What?"

She stretched, yawned. "I'm getting tired of negotiating. That's the offer. Otherwise, out the lock you go."

A look of grudging respect crinkled his eyes. "Okay." A pause, then he beamed. "I'll get my team to work—"

"Still, I'd say you need to work on your negotiating skills. Too brassy."

He frowned, but then gave her a grudging grin.

Subtlety had never been her strong suit. "Shall we discuss them—over dinner?"

Of What Is Past, or Passing, or to Come II

Ray Bradbury

Do you feel it? Time passing . . . time that unravels all the sleeves instead of knitting them up. The greatest living writer of imaginative fiction, the Martian Chronicler himself, offers this original poem that I hope one day will find its way into the complete asbestos edition of The Works. And a personal note: I wouldn't be working on this anthology if not for Ray. His encouragement for twenty-five years has played a crucial role in my pursuing the Holy Grail of science fiction, fantasy, and horror.

A chronicle of wits is what we act,
A history of dreams congealed to fact,
And then the rushing on to one more dream
Which, acted out, becomes an actual scheme.
So, leapfrogging astride a life too real,
Rough apeman's nightmares punish him to feel,
Then think, then reach, then probe the awful stuff
Of predawn ghosts, to which he cries: Enough!
He echoes bestial cries, he learns their dictions
To sketch on bare cave walls in science fictions,
That art at which apes laugh because it's dumb,
But artist apeman goes on with his sum

Until he's added panics, drawn them clear,
Predicting how to live another year.
Then out he prowls, abandons doubting wife,
And strides back with trapped fire, long spear, sharp knife.
He fetches meat and light and warms the cave,
His fictions now turned fact do apemen save.
Their laughter stops. He steps again to wall
And there blueprints new dreams to save them all.
He stares ahead in time, from that borrows
Fictions that can find and solve tomorrows.

TYRANNY

Poul Anderson

The future isn't a moment from now. It's much farther along, a place where spaceships travel between the stars; it's a universe where hundreds of intelligent species interact. No one is a better tour guide than the legendary Poul Anderson, winner of all the awards, one of the most significant *Astounding* writers of the 1950s on, and author of the Technic History and the Time Patrol series, not to mention the comic classic *The High Crusade*. With expertise in both physics and Scandinavian languages, and a longtime interest in the politics of liberty, Poul and his stories make you think. Here is a story that explores the implications of freedom and its corollary, responsibility.

The planet known as Jacob orbits its Sol-like sun in little more than a Terrestrial year, but with an axial tilt of twenty-five degrees and a rotation period of just under twenty-six hours. Thus the summers are warm even at high latitudes, and then the eventides grow long. It is a season for outlaws.

The five men reached the fence shortly after sunset, when twilight lay heavy beneath trees but the sky above was still bright. They breathed hard, and the reek of sweat overwhelmed any fragrances of leaf or blossom. They had been afoot since dawn, their aircraft left behind at an isolated campground, for they could not arrive openly. The trek through the Yellow Forest had been difficult, the ground overgrown, uphill, often broken by rushing streams, and none of them very skilled in woodcraft. Nevertheless a fierce energy upbore them yet, and ought to until they had completed their mission and vanished back into the wilderness.

Six meters high, ten kilometers in circumference, the fence closed off the top of Mount Arthur with a deceptively thin mesh that was soon lost to sight among the boles and brush growing close against either side. No animal, not even a saurobull, could have broken through. Yet its basic strength lay in the sensors woven into the molecules of it. Any attempt at forced entry, scaling, tunneling, or unauthorized overflight would trigger an instant summons to the guardian machines.

For a while the men stood mute except for their harsh breaths. After so long a walk, following so many months of planning and preparation, this landmark along the way to their goal did not at first seem quite real. Nor did they, in travel-stained coveralls and boots, loaded with backpacks and bedrolls, seem like either a military squad or a gang of desperados—and they weren't, actually. Only one among them, the soldier Eli de Coster, bore a firearm, and that was only against the unlikely event of attack by a wild beast. Nothing they could carry would be of any use if the robots caught them.

Joab Murray began unlimbering his special burden. Isaac Wong grinned a bit at him and drawled, "Well, here's where we find out whether that gadget of yours works as advertised."

"It does!" snapped the gaunt, gray physicist. "I've shown you the results from the laboratory, and you've watched the field tests. What we're going to find out is how well your leadership works."

"Sorry," apologized Wong. "That's more or less what I meant. The context that the projector gets used in. Murphy's Law is bound to spring something on us." He was a short, stocky man on whom the day's journey had perhaps told least. A commander must needs have endurance, both physical and psychic.

"¡A la chingada!" exclaimed Antonio Rueda. "Do not stand here yapping." His slender form jittered about; the dark features drew taut. "Let us get in, for God's sake, while we have light to see by."

"The enemy does, too," muttered big Uriel Barden.

"Day, night, it's the same to their sensors," de Coster reminded him. "But we are taking a needless risk if we dawdle."

"True," Wong agreed. "Go to it, Joab."

Murray nodded. He was already bent over his apparatus. Set on a tripod, it resembled a camera studded with meters and controls as much as it did anything else. He consulted his instruments, nodded again, and touched a stud. A faint buzz sounded for a moment. He turned about. "What are *you* waiting for?" he demanded.

Barden gaped. It was not long since he had been recruited. "That's all?"

"Yes," Murray said. "The projector emits a field derived from the electroweak force, which has knocked out the sensors for several meters to either side of us. The gap ought not to touch off alarms at the station. To date, the effect is considered no more than a laboratory curiosity. Its development has been a secret between me and the leaders of the Freedom League. But I am told that robots also patrol this fence line, on no set schedule, and I suggest that we proceed before one happens by."

The sarcasm of his lecture was lost on Barden, who took forth an ion torch while he listened and slipped goggles over his eyes. With hands made deft by the life's labor whose fruits he had lost, he cut a gap in the mesh barely large enough for the men to slip through. When they had done so, he tied the edges back together and draped a nearby vine over them to cover the traces, as if it had grown there naturally.

The band continued uphill. Wong came last, removing traces where they had trampled brush and squirting tree trunks from a spray bottle as he passed them. The paint was practically invisible, but would glow under the beam from an ultraviolet flashlight. It blazed the trail by which they would escape when they were done.

If no cruising spybug saw them first and informed the central intelligence at the station. In that case, robots with intelligence of their own would be on the trail, faster than men could run, armed and armored beyond men's power to fight. But such was the chance a guerrilla warrior took. Now when day had become a dusk deepening into night, the odds were not bad.

Darkness made the faring harder still than before. Feet snagged in unseen shrubs, hands scraped along thorns, shoulders brushed bruisingly against low boughs. The crackle and rustle seemed unnaturally loud. Somewhere an owl hooted; the voice from ancestral Earth sounded doubly mocking.

The men pushed on, though—it wasn't far now, was it?—until Wong said, "All right. Here's where we'll wait." Then they sighed, swore, or murmured thanks, and sat down one by one on thick sward. A breeze cooled their faces. Light flowed argent from above.

They had come into a glade. Though open to the sky, it was no less safe than anyplace else within the perimeter, and it afforded a view of their objective. On three sides the trees loomed and gloomed, a wall strippled with silver. Southward they thinned out. Farther on, the ground bore only turf, boulders, and scattered bushes. It rose sharply to the summit of the mountain. There bulked the great fusion power plant, also black and formless except where light from heaven touched it, for machines had no need of day. Its mass might have been that of an ancient castle, under the heaven-storming transmitter masts from which it hurled the energy beams, soundless and invisible, that supplied a third of a continent.

Low behind it, softly nacreous, glimmered the rings of Jacob. Both moons were aloft. Leah was a small crescent sinking toward the western treetops, but Rachel's half disk shone high and big, a radiance that drove most stars from sight and made a chiaroscuro of the world.

"Take it easy, boys," Wong counseled, still on his feet. "We've got hours."

"You . . . we're not supposed to linger," Rueda protested. "Are we?"

"Right now we are," Wong reassured him. "The extra time was to allow for unforeseen problems along the way. Well, we didn't meet any. Everything's according to plan and the map—so far, at least. When Rachel goes under the trees, we bring our friend into position, a little closer than here." Shrugging off his pack, he jerked a thumb at the bulge in it where the fission minibomb lay. A shaped charge would funnel its blast straight at the power plant. "And we set the timer and skedaddle."

"Do we *have* to wait for full dark? Robots see well under any conditions."

"My, my, you are eager, aren't you, Tony? You've clean forgotten your briefing. Our hope is that the machines, such of them as survive, will be too busy around the ruins, and too confused with the main brain here destroyed, to hunt for us. But police and militia will come zooming from Oropolis, and everywhere else around. Darkness handicaps men. We want it for our getaway."

"The League will have further uses for us," de Coster added.

"Yes, I know," Rueda said. He paused. "No, I'm sorry. I was being too impatient." He grinned without much mirth. "Patience is not easy when we are about to kick Northland Nucleonics in its bloated belly."

"And start bringing down the whole damned, heartless system," Barden growled.

"Only a start," Murray cautioned. "And we do not want to kill the society. Just the machines and their lackeys." He sounded more as though he was making an academic point than upholding an ideal.

"To set the people free," Rueda whispered.

"A long, hard road ahead," de Coster reminded them, "especially if we are not to cause more casualties than . . . we must."

Barden looked up toward Rachel. Its light reflected from his eyes like the glory of an angelic vision. One could well-nigh hear his thoughts—

Tonight, this very night. The sudden power blackout was to bring more than chaos and fear, more than a hindrance and distraction seizing upon the government and its armed forces over a vast area—indirectly, the entire globe. It would be the signal and the opportunity for the guerrilla bands of the Freedom League to make their first overt attacks. What they would accomplish before they must withdraw to their hiding places was unforeseeable. But it was secondary. The purpose was to show that their army existed, small but strong, utterly determined. That ought to draw more recruits, while it made the ordinary citizen wonder how secure the rule of the robots was, and— And thus the war would go on, year after year, as long and bitter as necessary, until the liberators entered Federal City and wrecked the Cyberon down to its last cryogenic coil.

Wong smiled under the moons. His voice went soft. "Relax, boys. Never mind the shining goals just yet. Take it easy, get your strength back. You'll be wanting it later, you know. If you're too high-keyed for a nap, how about a smoke and a talk?" He sat down, cross-legged, in the circle that the others had unconsciously formed. "We aren't as well acquainted as we might be."

"No," Mallory said. "The League leadership should not merely have picked us as most suitable for this mission, it should have given us more time to become integrated. I would like some idea of how much I can depend on the rest of you." He saw Wong's slight frown and added hastily, "Of course, you could do with more information about me."

Wong took a cigarette case from his pocket and offered it around. Everybody lit up. Jackwort smoke tasted good and soothed the nerves without turning mind or body slack. Presently the men were trading memories.

Sunlight fell gentle over the spires of New Cambridge University. Springtime made snowstorms of cherry blooms along a quad where boy walked hand in hand with girl through a breeze that smelled green. High overhead, a goldplume went winging and singing, *tilirra, tilirra, tili*. Standing at an open window, Joab Murray thought somewhere at the back of his mind how unjust this was, how cruel, that the weather should be so when the message arrived. There should have been rain and ruin.

"My application has been denied," he said. Each word fell like a stone. "Categorically."

Phyllis Diamond, who had come from her office down the hall to this one simply to convey, in person, a piece of cheerful news about her own research, half lifted a hand as if to lay it on his bent back, then let it fall. "Oh, I'm sorry," she murmured. After a silent spell: "Can you try again next year? I hear they've discovered the solar accelerator can be constructed for less than the original estimate. That ought to release fairly substantial funds." She ventured a smile. "Better start angling and politicking for your share right away."

"Categorically, I told you!" He swung about to glare at her. "No such project can even be considered for an indefinite time to come. The rejection was barely polite— No, that's meaningless. 'We regret to inform you—' How can a robot feel regret? What is it, what is the Cyberon, but a machine, a glorified computer, a *thing?*"

"It's rational," she argued, for he was questioning what she had always been taught was fundamental. "It draws on its database and continuing input from everywhere around the planet. And anyway, its power is limited. The Ministry of Science made that decision—people. What reason did they give you?"

"What I more than half expected, though I hoped, I hoped. . . . Gravity-wave studies are hugely expensive; they require access to a black hole and any amount of special equipment, oh, yes. And the work is already being done, by both Spacer and Federation scientists. Let me read their reports and use the data for whatever theorizing I care to do. Or let me get private funding." Murray's finger made a slashing motion below his jaw.

"Any chance of that?"

"None. Do you imagine I haven't looked into it? The work is in fact too costly and long range for anything less than a government or a consortium of fleets to support."

Diamond considered him before she said slowly, "Then you might go there and get onto one of those teams. You're brilliant in your field, Joab. Somebody or other would probably be glad to sign you on."

"While Jacob lags further and further behind."

"Do we have to do everything ourselves? The reports are published, after all. I never took you for a chauvinist."

"This is my home," he declared. "I wouldn't care to live anywhere else."

"Me neither. Not in the Federation, with some bureaucrat regulating everything I do and damn near everything I say." Diamond's gaze went out the window. "Nor inside a Spacer ship, or at best a . . . a habitat. The Founders were awfully lucky when they discovered a planet like this and secured it for themselves."

" *'And for our posterity.' * " On Murray's tongue the quotation became a curse. "Freezing it forever into their rigid, narrow, mean-spirited little ideology. Have you never woken in the middle of the night, gasping for breath, out of a dream where a dead man's hand had you by the throat?"

"No." Her tone sharpened. "Let's not get into that old argument again. I like it here, and I like being able to do what I want with my money and my life, and that's that. If you feel otherwise, you are free to emigrate."

"But what of the children?" Murray retorted. "Yes, I'm not married, but I have a niece and a nephew, bright and happy and growing up amidst vulgarity and short-sightedness, everything worthwhile being starved—"

"Not quite everything. And enough of this, for God's sake." Diamond sighed. "Oh, I had ambitious ideas, too, when I was younger, but I found that psychophysics has all the puzzles and potentials I could ever explore, and doesn't cost too much for the Blue Sky Foundation to give me my annual grant—" She broke off. "Joab, we're both being ridiculous. How often have we been over this ground, you and I? We've trampled it flat. Look, I'm sorry about your disappointment, and if I can help in any way—" She hesitated. "Might you be interested in collaborating with me? I could use a man with your kind of laboratory skill."

He managed a smile of sorts. "Thank you, but no. It isn't my area of interest."

"Do you have something else, then, something that'll fit inside the university budget?"

"Well, yes. Certain quantum mechanical paradoxes involving the electroweak force. I think it should be possible to demonstrate that a focused field will affect molecular bonds. . . ." Murray's lip lifted from his teeth. "It will be something to do, in between dismal teaching sessions. Something to do, to pass the time, and perhaps eventually another published article. While yonder in space, around the black hole, they— No!" he shouted. "If I'm a rat in a trap, I don't have to sit passive and feel sorry for myself!"

It could not be true. It must not be true. It was true.

Blindly, Antonio Rueda stumbled from the house and into the street. The sun was lowering, shadows were getting long, but summer's dry heat still hammered him; Carsonia lies on the Ephraimite Prairie. He didn't notice, nor heed the tumult around him.

Bubblecars made their slow way, hooting warnings that were mostly ignored, among pedestrians who spilled off the walks and across the thoroughfare, weaving, gesticulating, cackling, half of them drunk or drugged, the rest reckless or defiant or sunk in sullen apathy. Vendors clamored their wares, greasy food or tawdry trinkets. Two buckoes swaggered past in scarlet and gold, though when they saw a patrolman they spoke softly and moved along politely enough. Three troupers capered and tootled in their ragged costumes while a fourth held out a bowl for coins. A man stared and stared at the display in a sleaze shop but was obviously too poor to go in. Another who emerged was paunchy and jowly, with a breastplate of gold and jewels over a fur-trimmed velvite tunic to show off his wealth, however he had gotten it. A woman in an iridescent skinsuit plucked Rueda's sleeve, and shrank away from his snarl as he yanked himself loose. Something supposed to be music thuttered and screeched. Overhead fluorosigns glared against the day: FORTUNA CASINO, VENUS THEATER, HIGH SPIRITS TAVERN, LIQUORS ETC., HAPPINESS DOPE SHOP, CYBELE PSYCHIC, BEA & DEE, BLOODWELL FIGHT RING, MAMA'S—NEW GIRLS AND BOYS EVERY WEEK. The animations were generally quite explicit. A Redemptionist mission occupied one room on the ground floor of a crumbling tenement. People passed it by as if the saddened woman who stood outside with the invitation HELP, SHELTER, LOVE lettered on her robe did not exist.

Flori, wept Rueda within. *My little Flori, she's here.*

The district ended at Seventh Avenue, as abruptly as if chopped off by a laser gun. To cross over was like a dash of seawater in the face, cold and clean, a wave on the ocean where he had spent the past four years. Rueda walked onward among solid bourgeois facades, quiet traffic, respectable businesses, mannerly folk, while his head cleared.

He was almost calm when he boarded a slide going toward Nexus Plaza. He even noticed, as it gave him change for a moneta, that he had paid half the fare he used to. Competition, no doubt; at the time he left, Rollerways had barely commenced operations here.

The thought was vague and soon fluttered away. Resolution crystallized in him. Below its ice the grief lay calm, but black and bottomless.

Getting off at the square, he passed among its flowerbeds with long, stiff strides, took the rampway up into City Hall, and told the receptor, "I want to see the mayor. In live person. At once."

"He is quite busy," replied the machine. "An appointment can be arranged for the day after tomorrow if you wish, or you may enter a communication."

"At once, I said." Rueda produced identification. "Resident's privilege." He had maintained his legal address in this city without hitherto claiming the annual interruption to which it entitled him. Fascinating though his work for Westsea Development was— helping engineer a whole new community afloat in the Lucian Current!—he did not want to settle down elsewhere than in his birth home.

Or he had not, until now.

The receptor conferred with the circuits. "Very well, sir," it yielded. "In half an hour, if you please."

The compromise was reasonable, and Rueda found that the wait gave him a chance to plan his words. Make them count. Afterward, alone, he could scream his rage and shed his tears.

The mayor's office was spacious and airy. Behind his desk spread a mural of the Founders at the Constitutional Conference. It was only animated, ceremonially, on Adoption Day. *Appropriate,* the thought passed through Rueda: *a static image of men and women long dead, in their antiquated clothes, which once a year went through the same motions and uttered the same phrases, according to a program in a machine.*

Amariah Nash rose to offer a hand. Rueda took it for a bare moment. "Tony!" the mayor exclaimed. "This is a surprise. Your job yonder is nowhere finished, is it?"

"Leave of absence," Rueda snapped. "You know why."

"No, not really, except it looks like being something bad." Concern crossed the ruddy face. They had been friends from childhood. "Sit down, Tony. Want me to send for a drink or whatever? To hell with my appointments."

They lowered themselves. Rueda stiffened, as if the chair's adjustment to his contours were a whore's embrace. "No drinks," he said. "Not yet. Do you mean you haven't heard about Flori? I did, across a fourth of the planet."

"Your sister? No. We've been quite out of touch. Is she all right?"

"She is not," Rueda forced forth. "She's down in Stinktown, working at the Messalina House. A cousin of ours found out and called me."

Silence thundered.

"Oh, God," Nash whispered. "I'm sorry. I'm sorry."

"You had *no* idea?"

"None. When Micromulti folded, I remembered she'd been a production assistant there and tried to contact her, but got nobody. So I, well, I assumed she'd moved elsewhere, back with her parents or maybe off to join you." Nash spread his hands, a gesture of helplessness. "It's been so goddamn busy here."

"It has? When I left, you'd just gotten elected on the reform ticket. I haven't heard of any reforms, nor seen any changes today."

"She could have come to us, my family and me. We'd have been glad to give her what boost we were able."

"She's too proud for that. Especially since—" Rueda could not go on.

"Pride? If she was unemployed, she had a right—"

"Yes, to bed and board in a dormitory, medical attention at a clinic—processing."

"Or the churches, the charities—"

"They'd try to change her way of living. An employment agency would require it. Even friends like you would put pressure on." Rueda stared down at the fists in his lap. "She always was a bit wild, you know. When the company—*había bancarrota*—went broke, I think she decided she might as well enjoy herself a while, because she would not likely find another job fast, and so she played with recreational-use euphorin, mainly—and now she does not want the habit broken for her." His voice cracked across. "She told me she is quite happy and I should mind my own business."

"Tony, old fellow—" Nash squared his shoulders. "It was her decision."

Rueda looked up. "What about ten or twenty years from now?"

"She's not stupid. The schools, the Pro Bono Society, a million different books and dramas and everything else, they all explain and warn. We have philanthropies that try to pick up the pieces when that fails. What more can be done?"

"You could have cleaned out that Stinktown cesspool."

Nash's mouth bent briefly upward on the left side. "We meant to, Tony, my colleagues and me, once we were in office. We meant to. But you know we haven't got authority over consensual behavior except when it affects public health and safety, and the operators down there were quick to get smart about that. Also, they pulled back entirely into the district. The smug, respectable majority of local citizens don't feel threatened any longer."

Rueda leaned forward. "But you also promised poverty relief
that would amount to more than the bare necessities and a
personality-rehabilitation program that would truly get to the people who need it, persuade them, save them."

"Yes, we had our dreams, didn't we?" Nash shook his head. "I
found out what I probably should have realized from the first, even
our pilot-plant scheme wasn't affordable. We haven't the revenue
to pay for it. Bad enough when Micromulti went out of business.
If we raised taxes, Carson Atmospherics would move to Overburg.
They keep talking about it. And . . . taxes from Stinktown support
a lot of worthwhile things."

Rueda choked down a curse. "You were going to approach the
planetary government."

"Oh, we did. We presented our application for a grant, and described how we could provide a model and gain the experience to
make global action possible later. A bill for us was actually drafted
in Parliament. But on the advice of the Cyberon, it was quashed."

"And how did the Cyberon justify that?"

"The problems are too big and complicated for localities to handle, aside from encouraging education and charity. Anything on a
larger scale would be too expensive."

"Too expensive," Rueda mumbled. "Too much money for
human lives."

"There *are* other demands, Tony. Defense, environmental-
damage control—"

"Yes, yes. *Por consiguiente*—therefore we cannot spare the cost
of two or three small luxury items per person per year."

"I've not given up," Nash said. "More and more decent people
are becoming aware of the situation. There's any number of good
causes going begging, you know. If we can get the Constitution
amended, the expenditure limit raised—"

"You won't," Rueda said. "No matter how much you argue and
agitate and elect representatives, you won't. Not while the Cyberon
is in charge."

He could sit here no longer. "Thank you, 'Riah. I wanted to

know what your position is, and Federal City's. You have made them clear for me. I need bother you no more."

Nash rose, too. "Uh, Tony, wait a minute. Let's talk. Maybe we can do something after all for Flori."

"I doubt it," Rueda told him. "We are too late to do anything but avenge her. And make something better for the children she will never have."

Lean and straight in his uniform, young for his rank, Eli de Coster seemed altogether out of place in Micah Horan's country retreat. Understated sumptuousness glowed throughout the great room where they sat by themselves. A wall stood transparent to a lawn of Terrestrial grass kept smooth and soft as a woman's breast, pollarded hedges of Terrestrial boxwood, deer grazing under maples gone scarlet with autumn, all rolling down to a river and hills on the farther shore vivid with native blues and yellows. Backlit by the sun, the rings made a wan arch low above; after dark they would shine magnificent.

Horan took a leisurely pull on his cigar. "At ease, Colonel," he said with a smile. "This entire property is state-of-the-art secured, and what human staff it has are absolutely trustworthy. We can be as frank and honest as we please, and I promise you that nothing you say will give offense nor go past these walls without your leave." He was a big man, gray haired, distinguished looking in a portly fashion.

De Coster did not relax. "Very well," he said. "Why am I here?"

"Your invitation explained that I wish to honor your heroism by giving you what I hope will be a pleasant week's vacation, and to make your acquaintance."

"Thank you." De Coster's tone was dry. "However, plenty in the Service did more than me"—when the suppression of the Mechanoclastic Revolt got down to street-by-street, hand-to-hand combat—"and none of us move in quite the same social orbits as the chief executive officer of Andromeda Minerals."

"You are more interesting than most," Horan replied. "Although in your position you are constrained as to political advocacy, still you have expressed some very independent opinions, and your article in the *Proceedings of the Jacobian Military Institute* was as good an analysis of the long-range implications of our restrictive policies as I have ever seen."

De Coster gazed straight at him. "Shall we get to the point?" he asked quietly.

Horan's smile broadened. "Excellent, Colonel. I admit to a bad habit of pussyfooting and, yes, occasional smarminess. It comes from too many board meetings and too many dealings with politicians both domestic and, especially, foreign. Let us by all means be straightforward, here where nobody else is listening."

De Coster grinned a little and sipped the whiskey set by his chair before he responded. "All right. Andromeda got some lucrative concessions in the asteroid belt of Akkad. The new government on Sargon has expropriated those mine and told you to go whistle for your compensation. Our government has protested to no avail. That's what's on your mind, correct? Well, what do you imagine I can do about it?"

Horan set aside his blandness. "Nothing immediately or directly, I suppose. Unless perchance you have a suggestion for us?"

"I'm afraid not. And I have given it thought. It isn't as if those asteroids were Spacer property. We'd have some leverage there, as useful as Port Rachel is to them, and besides, Spacers would rather renegotiate a contract than abrogate it. Even with the Federation we could probably get some of their special interests to press our case—not that their bureaucrats would have granted so much to a private corporation in the first place. But Sargon is as sovereign a planet as Jacob, and the revolutionary government is committed to its ideology, whatever the consequences." De Coster grinned again, wryly. "Now I'm the one delivering the long-winded lecture about the obvious, eh? But I wanted to make my own understanding of the situation clear to you."

Horan nodded. "It is wise to spell things out. This is far too im-

portant for us to waste time talking at cross-purposes. So let me give
a lecture, too. The seizure is more than a dispute between Sargon
and Andromeda, with the Jacobian government merely obliged to
lend what good offices it can in aid of its citizens. It is a direct violation of the Treaty of Roma Nova. Our whole alliance with Sargon
will soon fall apart, unless we act. Jacob has not recognized the revolutionary regime . . . yet. What, then, besides making noises, does
Federal City propose to do?"

Bitterness surged up in de Coster. "You know full well. Sit on
its hands. The alliance always was meaningless anyway. If we're
ever attacked, we'll be on our own. The only real parts of the treaty
concern trade relations, and they're minor to both economies."

"Not so minor, in this case, to a good many Andromeda shareholders."

"The chance you take when you invest," de Coster said bluntly.
"I myself wouldn't care to spend Jacobian lives bailing out somebody's monetas."

"But it is a bad precedent, don't you agree? It makes Jacob look
weak. That will invite encroachments by the Federation."

De Coster was silent.

"Moreover," Horan pursued, "lives are in fact at stake. Your
coreligionists on Sargon. The latest reports I've received say that
the revolutionaries are already tightening the screws on them, exactly as promised. How long till outright persecution?"

De Coster's lips tightened. "You've got me there."

After a moment he added: "But I am an officer in the military
service, a citizen of Jacob, and ridiculous though it may be in this
self-centered society, a patriot. Yes, I would like to go on an expedition that cleaned those bastards out on Sargon and established
something reliable there." He made a gesture as of dismissal. "But
this is academic. We don't have the capability."

Horan regarded him through a veil of smoke while replying, "I
realize that. However, I've studied your writings and collected information about you. I also realize that Jacob's military weakness
is like a cancer in your soul."

De Coster's countenance froze. Red and white came in tides beneath the skin. "We are not impotent, sir. Whoever attacked us would lose more than he could possibly gain."

"Of course. But I tell you, I have read your writings, and the works of others who have thought like you, and I agree. It's all very well to keep a space-borne fleet of robot missiles than can slag the surfaces of several planets. It has indeed stayed the Federation's hand more than once. But when we have, essentially, nothing else except a small force to maintain peace in this one planetary system—a militia—we have no flexibility. Our only feasible policy becomes isolationism. They thumb their noses at us on Sargon because they know we are unable to do anything short of totally destroying them—untold innocent men, women, children—and we won't, when we are not facing a mortal threat. This is merely the latest instance, and by no means the worst. I need not go on. But you see, Colonel, I do understand."

De Coster drained his glass. The end table by his chair refilled it. "Why approach me?" he asked. "If you want things changed, the burden is on you and any other civilians you can rally, and you'll have a long, slow, grubby grind of politics ahead of you. Get enough money appropriated for a halfway adequate subdoomsday armed force. Then you and I can talk. But I won't be holding my breath."

"Nor am I hopeful, at present," Horan said. "There are too many claims on the skimpy funds available. We have to raise the limit on government revenues and expenditures."

"And that requires amending a supposedly unamendable article of the Constitution. You know the Cyberon would never let any such proposal reach the floor in Parliament."

"Exactly. The Founders turned Jacob's destiny over to a machine. Oh, a machine of the highest capabilities, with ongoing data input to a program subtle and adaptable as well as powerful—and the planet has prospered. I quote my old civics teacher." Horan's sardonicism turned to earnestness. "Nevertheless, a machine, limited, stubborn, inhuman."

"Times change," de Coster said very softly.

Horan nodded. "People do. Their wants, their needs. What provoked the rise of the Mechanoclastic cult, and at last the revolt, but a sense that life itself has become the slave of unlife? When the government proved powerless to stop settlers swarming into the Holy Meadows, that was just the breaking-point increment of outrage."

"The Mechos were lunatics," de Coster said harshly. "They'd have brought everything down around our ears. They needed suppression. People in general approved. Didn't you see on the news? When we held our victory parade down Union Boulevard, we nearly disappeared in the flowers they threw at us."

"Yes, yes, certainly. Still you're well read, Colonel. You know extremism is like a fever. It has to be reduced, but it's a symptom of an underlying, dangerous pathology. *I* say the Cyberon has outworn whatever usefulness it ever had, and we're overdue for a genuine democracy."

Silence fell. Outside, the sun went lower and a gust of cold sent fallen leaves awhirl.

"What are you implying?" de Coster demanded.

"You call yourself a patriot," Horan answered. "I believe you. Sometimes true patriotism requires making a hard, yes, cruel decision."

"You're not coming at me out of nowhere," de Coster said. "Since your agent first contacted me, I've been thinking. You have your personal agenda."

"Is it seriously opposed to yours, Colonel?" Horan responded. "Let us stipulate, for argument's sake, that Jacob has reached a point where it needs a revolution of its own. Nothing extreme, nothing dictatorial, simply a removal of the Cyberon—forcible, because that is the only way it can be done—so human beings can once again govern themselves. We both know that there is indeed such an underground movement, small, ill organized, and futile. It will always be small, but must it, should it, remain ineffectual? Given military expertise on one side, money on the other side, it could become a real force. We're concerned citizens, Colonel, you and I. Don't you think we should discuss these matters further?"

* * *

Rain roared straight down from an unseen sky, so thick that sight reached no more than maybe a hundred meters before drowning in darkness. It pocked the brown flood waters lapping around tree-tops, roofs of houses, crests of hills. Wreckage floated about, timber, plastic, pieces of furniture, now and then a dead animal, once a doll. Whatever little girl had cuddled it might have been rescued or might be in the mud on the bottom. In the raw chill of a Southland midwinter, corpses wouldn't start rising for quite a few days.

From the forked branch on which he huddled, Uriel Barden saw the boat at first as a shadow. "Hey-ey-ey! Help! Over here!" he shouted, aware his voice would be lost long before it got that far. The vague half-shape swung through an arc, drew near, became real.

Worn out, inwardly numb, he nonetheless recognized the type. A ten-meter hull bore a hinged deck as cover for cargo space, with a cabin and cockpit well aft. A detector at the prow included radar, infrared and sonic sensors, and a neural network; it had handily spotted him. Below it gleamed a name, *Hobo,* jauntily archaic. This was unmistakably the home and working equipment of Free-lancers, who had carried small shipments and done odd jobs along the Dragon River till it went berserk.

A single person stood at the controls. The boat lay to and ex-tended a grapple arm to the tree. The canopy over the cockpit retracted, the pilot beckoned. Barden crept down the bough and tumbled aboard. The pilot slid the transparent cover back, withdrew the grapple, and sent the boat smoothly off.

Looking up, Barden saw a woman, young, strongly built, blond, in garb spattered with water and muck. She gave the boat instruc-tions, relinquished her place at the console, and squatted before him. "Welcome." Her voice came hoarse and he saw how tired she was. "How're you doin'?"

"I'm alive, I guess," Barden said dully. He felt hollow, beyond fear or grief or joy.

"Anybody else hereabouts?"

"Not that I know of. I doubt it."

"Me, too. Nothin's registered on the screen 'cept you." She peered at him through the murk. "Family, friends?"

"I don't know. We're agrotechs, our farm's on Goddard Road, but I was on my way to help shore up the embankment when it— broke, I suppose. The flood went right over my car and wedged it against something. I got out and swam to where you found me."

The woman thought for a moment, then shook her head. "No, Goddard Road's well off my beat. Somebody else will've checked that area by now. You're the first I've picked up since, uh, three hours ago? No sense in cruisin' around here anymore. I'll take you straight to Bantry Ridge. They've set up a relief station there and're airliftin' people on to Rossville as fast as they can. Maybe you'll find your folks at one place or t'other. Me, I could use a rest 'fore I start out again searchin'."

She spoke to the boat, which changed course and wove its way amidst snags and flotsam. "C'mon below," she said. "You need attention, and we might as well both be comfortable. My name's Janice Wasilewski."

"Uriel Barden," he muttered, and crawled after her.

The cabin was compactly arranged and neatly kept, making it feel roomier than it was. Ports looked out on desolation. Doors forward led to a sanitor cubicle and a cook unit with well-stocked shelves. Lines in the deck showed that it could extrude chairs, a table, or a double bed as required; at present there were a padded bench and a small desk. Colorful costumes such as Freelancers wore in their leisure hung by a guitar, also a common sight among them. Either Wasilewski operated alone, which was not unusual, or any partners were elsewhere, probably helping out at Bantry Ridge. The thoughts plodded automatically through Barden's head.

She stepped into the galley and came back with a cup she thrust into his hands. "Drink this," she said. "Hot chocolate laced with stimulin." He obeyed. It was a miracle in his mouth. "Now for God's sake get out of those drenched clothes and into the shower."

He did, too dazed for embarrassment. She paid him no particular attention anyway, but tuned a flat comscreen and began collecting reports.

Steaming water followed by an airblast joined with the biochemical to clear his brain and revivify his body. He knew the lift would be brief and then he'd collapse altogether, but by then he'd have reached the refugee station and be in some kind of shelter, or in an aircraft, and he could sleep and sleep and sleep.

After he learned what had become of Hannah, Susie, Joey. If he did. It might take days, in all the misery. Fifty thousand human beings had lived in Kinshire.

Somehow that knowledge crowded to the fore. Anguish receded; it could wait, time enough to mourn when he knew the fullness of his loss. What rose in him like flood waters was rage.

He came out. Wasilewski had tossed his garments in a washer. She handed him a flamboyantly patterned robe, which he put on (yes, she was either married or had a close male friend), and gestured at two mugs of coffee on the desk beside a plate of sandwiches. The screen above displayed a parade of images interspersed with text news, most of it terrible, but she had turned the sound down till the rain fell louder.

"Eat, drink," she urged. He sank to the bench and took a mug. He wasn't hungry, however long he'd gone without food. His whole state was abnormal, he knew—but predictable, under the circumstances. This mood of anger might well be nature's mercy on him.

Still, he ought to show politeness. Cradling the warm vessel in his palms, he said, "I can't rightly thank you, freelady. Haven't got words to suit. But I owe you my life."

"Aw, that's all right." She leaned back against the bulkhead, legs braced against the frequent veering of the boat, and sipped. "Somethin' like this happens, everybody naturally does what they can. I've been checkin' up on things. More and more units are arrivin' from different outfits. Militia, of course, but also Knights of St. Martin, Helpin' Hand Society, churches, businesses—" She grinned, a bit maliciously. "Like the insurance companies. Oh, yes, them in full force."

"Why?" Barden asked. He saw immediately that it was a stupid question, but she was already answering.

"To cut down what they'll have to pay out. Why else? That's one thing the gover'ment's good for, watchdoggin' the big corporations to see they honor their contracts."

Wrath tasted like vomit. "About all it's good for!"

"Hey, I wouldn' say that. We've got defense, police and fire and health protection, courts— Never mind, you know the list. It's not very long, but what more do we need that people can't supply for themselves?"

"Flood control," he spat.

"Um, well— Look, Uriel Barden, I'm sorry for you and all those other poor folks, and I do hope there weren't a lot of you lost and that you'll manage a fresh start on good lives, but—" She paused. "Never mind," she repeated.

"Easy enough for you to say. You Freelancers can just motor north and ply your trades same as before."

"Not exactly. Competition from those already there. Me, I'm thinkin' of shiftin' way west, maybe even go coastwise."

"It's not so simple for us. And who will help? Who can, beyond hauling us out of the water? The government, why, it couldn't be bothered to channel and dike the river and prevent this."

"The gover'ment couldn't afford to."

"You mean the Cyberon wouldn't. It doesn't care. It's a machine."

Wasilewski took a drink. "You're wrung out and battered and grievin'. Drink your coffee, eat your food, lie down, and rest. Would you like a little music?"

"I'd like a little destruction!" Barden yelled. His fist crashed on the desk. Wasilewski had set her mug down. It jumped and fell to the deck. "Blow up the Cyberon, the whole rotten, centum-pinching, ice-hearted system!"

She bit her lip. She, too, was exhausted, stressed, close to the edge. After a few seconds: "All right, I'll say it. Nobody should ever have settled in a flood plain. The gover'ment did warn your parents or your grandparents against it, but when they insisted, how could they be stopped? What'd they have said if the law or some busybody official told 'em what to do with their lives and their sweat? Well, then, let 'em do their own embankin' and dig their own drainage canals. Why should taxpayers around the planet be forced to pungle up for a huge project that would've damaged the ecology of the whole basin for the benefit of those few, and in the end the dams and ditches would've silted up anyway? What funds were available could better go to stuff like eradicatin' disease vectors or enforcin' pollution limits or aidin' people in trouble through no fault of theirs—which is now goin' to include you, sir."

She was no ignoramus, Barden thought. For all their merry ways, Freelancers did as a rule educate their children adequately aboard their boats, using the Ultranet. He bent to retrieve the mug. "I'm sorry about this," he said. "Do you have something for me to clean up the mess with?"

Wasilewski softened. She patted his shoulder. "Naw, don't worry, that's a self-cleanin' surface. I'll just brew me a fresh cup, and maybe you'd like hearin' me caterwaul while we chug along. To chaos with politics, hey? We've got too damn much of it in our lives as is."

A thick sort of calm was congealing in him, but the fury beneath it would not let go. "We don't have enough," he replied. "Politics is the way people go about the affairs they've got in common. How much of that can they do, when the Cyberon ties them hand and foot?"

He decided she must have some deep convictions, for she didn't shrug his words off. "That's nonsense. It doesn't. All it's got authority over is money. Parliament decides how to spend it. Read the Constitution."

His civics lessons in school flashed back into him like a nightmare that had lain long forgotten. *In no year shall the total revenues of all branches and levels of government, from taxation or any other sources, exceed 10 percent of the gross planetary product of the previous year. . . . Total government expenditures shall at no time exceed current*

revenues and reserves, except that public debt may be incurred, which
shall at no time exceed the total revenues of the preceding ten years. . . .
This article is unamendable. . . . Its interpretation, together with any
specific provisions and measures for its enforcement, shall be permanently
and totally delegated to a machine of such design and programming as
the Parliament shall specify within five years of the adoption of this Con-
stitution. . . .

"Maybe that was needed once," he rasped. "The Founders were
breaking free of the Federation, yes, I know. But they had no right
to freeze everybody who'd come after them into the same mold.
Things change." Rivers, technologies, histories, souls.

"Then we do what we can inside the framework we've got,"
Wasilewski answered. "We can't repeal the laws of thermodynam-
ics either, can we? Me, I'm glad to live where they admit that."

Quite possibly she spoke for a majority around the curve of the
planet, Barden thought. There was the horror.

"But, Jesus, we don't have to argue, do we?" she went on. "What
use? Our proper business right now is survivin'. C'mon, let's ease
off, hey?"

And she made the rest of the time gentle for him.

But when he waded ashore onto the sodden ridge, he saw his
neighbor, old John Mkembu, standing aside from the crowd and
clutter, staring into the dark, and saying over and over while the
tears ran down to lose themselves in the rain, "It was so good here.
It was so good here."

Rachel was about to go behind the treetops. The glade lay full of
shadows. Cold had entered the night, and breath smoked ghostly
in what light remained.

"And what of you, *jefe?*" Rueda asked. "What brought you into
the League?"

Isaac Wong shrugged. "Nothing spectacular. Call it an intellectual conversion, very gradual."

"But there must have been a threshold of decision," de Coster said.

"And it must've been something almighty important to you," Barden added, "or you wouldn't have gotten as high in the organization as I reckon you are."

"Really, it's too long and complicated a story," Wong demurred. "We're getting near the time for action."

"We are not quite there," Murray replied, "and I for one would be interested to know what your intellectual issue was."

Wong sighed. "As you like, though it'll be the barest sketch. Call me a perfectionist." At their inquiring looks: "Not an original idea of mine. But surprisingly few thinkers have expressed it over the centuries. On the basis of what's known about psychology and physiology, I believe humans can make themselves, or at least their children, vastly superior to what they have generally been. On the basis of, well, philosophy, I believe we have a duty to do what we can toward that end, and only government can maintain the program with the thoroughness it will require."

"What precisely do you envision?" Murray persisted.

"Everyone physically strong and healthy, mentally stable and alert, free of superstition and prejudice, using every capability he or she is born with to the maximum. And I think that maximum may be beyond anything we today can quite imagine."

"I dunno," Barden said. "Seems kind of far fetched."

"No, not actually," de Coster observed. "We know what remarkable results training and discipline can achieve. Or consider everyday experience. You weren't born able to read and write and calculate, were you? Extrapolate from that."

Rueda nodded. "Yes," he murmured, "so many skills, so much knowledge—but we do not live long enough."

"Correction," Wong said: "We don't get the chance. By the time we're adolescent, it's too late for any but a few geniuses. The bad habits, the wrong thinking have taken firm hold."

Murray tugged his chin. "Y-yes . . . a scientifically designed program, starting from birth, to make the next generation more than a pack of selfish, thoughtless slobs—"

"Jacob seems like a poor place to begin," de Coster said dryly.

Wong smiled. "I think it may be the most promising place, once we've had our revolution," he replied, "precisely because this is a society of selfish slobs, as you put it, Joab. Destroy the Cyberon, liberate the will of the people for the common good— They won't *know* what the common good is, the concept's too strange to them; they'll be desperate for leadership that can make sense of the world and guide them along—"

The last silver sliver of Rachel's half disk went behind the forest wall. Only stars and the glimmer of the rings held back a total darkness. Wong sprang to his feet. "And here's where we begin!"

His four followers rose likewise. They had rehearsed aplenty, on similar terrain and in simulators. No flashbeam was needful. Swiftly they collected their gear and moved uphill to the open steeps below the power plant.

Wong gave a hand signal. The men halted. Silent, shadowy, they set about assembling their device for the overthrow of the world.

Out of the woods to right and left, and down from the black mass above, metal gleamed.

Rueda saw it first. He yelled. As if an instinct seized him, he dropped the crescent wrench in his hand and snatched for the sheath knife at his hip. It was no more than a tool of woodcraft. When he brandished it, crouched, spitting defiance, that was no more than a gesture. It merely said that his spirit would never surrender.

Barden groaned like a suddenly overloaded timber breaking. Murray shrieked an obscenity. De Coster unslung his rifle, hesitated, let it fall to the ground, and stood at attention. Wong's "Hold, boys, don't do anything foolish, it's hopeless" sounded emptily forth.

Huge and inhuman, the military robots closed in until they ringed the band around. Their weapons spoke for them. Rueda sheathed his knife. "What went wrong?" Barden sobbed. "What's going to happen?" But he stood as unbowed as his comrades.

Wong stepped aside and confronted the lead robot. Light flickered in its faceplate. He said a few words—only intermediately to it, for across the communications net he dealt with the whole integrated system and ultimately the Cyberon.

De Coster saw and understood. "You!" he cried. "You're who betrayed us!"

"Trapped us," Rueda then snarled, and moved as though to attack. Barden laid a cautionary hand on his arm and he stopped. They waited together, shoulder by shoulder. Murray shouted curses for a full minute before he too stiffened into silence.

The robot sheer at his back, Wong turned to face them. Starlight and ringlight limned him against night. "Yes," he said most quietly, "I did this."

De Coster bared teeth. *"Agent provocateur."* The phrase went beyond any of Murray's revilements.

"The saying goes," Wong replied, "you can't cheat an honest man. Who forced you into the League?" His tone mellowed. "But you are in fact honest men, in your different ways, and I do regret this. A dirty business. But it had to be done."

"All our units are infiltrated?"

"I hope so. This whole operation was meant to lure them into positions we covered. With luck, we'll have nearly the whole Freedom League under arrest before dawn." Wong nodded wearily. "Yes, by 'we' I mean the ad hoc federal security service. I'm one of those who gave several years to the job. How glad I'll be to go back to my own life."

"How much will they pay you?" Barden grated. "Thirty pieces of silver?"

Wong smiled a bit. "Very little. The government doesn't have a lot of money, you know, and nearly all of it's bespoken. What the government does have is a right to protect itself and the principles it stands for. What got me in was the fact that I have a wife and children, and expect we'll have grandchildren."

"Principles!" Rueda flung at him.

"Why, yes. Above all, the principle that ordinary people shall be free to lead their lives as they see fit—they, not some self-anointed elite."

"But that is exactly what the League fights for," Murray contended. He sagged. "Fought for," he whispered bitterly.

"In theory," Wong told them. "In practice, you'd have taken away the restraint our Founders laid on us against ourselves." He drew breath. "You've heard it countless times, every schoolchild has, but somehow, on too many people, it never takes. We all have our special interests or our noble causes. I really do believe humans can be improved . . . some. But anybody who supposes it can or should be done by decree is my enemy. Your particular wants, social welfare, expensive science, public engineering, foreign activism, they may offhand look less dangerous, and they have their desirable features. But any of them would open the gates for others beyond counting, with the taxation and regulation that come along but eventually become ends in themselves. Inside a hundred years we'd no longer be citizens but subjects, and Jacob might as well join the Federation."

He braced himself to meet their eyes. "Everything has its price, including liberty," he said. "In that case, self-discipline, a certain amount of self-denial, and as the proverb goes, eternal vigilance. Well, humans aren't capable of it. They'll amend and interpret any constitution out of recognizable shape, or just ignore it. So our Founders turned the vigilance job over to a machine. If technology has freed us from hunger and sickness, maybe now it can free us from enslavement. Come back in a thousand years and see. Meanwhile, I told you I hope for grandchildren."

And we four here? went unspoken beneath the stars.

Wong smiled again, with a measure of warmth. "You Freedom Leaguers for the most part aren't monsters," he finished. "From your viewpoint, you were fighting not only for justice but for democracy. The law could send you to the Isolate, but you don't deserve to live out your lives among crooks and psychopaths. I'm sure the courts will give you the option of emigrating to a Federation planet, and even find money for your passage."

THE KILLING OF DAVIS-DAVIS

Peter Crowther

Pete Crowther is known on both sides of the Atlantic as an editor and writer. As someone else who has coedited anthologies with Ed Kramer, he is uniquely qualified for this undertaking. Parenthetically, he accepted the absolutely strangest short story I have ever produced for *Tombs*. Turnabout is only fair, and the story he offers is an odd one—a sophisticated meditation about the game of power politics.

> "All my wishes end where I hope my days will end,
> at Monticello."
> —Thomas Jefferson

The sound was that of a gigantic pack of playing cards being fanned across the sky, echoing around the clouds in time to the distant flares of color that split the horizon into thick, weeping gashes. It reverberated and filled the entire cosmos and bounced off the weakening walls of time, dark winds whipping up great fragments of the continuum like street blocks of sidewalk and pavement, bombarding the billowing fabrics of the universe and sending them spinning and pirouetting like enormous gossamer curtains.

Amidst the carnage and the confusion, the voice screamed again, hoarse now, crying into the deathless winds. And deep within the maelstrom of movement and noise, a frail body writhed as if possessed.

Billion-mile rips, like gangrenous tears, breached the boundless heavens and pieces of history tumbled from the wounds onto the battlefield. Cries of the newborn mingled with the tearful oaths of the dying while, across the ground, the blood of the centuries ran, and formed pools, and then scabbed, and then disappeared.

And still the lone body amidst the ghostlike wraiths twisted and turned in a noiseless cry.

The air was filled with a multitude of odors.

Here a shape fell and decayed in seconds . . . only to reform its flesh and rise again screaming. Lying among the tortured souls, a fat man with a cigar gave a two-fingered sign as his legs crumbled into the river of entrails that washed around him. High above in the mists, red clouds scurried with crashes of thunder, and lightning raked the ground leaving craters and fires that later had never been but soon would be.

A young man slumped forward in his car as a bullet scattered pieces of brain across his driver, and the whole entourage plowed into the gates of a camp that made lamp shades out of the skins of babies. Above the scene, appropriately placed in a presidential box, a man raised high his weapon and screamed his assassin scream yet again . . . as peace was declared and war broke out.

All in sight was fading and returning, and still the body lurched and cried deep, sobbing moans . . . and he smiled as the gods tried to regain the balance.

And this was as it would always be.

Thus had it ever been.

The countdown for the final performance approached . . . and it was about time.

"Then it's the only way?"

"It's the only way. Will you do it?"

He turned a card, a red seven, and placed it on the eight of spades. "I'll do it," he said, fingering the pack.

*   *   *

The door slammed open and Mandrain burst in waving a piece of paper, his face pale and drawn.

"What is it?" asked DeFatz, his hand resting on the roulette wheel.

"The computer . . . it came up with this: We didn't know."

DeFatz spun the wheel, took the printout, and read.

"We didn't know!" screamed Mandrain, and he watched the little white ball bounce among the slots, waiting for the motion to stop.

"When will you leave?" she asked, stroking his head.

He stared at the spread of playing cards and gently rubbed those still to be turned. "Tomorrow, but you'll hardly know I've gone."

She sighed.

He turned a card.

The fire crackled.

"It's as simple as this," said Smutbath, waving his baton at the blackboard. "East Side Spare Parts now covers the world; from London to Adelaide, New York to Moscow." He paused and gesticulated wildly, unable to think of any other cities offhand. "In fact," he continued, "just about every damn place you can think of except—" And he turned again to the blackboard. "Except here." He prodded Jersey with his baton and stepped away from the blackboard.

"See," he started, "the past eighty, ninety years have seen massive progress in cooperation between the Federation and the . . ." He paused, seemingly trying to think of a word.

"The Jeffies, sir?" a voice shouted.

"The Spacers?" another voice enquired querulously.

Smutbath searched the room myopically, nodding. "Yes, quite," he said, "the Jeffies and the Spacers . . . indeed, such quaint pieces of terminology. Rather," he tapped the side of his leg with his baton, "let's call them free thinkers and free movers, shall we?"

There was no response.

"Anyway," Smutbath continued, "there has been, as I said, considerable progress between the Federation and the free-thinking and free-moving elements of our society in terms of business development and open communications . . . progress that has enabled East Side Spare Parts to expand beyond our one-time wildest dreams. Now"—he strode determinedly back to the blackboard and brandished his baton—"the Earth is effectively ours, at least in terms of strict commercialism, and similarly—thanks to last century's black hole discovery plus advancements . . . albeit of a limited success . . . in robotics and nanotechnology—delivery and production levels are off the scale."

Smutbath paused. "Everything in the garden is exceptionally rosy indeed . . . apart from one small slug wandering the flowerbeds." He pulled down the flip-chart and displayed Jersey Replacements' well-known emblem.

"Why don't we just bomb them?" asked Filbean, in a shrill voice that sounded like Smutbath's chalk on the blackboard.

Everyone nodded and muttered agreement.

"Because Jersey Replacements is too good a concern to just wipe off the map. Its reputation goes back decades . . . back to the early two-thousands I should think. Their ground-breaking work in spread-spectrum radio, steganography, and encryption, for example—and those are but a few of many such examples—has made them a highly respected element in the electronics and surveillance society of 2271."

Smutbath left the rostrum and all eyes followed him. "So, no," he continued, "we don't just bomb them. And Davis-Davis will not sell out—my God but we've tried."

"Then we kill Davis-Davis," said a voice.

Pilking, a small, sharp-faced man, rose to his feet and turned to face the speaker. "We have tried every way to blot him out. For years. The entire assassinations section has been geared to that very goal for the past eighteen months, even to the point of evaluating usage of the recently discovered black-hole singularity . . . but beams and devices used in that way cannot be effectively controlled.

"So . . . ," his voice trailed as he turned to face Smutbath at the front of the room. "We cannot get near him. The island of Jersey is impregnable, his bodyguards number in the thousands, and his clones exist in every corner . . . offworld as well as onworld, hidden, waiting to be called to duty should the Davis-Davis on the island be killed." He shrugged. "It would solve nothing even if we *could* kill him now. . . ." He paused and faced the room. "But if we had killed him as he moved up the company . . . that would have been different. We had opportunities then. We should have foreseen this situation when we killed his father." He nodded to nobody in particular and, turning, smiled up at Smutbath. "We blew it," he said. Then he sat down.

Smutbath returned the smile and walked quietly down the aisle between the desks until he reached the second desk from the back of the fourth row.

There, a dark-skinned man sat playing Patience.

The murmuring that had resulted from Pilking's words faded into absolute silence. The man looked up at Smutbath and then turned his eyes to Pilking, who had turned around in his seat and now sat staring at him through the sea of faces and backs of heads. The man held his cards tightly and said, "Then it's the only way?"

"It's the only way. Will you do it?"

He turned a card, a red seven, and placed it on the eight of spades. "I'll do it," he said, fingering the pack.

DeFatz ran from the data-control block to the management sector, horror in his heart.

Smutbath looked up from the four neat piles of playing cards on his desk as DeFatz burst into his office. "What the—"

DeFatz leaned on the desk, panting, and stretched out an empty right hand. "Read this," he gasped.

Smutbath frowned. "Read what?"

"This print—" DeFatz stopped and looked around the office. "Did you want me?" he asked.

"No." Smutbath lifted one of the piles and fanned it out, counting the points.

"Then why am I here?" muttered DeFatz, scratching his head.

"I've been expecting you," the man behind the desk said.

He kept the laser trained on the man and searched the smoldering office for opposition.

"This is the end, then," said Davis-Davis.

He nodded and pulled back on the trigger.

He turned an ace and moved it to the side.

"I have a feeling about this one," she said.

He said nothing and turned three cards, the three of clubs on the top. There was no red four and the ace of clubs had yet to be played.

"He's too clever for you," she said, reaching for her drink. "And Smutbath, and Pilking."

He turned more cards. Queen of hearts.

She held his head inches from her own and the tears trickled down her cheeks. "They've been trying for years to nail him and . . ."

But he wasn't listening.

She sighed and sipped her drink, feeling the soft coldness travel down her throat. "When will you leave?" she asked, stroking his head.

"It will be as normal," said Meatle, walking around his machine. "Just the initial dizziness, muscle recoordination—that's the tightness in the arms and legs," he interrupted himself, "and a sick feeling; then you're home and dry."

Smutbath stepped forward nearer to the console and thrust his hands deep into his pants pockets. "Any questions?"

The man continued to toss a coin, watching it twirl in the air and then land again on his outstretched palm. He checked the face of the coin and, tossing it again, said, "No."

"Even at that time, Davis-Davis had bodyguards, and the channel was constantly patrolled by Jersey Replacements vessels— although ships from France docked there daily, so that'll be your means of crossing. How you actually get onto the island will, I'm afraid, be your own problem."

He twisted the coin in his fingers and nodded.

"At the time," said Smutbath, "Davis-Davis was deputy managing director. It was three years before we assassinated his father, thereby allowing him to gain full control of the company. Perhaps he was even contemplating it then. We have no way of knowing, of course, but at least in retrospect, it would seem as though we did Davis-Davis a big favor.

"Eighteen months from the time you will arrive, key men in the cabinet were replaced by militants from the Davis-Davis camp. At that time, his father ceased to have any real control and thus merely became a figurehead, kept alive only, I'm sure, until new relationships with the rest of the world could be effected." Smutbath paused and shook his head. "If only we had thought, and paid more attention to the signs, then all of this might not have been necessary."

"But there is no real danger," Meatle said, rubbing his hand across the bulkhead of his machine. "And he has used it before," he added, turning to smile at the somber gathering.

"But this time we will be altering the entire time flow," Smutbath pointed out in a voice that bore traces of tiredness and something else. "This time, we will be removing a complete piece of history."

*　*　*

All in sight was fading and returning, and still the body lurched and cried deep, sobbing moans.

"Then it's the only way?"

"It's the only way. Will you do it?"

He turned a card, a black four, and started to place it on the eight of spades. He frowned and pulled back, puzzled. "I'll . . . do it," he said, fingering the pack.

DeFatz spun the wheel, took the printout, and read.

"We didn't know!" screamed Mandrain, and he watched the little white ball bounce among the slots, waiting for the motion to stop.

The paper carried the legend FILE AMENDMENTS. Under the subheading DELETIONS was the name Davis-Davis, complete with relevant date, time of death, time of birth, personal appraisals, and an estimated MAIN FILE CORRECTION run of 716,421,763 pages containing 8,162,946,344,446 entries. Beneath that was another name. **Finnegan.** It was double-printed, making the word stand out from the rest.

DeFatz looked up as the wheel came to a stop and the little white ball slowed. "Finnegan?" he asked.

Mandrain leaned across the desk, his wet face inches from that of DeFatz. "Look at the date of his death," he sobbed, grabbing the paper and pushing it toward the other man's face. "Look at the date!"

"That depends," said Captain Ferrarro, a grizzled one-legged Spacer who had left the FTL merchant trade and opted for onworld shuttle service.

"Depends?"

Captain Ferrarro gave a crinkly smile. "It depends on how much you've got."

His passenger smiled and placed his arm around the fat man. "There must be many ships bound for Jersey today, Captain: Am I right?"

The captain nodded nervously.

"Then I could just . . . kill you, now, right?" He smiled. "And then I could find someone else, someone more, shall we say, more willing to accommodate me. Am I right?"

A croak.

He leaned closer. "Pardon me?"

"You're right," came the reply.

"Good." He removed his arm. "Then you will accept the standard payment."

The captain smiled an uneasy acknowledgment.

"And please," he said, softly, inserting his index finger in Ferrarro's mouth and squeezing until blood ran down the man's face to meet his thumb, "let us keep to our little arrangement without any, shall we say, deviations."

Captain Ferrarro tried to smile, and swallowed some of his own blood.

"Because I just don't have the time." And he gave out a hollow laugh that was completely devoid of humor, while above the winds, the cries of the dying mingled with the tearful oaths of the newborn. . . .

Across the ground, the blood of the centuries ran, and formed pools, and then scabbed, and then disappeared.

And still the lone body amidst the ghostlike wraiths twisted and turned in a noiseless cry.

The door slid back and the guard walked briskly into the room. Davis-Davis nodded an acknowledgment to the salute and spoke.

"Yes."

"We have an infiltrator, sir." The guard stood rigidly, staring at a piece of the wall some four or five feet above the seated man's head.

"Where?"

"Block eight, sir."

"Casualties?"

"Four dead and seven wounded, sir."

Davis-Davis stood up and walked around the desk and behind the guard. "And what exactly is this person doing in block eight, Mr. Bissle?"

The guard winced. When names were used it invariably led to unpleasantness. "I think he's trying to get to you, sir."

"Then stop him."

"Sir." The guard saluted, pivoted, and left the room.

And the pomp and the circumstance were the seventh day.

Outside the sky grew dark and squalls of rain lashed the windows. "Bloody weather," said Mandrain. He turned back to his cards, chewed his bottom lip for a second, and said, "Okay, three diamonds."

"Where's the boss?" Drewjar asked, peering through a hatch.

Mandrain scratched his head and frowned. "Not really sure. I think he went . . . went to see Smutbath—" He hesitated. "Yes, to see Smutbath, about something or other. Why?"

Drewjar looked puzzled. "Well, I don't know if it's anything really, but the terminals are acting up."

"No bid," wheezed Flandell, the network controller. He placed his cards on the table and shook a cigarette from a crumpled pack. "Acting up? How?"

Across from Smutbath, Blick pushed his cards together and then fanned them out again. "Are we playing here or what?"

Drewjar studied Blick's cards as he spoke. "Well, they're giving out incorrect information all the time. Work's stopped on data prep until someone can have a look at it."

"Three spades," Blick said. "Now where the hell's—"

As if on cue, the door opened and DeFatz walked in. He looked uneasy.

Blick said, "It's your bloody bid."

Flandell shuffled around in his chair and coughed loudly. "My dear DeFatz, Mr. Drewjar informs us that the terminals are on the fritz. When did you last check the modem points?"

"Where've you been, anyway?" added Mandrain.

"Let me look at my cards, last Wednesday, and Smutbath's office," DeFatz said to each of the questioning faces, and he reached for his cards.

Drewjar raised his eyebrows in a what-do-I-do expression.

"What were you doing with Smutbath?" Blick asked.

DeFatz fanned his cards and counted. "Haven't got the faintest idea," he said with a chuckle. "When I got there, I'd forgotten. Must be going senile." He laughed again and stared at the cards.

Mandrain turned to look out the window. Outside, the sky was turning bright ginger in stages.

"You know," DeFatz said, "it's the damnedest thing."

Drewjar leaned back against the wall to wait until the conversation drifted back to the terminals.

"*What* is?" asked Blick in exasperation.

"These cards. I feel I've played this hand a million times."

And he laughed as the winds built up again.

He listened for footsteps.

All was silent.

He was into block four.

"Block four!" Davis-Davis screamed, his eyes aflame. "How the holy hell has he got all the way to block four?"

Bissle gulped and stared straight ahead. There wasn't a good answer. The intruder was there, and that was that.

"What are you all doing out there?" Davis-Davis continued. "He's one man, Bissle. One man! Why has he not been stopped?"

"He's good, sir. We don't seem to be able to get a trace on him."

Davis-Davis returned to his chair. As he sat down, his composure regained, he said, "I don't care how you do it, but I want him stopped."

All around, strange colors flashed and lit the heavens while voices boomed across the ever-changing landscape. Voices that screamed and sobbed; voices that laughed and altered tone and pitch, like bad recordings; voices that shook and shuddered, like the sound of a thousand bombs falling together, shaking the firmament.

He lay staring into the resulting voids with eyes of madness.

Hurried footsteps echoed on the tarmac outside the block four hatch. He slid beneath a large tarpaulin to the right of the hatch and waited, his heart thumping in his head.

The hatch creaked open.

All was silent save for the low hum of the machinery holding the door in place some five feet above the ground. Suddenly a hand appeared inside the hatch, and with a scurry, a guard dropped into the shadows in front of the tarpaulin.

He cursed silently.

He had not been ready.

He listened. The guard inside the block did not move.

He raised his air gun and waited.

A second figure appeared for a split second . . . and he fired. The air immediately in front of the guard swirled and compressed, and with the start of a shout, the body spun around and crashed into the hatch entry and slid to the floor.

With a scream of defiance, the guard inside the block leapt

from his cover in the darkness and fired two shots into the tarpaulin, which jumped into the air, smoking, and then settled again with a *fluump!*

He stood from his hiding place and fired point-blank at the guard's face, then turned and, with a flick of the controls on his air gun, sprayed the entry hatch. Two more guards exploded in a burst of skin and uniform.

He listened for a while and then stepped down.

He switched the hatch door to CLOSE and shouldered the gun.

At his feet was a torso with its left arm and shoulder missing. The legs were nowhere to be seen. The torso breathed in and out quickly, eyes open but unseeing.

The remains of a tag over its breast pocket said BISS.

And the fear and the horror were the sixth day.

"I know, I know . . . but I'm just supposing," said Flandell, mopping the sweat from his face.

Smutbath looked at him disdainfully and shuddered. "Well, don't suppose things like that too often—at least not while I'm around." He dealt the cards into four neat piles on his desk and then picked up one of the piles.

Flandell grunted. "There's just something strange happening and I don't know what it is."

"Must be an epidemic," Smutbath said, sorting the cards into suits.

"Hmmm?"

"Well, yesterday—at least, I think it was yesterday—DeFatz came charging into my office shouting abou—"

The door slammed open and Smutbath looked up.

DeFatz leaned on the desk, panting. "Read this," he gasped, holding out his empty right hand.

*   *   *

"Then it's the only way?"

"It's the only way. Will you do it?"

She frowned and stared into the empty fire grate.

"I've been expecting you," the man behind the desk said.

"Huh?" responded Flandell. He coughed and looked around the room he had just entered to ascertain where he was. It was Smutbath's office and Smutbath was dealing cards into four neat piles.

Smutbath finished dealing, picked up one of the piles, and fanned out the cards. Then he placed the fan of cards carefully on his desk and picked up another pile.

He looked up at Flandell, smiled, and then threw the cards onto the table. "Sorry," he said, "that wasn't my line. We'd better try it again." He dragged all the cards together with his hands and started to hum.

DeFatz burst into the office. "Read this," he gasped, holding out an empty right hand.

Outside, the clouds flashed past the mock-up building fronts and all the noise in the world rolled across the stage below.

For a second it all became clear to Flandell. He looked at Smutbath and DeFatz, saw Smutbath rest his head on the desk and start to sob.

The roar of eternity coming down the corridor outside the door mingled with the strange mauve clouds that had easily conquered the glassless windows and now swirled around the room, removing air.

Then the door disintegrated in a shower of splinters. "Here we go again," Flandell whispered to no one in particular.

When he awoke, he was sitting across from what appeared to be a statue of Smutbath, frozen in the act of arranging playing cards in his hands. A table was between them. He looked at his own cards. Seventeen points, seven diamond cards, no spades.

He laid the cards down in a neat fan and reached across to touch Smutbath's arm. It was pliant, cool to the touch, and slightly clammy.

"I know what's happening," he said.

Smutbath did not move.

Flandell rose to his feet and moved from the table to a large desk at the side of the room. On the desk was a tropical-fish tank, only partly filled with water. The water lapped against three small islands constructed from the sand and soil that lay at the tank's sides. In the water, several small fish swam lazily.

"He's dead," Flandell said. He pushed his hands into his pants pockets and turned to rest against the table. "We sent him back to kill Davis-Davis and he did it. But then, years after—or maybe even days after . . . or minutes—someone or something killed *him*. And that someone or something would not have been there or would not have happened if Davis-Davis had lived." He raised his voice and, looking around the room, said, "Is that about right?"

There was no answer. Smutbath remained deathly still.

"And so now," he continued, his voice lowered, "they're trying everything they can think of to put things right, letting different people know some of what's happening and what's happened in the process."

He moved away from the table and walked behind Smutbath. "Good hand," he said, looking at the cards frozen in the process of being sorted into suit order.

A slight movement from the fish tank caught his attention and he walked back to take a closer look. One of the fish had beached onto an island. It wiggled and squirmed, and when he bent closer, Flandell saw that it was sprouting tiny limbs as he watched.

Flandell started to cry.

The door burst open and DeFatz held out an empty hand. "Read this," he gasped. Flandell noticed grimly that DeFatz was holding out his *left* hand.

*   *   *

"See," said Flandell, "the modems are perfectly in order." He wiped his nose and grunted. "I knew it couldn't be anything to do with them."

"Well it must be something," muttered Drewjar with a scowl. "They shouldn't refuse information from files coded priority ten and under."

"And what the hell's this message?" Mandrain pointed to the terminal printout and read it aloud. " 'Code E005411: Information requested is under construction.' "

"Never heard of it. 'Under construction.' Hmmph." Drewjar snorted disdainfully and straightened up. "Never bloody heard of it."

Flandell remained bent over the machine. "Somebody get me a manual."

"I've got it here," Mandrain called from the rack of books at the other side of the room. "There's no message suite with a code prefix E."

"Cock!" said Flandell, and he jumped up and walked briskly over to Mandrain. Snatching the open book, he said, "If there's a message, then it must be explained in the manual."

The others watched as he studied the indices.

He snapped the book shut. "I'm going to see Smutbath," he said, and stormed out of the room.

"Yes?"

"Sir, Bissle's dead," said a voice through the intercom.

Davis-Davis swallowed hard and closed his eyes tightly.

"Sir?"

"Yes, I'm still here."

"What should we do, sir?"

"What's that noise? In the background?"

"That's Block Two, sir. It's on fire."

"He's into Block Two?"

"Yes, sir. What should we do?"

"I have no idea," said Davis-Davis, and he switched off the intercom.

A young paperhanger from Austria lazed on the front lawns of America's White House and the streets were awash with fire and screams, while inside the rambling multicorridored building, a man whose life and principles had in another deal of the celestial cards inspired an entire movement of so-called minarchists stood in an oval wood-paneled room, staring out of the windows.

The man, the third great leader of his great country, absently warmed his hands before a smoldering fire upon which had recently been thrown a revolving chair, the shards of a portable writing desk, a letter-copying device, and a cannonball-weighted clock that told the day of the week. As he watched the events unfolding outside he considered changing his name . . . a simple matter of making the first the last and vice versa. "Jefferson Thomas," he said, nodding, rolling the words around his tongue to see how they tasted.

On the next lot, Rasputin burned at the stake, his lips flecked with the saliva of the righteous.

Great seams opened and closed continually, spewing out more attempts while mercifully burying those that had no effect.

And the body laughed and clapped to the endless performances, its face dripping with the blood of the millennia.

And the applause and the shouting were the fifth day.

The door opened and Flandell walked into Smutbath's office. Smutbath was sitting with his feet on the window ledge, staring into the sky. On the table behind him were four small piles of cards. He turned around and smiled at Flandell. "It's all there," he said. "It's just the way you said—oh, yes . . . I could hear you."

"Hear me?"

Smutbath stood up and moved to the window. Outside, in the street far below the window, a tall, bearded man was trudging through the mud, jeered on all sides by the gathered crowds. On his back was a roughly made cross constructed from two planks. On one of the planks, the words ACME CONSTRUCTION could be seen clearly.

Smutbath turned from the window, chuckling. "Acme Construction," he said. "Sounds like one of the old cartoons from the twentieth century."

Flandell was frozen in the act of walking across the room, a code manual from the computer building clasped in his hands.

Smutbath walked around the other man, waved a hand in front of his eyes, pushed his shoulder . . . all to no avail. "You can't hear a word I'm saying, can you?"

There was no answer.

"No, you *can* hear. I heard you, after all. It's just that you can't do anything about it."

Smutbath walked back to the window. "I wonder how long they've been trying . . . how long this has been going on." He looked out and watched Jesus stagger to the end of the street. As he reached the mound, the figure stopped and the crowds quieted. All faces turned around and up to the window. It had no glass in it.

"Forgive them," Smutbath said softly, "for they know not what to do."

The sky turned a violent green and winds blew down the street, scattering both players and props alike.

Smutbath sobbed into his hands. "And *I* don't know what to do, either." When he pulled his face away, he saw that he had cried tears of blood onto his hands.

And the crucifixion and the stigmata were the fourth day.

"When will you leave?" she asked, stroking his head.

He stared at the spread of playing cards and gently rubbed

those still to be turned. "Tomorrow, but you'll hardly know I've gone."

She sighed.

He turned a card.

The fire crackled.

The man looked up at Smutbath and then turned his eyes to Pilking, who had turned around in his seat and now sat staring at him through the sea of faces and backs of heads. He held his cards tightly and said, "Then it's the only way?"

"It's the only way. Will you do it?"

"I've been expecting you," the man behind the desk said.

He kept the laser trained on the man and searched the smoldering office for opposition.

"This is the end, then," said Davis-Davis.

He nodded and pulled back on the trigger.

But he wasn't listening.

She sighed and sipped her drink, feeling the soft coldness travel down her throat. "When will you leave?" she asked, stroking his head.

"But there is no real danger," Meatle said, rubbing his hand across the bulkhead of his machine. "And he has used it before," he added, turning to smile at the somber gathering.

"But this time we will be altering the entire time flow," Smutbath pointed out in a voice that bore traces of tiredness and something else. "This time, we will be removing a complete piece of history."

DeFatz looked up as the wheel came to a stop and the little white ball slowed. "Finnegan?" he asked.

"That depends," said Captain Ferrarro, "on how much you've got."

"Because I just don't have the time." And he gave out a hollow laugh that was completely devoid of humor, while above the winds, the cries of the dying mingled with the tearful oaths of the newborn. . . .

"We have an infiltrator, sir." The guard stood rigidly, staring at a piece of the wall some four or five feet above the seated man's head.

"You know," DeFatz said, "it's the damnedest thing."

Drewjar leaned back against the wall to wait until the conversation drifted back to the terminals.

"*What* is?" asked Blick in exasperation.

"These cards. I feel I've played this hand a million times."

And he laughed as the winds echoed through the room and smashed the rostrum into the air.

Already it was the third day; and it was not good.

She sighed and stared into the empty grate.

He heard the sigh and turned his head on her lap. "Why worry about this one?" he asked. "There have been so many others in the past."

She laughed despite herself. "That's some play on words you've got there."

He smiled at his unintentional pun and sat up. "I've been back before. Please . . . just don't worry."

"But you'll be altering the entire time flow this time. Think about the things that Davis-Davis must have done in the last twenty years that we don't even know about." She shook her head and moved away from him. "If just one of those things—just one of those millions of things that he did, or would have done—was important, just think of what it could mean to the present. Think how things could change."

He laughed. "Even if something *did* change as a result of his death, then as far as you in the present are concerned, it would always have been that way." He looked into the fireplace. "Ever since whatever it was should have happened or shouldn't have happened . . . whichever the case may be." He frowned. Something seemed not to be right.

"I don't understand the paradoxes of time," she said with a brave smile. "Don't go."

"I must," he said, wondering why there was no fire in the grate.

The sign was directly above his head: BLOCK ONE.

Outside, down the wind, he could hear the voices and cries of the guards. In the last block there had been only the faint hum of machinery and equipment. He now stood against the block one hatch entrance and waited. The smell of burning was spreading everywhere, and his throat and nostrils were stinging.

He laughed to himself. He had made it. He was here.

One more block and he was *here*.

He checked the air gun. It was completely empty.

He bent down carefully, keeping his eyes scanning for any signs of movement, and laid the spent weapon on the ground.

Standing up, he decided it would have to be the laser rifle. He had always enjoyed using the laser rifle.

Unstrapping it from his back, he started across the block.

"It's kind of like a preemptive defense," Pilking said.

The audience did not respond.

Nobody moved.

One or two were frozen in the act of sleep; one was caught, his eyes half lidded, with a finger up his left nostril; several were looking this way or that; a few were writing.

But all were still.

Pilking walked along the aisles.

"They're playing the odds," he said. "They're trying every trick in the book to make a grand-slam contract."

He reached the front of the hall and, turning to face the immobile gathering again, leaned against the desk. "But how do you make seven of anything when you're missing the ace of trumps?"

"They'll try every permutation," he said, his voice almost a whisper. "They'll go back, and they'll go forward. They'll try it over and over again.

"They'll have Germany winning the Second World War . . . they'll have Gorbachev assassinated . . . maybe Clinton, Dole, Erikson, Mondayo . . . all of them, all the ones ever since . . . and then they'll rerun the whole thing, bringing it up to date, and see if it's worked. Because, let's face it: There's no law anywhere that says gods have to be intelligent."

"And maybe they'll try name-changes, too." He smiled and thrust his hands into his pants pockets, nodding. "Yeah, maybe they'll change your names—all of your names—and my name, too. Hell, maybe they'll even change the Earth's name . . . change it to—" He stopped and lifted his head, searching for inspiration. "To Valhalla, maybe, or Armageddon." He thought of his beloved president, Jefferson Thomas—ignoring the nagging small voice that seemed to question some important element of that memory—and laughed. "Or maybe they'll even call it Monticello, forgetting the old space station." He placed an arm across his chest and said, in deep sepulchral tones, " 'All my wishes end where I hope my days will end, at Monticello.' "

He walked onto the rostrum and sat on the desk. "This is what it's about now: cause and effect, action and reaction.

"And if it doesn't work, then they'll take it all back and try something else . . . bring it forward again, check it out—no, didn't work—take it back, try something else . . . and so on."

He smiled and ran a hand through his hair. "Sounds boring, doesn't it? But *they* don't get bored doing things like this. Hell, *they* enjoy it. Death, destruction, pain, confusion . . . these are the trademarks of a god's work. No sense, no reason, no logic.

"Air crashes, earthquakes, famines . . . none of it makes any sense.

"So, *why do it?* do I hear you say?" He laughed. "Why indeed." He shrugged. "Because. It. Passes. The. Time.

"That's all. Nothing more."

He rubbed his crotch through his pants and then held up his hand. "See this? What I just did with it?"

Nobody responded.

Nobody moved.

Nobody even breathed, at least not in the usual way.

"I scratched my balls. There. What about that?"

Nothing.

"Important? Nah! But when you get to the stage where you've considered everything else, the seemingly unimportant things suddenly seem like they might be important after all. So.

"I scratched my balls with my right hand. I always do it with my right hand. . . . I'm right handed, for Crissakes.

"What they may do now is go back to every time I scratched my balls—or you . . ." He pointed to a man on the front row.

"Or you." One on the fifth row.

He pointed to the man with his finger up his nostril. "Maybe they'll go back to every time you picked your nose."

The man, his finger permanently fixed up into the darkness and moist dirt, didn't move.

"And they'll have us do it with our other hand," Pilking continued. "The one we don't usually use. Then they'll run it through again and see if it's worked out."

He sat and watched for a while.

Nobody moved.

"But it *won't* work out. I mean . . . it's all just a big gamble. And, in the long run, nobody ever wins by gambling."

He stretched out on the table and looked up at the sky. "Hah," he said. "I hadn't even noticed that the ceiling was gone."

And the second day was a load of balls.

It was/is/soon would be the first/last day.

A time of endings and beginnings.

The possibilities were, at last, exhausted. It would have to be this way.

The hatch was open and all was quiet.

He looked around carefully before he moved inside.

The fires had swept fiercely through the block-ventilation system and the Home Block was already smoking.

He released the catch on the laser rifle and stepped through the hatch to find Davis-Davis, looking very old and very tired, seated behind a large mahogany desk.

"I've been expecting you," the man behind the desk said.

He kept the laser trained on the man and searched the smoldering office for opposition.

"This is the end, then," said Davis-Davis.

He nodded and pulled back on the trigger.

And the winds came crashing through the blocks and whistled across the gashes in the dead man's chest and face; and he felt a tugging in his stomach and tasted the bile in his mouth.

The screams echoed in the tiny office and he dropped the laser rifle and ran. And as he ran back through the blocks, the way he had come, he watched with fascination as the bodies of the dead guards leapt from the ground and ran, first backward and then forward, screaming gibberish in reverse, speeded up and then slowed down. But nobody seemed to notice him as he passed through.

"Then it's the only way?" he panted into the wind. "It's the only way," he replied.

He screamed a frantic refusal and was answered with a sound like mad static.

And now the blocks were gone. All around was bare and deserted.

And in his head, he heard the voices.

*   *   *

DeFatz spun the wheel, took the printout, and read.

"We didn't know!" screamed Mandrain, and he watched the little white ball bounce among the slots, waiting for the motion to stop.

The paper carried the legend FILE AMENDMENTS. Under the subheading DELETIONS was the name Davis-Davis, complete with relevant date, time of death, time of birth, personal appraisals, and an estimated MAIN FILE CORRECTION run of 716,421,763 pages containing 8,162,946,344,446 entries. Beneath that was another name. **Finnegan.** It was double-printed, making the word stand out from the rest.

DeFatz looked up as the wheel came to a stop and the little white ball slowed. "Finnegan?" he asked.

Mandrain leaned across the desk, his wet face inches from that of DeFatz. "Look at the date of his death," he sobbed, grabbing the paper and pushing it toward the other man's face. "Look at the date!"

DeFatz looked again at the paper and studied the information carefully. "He was killed sixteen years ago . . . *after* Davis-Davis was assassinated." His voice trailed off and he looked up at Mandrain. "But if that's true, then how could he go back? What does it all mean?"

Mandrain pulled out a chair and sat down. "It means that Davis-Davis was somehow responsible for the death of the would-be killer of our assassin." He pointed at the paper hanging limply from DeFatz's hand. "Finnegan."

"Oh no," DeFatz said, his eyes wide in understanding.

"Oh *yes,*" Mandrain corrected. "And because we had Davis-Davis assassinated, Finnegan lived. Therefore, Finnegan killed our man before he could possibly have set off back to kill Davis-Davis. Thus, Davis-Davis didn't die after all. Therefore, our man *did* go back, and Davis-Davis *did* die, and Finnegan *did* live, and our man *did* die, and so Davis-davis *did* live, and Finnegan *did* die, and our man *did* live. . . ."

DeFatz was openly weeping.

Mandrain was almost out of breath. "It's beautiful," he said, clapping his hands together in mock glee. "It's beautiful but it's impossible." He looked at the stationary ball in the roulette wheel. "The number is decidedly up and it's a no-win situation. And . . ." He pointed to the ceiling. "Anytime now, they're going to figure that out for themselves."

He screamed.

He screamed loud and long as strange forces jostled for control of his body.

Then there came the first and last sound.

The sound was that of a gigantic pack of playing cards being fanned across the sky, echoing around the clouds in time to the distant flares of color that split the horizon into thick, weeping gashes. It reverberated and filled the entire cosmos and bounced off the weakened walls of time, dark winds whipping up the last great fragments of the continuum like street blocks of sidewalk and pavement, bombarding the billowing tattered fabrics of the universe and sending them spinning and pirouetting like enormous gossamer curtains.

The final sound of all amidst the confusion was a rending crash, a clapperboard that signaled the last take.

And the show was abandoned.

As one, all the lights went out.

Everywhere became dark and silent.

And it was good.

> What of liberty and slavery among them, what they
> thought of death and the soul,
> Who were witty and wise, who beautiful and poetic,
> who brutish and underdevelop'd,
> Not a mark, not a record remains—and yet all remains.
> —Walt Whitman, from *Unnamed Lands* (1881)

DEMOKRATUS

Victor Koman

The only guy in the universe to do editorial work with Samuel Edward Konkin III for *New Libertarian* and also sell a story to Kris Rusch for *The Magazine of Fantasy & Science Fiction* (read these magazines back-to-back if you would fully appreciate the magnitude of his achievement), Vic Koman is a natural for this anthology. He did a story for the previous book on which I worked as coeditor (*Weird Menace*, the brainchild of movie producer Fred Olen Ray), so I wasn't about to let the author of *The Jehovah Contract*, *Solomon's Knife*, and the forthcoming *Kings of the High Frontier* get out of tackling one of my pet peeves—mob rule wearing a pretty name.

Welder Volnos, grimly serious, looked at the man across from him and said, "My mind's made up. Banishment."

"Are you crazy?" his friend Tom Hacker asked. "Banish yourself? Is that even possible?"

They sat together in the sky lounge of the trader *Spirit of Bob*, drinking sudabsinthe and gazing at the hypnotic swirl of color and light that illuminated their trip through space on a soliton wave. The curious rippling of starlight as the ship's engines compressed space at the bow and expanded it mightily at the stern—propelling them at faster-than-light speeds while satisfying Einstein's jots and tittles—had long ago lost its wonder for the lifelong spacefarers, yet it still imparted a hypnotizing calm to the men, much as watching a fireplace or a television might have soothed their ancestors. In that calm, Volnos had grown contemplative.

"Self-banishment is not only possible," Welder said to Tom, "I've heard it happens more often than you might think."

Tom mused on that for a moment, then took a deep draft of the liquor. "I can't imagine it," he said in a low, astonished tone. "To go from the universe to nothing?"

"A planet's quite a lot of something." Volnos finished his own drink and tossed the slender glass into the air. A waiter darted down from the overhead, extended a gripper, and snatched the glass into its chamber, cleaning and polishing the fine crystal as it flew back to the bar. "You could roam around one single planet your entire life and not see everything. The star routes may seem vast to you, but admit it: You've managed to travel them all in just eighty years, haven't you?"

"There are new ones opening up every day, Welder."

"Not that many. Habitable planets are few and far between in *this* sector of the galaxy; we've only found profitable routes to a few thousand star systems."

"I hear that the Federation's discovered a nebula where every star has planets and every one of them harbors some form of life."

"That's an easy lie for them," Volnos said with a sarcastic laugh. "They refuse to offer any proof by falling back on that protectionist noninterference nonsense. What a bunch of"—he glanced around to see if any women were present—"*taxers!*"

Hacker's ears reddened at Volnos's casual use of profanity. Maybe he *had* been plying too many trade routes. "Why self-banishment, though? If it's roaming around you want to do, why not—"

"It's the people, Tom. Nothing personal, but waverunners are getting on my nerves. We dart around from system to system making our fortunes, buying, selling, haggling, evading Feds, harassing Jeffies. Every now and then we discover an alien artifact or a new race. I mean, what's the point? After three or four hundred years, you're going to be dead anyway."

Hacker cocked an eyebrow at his friend. "You need a woman." he said. "And kids. Fast."

Volnos snorted as the sudabsinthe hit his brain, his gestures becoming as expansive as a neurevangelist's. "Oh, yeah. I need *more* complication in my life. Forget it. I just want to go someplace where I don't have to be so . . . *responsible* for my life. Where I can take a breath of air without being reminded that at some point I'll have to recharge the oxygen converters, or take a drink of water without remembering that it's somebody else's sweat or urine that's been recycled and purified. Where I don't have to make life-or-death decisions day in and day out. I just want a simpler life. I can find that on a planet."

Hacker shuddered. "Unfiltered air full of allergens? Water that Reason-knows-what has swum in or worse? Food grown in *dirt?*" He waved his glass around. The waiter buzzed by to refill it with the bitter green liquid. "And worst of all, *bugs!* I've been planetside a couple of times with the New Worlds Exploitation Syndicate, you know. Planets are lousy with insects."

Volnos's expression turned from wistful to grim. "I'd endure a *dozen* bug bites if it meant I never had to put on a pressure suit again. My mind's made up." He stood, a little wobbly but filled with resolve. "Next planet we pass, I'm going gravitational!"

Hacker just stared in amazement. "You don't even want to choose your planet?"

"I'm sick of choice."

"Don't you at least want to pick a form of"—his voice dropped to a whisper—*"government?"*

Volnos punched his drinking buddy in the shoulder. "What's the difference? They're all the same. The State tells you what to do and you do it. You're *free* down there. Free of all responsibility, all worry. Just do what you're told and enjoy living!"

Self-banishment was not as easy as he had thought. The toughest part turned out to be getting down to a planet. Banishment almost exclusively served as extraordinary punishment for violating the customs of Free Space. Self-banishment was considered evidence of mental incapacity, and very few Spacers had the time or desire to indulge a madman.

He found one, though, at Moon Poul's Trading Post and Fuel Dump, a space station drifting casually in deep space almost exactly halfway between Deneb (a stellar system that most decent Spacers deigned not to discuss) and the Stars of Africa: Kyng (whose most populous planet, Garvee, was, at 1.5 terramass, the birthplace of the galaxy's finest athletes) and Jak's Sun, whose five vibrant worlds were the source of most of the music filling the spaceways.

With little more than a pound of slender gold rods strapped on each wrist, Volnos jumped ship and wandered casually through the cramped space station, ignoring the imprecations of the buyers and sellers. He stopped at a PirogiMat to buy one of the fist-sized, grenade-shaped meat pastries that proved to be the current regional food fad. Tom Hacker found him at the counter and plopped down by his side.

"That was a draft-headed thing to do," Tom said out of the side of his mouth. "Captain Hudson's as mad as a Fed at you."

"Fine," Volnos muttered. "Let her banish me. I bought out my contract, fair and square." He finished the meaty meal in one last bite and strode into the main promenade of the wheel-shaped space station. Hacker followed him as he elbowed his way through the bustling crowd of spacefarers and post traders, each intent on business and deal-making.

"It's not the contract," Hacker insisted, dodging Spacers in an effort to keep up with Volnos. "She doesn't want to see a good man banished!"

Welder Volnos splayed his fingers wide in that Spacer gesture that signified a shrug of indifference. "I'm hitting the dirt. And that's the last choice I'll ever have to make."

He noticed a sign at a small booth recessed into a bulkhead.

Planetary Excursions Limited (Extremely)
"We Drop You Like a Hot Pirog"

Wedged inside the booth sat an unusually corpulent fellow who smiled at Volnos as he and Hacker approached. His rumpled cloak was the color of liquid methane and his face as florid as the Great Red Spot.

"Good trading, Freemen, good trading," he said in a spiel undoubtedly oft-repeated. "Welcome to Planetary Excursions! Tired of endless runs through the airless void of Free Space? How about a little sustenance for the soul? Leviathan Smith can get you anywhere you want to go! How about a visit to a *real* planet teeming with *real* life? Pharmaceutical-rich jungle planets, snow-covered ski worlds, ocean planets packed with the most amazing trophy fish! Worlds of excitement and delight!" He leaned toward the pair as best his bulk would allow. "Bring a date along and try one-gee sex, hmm? It's delightfully different. No floating around, just lying there in one—"

"I'm not a tourist," Volnos uttered in a low, even tone. "I want a one-way ticket to an inhabited Federation planet!"

Leviathan Smith frowned, his broad forehead furrowing like rills on a great airless moon. "You want to *live* on a *planet?* A planet polluted with Fed subjects?" He gave Volnos a look of shock, then gazed inquiringly at Hacker.

Tom shook his head and pointed at Volnos. *"He's* the self-banisher. *I'm* trying to talk him out of it."

The huge man in the tiny booth took a deep breath—which caused the walls of the booth to bend outward with many a creak and pop—and sighed. "Self-banishment does not work," he muttered in a low rumble. "And I'm not just speaking as a Spacer who wants repeat business for his agency. I promise that while you may love *visiting* a planet, you will hate *living* on one. There's no reason a Spacer should ever touch foot on a Federation planet. Everything we need we can get from planetoids, asteroids, and comets! What planet as easily yields up its iron, nickel, cobalt, molybdenum as a FeNi asteroid, not to mention my perennial favorites platinum, gold, and silver? And how easy is it to drill or mine a planet for highly prized organic compounds compared to breaking up a carbonaceous-chondrite asteroid?"

Tom nodded eagerly in agreement. "That's what I've been trying to tell him!"

"Yeah, yeah," Welder added sarcastically. "And we can get all the water we need from comets in the Oort haloes around stellar systems. But I—"

"So why plunge down into the thick, germ-and-allergen-laden soup called an atmosphere to tromp around in gravity that drags your every cell down with excruciating, relentless force?" Leviathan grimaced at the thought. "There's only one reason, and it's certainly not to squat on some real estate. No. A Spacer only touches down on a planet if he's a Cheater!" Smith gave him the once-more-over. "And you don't look like Cheater material."

"I'm not interested in Cheating!" Volnos pounded a fist on the narrow counter. "I just want to settle down!"

"Hoi!" a voice screamed from farther up the curving promenade. Welder and Tom turned to see Captain Hudson race toward them, frannie drawn, taking aim. "Volnos!" she shouted, her deep crimson hair flowing wildly in the low g of the trading post. "Freeze, you AWOL son of a groundhog!" The muzzle of the frangible-round pistol held steady, the laser dot painted on a spot right between Volnos's eyes. It danced about with each pounding footfall of her gait, but never wavered more than an inch from center.

He jumped straight up just as she fired. The round missed him and spattered into pinkish bismuth dust against the bulkhead behind Leviathan Smith's booth. Volnos kicked off the overhead and hit the deck running. His only chance lay in the docks. If he could lose her and stow away somewhere . . .

He reached the docks and plunged through an inner airlock just swinging shut. With swift hands he pulled an emergency helmet from its wall unit and slipped it on. Since Spacers always wore their skintight pressure suits as underwear, he had only to fasten the neck seal. The rebreather operated automatically, allowing him to turn and wave at the livid captain beyond the 'lock.

Air hissed away, pumped into its storage tank, and the outer hatch opened in vacuumed silence. Volnos gazed at the ship he would be boarding along with the cargo.

Uh oh, he thought. *Cheaters!*

The emergency rebreather did not last long. Scrambling to reach the cargo hold, Volnos maneuvered through the voids between shipping containers, well aware that a slow-moving, weightless container had enough inertia to crush him with a force of several thousand g pounds. Barterships carried unconscionable slugs of mass. He scrambled through the outer, unpressurized holds until he found an airlock. Cycling atmosphere in, he gazed through the plate-plastic viewport at the pair of suspicious eyes peering at him from inside the spacecraft.

The barterships held a peculiar place in the hearts and minds of Free Spacers. Run by the Cheaters, the barterships essentially traded with the enemy, yet served as a subversive force in their own right. The planets of the Federation existed under a virtual quarantine, visited only rarely by Federation taxships, ignored and despised by most Spacers except as a dumping ground for the banished. The Cheaters violated this firm custom with impunity, their smuggling of Spacer goods to the planets impossible for Federation taxships to control, their importation of planet-dwellers' artifacts a hot commodity among the inhabitants of other worlds (not to mention among the few Spacer aficionados of the bizarre and perverse).

Volnos sat in a cramped hold on the bartership *Hinman* and gazed at Brigadier Cheater Aldrin D'Asaro, who ranked just below his commander, Major Cheater Davy Crockett XIX. Crockett—seldom seen by any of the crew—existed more as a Cheater legend than as a functioning trader. Running all aspects of the ship from his virtual bridge, he was as reclusive and eternal as his rival, the Dread Cheater Roberts.

D'Asaro leaned back in his chair. A comfortably stout man in a trade where liftoff mass mattered immensely, his dark-hued bulk filled the chair as fully as a smile filled his expansive face.

"We take the slow way down," he said. "Minimizes the ionization trail." Glancing at the vidscreen set into the antique mahogany desk that separated him from Volnos, he added, "We'll be miles from the city. You in good shape? I can sell you enduropatches if you need to boost the stamina." He fingered the half pound of gold rods that had until recently resided on the stowaway's wrist.

Volnos demurred. A stroll along something other than a metal corridor sounded divine.

"Almost there." The bartership shuddered, touched planet, and slowly the throb of reaction engines wound down to silence.

Welder stood. "I'm lighter!"

"Demokratus is four-fifths standard gee." D'Asaro's ebon face lost its pleasant expression for a moment. "Are you sure you want *this* planet?"

Volnos shrugged. "One's pretty much the same as another, right? All have governments that free you from having to think or provide for yourself."

D'Asaro pursed his lips and took a breath. "Well . . . there are States and there are States. This one is called Demokratus."

Volnos rolled the planet's name over in his mind, then said, "Demokratus. Almost sounds like a swear word."

D'Asaro grinned broadly as if at some secret joke. "Get used to it," he said. Rising, he extended his left hand, palm up. "Take it easy," he said cheerfully. "But take it! Lazy's Fair."

Welder held his right hand over the proffered hand, his fingers curved and touching, as if about to drop something. "Lazy's Passé."

There's another stupid custom I won't have to bother with. . . .

*   *   *

He emerged into night as the Brigadier Cheater and his minions
made their deals with the local countereconomists who gathered
at what must have been the appointed place at the appointed hour.
Buying an outfit that one of the groundhog barterers assured him
was local clothing (consisting of loose white slacks, a tunic-style
shirt, and leather sandals made from the skin of a local bird called
the grack), Volnos left his old Spacer clothes—and his Spacer
past—behind and took a deep, full breath of genuine, natural
planet air. It smelled good and sweet and pure.

He sneezed.

And sneezed.

And sneezed again.

His nose began to run, his eyes to itch. Suddenly, he remembered what his mother had told him once; he thought it was merely
a new wives' tale meant to mold children's character: *Stop being so
dependent and obedient or we'll put you on the next planet we pass and
you'll come down with Banishee's Bane.*

Great, he thought, wiping a sleeve against his nose. *I'm allergic
to planets.*

He sniffled his way toward the city lights, gazing at the night
sky, marveling at how few stars were visible beneath the miles of
air, thrilling at the slate-gray color between the dozens of points of
light. Now *that's* something he'd never seen before!

The road consisted of an uneven strip made from something
brown and powdery. He had seen dirt before, of course—small
vials of genuine Terran, Lunar, or Martian soil were a perennial gag
gift. He had simply never seen so much at one time. And it
stretched for miles.

By dawn, feet aching, soles sore, nose raw, shirt cuffs soaked
and beginning to crust over, desperately wishing he had bartered
for a few handkerchiefs, he reached the city of Suffragium. Though
he didn't like the ominous sound of the name, the city itself possessed all the regal beauty of a capital city. Tall buildings towered

over vast open squares. No technological backwater, groundcabs zipped this way and that across the squares and subsonic aircraft slowly arrowed through the sky.

He reached the city limits, where the dirt road became a paved street. At the borderline stood a white-washed guardhouse from which extended a wobbly red plank that served as a crossing gate. Volnos glanced to either side. No fences or anything. He could have easily walked around it, but he felt a sudden warmth for the quaint trust this government put in its subjects.

As he boldly approached the gate, he batted the word about in his mind. *Subject. Rolls off the tongue easier than that harsh phrase "Citizen of the Galaxy." "Subject to the jurisdiction of the State." Never have to make a choice again.*

Volnos sighed. *Freedom at last. Freedom from choice.*

A wrinkled old man—utterly hairless from pate to chin, including his eyebrow ridge—sat by the gate reading a slip of plastic. Every time he reached the bottom of the page, he gave it a little shake and read the next page that appeared. He touched the edge of the scrim every now and then, as if ticking off points. He appeared quite content.

He wore clothing similar to what Volnos had bought, but of a turquoise shade and less puffy. He glanced up at the sniffling newcomer, then wrinkled his face even further, as if viewing a plate of bad food. "Greetings, elect one," he said. "Dressed for a costume party? I don't remember one being polled." Then he glanced at the other's wrists. "Ah," he said. "Greensleeves. What is it with you foreigners? No fashion sense and can't stand fresh air!"

"I guess not." Volnos had difficulty with the old man's accent, but the language—except for some idiomatic differences—was standard. He wasn't sure whether "poled" meant something different on this world; certainly the man wouldn't have used the *other* word in front of a complete stranger.

"You want in?" the guard asked.

"Yes indeed," Volnos replied, more than familiar with toll gates. Every spaceport had its share of private airlocks, owned by similar geezers who demanded TIPS: To Insure Pressure Seal. He wiped his runny nose on his sleeve and asked, "How much?"

The guard shrugged as if the question itself were strange. "One entry, one vote. All in flavor?" He raised his right hand to poke his middle finger in his eye, then stared at Volnos with the other. "Well?"

Volnos hesitantly raised his right hand and inserted finger into eye.

"Looks unanimous," the old man said. "C'mon through." He raised the flimsy board. "Welcome to Suffragium, voter."

Volnos clenched his fists suddenly, a wave of anger surging over him. *"What did you call me?"*

The old man looked shocked, as if he had made some terrible blunder that he could not imagine. "Voter?" he repeated. "We're all voters here."

Welder Volnos lowered his fists, stared at the terrified little man, and then began to laugh. He would have a hard time maintaining a straight face on a planet that used one of the spaceway's foulest profanities as an honorific. Clapping a hand on the gatekeeper's shoulder, he said, "My apologies, fellow . . . *voter*." He suppressed the urge to snicker and instead passed the border into his new life.

The old man took a rag to the sticky smear left on his clothing and shook his head, muttering, "Damned greensleeves . . ."

The city began as a few outlying homes surrounded by verdant beltways, then seamlessly merged into light industry, vast hexagonal aquaculture lakes (he presumed—he saw no pleasure craft), then grew to the taller buildings of the central city. Most of the outer buildings stood no more than twelve stories tall. Only the government buildings soared to lofty, impressive heights. Several had skyship pads at mid- and roof-level. These saw constant use as small flitters raced to and fro, ferrying (Volnos assumed) the planetary rulers about the city and continent in their tireless quest to create an ordered lifestyle for their subjects.

Volnos would fit right in, a totally carefree drone for the State.

First, though, he required lodging. Wandering the streets, groundcabs zipping up and down past him, he noticed the profound absence of advertising. No holobills thrusting into his face, no sublims whispering amid the background noise, not even a commercial nanobot beaming an ad onto his retina and then buzzing away. Nothing.

He found—by noticing its modest steel plaque—a nicely maintained tenement with rooms to let. He bounded up the painted steps to enter a lobby filled with boisterous noise.

The tenement's inhabitants—a dozen or so men and women wearing tight, efficient tunics and slacks in either crimson or gray—stopped whatever they were loudly discussing to stare at the interloper.

Volnos sneezed into the crook of his elbow, then sniffled and said, "Greetings, uh, fellow . . . *voters.*" He still had a hard time with that word. "Is there a room to rent?"

"Eieuw," one woman said. "Another greensleeves!" Turning to the others, she said, "Do we let Soozinbee rent to him?"

"Move to discuss," a skinny man said. "Can he afford it?"

"Have you got the ten thrallers a week it takes?" a stout woman asked.

Volnos hesitated, then said, "I have gold."

The others fell silent and stared. The first woman said, with extreme caution, "Gold was voted out of use as money ten years ago." She narrowed her gaze and swaggered over to peer at him very nearly eye to eye.

Volnos felt a choking dread envelop him. How did anyone ever survive banishment, when the dangers of violating a Federation planet's laws and customs lurked at every turn?

Her stern expression broke into a grin. "I vote that we convert his gold to thrallers at a rate of one hundred seventy-five per decagram. All in flavor?"

The majority of the others stuck their middle fingers in their eyes.

"Or posed?" A few inserted index fingers up their nostrils.

The woman—black hair contrasting sharply with her crimson outfit—counted the votes. "The Eyes are above the Nose!" she announced. "Welcome! Now give us your gold."

Bewildered by it all, but grateful to receive an order about which he need not think, he swiftly unstrapped the small gold rods from his wristlets and handed them to the scrawny young man while mentally converting ounces to the arcane metric system, long abandoned by Spacers as a utopian attempt to dumb down science. Among Spacers, anyone lacking the mental acuity to multiply and divide by twelve, sixteen, or two thousand was considered . . . well, a bit of a dope, to put it graciously.

With a handful of crinkly flaxpaper thrallers in hand, he paid Soozinbee when she appeared at the service counter. Noting that her name was Kennadie Soozinbee, he guessed that Demokratusians (or would it be Demokratists? Demokratites? He'd better check before he opened his mouth) put their surnames first. A quick glance at the register bore that out. He scanned it for common names and combined two to yield the name Wulsie Freechoice, which he signed on the register with a fountain pen—a gravity-powered item no Spacer would ever use.

Soozinbee, a worn older woman with gray hair in a bun and a suspicious cast to her eyes, gave him the once-over, then accepted his money. Looking at the new name, one of the crowd said, "I knew a Wulsie Freechoice at Nyksun Electoral College. Where'd you attend?"

Wulsie decided to evade. "It wasn't a very good one. . . ."

"Oh," the other said knowingly. "Rusaveld, right? Or maybe Leenkun?"

"I really need to get some rest." He turned to Soozinbee. "Could I have the key?"

Her suspicious face wrinkled up even more. "Keys were voted

out of existence back in 'sixteen. Where have you been?"

With a weak smile and laugh, Freechoice turned and headed for the stairs. When he reached his room, he found a bicycle seat and cranks extending from the wall next to the door. Mounting it, he began to pedal furiously. The ExerLok slowly cycled the door open while sounding a buzzer to alert anyone inside of impending intrusion. He had to admit it provided some small level of security in addition to its aerobic benefits.

Inside, the room was not particularly lavish: bedroom, efficiency kitchen, and a media room. The media room, though, possessed its own built-in vidscreen of fairly sophisticated design. "Vid on," he said to it. Nothing happened. *Great. Now I have to embarrass myself again, asking how to turn on a common home appliance.*

The problem solved itself when the screen suddenly lit up to display a menu of items.

"Attention! Attention!" the unit announced. "The People have spoken! The following propositions are submitted for immediate vote.

"Shall Sewage Street be renamed Avenue of the Recyclers? All in flavor? Or posed?"

Wulsie said nothing. After just a moment's pause, the machine said, "The Eyes are above the Nose. Long live democracy! Long live Demokratus! Next: Shall skycar landings be forbidden between midnight and dawn on weekends? All in flavor? Or posed?"

"No?" Wulsie ventured.

"The Eyes are above the Nose. If you vote you can't complain! Next . . ."

And so it went for a good fifteen minutes: quickly phrased propositions followed by immediate voting. The former Welder Volnos now understood why Freechoice was such a common given name—these people were voting fools!

Wulsie Freechoice flopped onto his new bed and—weary from his first day of self-banishment—fell fast asleep.

*   *   *

"Good morning! Good Morning! The People have spoken! It is to be a good morning today!"

The cheerful voice of the Ballot Box roused Wulsie Freechoice from his slumber. He rolled over and tried to drift off again.

"Wake up! Wake up!" The Ballot Box, as he had discovered the vidscreen was called, blared away at the drowsy man. "The People have spoken! Sunrise is too beautiful to waste! By popular vote, the fine for missing sunrise has been increased to four thrallers."

Wulsie Freechoice released the safety restraints and rolled out of bed onto the soft, spongy bedroom floor. His long legs ached with cramps from sleeping on the overly soft mattress. He had voted against that particular home feature, but—as seemed to be the case—had lost by a narrow margin.

He had been on Demokratus for less than a week and he was about to go insane.

The Ballot Box chimed, a note of derision in its voice. "Voter Wulsie! You have slept in underwear! The People have chosen Cleisthenesday as a nude sleeping day. You will be billed a two-thraller fine."

Is it a nude breakfast day, too? Wulsie wondered, not sure whether to remove his briefs or to dress. His hair, cut to voter-approved neck length, shot off in all directions as it did every morning after sleeping on the incredibly fluffy headrest that had won approval one day after a disastrous vote had temporarily made sandbags the planetary pillow.

"Hurry!" the BB cried with urgency. "The vote on breakfast is about to begin!"

Wulsie raced to the kitchen and slid into the dining cubicle. A long menu of items appeared on the flimsy scrim before him that served as a remote Ballot Box. He had heard good things about spamalope bacon and grack eggs, two of the planet's indigenous delights. He selected his menu from the list of choices, registered his vote, and awaited the outcome.

The power of the BB was its hyperfast computer that could poll the entire time zone (or even the world population, if necessary) within seconds and deliver the result of the vote instantaneously. It made direct democracy not merely possible but intrusively ubiquitous. And mandatory.

"The People have spoken!" it announced with a fanfare. "Breakfast shall be blen flakes and sneft milk once more!"

Wulsie sighed, comforting himself with the thought that, at least, he had voted. And since he had voted, he had to accept the outcome; he could not complain.

He *wanted* to complain, though, and knew what he would say if there were anyone to whom he could complain: What in Reason's name was going on with a government that demanded so many choices from its subjects?

He had spent the last few days wandering around the city, sightseeing. What he saw mystified him. He saw no police, no military, no organized instrumentality of force whatsoever. A tour of the vast squares at the center of the city uncovered no massive, orchestrated pro-government demonstrations, no forcefully suppressed protests. In fact, the downtown buildings did not seem to be anything more than tall office buildings. Where were the bureaucrats eager to hand out "benefits" in exchange for obedience? Where were the agencies ready and willing to issue commands: Work there, live here, build this, buy that?

Where were the signs that said No?

He found no local library in which to research his questions, and the popular holos offered little in the way of history—most seemed to be about personal crises finally decided by a vote of the characters involved. Usually, the dramatic climax was that the decision passed or failed by a single vote. Even more confusing was that the viewers could determine the outcome of the story by voting on their portable mini-BBs—the little plastic slip that had so absorbed the gatekeeper.

Wulsie Freechoice had almost no money left. He had hoped to find an employment agency to tell him where to work, but after four solid days of searching, he feared that he would have to make the decision on his own. He hated that.

Alone in his room, afraid to pinion his neighbors and ask questions that might reveal his illegal alien status, he silently fumed. Of all the planets in the Federation, he had to land on the one where choice was not merely permitted, it was relentlessly demanded!

"Who the hell's in charge here?" he muttered.

The Ballot Box flicked on. "Why, *you* are, Voter Wulsie," it replied.

Wulsie suddenly regretted the number of times in his life he had encountered situations in which the operative response could—charitably, at best—be summed up as: *Well, duh.*

"Are you the city library, too?" he asked.

"An uninformed electorate," it answered, "is the joy of tyrants."

"I was never good at history or civics," Wulsie ventured, pulling a chair over to the vidscreen. "Could you review for me how government operates on Demokratus?"

After a pause that caused Wulsie to wonder whether the machine was polling itself, it answered, "Demokratus was settled two hundred forty-seven years ago by a Terran political movement called People for a Democratic Society. Displeased with the flaws of a representative republic such as the United States of America back on Old Earth, their goal was to create the first truly democratic society in which all decision-making was the right and duty of the people. With the aid of the Ballot Box, this was achieved and maintained even as the settlement grew into scores of cities with a planetary population of millions.

"All decisions that affect the population as a whole are relegated to a vote. A simple majority is all that is needed to win."

Wulsie pulled his chair closer to the Ballot Box, as if somehow to confide in it. "So fifty-percent-plus-one voters can rule the rest of the people?"

"Affirmative."

"How are the rights of the minority protected?"

"They are protected by their freedom to persuade a majority to vote with them."

This began to sound ominous to Wulsie, who had heard enough

bedtime stories about the Federation to know how people have voted themselves into tyranny time and again. "Is there no document that protects the people against the State?"

The Ballot Box mulled this one over for a few nanoseconds. "The people *are* the State. Any document or constitution restricting the State restricts the people in their exercise of pure democracy."

"Then how is the government organized?"

"However the people elect to organize it."

Wulsie wanted to smack the box upside its chips. "I mean, who works for the government and who runs its day-to-day affairs?"

"The question is oddly phrased. Everybody works for the government and everybody runs it."

"Even children?"

"Children are people."

"Oh, for taxing out loud!" Wulsie shoved his chair back and stormed out of his room. Pounding downstairs, he sought out the little discussion group in the lobby. "May I ask you all a question?"

They stopped to gaze at the rude intrusion. Then the sable-haired woman who had first greeted him—Pankirst Electora—asked the others if his question should be heard. Fingers darted quickly to eyeballs.

All were in flavor.

"All right." Wulsie took a deep breath and began. "If we're supposed to vote on matters that affect the majority of people, why are we voting on minor personal things such as what to eat for breakfast and what to wear and how to sleep?"

A big guy, who looked as if he ought not to have a brain in his head, turned out to be surprisingly articulate. "Everybody eats breakfast, wears clothes, sleeps. A vote on any of those matters affects everyone."

Wulsie's voice grew agitated. "It taxing well does, but how does anyone's personal decision to dress one way or another, or eat one meal or another, affect everyone *else*?"

They all stared at him as if he had come from another planet.

The large man again answered. "What you eat determines what you buy. What you buy determines what others sell. What others sell determines what *they* must buy. And back and back until *everyone* is touched by the decisions you make. The sum total of all those choices—votes, every one of them—determines what our society is."

"But people make thousands of choices every day!" Something began to tighten in Wulsie's throat.

Pankirst nodded. "And as the Ballot Box increases its processing speed and response time, more and more of those decisions shall be subject to a vote." She shrugged and smiled. "Our system may not be perfect, but it's the best this world has ever seen."

Wulsie Freechoice gazed in stunned disbelief at the smiling faces around him . . .

. . . while Welder Volnos mentally chose to unbanish himself, and began to formulate a desperate plan to get back to Free Space.

"Ballot Box!" he called out upon returning to his room exhausted from cycling the door open and closed.

"Yes, Voter Wulsie?"

He still bristled at the appellation, but now was not a time for natural Free Spacer reactions. Now he had to play the game for all it was worth. "Who determines what motions come up for a vote?"

"Anyone can submit a motion for immediate vote during daylight hours. The rest of the planet votes at the appropriate time. If the results can be enacted locally, the law takes force immediately. If the effect is global, passage must wait for the total world results."

Something stank in that answer, and Freechoice homed in on it. "You can't be conscriptin' serious! There are millions of people on Demokratus—if every one of them could make a motion anytime they wanted, your chips would fry!"

He thought he heard an almost human concern in the machine's reply. "In the nearly two-and-a-half centuries of the Ballot Box's existence, recurring periodic motions—daily, weekly, monthly, and annual—have increased moderately, but individual motions have not kept pace with population growth."

"Voter apathy?" Wulsie perked up at the thought. "Any reason for that?"

"The dissident writer Hunter Leon suggested in an article published in 164 that generations of Demokratani subsequent to the Founding Parents had grown up accustomed to the reflex action of voting, but that the much more dynamic act of introducing motions was a dying art. She predicted that a point would come when the Ballot Box would merely 'wither away.' "

Wulsie smiled. "Is that point near?"

"Voting is natural and habitual to Demokratani, but the content of most introduced motions is trivial."

His smile widened. He had found the weak point.

"Good Morning! Good Morning! The People have spoken! It is to be a good morning today!"

Wulsie snapped to wakefulness, realizing that he must have fallen asleep at the Ballot Box. No need to wonder what time it was—the BB now went off at 6:05 A.M. after a vote the previous week to move it ahead five minutes.

He had been up all night talking to the supercomputer's electronic librarian, learning all he could from its memory. When he found out how to introduce motions for a vote, he was ready for the dawn of a new day on Demokratus. After the vote on breakfast (blen flakes and sneft milk yet again), Wulsie Freechoice got down to business.

"Ballot Box," he said. "Submit saved motion, title 'Space Travel Act of 248,' for general vote." Within seconds, the Ballot Box spoke and everyone on the daylight side of the planet heard a new proposition.

"Attention! Attention! The following motion is submitted for voter approval: Moved, that the planet Demokratus shall build a spaceship for the purposes of exploration, trade with the Federation, and promotion of democracy throughout the galaxy. An Eye vote will authorize immediate construction. All in flavor? Or posed?"

He swore he could hear puzzled gasps from the other flats in the building. It took only seconds for him to hear the results.

"The Eyes are above the Nose. Pending final global returns, the motion passes."

Wow! Wulsie stared at the screen. *This is going to be easier than I thought!*

"Submit saved motion, title 'Space Exploration Council Amendment.' "

Within seconds, the BB submitted the motion to form a council with Wulsie Freechoice as its chief administrator. Within a few more seconds, it passed.

He could not contain the yelp of excitement. People were actually voting him a way to get off this crazy planet. On the other hand, what if he stayed? What if these knee-jerk voters handed him the entire planet?

He discovered with mild surprise that his will toward power could so easily overcome his urge to dodge decisions. It took him less than a minute to formulate his next proposal, which the Ballot Box dutifully introduced to the planet Demokratus.

"Attention! Attention! The following motion is submitted for voter approval: Moved, that the planet Demokratus shall be ruled by Voter Wulsie Freechoice, who shall be granted by this vote all the powers of planetary governance. An Eye vote will authorize his immediate inauguration. All in flavor? Or posed?"

Mere seconds ticked by before the BB announced the decision. "The Eyes are above the Nose! The People have spoken! Ballots are the moral alternative to bullets!"

Breathless with victory, Planetary Dictator Wulsie Freechoice cycled the ExerLok and strode down into the lobby to greet his subjects. They lounged about, engaged as ever in their discussions. Wulsie cleared his throat. No one noticed. He cleared it louder and more theatrically. When he cleared it loud enough to cough up his larynx, the raven-haired Pankirst Electora turned to see him.

"Hello, Freechoice," she said casually. "Good morning, isn't it?"

"The People have declared it so," he said with more than a bit of bewilderment. "Did you, um . . . *vote* just now?"

She had already turned back to a spirited argument about manufacturing goals for the city's industry. He tried to get her attention again, his newfound tyrant's displeasure growing.

"*Hoi!*" he shouted. The rude outburst silenced them. Every head turned toward Wulsie. "Weren't you listening to the BB?"

Shrugs and nods.

"Didn't you hear the outcome of the last vote?" Wulsie tapped his fingers against his breastbone. "I just got elected leader of Demokratus. I'm president. King. Ruler. The People have spoken. Now I want someone to bring a skycab around so that I can go to the BB station and address the planet—" He gazed at the immobile crowd. "Why are you all just standing about? I told you, I've been elected as your ruler!"

Electora looked at him with a smiling frown halfway between puzzlement and amusement. "That Wulsie Freechoice was *you*? I thought some child had gotten hold of a BB remote. You think you've been elected?"

The others began to snicker. As more of them realized what Wulsie had done, the merriment grew until most clutched at their bellies, doubled up in paroxysmal laughter.

"Hey, you can laugh," the new dictator yelled, "but a vote's a vote. 'If you vote, you can't complain.' The decision's binding."

"Binding?" Pankirst Electora managed to sputter between great heaving horselaughs. "What makes you think votes are binding?"

Wulsie stared about at the chortling masses surrounding him. A sudden, sick sensation crashed over him like icy seawater. "But . . ." was all he could get out for several seconds. "But . . . this is a *democracy!* You vote on *everything!* I've eaten nothing but blen flakes and sneft milk because of your damned voting!"

"You eat blen flakes and sneft milk?" Electora wrinkled her nose. "*Eieuw!*"

"That was the vote!" Wulsie grew uncomfortably warm. "The Ballot Box told me to!"

The big dumb-looking guy—a bewildered expression on his face—stopped laughing long enough to ask, "If the BB told you that the People had voted to jump in a lake, would you?"

Wulsie did not have to mull that one over. "Well, no. That would be stupid, but—"

"Most proposals in a democracy are stupid, Freechoice." Electora wiped her eyes and put a consoling arm around the newcomer. "Most people learn—while children in *kindervotum*—to ignore the stupid laws and obey the reasonable ones. They also go through their 'duly-elected dictator of the world' phase while there, so they don't clog up the real BB with such drivel."

"What about the fines?" Wulsie demanded. "I've run up hundreds of thrallers in fines for ignoring the will of the People!"

Electora shook her head. "Then you haven't been here very long." She pulled out her pocket BB and touched the scrim a few times. "I've run up—since the age of majority—five million, eight hundred seventy thousand thrallers and change. What do you think happens, someone comes around to *collect? We* are the government. We owe it to ourselves. If someone collected our fines, it would be going to someone other than us. Where's the logic in that?"

Wulsie's voice had gone from flabbergasted to shrill. "Why vote at all, then, if nobody bothers to obey the outcome?"

Soozinbee, the landlady, put in her two centithrallers worth. "Voting is a part of life."

"No, it's not," Wulsie said, straightening up to stare them all down. "Ninety-nine percent of the galaxy doesn't vote, at least not as compulsively as you do here."

"Nonsense!" someone muttered loudly. "Everybody votes."

"I wasn't born here. My real name is Welder Volnos and I'm a Free Spacer. I banished myself here because I thought this planet had a state that would tell me what to do with my life. Instead, your insane concept of democracy forced me to make endless choices, day in and day out! I voted myself in as ruler so I could mobilize you . . . you *voters* to build a spaceship to get me off this backward dirtball and on to some damned dictatorship that will free me from making so many damned choices!"

Soozinbee shook her head in bemusement. "Don't you realize, Spacer, that every time you'd receive an order, you'd still have to choose to obey or not?"

Volnos began to sweat. "What?"

"In fact, you'd have to vote—in your own mind—whether to obey, disobey, stand, run, retreat, bargain, plead, grovel, or ignore. Tyranny has as many choices in it as Anarchy—and no fewer than Democracy. You can't run away from choice. There's no place in the galaxy that far. Communal public choice—what we call voting—comes naturally to us. If it doesn't to you, you should go back to where your choices are individual and private."

Volnos slumped down onto the sofa. "I can't. I told you, I've banished myself and Demokratus doesn't have any rockets to get me back to Free Space."

Electora shook her head, smiling. "Since you have to make choices anyway," she said in a soothing tone, "you couldn't do any better than Demokratus, where we know the difference between good and bad ones."

He looked into her sapphire eyes and saw something replacing the friendly mockery of a moment before.

"If," he asked, "I choose to stick around, would you choose to have dinner with me tonight?"

"Maybe," she said lightly.

"When do I find out?"

She raised her middle finger and gazed at him with a sardonic smile. "As soon as you and I vote on it. All in flavor?"

The Eyes had it.

THE HAND YOU'RE DEALT

Robert J. Sawyer

At the Nebula Award banquet, aboard the *Queen Mary* no less, I saw Rob Sawyer win the award for best novel of 1995: *The Terminal Experiment*. He is the author of five other science-fiction novels including *End of an Era* and *Golden Fleece*. One of the new breed of Canadian science-fiction writers, Sawyer embodies today's *Analog*. In the overworked area of hard-boiled SF noir, he pulls off something new. Grappling with a contemporary problem, he offers a solution only to be found in science fiction. I'm glad he's cutting the cards.

> And ye shall know the truth, and the truth shall
> make you free.
> —John 8:32

Got a new case for you," said my boss, Raymond Chen. "Homicide."

My heart started pounding. Mendelia habitat is supposed to be a utopia. Murder is almost unheard of here.

Chen was fat—never exercised, loved rich foods. He knew his lifestyle would take decades off his life, but, hey, that was his choice. "Somebody offed a soothsayer, over in Wheel Four," he said, wheezing slightly. "Baranski's on the scene now."

My eyebrows went up. A dead soothsayer? This could be very interesting indeed.

*   *   *

I took my pocket forensic scanner and exited The Cop Shop. That was its real name—no taxes in Mendelia, after all. You needed a cop, you hired one. In this case, Chen had said, we were being paid by the Soothsayers' Guild. That meant we could run up as big a bill as necessary—the SG was stinking rich. One of the few laws in Mendelia was that everyone had to use soothsayers.

Mendelia consisted of five modules, each looking like a wagon wheel with spokes leading in to a central hub. The hubs were all joined together by a long axle, and separate travel tubes connected the outer edges of the wheels. The whole thing spun to simulate gravity out at the rims, and the travel tubes saved you having to go down to the zero g of the axle to move from one wheel to the next.

The Cop Shop was in Wheel Two. All the wheel rims were hollow, with buildings growing up toward the axle from the outer interior wall. Plenty of open spaces in Mendelia—it wouldn't be much of a utopia without those. But our sky was a hologram, projected on the convex inner wall of the rim, above our heads. The Cop Shop's entrance was right by Wheel Two's transit loop, a series of maglev tracks along which robocabs ran. I hailed one, flashed my debit card at an unblinking eye, and the cab headed out. The Carling family, who owned the taxi concession, was one of the oldest and richest families in Mendelia.

The ride took fifteen minutes. Suzanne Baranski was waiting outside for me. She was a good cop, but too green to handle a homicide alone. Still, she'd get a big cut of the fee for being the original responding officer—after all, the cop who responds to a call never knows who, if anyone, is going to pick up the tab. When there *is* money to be had, first-responders get a disproportionate share.

I'd worked with Suze a couple of times before, and had even gone to see her play cello with the symphony once. Perfect example of what Mendelia's all about, that. Suze Baranski had blue-collar parents. They'd worked as welders on the building of Wheel Five; not the kind who'd normally send a daughter for music lessons. But just after she'd been born, their soothsayer had said that Suze had musical talent. Not enough to make a living at it—that's why she's a cop by day—but still sufficient that it would be a shame not to let her develop it.

"Hi, Toby," Suze said to me. She had short red hair and big green eyes, and of course, was in plain clothes—you wanted a uniformed cop, you called our competitors, Spitpolish, Inc.

"Howdy, Suze," I said, walking toward her. She led me over to the door, which had been locked off in the open position. A holographic sign next to it proclaimed:

SKYE HISSOCK
SOOTHSAYER
LET ME REVEAL YOUR FUTURE!
FULLY QUALIFIED FOR INFANT AND ADULT READINGS

We stepped into a well-appointed lobby. The art was unusual for such an office—it was all original pen-and-ink political cartoons. There was Republic CEO Da Silva, her big nose exaggerated out of all proportion, and next to it, Axel Durmont, Earth's current president, half buried in legislation printouts and tape that doubtless would have been red had this been a color rendering. The artist's signature caught my eye, the name Skye with curving lines behind it that I realized were meant to represent clouds. Just like Suze, our decedent had had varied talents.

"The body is in the inner private office," said Suze, leading the way. That door, too, was already open. She stepped in first, and I followed.

Skye Hissock's body sat in a chair behind his desk. His head had been blown clean off. A great carnation bloom of blood covered most of the wall behind him, and chunks of brain were plastered to the wall and the credenza behind the desk.

"Christ," I said. Some utopia.

Suze nodded. "Blaster, obviously," she said, sounding much

more experienced in such matters than she really was. "Probably a gigawatt charge."

I began looking around the room. It was opulent; old Skye had obviously done well for himself. Suze was poking around, too. "Hey," she said, after a moment. I turned to look at her. She was climbing up on the credenza. The blast had knocked a small piece of sculpture off the wall—it lay in two pieces on the floor—and she was examining where it had been affixed. "Thought that's what it was," she said, nodding. "There's a hidden camera here."

My heart skipped a beat. "You don't suppose he got the whole thing on disk, do you?" I asked, moving over to where she was. I gave her a hand getting down off the credenza, and we opened it up—a slightly difficult task; crusted blood had sealed its sliding doors. Inside was a dusty recorder unit. I turned to Sky's desk and pushed the release switch to pop up his monitor plate. Suze pushed the recorder's playback button. As we'd suspected, the unit was designed to feed into the desk monitor.

The picture showed the reverse angle from behind Skye's desk. The door to the private office opened and in came a young man. He looked to be eighteen, meaning he was just the right age for the mandatory adult soothsaying. He had shoulder-length dirty-blond hair, and was wearing a T-shirt imprinted with the logo of a popular meed. I shook my head. There hadn't been a good multimedia band since The Cassies, if you ask me.

"Hello, Dale," said what must have been Skye's voice. He spoke with deep, slightly nasal tones. "Thank you for coming in."

Okay, we had the guy's picture, and his first name, and the name of his favorite meed. Even if Dale's last name didn't turn up in Skye's appointment computer, we should have no trouble tracking him down.

"As you know," said Skye's recorded voice, "the law requires two soothsayings in each person's life. The first is done just after you're born, with one or both of your parents in attendance. At that time, the soothsayer only tells them things they'll need to know to get you through childhood. But when you turn eighteen, you, not your parents, become legally responsible for all your actions, and so it's time you heard everything. Now, do you want the good news or the bad news first?"

Here it comes, I thought. He told Dale something he didn't want to hear, the guy flipped, pulled out a blaster, and blew him away.

Dale swallowed. "The—the good, I guess."

"All right," said Skye. "First, you're a bright young man—not a genius, you understand, but brighter than average. Your IQ should run between one hundred twenty-six and one hundred thirty-two. You are gifted musically—did your parents tell you that? Good. I hope they encouraged you."

"They did," said Dale, nodding. "I've had piano lessons since I was four."

"Good, good. A crime to waste such raw talent. You also have a particular aptitude for mathematics. That's often paired with musical ability, of course, so no surprises there. Your visual memory is slightly better than average, although your ability to do rote memorization is slightly worse. You would make a good long-distance runner, but . . ."

I motioned for Suze to hit the fast-forward button; it seemed like a typical soothsaying, although I'd review it in depth later, if need be. Poor Dale fidgeted up and down in quadruple speed for a time, then Suze released the button.

"Now," said Skye's voice, "the bad news." I made an impressed face at Suze; she'd stopped speeding along at precisely the right moment. "I'm afraid there's a lot of it. Nothing devastating, but still lots of little things. You will begin to lose your hair around your twenty-seventh birthday, and it will begin to gray by the time you're thirty-two. By the age of forty, you will be almost completely bald, and what's left at that point will be half black and half gray.

"On a less frivolous note, you'll also be prone to gaining weight, starting at about age thirty-three—and you'll put on half a kilo a year for each of the following thirty years if you're not careful; by the time you're in your midfifties, that will pose a significant health hazard. You're also highly likely to develop adult-onset diabetes. Now, yes, that can be cured, but the cure is expensive, and you'll have to pay for it—so either keep your weight down, which will help stave off its onset, or start saving now for the operation. . . ."

I shrugged. Nothing worth killing a man over. Suze fast-forwarded the tape some more.

"—and that's it," concluded Skye. "You know now everything significant that's coded into your DNA. Use this information wisely, and you should have a long, happy, healthy life."

Dale thanked Skye, took a printout of the information he'd just heard, and left. The recording stopped. It *had* been too much to hope for. Whoever killed Skye Hissock had come in after young Dale had departed. He was still our obvious first suspect, but unless there was something awful in the parts of the genetic reading we'd fast-forwarded over, there didn't seem to be any motive for him to kill his soothsayer. And besides, this Dale had a high IQ, Skye had said. Only an idiot would think there was any sense in shooting the messenger.

After we'd finished watching the recording, I did an analysis of the actual blaster burn. No fun, that: standing over the open top of Skye's torso. Most of the blood vessels had been cauterized by the charge. Still, blasters were only manufactured in two places I knew of—Tokyo, on Earth, and New Monty. If the one used here had been made on New Monty, we'd be out of luck, but one of Earth's countless laws required all blasters to leave a characteristic EM signature so they could be traced to their registered owners, and—

Good: It *was* an Earth-made blaster. I recorded the signature, then used my compad to relay it to The Cop Shop. If Raymond Chen could find some time between stuffing his face, he'd send an FTL message to Earth and check the pattern—assuming, of course, that the Jeffies don't scramble the message just for kicks. Meanwhile, I told Suze to go over Hissock's client list, while I started checking out his family—fact is, even though it doesn't make much genetic sense, most people are killed by their own relatives.

Skye Hissock had been fifty-one. He'd been a soothsayer for twenty-three years, ever since finishing his Ph.D. in genetics. He was unmarried, and both his parents were long dead. But he did have a brother named Rodger. Rodger was married to Rebecca Connolly, and they had two children, Glen, who, like Dale in Skye's recording, had just turned eighteen, and Billy, who was eight.

There are no inheritance taxes on Mendelia, of course, so barring a will to the contrary, Hissock's estate would pass immediately to his brother. Normally, that'd be a good motive for murder, but Rodger Hissock and Rebecca Connolly were already quite rich: They owned a controlling interest in the company that operated Mendelia's atmosphere-recycling plant.

I decided to start my interviews with Rodger. Not only had brothers been killing each other since Cain wasted Abel, but the fingerprint lock on Skye's private inner office was programmed to recognize only four people—Skye himself; his office cleaner, who Suze was going to talk to; another soothsayer named Jennifer Halasz, who sometimes took Skye's patients for him when he was on vacation (and who had called in the murder, having stopped by apparently to meet Skye for coffee); and dear brother Rodger. Rodger lived in Wheel Four, and worked in One.

I took a cab over to his office. Unlike Skye, Rodger had a real flesh-and-blood receptionist. Most companies that did have human receptionists used middle-aged, businesslike people of either sex. Some guys got so rich that they didn't care what people thought; they hired beautiful blond women whose busts had been surgically altered far beyond what any phenotype might provide. But Rodger's choice was different. His receptionist was a delicate young man with refined, almost-feminine features. He was probably older than he looked; he looked fourteen.

"Detective Toby Korsakov," I said, flashing my ID. I didn't offer to shake hands—the boy looked like his would shatter if any pressure were applied. "I'd like to see Rodger Hissock."

"Do you have an appointment?" His voice was high, and there was just a trace of a lisp.

"No. But I'm sure Mr. Hissock will want to see me. It's important."

The boy looked very dubious, but he spoke into an intercom. "There's a cop here, Rodger. Says it's important."

There was a pause. "Send him in," said a loud voice. The boy nodded at me, and I walked through the heavy wooden door— mahogany, no doubt imported all the way from Earth.

I had thought Skye Hissock's office was well appointed, but his brother's put it to shame. Objets d'art from a dozen worlds were tastefully displayed on crystal stands. The carpet was so thick I was sure my shoes would sink out of sight.

I walked toward the desk. Rodger rose to greet me. He was a muscular man, thick necked, with lots of black hair and pale gray eyes. We shook hands; his grip was a show of macho strength. "Hello," he said. He boomed out the word, clearly a man used to commanding everyone's attention. "What can I do for you?"

"Please sit down," I said. "My name is Toby Korsakov. I'm from The Cop Shop, working under a contract to the Soothsayers' Guild."

"My God," said Rodger. "Has something happened to Skye?"

Although it was an unpleasant duty, there was nothing more useful in a murder investigation than being there to tell a suspect about the death and seeing his reaction. Most guilty parties played dumb far too long, so the fact that Rodger had quickly made the obvious connection between the SG and his brother made me suspect him less, not more. Still . . . "I'm sorry to be the bearer of bad news," I said, "but I'm afraid your brother is dead."

Rodger's eyes went wide. "What happened?"

"He was murdered."

"Murdered," repeated Rodger, as if he'd never heard the word before.

"That's right. I was wondering if you knew of anyone who'd want him dead?"

"How was he killed?" asked Rodger. I was irritated that this wasn't an answer to my question, and even more irritated that I'd have to explain it so soon. More than a few homicides have been solved by a suspect mentioning the nature of the crime in advance of him or her supposedly having learned the details. "He was shot at close range by a blaster."

"Oh," said Rodger. He slumped in his chair. "Skye dead." His head shook back and forth a little. When he looked up, his gray eyes were moist. Whether he was faking or not, I couldn't tell.

"I'm sorry," I said.

"Do you know who did it?"

"Not yet. We're tracing the blaster's EM signature. But there were no signs of forcible entry, and, well . . ."

"Yes?"

"Well, there are only four people whose fingerprints opened the door to Skye's inner office."

Rodger nodded. "Me and Skye. Who else?"

"His cleaner, and another soothsayer."

"You're checking them out?"

"My associate is. She's also checking all the people Skye had appointments with recently—people he might have let in of his own volition." A pause. "Can I ask where you were this morning between ten and eleven?"

"Here."

"In your office?"

"That's right."

"Your receptionist can vouch for that?"

"Well . . . no. No, he can't. He was out all morning. His sooth says he's got a facility for languages. I give him a half day off every Wednesday to take French lessons."

"Did anyone call you while he was gone?"

Rodger spread his thick arms. "Oh, probably. But I never answer my own compad. Truth to tell, I like that half day where I can't be reached. It lets me get an enormous amount of work done without being interrupted."

"So no one can verify your presence here?"

"Well, no . . . no, I guess they can't. But, Crissakes, Detective, Skye was my *brother.* . . ."

"I'm not accusing you, Mr. Hissock—"

"Besides, if I'd taken a robocab over, there'd be a debit charge against my account."

"Unless you paid cash. Or unless you walked." You can walk down the travel tubes, although most people don't bother.

"You don't seriously believe—"

"I don't believe anything yet, Mr. Hissock." It was time to change the subject; he would be no use to me if he got too defensive. "Was your brother a good soothsayer?"

"Best there is. Hell, he read my own sooth when I turned eighteen." He saw my eyebrows go up. "Skye is nine years older than me; I figured, why not use him? He needed the business; he was just starting his practice at that point."

"Did Skye do the readings for your children, too?"

An odd hesitation. "Well, yeah, yeah, Skye did their infant readings, but Glen—that's my oldest; just turned eighteen—he decided to go somewhere else for his adult reading. Waste of money, if you ask me. Skye would've given him a discount."

My compad bleeped while I was in a cab. I turned it on.

"Yo, Toby." Raymond Chen's fat face appeared on the screen. "We got the registration information on that blaster signature."

"Yeah?"

Ray smiled. "Do the words 'open-and-shut case' mean anything to you? The blaster belongs to one Rodger Hissock. He bought it about eleven years ago."

I nodded and signed off. Since the lock accepted his fingerprint, rich little brother would have no trouble waltzing right into big brother's inner office, and exploding his head. Rodger had method and he had opportunity. Now all I needed was to find his motive—and for that, continuing to interview the family members might prove useful.

Eighteen-year-old Glen Hissock was studying engineering at Francis Crick University in Wheel Three. He was a dead ringer for his old man: built like a wrestler, with black hair and quicksilver eyes. But whereas father Rodger had a coarse, outgoing way about him—the crusher handshake, the loud voice—young Glen was withdrawn, soft spoken, and nervous.

"I'm sorry about your uncle," I said, knowing that Rodger had already broken the news to his son.

Glen looked at the floor. "Me, too."

"Did you like him?"

"He was okay."

"Just okay."

"Yeah."

"Where were you between ten and eleven this morning?"

"At home."

"Was anyone else there?"

"Nah. Mom and Dad were at work, and Billy—that's my little brother—was in school." He met my eyes for the first time. "Am I a suspect?"

He wasn't really. All the evidence seemed to point to his father. I shook my head in response to his question, then said, "I hear you had your sooth read recently."

"Yeah."

"But you didn't use your uncle."

"Nah."

"How come?"

A shrug. "Just felt funny, that's all. I picked a guy at random from the online directory."

"Any surprises in your sooth?"

The boy looked at me. "Sooth's private, man. I don't have to tell you that."

I nodded. "Sorry."

Two hundred years ago, in 2029, the Palo Alto Nanosystems Laboratory developed a molecular computer. You doubtless read about it in history class: During the Snow War, the U.S. used it to disassemble Bogotá atom by atom.

Sometimes, though, you *can* put the genie back in the bottle. Remember Hamasaki and DeJong, the two researchers at PANL who were shocked to see their work corrupted that way? They created and released the nano-Gorts—self-replicating microscopic machines that seek out and destroy molecular computers, so that nothing like Bogotá could ever happen again.

We've got PANL nano-Gorts here, of course. They're everywhere in Free Space. But we've got another kind of molecular guardian, too—inevitably, they were dubbed helix-Gorts. It's rumored the SG was responsible for them, but after a huge investigation, no indictments were ever brought. Helix-Gorts circumvent any attempt at artificial gene therapy. We can tell you everything that's written in your DNA, but we can't do a damned thing about it. Here, in Mendelia, you play the hand you're dealt.

My compad bleeped again. I switched it on. "Korsakov here."

Suze's face appeared on the screen. "Hi, Toby. I took a sample of Skye's DNA off to Rundstedt"—a soothsayer who did forensic work for us. "She's finished the reading."

"And?" I prompted.

Suze's green eyes blinked. "Nothing stood out. Skye wouldn't have been a compulsive gambler, or an addict, or inclined to steal another person's spouse—which eliminates several possible motives for his murder. In fact, Rundstedt says Skye would have had a severe aversion to confrontation." She sighed. "Just doesn't seem to be the kind of guy who'd end up in a situation where someone would want him dead."

I nodded. "Thanks, Suze. Any luck with Syke's clients?"

"I've gone through almost all the ones who'd had appointments in the last three days. So far, they all have solid alibis."

"Keep checking. I'm off to see Skye's sister-in-law, Rebecca Connolly. Talk to you later."

"Bye."

Sometimes I wonder if I'm in the right line of work. I know, I know—what a crazy thing to be thinking. I mean, my parents knew from my infant reading that I'd grown up to have an aptitude for puzzle-solving, plus superior powers of observation. They made sure I had every opportunity to fulfill my potentials, and when I had my sooth read for myself at eighteen, it was obvious that this would be a perfect job for me to pursue. And yet, still, I have my doubts. I just don't feel like a cop sometimes.

But a soothsaying can't be wrong: Almost every human trait has a genetic basis—gullibility, mean-spiritedness, a goofy sense of humor, the urge to collect things, talents for various sports, every specific sexual predilection (according to my own sooth, my tastes ran to group sex with Asian women—so far, I'd yet to find an opportunity to test that empirically).

Of course, when Mendelia started up, we didn't yet know what each gene and gene combo did. Even today, the SB is still adding new interpretations to the list. Still, I sometimes wonder how people in other parts of Free Space get along without soothsayers—stumbling through life, looking for the right job; sometimes completely unaware of talents they possess; failing to know what specific things they should do to take care of their health. Oh, sure, you can get a genetic reading anywhere—even down on Earth. But they're only mandatory here.

And my mandatory readings said I'd make a good cop. But, I have to admit, sometimes I'm not so sure. . . .

* * *

Rebecca Connolly was at home when I got there. On Earth, a family with the kind of money the Hissock-Connolly union had would own a mansion. Space is at a premium aboard a habitat, but their living room *was* big enough that its floor showed a hint of curvature. The art on the walls included originals by both Grant Wood and Bob Eggleton. There was no doubt they were loaded—making it all the harder to believe they'd done in Uncle Skye for his money.

Rebecca Connolly was a gorgeous woman. According to the press reports I'd read, she was forty-four, but she looked twenty years younger. Gene therapy might be impossible here, but anyone who could afford it could have plastic surgery. Her hair was copper colored, and her eyes an unnatural violet. "Hello, Detective Korsakov," she said. "My husband told me you were likely to stop by." She shook her head. "Poor Skye. Such a darling man."

I tilted my head. She was the first of Sky's relations to actually say something nice about him as a person—which, after all, could just be a clumsy attempt to deflect suspicion from her. "You knew Sky well?"

"No—to be honest, no. He and Rodger weren't that close. Funny thing, that. Skye used to come by the house frequently when we first got married—he was Rodger's best man, did he tell you that? But when Glen was born, well, he stopped coming around as much. I dunno—maybe he didn't like kids; he never had any of his own. Anyway, he really hasn't been a big part of our lives for, oh, eighteen years now."

"But Rodger's fingerprints were accepted by Skye's lock."

"Oh, yes. Rodger owns the unit Skye has his current offices in."

"I hate to ask you this, but—"

"I'm on the Board of Directors of TenthGen Computing, Detective. We were having a shareholders' meeting this morning. Something like eight hundred people saw me there."

I asked more questions, but didn't get any closer to identifying Rodger Hissock's motive. And so I decided to cheat—as I said, sometimes I *do* wonder if I'm in the right kind of job. "Thanks for your help, Ms. Connolly. I don't want to take up any more of your time, but can I use your bathroom before I go?"

She smiled. "Of course. There's one down the hall, and one upstairs."

The upstairs one sounded more promising for my purposes. I went up to it, and the door closed behind me. I really did need to go, but first I pulled out my forensic scanner and started looking for specimens. Razors and combs are excellent places to find DNA samples; so are towels, if the user rubbed vigorously enough. Best of all, though, are toothbrushes. I scanned everything, but something was amiss. According to the scanner, there was DNA present from one woman—the XX-chromosome pair made the gender clear. And there was DNA from one man. But *three* males lived in this house: father Rodger, elder son Glen, and younger son Billy.

Perhaps this bathroom was used only by the parents, in which case I'd blown it—I'd hardly get a chance to check out the other bathroom. But no—there were four sets of towels, four toothbrushes, and there, on the edge of the tub, a toy aquashuttle . . . precisely the kind an eight-year-old boy would play with.

Curious. Four people obviously used this john, but only two had left any genetic traces. And that made no sense—I mean, sure, I hardly ever washed when I was eight like Billy, but no one can use a washroom day in and day out without leaving some DNA behind.

I relieved myself, the toilet autoflushed, and I went downstairs, thanked Ms. Connolly again, and left.

Like I said, I was cheating—making me wonder again whether I really was cut out for a career in law enforcement. Even though it was a violation of civil rights, I took the male DNA sample I'd found in the Hissock-Connolly bathroom to Dana Rundstedt, who read its sooth for me.

I was amazed by the results. If I hadn't cheated, I might never have figured it out—it was a damn-near perfect crime.

But it all fit, after seeing what was in the male DNA.

The fact that of the surviving Hissocks, only Rodger apparently had free access to Skye's inner office.

The fact that Rodger's blaster was the murder weapon.

The fact that there were apparently only two people using the bathroom.

The fact that Skye hated confrontation.

The fact that the Hissock-Connolly family had a lot of money they wanted to pass on to the next generation.

The fact that young Glen looked just like his dad, but was subdued and reserved.

The fact that Glen had gone to a different soothsayer.

The fact that Rodger's taste in receptionists was . . . unusual.

The pieces all fit—that part of my sooth, at least, must have been read correctly; I *am* good at puzzling things out. But I was still amazed by how elegant it was.

Ray Chen would sort out the legalities; he was an expert at that kind of thing. He'd find a way to smooth over my unauthorized soothsaying before we brought this to trial.

I got in a cab and headed off to Wheel Three to confront the killer.

"Hold it right there," I said, coming down the long, gently curving corridor at Francis Crick. "You're under arrest."

Glen Hissock stopped dead in his tracks. "What for?"

I looked around, then drew Glen into an empty classroom. "For the murder of your uncle, Skye Hissock. Or should I say, for the murder of your brother? The semantics are a bit tricky."

"I don't know what you're talking about," said Glen, in that subdued, nervous voice of his.

I shook my head. Soothsayer Skye *had* deserved punishment, and his brother Rodger *was* guilty of a heinous crime—in fact, a crime Mendelian society considered every bit as bad as murder. But I couldn't let Glen get away with it. "I'm sorry for what happened to you," I said. The mental scars no doubt explained his sullen, with-drawn manner.

He glared at me. "Like that makes it better."

"When did it start?"

He was quiet for a time, then gave a little shrug, as if realizing there was no point in pretending any longer. "When I was twelve—as soon as I entered puberty. Not every night, you understand. But often enough." He paused, then: "How'd you figure it out?"

I decided to tell him the truth. "There are only two different sets of DNA in your house—one female, as you'd expect, and just one male."

Glen said nothing.

"I had the male DNA read. I was looking for a trait that might have provided a motive for your father. You know what I found."

Glen was still silent.

"When your dad's sooth was read just after birth, maybe his parents were told that he was sterile. Certainly the proof is there, in his DNA: an inability to produce viable sperm." I paused, re-membering the details Rundstedt had explained to me. "But the soothsayer back then couldn't have known the effect of having the variant form of gene ABL-419d, with over a hundred T-A-T repeats. That variation's function hadn't been identified that long ago. But it *was* known by the time Rodger turned eighteen, by the time he went to see his big brother, Skye, by the time Skye gave him his adult soothsaying." I paused. "But Uncle Skye hated confrontation, didn't he?"

Glen was motionless, a statue.

"And so Skye lied to your dad. Oh, he told him about his steril-ity, all right, but he figured there was no point in getting into an argument about what that variant gene meant."

Glen looked at the ground. When at last he did speak, his voice was bitter. "I had thought Dad knew. I confronted him—Christ sakes, Dad, if you knew you had a gene for incestuous pedophilia, why the hell didn't you seek counseling? Why the hell did you have kids?"

"But your father didn't know, did he?"

Glen shook his head. "That bastard Uncle Skye hadn't told him."

"In fairness," I said, "Skye probably figured that since your father couldn't have kids, the problem would never come up. But your dad made a lot of money, and wanted it to pass to an heir. And since he couldn't have an heir the normal way . . ."

Glen's voice was full of disgust. "Since he couldn't have an heir the normal way, he had one made."

I looked the boy up and down. I'd never met a clone before. Glen really was the spitting image of the old man—a chip off the old block. But like any dynasty, the Hissock-Connolly clan wanted not just an heir, but an heir and a spare. Little Billy, ten years younger than Glen, was likewise an exact genetic duplicate of Rodger Hissock, produced from Rodger's DNA placed into one of Rebecca's eggs. All three Hissock males had indeed left DNA in that bathroom—exactly identical DNA.

"Have you always known you were a clone?" I asked.

Glen shook his head. "I only just found out. Before I went for my adult soothsaying, I wanted to see the report my parents had gotten when I was born. But none existed—my dad had decided to save some money. He didn't need a new report done, he figured; my sooth would be identical to his, after all. When I went to get my sooth read and found that *I* was sterile, well, it all fell into place in my mind."

"And so you took your father's blaster, and, since your fingerprints are the same as his . . ."

Glen nodded slowly. His voice was low and bitter. "Dad never knew in advance what was wrong with him—never had a chance to get help. Uncle Skye never told him. Even after Dad had himself cloned, Skye never spoke up." He looked at me, fury in his cold gray eyes. "It doesn't work, dammit—our whole way of life doesn't work if a soothsayer doesn't tell the truth. You can't play the hand you're dealt if you don't know what cards you've got. Skye deserved to die."

"And you framed your dad for it. You wanted to punish him, too."

Glen shook his head. "You don't understand, man. You can't understand."

"Try me."

"I didn't want to punish Dad—I wanted to protect Billy. Dad can afford the best damn lawyer in Mendelia. Oh, he'll be found guilty, sure, but he won't get life. His lawyer will cut it down to the minimum mandatory sentence for murder, which is—"

"Ten years," I said, realization dawning. "In ten years, Billy will be an adult—and out of danger from Rodger."

Glen nodded once.

"But Rodger could have told the truth at any time—revealed that you were a clone of him. If he'd done that, he would have gotten off, and suspicion would have fallen on you. How did you know he wasn't going to speak up?"

Glen sounded a lot older than his eighteen years. "If Dad exposed me, I'd expose him—and the penalty for child molestation is also a minimum ten years, so he'd be doing the time anyway." He looked directly at me. "Except being a murderer gets you left alone in jail, and being a pedophile gets you wrecked up."

I nodded, led him outside, and hailed a robocab.

Mendelia *is* a great place to live, honest.

And, hell, I did solve the crime, didn't I? Meaning I *am* a good detective. So I guess *my* soothsayer didn't lie to me.

At least—at least I hope not. . . .

I had a sudden cold feeling that the SG would stop footing the bill long before this case could come to public trial.

How Do You Tell the Dreamer from the Dream?

Wendy McElroy

Reviewed in *The New York Times Book Review* for her ground break-ing *XXX: A Woman's Right to Pornography*, Wendy is the only babe I managed to talk between the covers of this book. No, wait, I mean woman . . . and what a woman! McElroy is a real force in lib-ertarian circles and I've been honored to write for some of the same publications in which she appears. In common with Victor Koman, she has sold to the prestigious *F&SF* (but in her case it was a poem). She has a vision of human rights that even cheers up a cynical bastard like your faithful editor. Following is a distillation of hope.

Luna was prelude to using Mars
for military-industrial orbit.
As parched as mortality, frigid
when dark, the moon was training . . .
'til filters failed.
The radio crackled:
"The virus is rapid."
Transmission collapsed to static.

Terra declares: **"Human error."**

Next came Mars, with polar water
and precious volatiles.
Under a cover of oxide dust,
beneath a permafrost ceiling,
colonies bubbled like submarines,
rarely heeding a coralline sky.
A meteor . . . Number Three pleaded
for permission to evacuate.
Death resulted from impact-cracks,
where atmosphere bled to near-vacuum.

"Act of God," they announce.

On Ganymede—they blasted beneath
winters of nitrogen and CO_2,
into caverns heated by fusion.
Then . . . one reactor down for care.
The wrong spare parts;
the backup coughs.
"Bypass safeties for one more day."

"Human error . . ." the deaths are labeled.
Before the review committee rolls forward,
a member declares, "It wasn't error.
It's the way we are:
It's how technology's shaped us.
By sating appetite, it killed our hunger.
By offering god, it destroyed our wonder.
We're no longer pioneers."

Another member quickly scorns, **"Oh <u>you're</u>
the historian. I should have known. . . .
Peddle philosophy. Leave the future alone."**

"Space is a dream, like flight was.
And dreams need dreamers to become real . . .
people who dance on the cliff for answers
to "Why?" and "How?" . . . "What if?"

"Space is freedom, the primordial dream.
It breeds—raw and beating—
in bone and the genes.
But it can be dulled
by push-button comfort.
Dreamers must hunger and need."

Where to find utopians?
Not among those whose lives
have drooped—sweet and leisurely—
like succulent fruit. Not from
those with precleaned air,
born under bell jars of delicate form,
polished by science . . . half-forgotten . . .
purchased by long-dried sweat.

From where?
"Cryonic suspension—
the rebels against death—from every one
who never accepted mortality."

"Cryonics is against our law."

"But hundreds of cryonauts remain . . . floating
in stasis. The last Quixotes,
the lotus-eaters . . . Perhaps,
these ghosts should meet the machine."

They began with the last suspension,
where damage to shrunken cells was less.

After months, her eyes flutter open,
her arid throat utters: "When?"

Then . . . others.
Bloodstreams teem with microbic machines
that clear the ice and leave link-
fibers along which data can sing.
Then, nanocomputers orchestrate
a majestic ballet to recreate
vital humans from wintered cells.
The information that is "them"
sluggishly stirs . . . then
it quickens.

At first, the revived quiescently listen
to the webwork of laws that are laced
about them, like chains around a wind.
Then a spokesman confronts the committee.
"What do you need?" they brusquely demand.
"Knowledge and freedom . . . ," the answer
is hot. "Teach us and leave us alone."

"You're alive because we revived you."
"You needed us," he dryly reminds.
"And people we loved
—family and sweethearts—
are rotting like meat,
because technology seized you
with terror, not wonder.
Damn your Luddite souls!"

"You were revived to colonize . . .
admonition slides to threat.
Legally . . . you're still 'dead.' "

They went to Luna, where meters deep,
they painted the tunnels azure and green.
They potted trees and edged the "streets"
with blossoms and night-blooming jasmine.

No contact. But Terra waited,
knowing the colony would need supplies.
Weeks.
Then months.
No contact.
Advise of status.

Abruptly, revelation . . .
Luna was now a private venture
to cryoprev Terrans
of wealth and position.
With the moon as base,
the cryonauts stretched
up and out to the stars.

Advise of status!
The last message radioed:
Laissez passer. Laissez nous faire.
Let it pass. And leave us to be.

IF PIGS HAD WINGS

William Alan Ritch

Rites of passage ain't what they used to be. As technology marches on, and the young mature earlier in certain ways (while not in others), the future becomes more frightening to those who already fear adolescence. Inspired by the Heinlein juvies, Bill offers a story that could only happen in Free Space. The previous editor of *Prometheus*, The Journal of the Libertarian Futurist Society (the current editor is Anders Monsen), Bill has been involved with numerous WorldCon presentations of the awards. He has also written for other anthologies and the Atlanta Radio Theatre Company.

M y parents almost caught us at it again last night. My sigpair, Hank, and I were up in my room when they came home ten kilosecs early. Immediately we switched the light, moved the bookdiscs, and adjusted our clothes before they shifted through the door and . . .

But I'm getting ahead of myself. Hank says I should start at the beginning. OK. My name is June Bulmer. I'm 442 megasecs old, and in the fourteenth form. And I'm a groundhog stuck here on New Bohemia!

If you're listening to this diary and not familiar with Federation worlds, New Bohemia is an "Artists' Colony." Which means we export the official art for the Federation. Everyone here is supposed to be some sort of artist, musician, dancer, whatever. There are some transient Fed workers here who maintain the automated equipment and do the stuff that the computers can't. They're not Bohemians, so they don't count. Of course the Jeffersonians run the spaceport here, like they do everywhere else.

That's where I was yesterday for my ComServe. I was on the grunt run when the Free Spacer's ship landed. At first, I didn't know what it was. It was like the sound of a million gears grinding against each other coming from somewhere in the sky. Looking up from the hovercart, I couldn't find the source of the noise. Odd. When a Jeffie ship lands you don't hear anything until it's less than a kilometer from the ground.

I searched the cloudless sky for several seconds while the horrible sound got louder. Finally, I spotted a strangely colored ship warping the atmosphere as it descended. I still couldn't see it very well, but it wasn't like any Jeffie ship *I'd* ever seen.

The noise was so deafening that I did not notice her standing next to me until I felt a small hand touch my shoulder. I looked down to the short brunette at my side. Alicia. Unable to talk we just stood there looking up at the sky. Just like the day we first met.

That had been on my second day of ComServe. When we start twelfth form the Council issues us students ComServe assignments. Nothing very complicated. At the port, we mostly delivered afternoon snacks—nothing that couldn't be automated. But then, as Hank points out, ComServe is to teach us duty and humility. Where would the community service be in letting a robot do something we could?

As the only twelver assigned to the spaceport, I had been given the grunt run. None of the older students like driving the hovercarts out to the mechanics. They prefer serving the admins, the planet hoppers, and the SecPols. They're all indoors, in clean, climatized rooms. The grunts are outside where the ships are.

Although at first I had been excited, I rapidly got discouraged. The mechanics were rude. They called me a lot of slang words I'm sure were insults, like "groundhog." The heat was stifling, as was the stench of the lubricants. Then I saw a ship launch.

When a ship goes up, nothing stands still. It's not so much the noise; Hank says the old rocket engines were much louder. With these modern ships the only real sound is the sonic boom about four kilometers up. No, it's more the wind, rushing to follow the ship upward, pulling with it all the heat and smells, leaving a brief patch of crisp air, tingling like after a thunder shower.

I left the hovercart to stare up at the fleeing spaceship. *How beautiful,* I thought. I must have said it aloud, because the mechanic next to me remarked sarcastically, "Yeah, just like a giant bird."

"No," I said to her without moving my eyes, "precisely unlike one."

A moment of silence passed before she said, in a much warmer voice, "Alicia DuBarry. Never call me a grunt and we'll get along fine. I'm a mech."

"June Bulmer," I returned, "and don't call me a *groundhog.*"

We both stood transfixed by the departing ship, waiting for the telltale green-shift smear as it hypered away. I never wanted to see a launch from indoors again.

The noise from the landing ship stopped abruptly, interrupting my daydreaming. "They've cut the drive and are landing with just the a-grav," Alicia explained.

"What is it?" I asked. "It's so small, and I don't recognize the markings." The ship was a tenth the size of any Jeffersonian ship I'd seen. And it was dirty. All the Jeffie ships were polished until they gleamed. They have flags and banners and insignia on their sides. This ship was scorched and scored. I could see different-colored layers of paint peeling off.

"It's not one of ours," Alicia answered. "It must be a Free Spacer."

A Free Spacer. In the universe beyond New Bohemia there is this three-way game between the Federation, the Jeffersonians, and the Free Spacers. What I understand is that the Free Spacers and the Federation hate each other, but both use the Jeffies as go-betweens. This sort of interstellar politics isn't taught at my school.

I've picked it up from my forbidden political conversations with Alicia. And from Hank.

"It's landing near the hangar," I said.

Alicia shushed me. She was listening to her comlink. "I've got to go," she said excitedly. "They're calling in all the mechs to work on the Spacer's ship. What an opportunity!"

I offered to take her in the hovercart. "It'll be faster than walking." And it was a good excuse to get closer to the Spacer's ship.

Well, a hovercart *is* faster than walking, but it's not faster than running. Oblivious to the whining fans of the hovercart, Alicia and I talked about the Free Spacer. Although she had seen her share of Spacers, she had never been inside one of their engines.

For the past two forms, Alicia and I have been best friends. Or least as best as we can be considering she's almost twice my age, and the Jeffies aren't supposed to fraternize with us Feds. I never had anyone to *talk* to until I met her. Unlike my parents, she understands why I worry about how things work instead of how they look. Alicia has surreptitiously taught me all she can about ships, their engines, and how they're put together. I talk with her about my failed attempts to fit into Bohemian society. And my fear of being shipped off like my cousin Lee. We've even talked about our problems with sigpairs.

The hangar is easy to find—you can see it from all over the port. It's an enormous green geodesic dome built to house any Jeffie ship that could land on New Bohemia. It's the largest single building at the port, maybe even on the planet.

Usually a calm place, the hangar was alive with a flurry of activity around the Spacer's ship that betrayed its location. It looked like every mech in the port was there. In their dull orange coveralls they looked like autumn bees buzzing about a hive. However, the hot, dry wind reminded me it was still summer.

A SecPol stopped my hovercart. I saw a clutch of SecPols, all surrounding a wizened, old man with white hair and a stubby white beard. Now Hank always tells me that when I see SecPols I should get out, but I was fascinated. In addition to the gray uniforms of the Federation I saw a few sky-blue ones. It took me a few seconds to realize these were Jeffie SecPols. I wasn't even sure they existed.

The old man wasn't wearing any kind of uniform. He had a bright multicolor shirt that danced in the wind. His pants were dark blue and looked substantial and rugged. All this was *over* some kind of form-fitting space suit.

He turned his oversized head back and forth like a radar dish. Then he spotted me. I don't know why, especially with Alicia next to me. Where I'm gangly, gawky, and let me be truthful, flat, she is full and curved, with just a hint of plumpness. I keep my orange-red hair cropped short, otherwise it's thin, wiry, and unruly. Alicia's long black hair always seems composed. Maybe he looked at me because I was the only one in a school uniform. Maybe he liked my freckles—or my eyes. Hank tells me my eyes are bright as emeralds.

The Spacer's stare was intense, like he was evaluating me. Sweat pasted my clothes to my body. I was aware of my slightest curve. I suddenly felt embarrassed and inadequate. Even when I'm naked with Hank I've never felt so—so sexual. And then he winked at me. I turned away quickly.

The SecPol admitted Alicia to the circle of mechs and sent me on my way. It was just as well. My shift was over and I had to hurry to make it to my afternoon sculpting class.

Which was a bore. My parents are both painters, so naturally they wanted me to be a painter, too. Unfortunately, I just don't have their color sense, so I'm stuck learning sculpture because my psych evaluation said that I had "excellent three-dimensional visualization and digital coordination."

At least I fared better than my cousin Lee. He failed all his classes and then was evaluated and sent to an ag world where he was horribly mangled in a harvester. Hank says that the Federation doesn't bother with safety on farms because replacement operators are so cheap.

We were modeling in Plasteel, which you work with your hands like clay, but is not as messy. As usual, I was not paying attention. I felt the warm ooze of the Plasteel as I let myself think about the Free Spacer landing. I wished Hank had been with me at the spaceport to see it.

I worked the Plasteel into a sphere, and then chopped it in half with my u-knife.

Henry Rankin was the only good thing that happened in painting class last form. He was modeling for us. All the students have to take turns modeling for the art classes. I was just lucky that he had shown up in mine. Mostly I don't notice the models. Hank was different. I hadn't been able to take my eyes off him. I thought he was human perfection.

I formed the Plasteel into several long cylinders, hardening them with freeze-gel. I attached the cylinders to the hemisphere.

I had willed him not to notice me. Trying to hide my painting, I attracted his attention. He looked at my work, took a deep breath, and told me that it was terrible. I wasn't expecting honesty. I agreed and detailed everything *I* thought was wrong with the painting. He laughed his deep, good-natured laugh. It was at that point that I fell in love with him.

I continued to work the Plasteel. I formed section after section of long, curved, flat panels, hardening each as I finished. The addictive, sweet odor of the freeze-gel made me smile.

Hank's a lot nearer graduation than me—in twenty-second form. Mom and Dad want to tell me that he's too old to be my sigpair, but they can't come right out and say it since we're both still students. He's listened to a lot more instructional discs than me. He can even read, something that's forbidden until twentieth form. Despite that, he's teaching me how. My folks say he's a bad influence on me. They're right about that.

When the panels were finished I stuck them together. Then I added loose Plasteel, shaping around the framework.

We've spent many nights on the hill near the spaceport staring up at the stars, the sharp blades of grass jabbing into our bare skin, watching the ships come and go. Federation citizens aren't allowed much space travel. We're supposed to stay on the planet where we're born, unless we're ordered somewhere else. I've tried to talk to Hank about all my doubts and fears but he really doesn't discuss things with me. He's just offered me solutions to my problems. Some of them were pretty drastic.

It came to me as I was heating one of the Plasteel sections to remold it into a different shape. Hank and I had talked about this before. I didn't need to fit in. I could leave. Hank and I could leave. Surely that old man would take us with him—as refugees. Maybe we could give him something.

Then I remembered his stare. I remembered the way he looked at me. If that's what he wanted, well, I could give him *that*.

One of the instructors came over to evaluate my progress. "Better, June, better," she said. "I like your use of the transverse line, and the curved surfaces are most intriguing. It's still a little mechanical, but at least it's not another one of your spaceships. Don't be so representational. Remember: The important thing is to express yourself."

She left, scribbling on her grade-pad. I hadn't been paying attention to what I was molding: the Free Spacer's ship. I *had* been expressing myself. I put a few finishing touches on it and slipped it in a stasis bag. *This* project I would show to Hank.

Hank was late when he came by my house. We were supposed to go to a porno party at one of his friends' houses. I was so excited about the Free Spacer and the thought of escape that I just wanted to stay at home with Hank and talk about that. My folks were at an exhibit opening, and wouldn't be back until late.

"You haven't seen a porno cube before, have you?" he asked.

"No," I replied, reluctantly, "but I've heard all about them from the Council."

"And you *always* believe the Council don't you?" he laughed. "You're the one who wants to live with the Spacers. Don't you think you should learn something about them?" Everyone knows that the Free Spacers make the porno cubes. I relented.

We went to Robert's house, since his parents were away. Someone else brought the porno cubes. I wondered how they got them. The Council carefully monitors our cultural influences. I had asked Alicia if the Jeffies distribute them. She had said they were so worried about their treaties that she doubted it. One of the kids at school told me that the Spacers beamed the porno to us using gravity waves from a singularity. Right. Even Hank was not much help. He just said that any controlled substance automatically creates a black market.

At first I felt out of place at the porno party. It was all a bunch of older kids, at least four forms ahead of me. My discomfort vanished as I watched the cube.

The way the Council talks I expected them to be badly made, with abysmal acting and no production values. Nothing could be more untrue. In contrast, *our* cubes look two-dimensional and monochrome.

Everything looked *real*—believable. In less than half a kilosec, I felt that I was no longer watching a cube, but instead peeking into someone's real life. The story was about this asteroid miner who was found dead floating in space. Then an "assessor" was hired by the miner's partners to determine who killed him. After interviewing tens of people, the assessor determined the culprit and, in a dramatic confrontation, killed the murderer in a derelict space station.

I'm not sure what was supposed to be wrong with what we saw. Why does the Council forbid these cubes? Robert insisted it was due to the propaganda. Perhaps this cube was atypical, but I failed to see any propaganda whatsoever.

We all talked about the cube for several kilosecs. Where did the assessor get his authority? Why would anyone solve crimes if he weren't a SecPol? Why did the partners hire him—why not just contact the Security Police?

Our discussion ran longer than the actual porno cube, and was just as much fun. Hank told us to compare this discussion to any of the organized conversations we had in school after one of the cubes that they made us watch. Those discussions were always so dull, filled with long silences while we waited for the teacher to hint at what we were supposed to say. Here we could all be ourselves and say what we really thought.

Emboldened by this, I casually mentioned what I had seen at the spaceport. A brief moment of silence preceded the deluge of questions. Some of the students had heard about the ship, others knew nothing. When the din quieted the only new thing I learned was that the old man I had seen was the spaceship's sole occupant. I never realized you could operate a ship by yourself.

When we got back to my house it still wasn't very late, so Hank insisted that we have a reading lesson. He carefully removed the bookdiscs from his jacket and we began.

Usually, I'm the one that wants to start the reading lessons. That night I was distracted. All I could think about was the Free Spacer taking us away.

"You're daydreaming again," Hank said in his beautiful deep voice. No wonder he was training to be an opera singer. I even loved the way he told me I was wrong.

"It's possible," I insisted. "I know a way to get into the hangar— and then on board the ship."

I was beginning to convince him when I heard my parents activate the door. Ten kilosecs early! We weren't ready. I quickly switched off the light. Hank and I tore off our clothes and hid the bookdiscs under them. I threw a glass of water at Hank so it would look like sweat. We hid under the covers as my parents came up the stairs. We hoped that the covers would hide the fact that we were still wearing our underwear.

Hank and I were kissing as Mom and Dad shifted through the door to my room. I sat up a bit as I said "hi" to them so they could see my breasts. For once I was glad that I don't need to wear a bra yet. I didn't have time to extricate myself from one. Hank said "hi," too, and they frowned a bit as they acknowledged his existence. There was that little embarrassing silence before they apologized for interrupting us. We forgave them and promised to see them in the morning for breakfast.

When the door shifted shut behind them we got out of bed, stripped away our underwear, and carefully concealed the bookdiscs. We fell together on the bed, laughing and relieved. I'm sure it sounded like we were still pairing. Good.

Well into the night we planned our escape. I convinced Hank that I could at least get us into the hangar, if not all the way to the Spacer's ship. It was worth a chance.

When we ran out of plans, we paired. Since last form we've been pretending it, because I was always hesitant, and Hank was always understanding. That night I was hesitant no longer. The possibility of our escape had excited me, and *I* initiated the pairing. I could tell you, in intimate detail, what I felt, how I acted—I remember each delectable second; but a girl has to have *some* privacy.

This morning, I know I must have gone to school. I just can't remember anything about it. I thought only of the spaceport and our escape.

Getting into the port was no problem. The Jeffies are used to the students swapping ComServe days. We put our chops on the roster and stepped through the force membrane and into port. We did a few turns on the grunt run, in a pattern calculated to bring us by the hangar at a mech entrance.

I parked the hovercart near the showers. We were several kilosecs away from a shift change, so it was deserted. Rows of the dull orange coveralls stood waiting for the next shift. We found two that fit and quickly put them on. I took a tub of lubricant and smeared it on our coveralls and our exposed skin so we would look like we'd been working. I was used to the smell. Hank curled up his nose and made a face. He knows how to make me laugh.

A few SecPols stood guard at the Spacer ship. Following Hank's lead I sauntered past them with my head held high. We were proud mechanics here to do our job. We didn't salute them or anything since grunts are mere civilians. The SecPols acted like they didn't notice us, but they did notice the lubricant. I don't think they were checking any mechanics, because if they had to talk to them they had to smell them.

Once past I began to panic. What if we were caught? What if there wasn't room for us on the ship? How could we communicate with the Free Spacer? Did he speak our language?

Hank must have noticed my hesitation. He grabbed my hand and gave it a little squeeze. That was all I needed. I buried my fears.

We followed a group of mechs into the ship. It was as dingy on the inside as the outside. Many of the lights didn't work. As we walked along a corridor I noticed some of the interior panels were missing. The most surprising thing was the smell. We were near the galley because the smell of *food* was overwhelming. I caught whiffs of spices and oils that I could almost identify.

We had planned to hide in the cargo hold. What we found was better. The pantry was large and packed with food, stored in rows. You could open its door and not have a clear view of the back. No one should come here until after the ship launched.

We waited there, reading bookdiscs, until I couldn't hold my bladder any longer. Night had fallen and it had been kilosecs since I last heard any mechanics working on the ship. I motioned my desperate need to Hank and he nodded in agreement.

The head was easy to find, not far from the galley. Hank let me use it first, then I stood guard while he was inside. It's one thing to pair with someone and quite another to stand around and watch them pee. I paced back and forth. I was about three meters from the head when I heard something.

So I'm not a spy. So I'm no good at this. I didn't know someone was sneaking up on me. I didn't know until I heard her say, "Turn around!"

"Alicia?" I shouted, warning Hank inside the head.

"I knew you would do this, June. I knew it when I saw the ship land." She was obviously tense and uncomfortable. Sweat poured from her dark face. There was something in her hand—some sort of a weapon.

"You knew?" I found it hard to breathe. My brain started spinning like a rotor. "How? I didn't even know then."

"I've been listening when you talk to me. I know you aren't

happy here. Can't be happy here. But I can't let you go."

"Why not?" I asked as I backed away from her and moved to the left. "You're not a SecPol." She followed, keeping her weapon trained on me. I had to get her back against the door to the head.

"Please," I continued. "You're one of the few people that understands me. You know that sooner or later the Council's going to figure out that I'm no artist and I'll end up like Lee."

"You don't understand," she pleaded, her hands shaking. *She* had the weapon and *she* was the nervous one. I had the cool resolve of desperation. "Things are very strained between the Federation and the Jeffersonians right now. Your SecPols didn't want us to let this ship land. They certainly didn't want us to fix it. Now, if you escape it could be the spark that blows everything up."

I moved a few more centimeters to the left. "I can't go on living here," I said to her softly. "If you won't let me go, you'll have to kill me. You've got to decide between your country and your friend."

The head was directly behind her. I yelled Hank's name. The door, old fashioned and metal, flew open and sent Alicia sprawling. Annoyingly, she held on to her weapon as she rolled across the floor. Hank threw himself on top of her and tried to wrestle it away from her hand. He was twice her size, but still no match for her speed and skill. Alicia kicked straight back, knocking him a couple of meters away. Then she aimed her gun at me.

I've heard about time slowing down. Her thumb jammed down on the butt of the weapon, her forefinger moved toward a red button on its grip. She looked straight at me and said one word: "Down!"

I threw myself to the grungy floor. A particle beam zipped past my ear as I fell. I felt the tingling in the air as it passed. My head jerked back involuntarily and I saw the target of Alicia's beam. A Federation SecPol collapsed to the floor, his hand clamped on his gun and his head a charred mass.

Rolling toward the corpse, and fighting the urge to vomit, I pried his still warm fingers from his gun, then held it tightly in my hand. I glanced back at Alicia, who was furtively searching for more SecPols to shoot.

Hank was still breathing hard from where Alicia had kicked him. Blood drained from his face as he stared at the dead man. The smell of the burnt flesh filled the corridor.

"Now that's what I call a welcome."

I swerved. Instinctively I pointed my new possession in the direction of the voice.

"Sorry, Captain," Alicia said to the Spacer as she lowered her gun. "He was going to shoot. . . . I couldn't . . ."

"No need to apologize, He *was* gettin' to be a damned nuisance." He spoke in a strange accent that I can't mimic. Alicia told me that Spacers spend their lives acquiring and developing accents. They think it gives them character.

"You can drop the 'Captain,' too. It's just O'Malley. It's a good thing you Jeffies fixed up my ship." Then he added under his breath, "Charged me enough for it, too."

"Nice shot," he continued. "I think we can salvage the uniform. Now help me get this thing off him."

Alicia complied like she was on autopilot.

"And you, boy! Stop pointin' that thing at me. I get kinda nervous with the safety off."

He was talking to me! I lowered my pistol, doubly embarrassed.

"I'm a girl!" I retorted.

"Yeah?" he drawled suspiciously as he and Alicia stripped the corpse. "Yeah, I can see that you're a girl now. Wait a minute, you're the cutie I winked at yesterday, ain't you? I didn't know I was that irresistible."

I tried to explain things. O'Malley listened intently, but stopped me before I got very far. "That's enough. Heard it all before. Seen enough Federation worlds to recognize the pattern. I'd be honored to take you outta here. Later, when you get a job, you can pay me back for the transport. Now let's get your boyfriend here into this uniform."

"What?" I screamed.

"We've got us a sticky problem. The Feds sent a SecPol up with me and they expect to get one back. They ain't gonna look too carefully at who comes *out*—"

"No!" I stopped him. "Hank's coming with me. I love him. I won't leave without—"

Hank squeezed my hand. My voice stopped working. A cold blast blew across my heart. Somehow I knew each word before he spoke. "No," he said, "O'Malley's right. I fit in here well enough. I don't *need* to leave, the way you do. And I don't think I have the courage you have to go."

I wanted to argue with him. I wanted to tell him that I would be with him forever. The words died stillborn. He knew there was nothing I could say. I knew it. Everybody knew it.

"Don't mean to shorten this farewell, but time is pressin'. If Hank here's any good at all, he should be able to lose himself outside before they start noticin' him."

"I'll help you," said Alicia slowly, "I know this port—"

"Hold on, missy. I don't think you understand the temperature of the fire you've jumped into. The Feds don't take kindly to folks fryin' their Security Police. The Jeffies ain't so hot about it either. They don't have my enlightened attitude."

"You want me to come with you?" she asked, amazed.

"There's the girl. Always wondered what it would be like to expose a Jeffie to a little *real* freedom. Now let's get a-goin'. I won't be happy 'til I'm in hyper, well away from this sinkhole."

Getting Hank into the uniform was a lot easier than saying good-bye to him. I could barely watch him walk away from me through my tears. I suppose his subterfuge worked. The Jeffies towed us out to the launch site without question.

I continued crying through the launch. There's no sense of motion at all, until you hyper. Alicia sat hugging me as she stared out the viewport.

"You should have killed me," I whimpered, my tears soaking her lap. "I'll never see him again. I shouldn't have left."

"Stop that," she ordered. "You couldn't have gone on—even with Hank. You know that, don't you?"

I nodded. "Will I ever stop hurting?"

"I won't lie to you. No. But each day will dampen the pain a bit. You'll never stop missing"—her voice began to trail away—"loving him. I know."

I sat up next to her, drying my tears as best I could. Alicia smiled abruptly. She squeezed my hand, pointing to the beautiful pink and purple of New Bohemia receding beneath us. I was surprised to feel a little homesick.

"Look at my little groundhog now," she said. "You've sprouted wings."

I felt a tiny glow beginning inside my breast. "What the hell," I giggled, "is a groundhog?"

A MATTER OF CERTAINTY

L. Neil Smith

This collection would not feel right without the presence of L. Neil Smith. If fans only knew of one Prometheus Award–winning novel, that book would be *The Probability Broach*, the most popular libertarian SF novel of our generation. This is the novel that launched the North American Confederacy series. If the condition of old paperbacks is any indication of success, the dog-eared copies of *Broach* provide mute testimony to why he must be the tour guide to Free Space. One of the most prolific novelists in SF, he is author of *Henry Martyn*, about which I said in a review: "This book reads as though there had been a three-way collision between *Star Wars*, *Treasure Island*, and *The Story of O.*" Neil certainly knows how to deliver the goods.

I n the sixth month of the thirtieth year of the Eighth Akufik War, *Vettlos*-major Loxeh Wasahof, decorated veteran of three previous such wars, gave an order.

"Get up, Ehrahfi. You're wrinkling your uniform."

"But sir—" Senior *Lesuneh* Vonlos Ehrahfi, another seasoned campaigner, had abased himself on threading through the frayed weather-strands at the entrance of his commander's tent, flopping onto his broad abdomen on the canvas floor, lifting all four limbs—the faces at their ends shut tightly—in a display of willingness to accept whatever his superior desired to impose on him.

"Up, I said. You're too old and—considering our circumstances upon this pesthole planet—it's pointless."

The *lesuneh* opened two of his good faces, lowered his limbs, placed the unopened ones—one had been blinded in a mortar attack—beneath his bulk, and heaved himself upright. Closing an erect face as an afterthought, he brushed the faded, vegetation-printed fabric about his person, straightened the patched harness across his broad-domed back, then opened it again, eyeing his commander.

They were as close to being friends as their differing stations allowed. Nor was this the first war they'd fought together.

"Tell the truth, sir, it was never comfortable at any age."

The ancient noncom made a rasping noise his superior knew from long acquaintance was less to clear his breathing passages than to change the subject.

"Sir, the emissary we were ordered to receive 'with every hospitality' was scope-sighted minutes ago. It'll touch down any moment—or momentously; computer's getting sloppy—outside our perimeter, in an Akufik Silly 14-D."

Wasahof absently nodded a face, speaking more to himself than his *lesuneh*. "It might be expected. I imagine this emissary's anatomy approximates that of our enemy better than ours."

Ehrahfi cleared his breathing passages again. " . . . sir?"

Wasahof recognized the tone. He shifted from his ruminations with difficulty. "Very well, what do your tentmates wish to know?"

"Rumors, sir—this emissary's from some bug-eyed thin-blooded, cowardly species as hasn't fought a war in a million years. . . . "

Wasahof swung his faces toward each other and away again. "It has all the truth of barracks rumors, Ehrahfi. Your bug-eyed, thin-blooded, cowardly aliens have fought no war merely in *five hundred* years." He stepped toward the *lesuneh* and melodramatically lowered his left voice. "The Plenum and Commonage have joined our enemy in accepting their offer to show us how to be thin blooded and cowardly, too."

It was the *vettlos*-major's turn to rasp a subject-change: "This may be another Akufik trick, Ehrahfi. Have a quatroon of grenadiers surround the designated area. I'll be there directly. No one's to loose a rocket unless I order it."

"Sir!"

Ehrahfi slapped walking limbs together, dipped his aged body in defiant token of an abasement he saw as a prerogative of his class, turned—smartly for a wounded elder—and left in a swish of tattered weather-strands.

Merely five hundred years.

Wasahof sighed, closed his faces, let the limbs touch the floor. He lifted another pair—his fourth was artificial from the mid-point—opened his remaining face, and blinked his eye, a concession to fatigue he'd resisted while Ehrahfi was present. It seemed he'd always been tired, marooned upon this accursed globe, a disputed colony his people named Vylmybb Awign and the Akuf called Xungufa.

Again he placed limb-ends on the canvas floor, raised the other pair, and opened their faces. Tidying his own much-mended uniform, he pushed aside the weather-strands at the entrance and stiffened his posture to acknowledge a weary abasement from an emaciated throng-runner awaiting his will outside. He peered at the grenade projector riding the harness on the younger Meyhmaan's back.

"Weapon's dirty, splitling, see to it before lights-out."

The youngster hesitated. "Solvent's gone, sir—and I've only half a clip of ammo left."

Wasahof reflected. If an officer's weapon is the army he commands, he wasn't doing any better than this tired halfeling.

"Boil it in the cooktent. Dry it before you reassemble it. Nothing to do about ammunition, resupply's overdue. You've your barrel-knife."

"Sir!"

The junior officer snapped to as close as he could come to attention. Wasahof let it pass: His command was overdue for more than ammunition. They hadn't had enough to eat since . . . he gave up trying to remember, acknowledged the throng-runner's salute, and limped off through the stink and litter of an exhausted, starving command.

Five *hundred* years.

Just what the galaxy needs, he thought, *another* sapient species.

Silhouette 14-D in the Observer Manual was an Akufik *Harbinger*-class reconnaisance-courier, unarmed, crewed by three ugly little beings, incapable of spaceflight.

Dropping through the overcast, the vessel throbbed. It was, Wasahof knew, supposedly equipped to muffle any warning of its approach. The Akuf had maintenance problems, too. Below, his soldiers prudently cleared the area its inertia-field would contact. Outside that deadly circle, forty blunt-barreled rocket launchers, worn handles locked in the practiced jaws of forty grenadiers, followed its descent.

"Have them rest easy, Ehrahfi." As he joined his *lesuneh*, Wasahof indicated the maze of ruptured sandbags and artillery-ravaged acreage where the quatroon concealed itself. "Gently: We haven't many rockets left, and we don't want anyone biting a trigger because we startled him by telling him *not* to."

"Sir!" Ehrahfi shambled off to do his bidding.

I hope something comes of this, Wasahof thought. He watched the 14-Ds underlubricated landing-limb shudder out from its dented fuselage. *Ehrahfi's stiffening up worse than the rest of us. If he fails to reproduce before long, he'll die.* Antigenerative drugs, combined with antigeriatrics (for Meyhmeen they were much the same), can only do so much.

How terrible to die forever.

The *vettlos*-major glanced at the knobby flesh exposed at a threadbare cuff of his own uniform, blue, like the skin of all Meyhmeen, growing darker with advancing age. Ehrahfi's was virtually black. Fresh-fissioned Meyhmeen were the color of a cloudless sky.

If the old fellow does reproduce, if our supplies dry up and we do as we must, the Akuf, with reproductive habits as perverted as their appearance—immune to the vulnerability reproducing Meyhmeen suffer—will slaughter us while we're helpless infants.

The noisy Akufik vessel's support field touched down, churning dust into incandescent plasma. The field cut, dropping the craft onto its extended limb, where it balanced, bouncing on worn springs. A hatch gritted aside, but no Akuf floated out. Instead, metal clashed—he was glad he'd had the quatroon stand easy— and something like chains for all-weather vehicles jerked to a swinging halt at ground level.

The newcomers cannot fly, Wasahof noted. In this, they're more like us than the Akuf.

What emerged wasn't at all like an Akuf, nor was it like a Meyhmaan. A billow of fabric—eye-curdling orange visible for many *faowya* on a clear day—an arhythmic unfolding of oddly articulated limbs. The thing climbed down the chains and moved across the freshly stirred soil. It stood—Wasahof guessed it stood—looking from a single face with a pair of eyes as blue as the skins of splitlings.

Behind it, a shapeless bundle struck the ground. Without warning, the *Harbinger* groaned and lurched upward a dozen *lanaht*.

After a brief silence: "I'm an emissary commissioned by the Plenum and Commonage on Meyhmaandela." It named Wasahof's home planet, employing a speech synthesizer concealed within its nauseating billows. "Will *Vettlos*-major Loxeh Wasahof kindly identify himself?"

"I'm Wasahof." He trudged to within limb's reach of the thing, which he judged to be two-thirds his height and a quarter of his mass.

"Greetings, *Vettlos*-major. To spare your people's curiosity and avoid further distraction . . . "

The thing placed limb-ends on the fabric it wore. With a tearing noise, it pulled the fabric in two directions, dropping what it had worn onto the ground. Save for an abbreviated weapons harness about one of its upper appendages, it wore nothing.

" . . . *this* is what we're like."

It pivoted, that all might see it. A murmur swept through the ranks of grenadiers. One soldier let his launcher fall from horror-slackened jaws. It struck the ground with a thump.

Finally, the alien spoke again. "Now that I've introduced my species, I'm personally called Rene Aurelius."

The *vettlos*-major had barely kept from recoiling at the sight of this travesty of Meyhmaanese anatomy, harsh planes and corners rounded only by sickly translucent flesh the color of concrete, punctuated by dirty patches of brownish fungus.

By comparison, the Akuf seemed wholesome.

Possessing *five* limbs, it stood on two, without any of a Meyhmaan's eye-pleasing symmetry. The uppermost was hideously truncated, terminating in the creature's single, two-eyed, *lidless* face. Most of the fungus found root at its tip. The remaining four each ended in a *kind* of face, elongated manipulatory lips without trace of a mouth in their empty center, nor a nostril, nor the large, beautiful eye adorning a proper face. Again, there were no enveloping facelids.

He'd seen unsuccessful splitlings resembling this alien—days after they'd died. He summoned up a lifetime of self-discipline, fighting an urge to vomit from four mouths at once. That wouldn't be diplomatic, he told himself. Instead, he pointed a not-quite-trembling limb at the alien's polished harness.

"You arrive strangely accoutered to negotiate the end of conflict, Rene Aurelius." His mouth-parts stumbled over syllables as obscene as the being's appearance. "It's said your people haven't waged war for a million years."

It flexed a thin upper appendage at an acute angle, tapping its weapon-grip. "Before negotiation begins, *Vettlos*-major, there must be philosophical agreement. I'm properly equipped for what I am." The words issued from the fabric crumpled at its nethermost extremities. It bent, snatched up the garish drapings, swirled them about itself, and was clad.

Relief rippled through the quatroon.

The emissary turned and picked up a bag almost as large as itself. The battered Akufik craft thrummed, whined, and disappeared into the overcast.

"Shall we go to your quarters, *Vettlos*-major, and discuss this first lesson of peace?"

Within the privacy of the *vettlos*-major's tent, the alien again shocked the commander. Setting its bag at the entrance, it touched a deformed right upper limb to Wasahof's left, its left upper limb to Wasahof's right, and managed to tread on the limb-tips—one of them prosthetic—supporting the *vettlos*-major's greater bulk.

"We exchange essence," they both intoned, the astounded officer from lifelong reflex. It was a ritual conjugation, formal and meaningless even between Meyhmeen. Awkwardly, the alien bore an extra limb above its body that the Meyhmaan's four-limbed body couldn't meet.

The being called Rene Aurelius stepped back.

Trying not to mutter, Wasahof settled on a soil-mound built beneath the floor before the tent had been pitched. Aurelius perched on another, looking uncomfortable.

"Sir?" Ehrahfi peered from behind a patched partition, a serving tray of dented plastic dangling in his left mouth, on his right face a questioning expression. Wasahof contracted both upper limbs, a Meyhmaanese shrug. The *lesuneh* nodded and disappeared. A subdued clatter of dishware followed, filling the embarrassed silence.

What will I do, Wasahof thought, *without Ehrahfi? As the situation stands, he'll leave nothing of himself behind, not even any mindless little splitlings to bring up as their older self would approve. Anyday, he'll pass away in the midst of obeying one of my foolish orders and be gone, leaving me to face things as they've become.*

One of those *things* cast its gaze about, upper limbs wrapped about folded lower ones, as if the meager artifacts and time-abused furnishings it saw were of actual interest. It seemed to be up to Wasahof to start the conversation.

"Emissary, my orders were necessarily brief, zipped through a break in Akufik jamming. Are we to have another cease-fire, the thousandth in my lifetime? When do I begin the endless, pointless meetings with my Akufik counterpart?"

Aurelius rearranged itself, resting its face on the end of one of its longer limbs. There was no equivalent Meyhmaanese gesture. "You're cynical, *Vettlos*-major. I'll be direct. Our analysis indicates what you already know: This garrison can't survive another season. Your Plenum and Commonage have no resources to get you and your troops offplanet, and won't have again for a century."

Stiffening against a truth he'd long avoided, Wasahof almost missed the next words.

"—are in the same shape. This world was chosen for its desperation. We thought you'd be inclined to listen."

"And a cease-fire?" This time there was sincerity in Wasahof's voice.

"On Vylmybb Awign, the war's over. You're to suspend hostilities and begin establishing a self-sufficient colony, while the Akuf—"

Wasahof shook both upper limbs in outraged denial. "Have they told you nothing of our biology? If we reproduce, we'll be helpless, our memories erased with the stress of starting over. While the Akuf..." He let the sentence die for lack of words to do the catastrophe justice. At least the alien had called the planet by its right name.

Now it bobbed its fungus-covered limb. "One of my kind is speaking with Xungufa's Akufik leaders now—having arrived, symmetrically enough, in a Meyhmaanese vessel."

It broke off as the *lesuneh* limped in with his tray and the *vettlos*-major's last bottle of refreshment. Employing proper form, the alien thanked him, reached for a funnel of *rhusb,* and used one faceless limb to tip the liquid into its horrible mouth.

"The Akuf have equivalent problems, *Vettlos*-major. Through misfortunes of war—for which you're tactically responsible—they've lost all but a few of the symbiotes that facilitate *their* reproduction."

Wasahof suppressed the customary rejoinder concerning what he knew of Akufik reproduction. They were beginning to seem homely and familiar to him. Instead, he forced himself to listen to the more alien thing before him.

"Fighting halted, their priority will be cloning symbiotes. They'll be too busy starting a postwar baby boom to give you any—"

Wasahof began an angry reply. The creature cut him off with a display of a limb-end.

"Yes, *Vettlos*-major, an Akufik colony, too. Do you care who your neighbor is, if your holdings are secure and he minds his own business? They're no better equipped to leave this world. Besides, the first condition for peace is that both sides have a tangible stake in it. Settlers have such a stake. Occupying forces don't."

There was another, considerable silence.

Wasahof seized the neck of his own *rhusb* funnel, meaning to tip it, from habit, into that limb's mouth. Instead, he poured it into his other mouth. Aurelius watched the anatomical experiment, saying nothing.

"A colony," Wasahof answered, "with the Akuf respiring down our humps. That's how fighting *started* here! This command is from the Plenum and Commonage?"

Aurelius made a barking sound the commander would discover was its laugh.

"Perhaps, *Vettlos*-major. Or perhaps not. Perhaps we inscrutable aliens made it all up, for reasons as sinister and repulsive as we appear. Perhaps it contravenes the wishes of those who issue orders on your homeworld." It took another sip of *rhusb* while the commander stared. "*You* must decide, from now on, what's in your best interest."

Another gesture of denial: "I cannot accept this. I'm a soldier. If I had orders . . . "

Aurelius finished its drink. "Beg pardon, *Vettlos*-major, I've traveled far today. I must attend to my own biological necessities." It crossed the tent with a misarticulated gait and picked up its bag. Halfway through the weather-strands, it turned. "The second lesson of peace, Wasahof, is learning not just to disobey orders, but neither to give them nor give a damn about them."

Acrid smoke from refuse-burning cookfires mingled with the odor of latrines that should have been abandoned months ago. The evening sky was clear, but cooling temperatures blanketed the campsite with its own contamination.

Nevertheless: "You were correct, Rene Aurelius." Wasahof suppressed a shudder at his memory of the creature's appearance. "It's more pleasant outdoors."

The alien bobbed its face. "I know I've afforded you little time for reflection, *Vettlos*-major. I've little to spare. But there can be no unprecedented effects without unprecedented causes."

After a lifetime of war, the commander remained unconvinced that there could be peace between his people and the Akuf. The sun had been down an hour when Aurelius had returned. Vylmybb Awign was moonless. Alien and Meyhmaan spoke in darkness unrelieved by scattered starlight. Wasahof found it helpful—comforting, he admitted—to perceive the creature as an indistinct blob. He suspected the emissary had proposed an outdoor conference for that reason.

It had exchanged the fluorescent robe it had worn for a muted garment fitting its nightmare form. Perhaps, thought Wasahof, it had concealed itself in the beginning to spare them an unfortunate first impression. It had failed. Even now he had to concentrate to let the import of its machine-generated words—Aurelius understood the language; the synthesizer shaped syllables its mouthparts couldn't manufacture—sift through layers of instinctive terror he felt toward this malformed entity speaking to him out of the shadows.

"We begin," Aurelius continued as if unaware of the struggle going on nearby, "with agreement about not only what our words mean, but what their *meanings* mean."

Light and motion startled Wasahof. Shrouded by Aurelius's manipulators, an igniter flared. The alien touched flame to the end of a tube protruding from its mouth. Smoke trickled from orifices in its horrifying face, back-lit by the glare. Then blackness reigned, punctuated by a tiny, glowing coal. Wasahof realized that Aurelius believed in the promised cease-fire: That coal would have made a perfect target for the infrared sight of an Akufik sniper.

"It puzzles everyone," the alien mused, "that few sapient beings *relish* mortal conflict. War is everywhere regarded as a waste. What makes war possible despite our fervent desires?"

Wasahof spoke: "The term 'sapient' is wishful thinking. People are more often stupid and irrational."

The alien made the same barking noise as before. "I hesitate to argue—except that, if you're right, there's no use continuing this conversation."

Wasahof laughed, too, a high-pitched keening he didn't know was at the edge of Aurelius's auditory capability. "Alternatively, it's a common belief," he offered, "that sapients are, by nature, evil. Even the Akuf believe this."

Aurelius bobbed agreement. "Among us, it's called 'Original Sin.' " It sucked its fire-cylinder, lighting its face horribly. "Worse than untrue, it's irrelevant. By their nature, most sapients can't fly. Even the Akuf aren't good at it, any more than I am at running. Yet fly we all do, up in the air, among the stars. We all seem to have progressed more quickly at it than we have at the art of war."

"You say nothing new, Rene Aurelius," Wasahof stated. "Evil by nature, yet we might teach ourselves to be virtuous, as we've taught ourselves to fly. It's the basis for many philosophies, most of them brutal."

"My experience with other sapients is limited," Aurelius admitted. "Yet the idea that we may be better at flying than fighting gives me comfort. I don't think we're evil: Sapience simply offers choices for greater evil—and greater good. Sometimes people weary of the responsibility for making choices. At such times, sapience seems a burden."

Wasahof thought a while: "Meyhmeen and Akuf are flesh-eaters. I expect the same is true of your kind; there's a theory that only flesh-eaters achieve sapience. Perhaps we're predators who, running out of challenging prey, turn upon one another."

The barking came again. "Original Sin, tarted up for another century. One of our thinkers called this the PANG Principle: People Are No Good. It, too, is a basis for brutal philosophies. One generality I do accept: Sapience is, by nature, complex. There's enough variety among us—or in any individual, day to day—that you can prove this or any other principle if you're determined."

It was quiet, for a time, under the starlight.

"Economics?" Wasahof suggested. "War as a struggle for food and room to live?"

"My understanding of Meyhmaanese history," Aurelius answered, "tells me this is insufficient to explain your ugliest wars—or those of my species, for that matter."

It was as if Wasahof hadn't heard the reply. "Individual greed—arms-makers, growing rich in wartime."

"Not to mention media reporters." Laughter mingled with the alien's words. "Few think to blame them for the existence of the market wherein they ply their trade. Why not blame baby-sitters, profiting excessively while parents work in war-plants?"

Wasahof joined the laughter, offering no other reply.

"Better focus," Aurelius switched topics, "on pragmatics—what makes war possible. *Vettlos*-major, how do the Plenum and Commonage persuade individual Meyhmeen to fight?"

Wasahof snorted. "No loyal Meyhmaanese stands idle in sight of threats to the Plenum and Commonage."

"What," asked the alien, in a tone Wasahof suspected denoted skepticism, "if some refuse?"

"Conscription! By my oath, no nation can fight a war without—"

"*Precisely.*"

Aurelius let the word hang between them. "We've one answer: War is made possible by conscription. Now another: How do the Plenum and Commonage acquire resources to wage war? Don't tell me about patriotic contributions—in your parlance, I wasn't halved yesterday."

"By imposition," replied the officer, "of a periodical obligation upon members of the Commonage by the Plenum."

"Textbookish," Aurelius observed, "but lucid. We've identified two practices that make war possible, conscription and taxation. What have they in common?"

"You'll say," Wasahof growled, "they're involuntary. Yet the benefits of civilization imply duties, which if not willingly performed, must be forced upon the beneficiaries if civilization is to survive."

Wasahof's eyes had adjusted. He watched the alien swivel its head from side to side.

"What of the ruin that conscription and taxation make possible? Look around, *Vettlos*-major. How conducive is *this* to civilization?"

A pause, unfilled by either voice.

"Let it pass," Aurelius sighed. "Ponder another question: For how many millennia have Meyhmeen prayed for peace?"

Wasahof grunted. "You'll say that praying is as invalid as—what did you call it? 'Original Sin.' " He shook his heads, unconsciously imitating the alien. "Well, given its record of effectiveness—"

"And political agitation against war?"

It wasn't a thing Wasahof was proud of. "Occasionally, during the First and Third Akufik Wars, groups of Meyhmeen massed—"

"Providing exercise for policemen," Aurelius interrupted, "local focus for popular hatred of faraway enemies, excuses to make laws harsher, and no answer to the questions we ask. I know little of Meyhmaanese peace movements, Wasahof; I predict they advocated disarmament, a cure without recovery, and pacifism, a remedy that only works on the wrong parties."

No military Meyhmaan disagreed: "The most pacific entity's a corpse."

The alien tapped the weapon under its limb. "Pacifism renders one helpless against those with no desire for peace. My people—the five hundred warless years we've enjoyed—began by assuming you can never end conflict among sapients. It's part of our nature. But you can limit its scope."

"Abolishing conscription?" anger colored Wasahof's voice. "Rendering the collective helpless? Eliminating taxation? Forget defense—if we've no means to provide for the unfortunate, how will they survive?"

Aurelius stretched its limbs and widened its mouth. "Pardon, *Vettlos*-major. The gesture indicates that I've sat too long within vibrating metal hulls, in seats not made for my kind."

The entity took another breath and expelled it.

"Majoritarianism, like you Meyhmeen practice, is a matter of avoiding reality, then avoiding the consequences of the first avoidance. There's no 'purely social' measure that, once taken, can't be converted to military use. Welfare registries provide data for conscription. Education atrophies into indoctrination. Disease research can't be distinguished from that dedicated to biological warfare. In my world's history, some came to see no difference between nuclear energy and nuclear weaponry. In the narrow context they lived with, maybe they were right."

Wasahof, too, suppressed a yawn. "Which gets us where?"

"To the choices reality imposes on us. It may be better to let the poor go hungry, to prevent them being incinerated along with everyone else. If they're provided for, it must be by means that don't threaten racial extinction. Those concerned must do the providing because, if means exist to *force* the feeding of the poor on everyone, they'll inevitably be employed to feed the machinery of war."

Tired of the strain of tolerating alien company—and even more alien ideas—Wasahof snapped, "Of what relevance is this upon Vylmybb Awign? We're a military establishment. We've no poor to feed but ourselves!"

"You aren't a military establishment any longer, remember?" Wasahof grunted belligerently.

"Remember?"

"How could I forget?"

"Look: You're bound to make mistakes. Better to make new ones than repeat old ones. Take my advice, *Vettlos*-major: Do *more* than eliminate taxes and conscription. Avoid creating the authority capable of imposing them. My world's history demonstrates that this won't impair your ability to defend yourselves. Taxation and conscription have nothing to do with that. They only serve the interests of—"

"Vettlos-*major!*" It was the throng-runner Wasahof had spoken to—had it only been this morning? The young Meyhmaan approached, uniform tatters flapping.

Wasahof arose. "What?"

"The *lesuneh, Vettlos*-major. I begged him to let me go for water, but he wouldn't . . . halfway there, he fell. We got him to your tent, then couldn't hold him. The medic said *convulsions!*"

Cursing the prosthetic slowing him, Wasahof hastened to the lantern-illuminated tent glowing before him. Tearing through the strands, he stumbled to a mound where figures crowded about the form of the *lesuneh*.

He pushed a pair of grenadiers aside. "What's happening, medic?"

The medic snapped at his superior as he went on tapping and poking the unconscious noncom. "Got the twitches under control—used up the *lehgdusa*. No cure for *time,* though, which is what's killing him."

"*Killing* him?" He'd never heard it said by anyone else before.

Permanent.

Irrevocable.

Death.

"Killing us all," the medic muttered. Straightening, he looked at Wasahof. "That and our glorious—"

Wasahof stiffened, left mouth opening for a reprimand.

"Barefaced sedition, *Vettlos*-major." The medic shrugged. "Attempted, anyway. Go ahead and shoot me. I could use the rest."

Wasahof sagged. "Later—I'm too tired now, myself. What can we do?"

The medic thought. "Ask *that* if it brought along any anticoagulants."

Wasahof whirled; Aurelius had followed. He bit back a savage command. He wanted the abomination out of sight, away from his dying friend.

Aurelius shook its face. "Sorry, wrong blood chemistry." To Wasahof: "The Akuf have Meyhmaanese prisoners scheduled for release in a few days. They may have—"

"Throng-runner!"

"Sir!" Limbs clicked.

"Find a working communicator. Salvage parts from others if necessary. Contact the enemy. See if this monster's idea is any good."

"Sir!"

Strands swished as the runner disappeared. Wasahof stood, breathing hard, staring at the alien, not caring that he'd just insulted an official emissary from Meyhmaandela.

Aurelius asked, "Might there be time, medic?"

Preoccupied, the medic grunted an affirmative.

A quiet barking came with the alien's next words. " 'Contact the enemy'? You're learning, Wasahof."

Through the night, they kept watch beside the body of the *vettlos*-major's comatose friend.

They talked. Aurelius was saying, " . . . secret of lasting peace lies in accepting the inevitability of conflict—" when the runner returned with news that the proper medicine was in good supply in the Akufik encampment, half a continent away.

He was breathless. "The enemy have dispatched their last operating flyer to bring it!"

"I wonder," mused Aurelius, "whether 'enemy' is the word to use in such a context."

"I don't . . . " The throng-runner blinked.

"I know you don't," Aurelius answered. "That seems to be the trouble."

Across the tent, the dozing medic nodded as if the exchange included him. The confused throng-runner was dismissed. To his own surprise, it was the tired *vettlos*-major who took up their earlier conversation.

"Assume—you argue—that when conflict arises, everyone is right. Let each do, accordingly, as he wants, with his *own* life."

The alien nodded. "At the same time, assume that everybody's wrong—unentitled to impose his views on anyone else. Prohibit one form of behavior—*initiation* of force—since that's the only means by which a nonaggressive individual may be prevented from doing what he wants. You'll find an armed populace will take care of any enforcement this one prohibition requires."

Wasahof's brain spun. His best friend was dying. His last command was doomed. This repulsive creature—with even more repulsive ideas—was all the comfort he'd been offered by a government he'd given a lifetime of service.

"You'd have us scrap every value we possess, every tradition we treasure."

The creature was unmoved. "You'd prefer to scrap your species?"

Silence.

Finally: "This . . . this anarchistic *nonsense* is all you came to teach us?"

Aurelius arose, stretching. "To convince you of its necessity, Wasahof, a different matter altogether. Both sides—you, the Akuf—must begin by learning to distinguish between the needs of personal survival and group demands that threaten it."

"Talk!" Wasahof retorted without enthusiasm. His gaze lingered on his dying friend, weakening his resolve. "Nothing but talk . . . "

Aurelius shaped its face into a grimace. "You're curious and we both know it. Regarding that prohibition I mentioned, learn to avoid a temptation you'll feel, sooner or later, to extend the concept to unrealities like 'moral compulsion' or 'economic coercion.' Focus on the actuality of initiated physical force. It won't solve every problem, but it inhibits the creation of new ones. There's more to learn, Wasahof, but for now, living in peace should be enough."

Wasahof sighed, "Five hundred years is a long time. Monster"—despite the word, his tone was gentle—"why do you care what happens to us?"

Aurelius laughed, throwing its face back. "It's *business.* You get a Ninth Atomic War that doesn't happen. We . . . " It stopped laughing and thrust manipulatory appendages into slots in its clothing Wasahof hadn't noticed. "Okay, I'll tell you: Like your people, Wasahof, we learn the hard way. Our species is divided into two groups, those willing to trade their liberty for comfort and safety. They live on planets, mostly, throughout our sector of the galaxy, and prefer a warm, cozy state, snugged up nice and tight around their necks and genitals."

From somewhere in its clothing it acquired another fire-cylinder, and with a guilty glance toward medic and patient, lit it.

"Then there're we Free Spacers, who crave more room, breathing, living, elbow—we live anyplace that *isn't* a planet, anyplace we won't feel trapped by government and gravity, both of which, according to a proverb, *suck.*"

The coal at the end of its fire-cylinder brightened, then faded.

"We'd an artificial habitat called *Edgar Friendly,* five miles long, an engineering triumph, Wasahof, until it was obliterated by a pebble the size of your thumbnail—the size of mine, anyway—tearing along at fifty thousand mile-seconds. We survivors have indentured ourselves to finance construction of an even better habitat, *Edgar Friendly II.*"

"Indentured?"

The alien bobbed its face. "My mate and I taught history. Now we're mercenary philosophers, surviving by teaching *you* to survive. This scenario's being repeated *everywhere* Meyhmeen and Akuf are fighting, because your leaders finally realized that this war must end if there's to be anything left of your species. They've hired us to end it, by whatever means, although we're not sure how far we can push it. Converting military outposts into independent colonies may be going too far. . . . "

Lifting its face toward the ceiling, it made barking noises as it left the tent.

Morning.

As the Akufik vessel waited, the thing called Rene Aurelius looked over what had been a battlefield. Everywhere lay charred vehicles, sandbags, a litter of equipment, military and personal.

Stretching down to a dark spot that had begun as a pool of Meyhmaanese blood, it sifted soil through its manipulators. "More than five hundred years ago," its voice was a whisper, "my people fought like this. It wasn't the last time, but it was among the last."

The alien rose, brushed manipulators together, and turned to Wasahof. "Afterward, a famous philosopher, six *million* of whose kinsmen had been slaughtered by one party to the conflict, took media to one such slaughtering site. Before them, he reached into a shallow pool and brought up a handful of sediment consisting, he said, of the ashes of those who'd been slaughtered."

Wasahof made sympathetic noises, but didn't interrupt. His thoughts were with Ehrahfi, being given further care in the tent they'd just left.

Aurelius spoke again. "What do you suppose he claimed was the essential nature of the crime? I've heard him myself, in recordings of the moment, although he's been ashes himself for half a millennium. *Certainty*. The murderers, he said, were *certain* they possessed the truth. Thus they felt entitled to kill their enemies like animals, burn their remains like garbage."

"I take it," stated the *vettlos*-major, "you believe this not to be the case." Wasahof was finding, now that Aurelius was leaving, that he'd enjoyed its company. Looking at it in the light of day, however, was something he was glad he wouldn't have to get used to.

"What they were guilty of," Aurelius answered, "was proceeding from certainty to license, killing those who wouldn't agree. The one doesn't follow upon the other, yet it's an indication of the state of our culture then, that nobody questioned such faulty logic, applied by mass-murderers *or* famous philosophers."

Wasahof nodded his upper limbs. "There are degrees of certainty. We're justified in believing that the sun will rise tomorrow upon the horizon leading a planet's rotation."

The alien agreed. "Yet philosophers like the one I spoke of came to regard *un*certainty as a token of intellectual trustworthiness. Everyone has a right to—a desperate need for—certainty. Otherwise, motion stops. People stagnate. The resulting slaughter is wider and agonizingly slower than any meted out by mere murderers."

They looked out over the ravaged landscape.

"The real crime," Aurelius said, "is acting on a belief that certainty entitles you to impose your views on others. That was what they were guilty of, a crime the philosophers—with an ethic of cultivated uncertainty—were helpless to prevent. So, of course, it happened again."

Wasahof pulled himself into a formal posture. "Not here. We'll cast off our weapons—"

"You *can't,* Wasahof. You need them for hunting, protection from predators. And people deprived of weapons are subject to authority. You might forget, try to go back to organization-by-coercion. Or, should the Plenum and Commonage recover, they may disapprove of what you've built here."

Wasahof fought the urge to glance about, see if anyone was listening. Hearing these words, thinking these thoughts, living this treason—for a being like himself—was going to take getting used to.

"You'll have to achieve peace the hard way, with a gun in your hand. Civilizations can't *disinvent* technology. They either die of it or learn to live with it."

Wasahof sagged. "Easy to say when you're going away from where the living or dying will be done." To himself: *At least it's leaving.*

For the first time, Aurelius stared in disbelief. "The Plenum and Commonage are in no shape to transport *anyone*. I've the same stake here that you have. Otherwise I couldn't do my job."

Hefting its bag, it started toward the waiting vessel. "The human in the Akufik camp is my mate. Like you, we practice direct conjugation. Like the Akuf, two reproducing humans generate a third, independent individual. Unlike either, it's carried within our bodies—one of them, anyway—until it's ready to enter the world."

From within the tent came the brassy squall of a new pair of splitlings. It would be Wasahof's honor to find names for each and look after them until his own time came. He wondered what Rene Aurelius's mate was called.

"We're staying," it said, "We were Free Spacers once; our children will be again. But it's sink or swim for Meyhmeen, Akuf, *and* humans of this generation. If your former enemies keep this flyer running, I'll be back to introduce you to my mate."

Perhaps, Wasahof thought, my splitlings upon Vylm—Xung-ufa—will be able to look at yours without wishing to regurgitate.

But what he said was, "Good-bye."

PLANET IN THE BALANCE

John DeChancie

And now for something completely different. DeChancie's natural gift for satire serves him well in a story exploring a different kind of tyranny. The author of the Skyway trilogy is noted for a great comic sense. He was the first to put trucks in space! The author of the *Castle Perilous* series is well acquainted with the Theater of the Absurd. Finally, this man worked on *Mister Rogers' Neighborhood*. Talk about qualifications! His story should leave some readers green with envy.

You can't land here," said the voice on the ship-to-planet channel. George Gross, freelance planetologist, let out a weary sigh. "For the *n*th time," he said, "this is a legitimate distress call. My ship is experiencing massive systems failure. I have about three hours of breathable air left, and the recycling system is down. None of my recycling equipment is functioning. I have no potable water to speak of, nor much food. I must attempt a landing on your planet, because, as you said, you have no ship ready to come up here and rescue me in orbit."

"Under no circumstances will you be permitted to land on St. Rachel," the voice said adamantly. "This entire world is a protected environmental preserve. No landings are allowed except those granted by permit. You may apply for a landing permit by facsimile transmission."

"How long does processing usually take?"

"A few weeks at the minimum."

"I'll be dead by then," Gross said.

"Sorry, but we can't help that. An unauthorized landing can cause serious and irremediable damage to the very, very, very delicate biosphere of this planet."

"I'll be very, very, very careful. I have a doctorate in planetary ecology, you know."

"I'm sure you do. You're a worldscaper. A planetbuster. You practice the crime of terraforming. You rape planets."

"Only if they're consenting adults."

"And you do it with nanotechnology, the most dangerous and potentially destructive technology in the known universe."

"That's why it's the most jealously guarded secret in the known universe," Gross answered. "The Nanotech Guild doesn't like its members giving away trade secrets."

"It's an infernal science, tampering in the domain of the Great Universal Spirit. We don't want your kind here. Go away."

"Nevertheless, bunkie, I'm landing on your world."

"The hell you are."

"The hell I'm not. How are you going to stop me?"

That stumped the voice.

George Gross said, "I happen to know that you have no military vessels to speak of. Do you have an aerospace defense network? Have any missiles down there? Beam weapons?"

"Yes."

"You lie badly. Sorry, I'm coming down. I really have no choice."

"You'll be arrested the moment you land," the voice told him.

"If I live," said George Gross.

If you can find me in that endless jungle down there, he added to himself.

The planet really was a tropical hell. Vast rain forests, ringed with white mountains, dominated the main landmass. The only other continent-size chunk of dirt was under miles of ice at the south pole. The rest was water, bright, blue, and beautiful, wreathed with complex networks of islands. Slap another polar ice cap on the top, and you had a dandy planet for homesteading. That jungle was a cornucopia. If you didn't mind exploiting it a little. It was all at the bottom of a costly gravity well, sure. But if you liked planets, this one was potentially lucrative.

The local solar system was a typical double-star system. Twin primaries, close enough to orbit each other, but far enough apart to shepherd separate planetary flocks. St. Rachel orbited the yellow component of the binary. The other component was bluish and a trifle hot. There was no true night on St. Rachel during most of the solar year. Lots of sunshine, lots of energy. Hence, lush vegetation and tropical climate all through what would have been the temperate zone.

The stubby lander detached from the huge planeteering vessel, drifted off, farted flame, and began its descent into the atmosphere.

"Here we go," Gross told Systems, the chief operating intelligence of his ship.

"Wheee," Systems said in mock elation.

"Cheer up," Gross said. "Worst thing that can happen is, we can die. Better than getting repossessed."

"Look," Systems said. "Foreclosure affects you, not us. You go, we stay, no matter who the ship's new owner is. But if you smash us . . ."

"Hey, I'm the one in the flipping lander, not you," George said. "Keep that in mind. You're only linked through telemetry."

"There are subsidiary systems aboard that lander, and while they're not an integral part of me, they're kin, so to speak. So, death before dishonor? We'd rather not, if you don't mind."

"This is not a suicide mission. I fully expect to walk away from this landing. Or hobble."

"Good luck," Systems said.

"Thanks."

Bright flags of plasma fluttered around the craft as Gross checked the instruments.

"Found a landing spot for me yet?"

"Not yet," Systems said. "Still mapping."

"You'd better get a move on," Gross said. "Speed's already dropped to Mach twelve. I have very little flying-around fuel on this craft."

"I'm well aware of the fuel capacity of a standard planetary lander."

"Are you sure the inhabitants live on this continent? The forest is as thick as thieves. Might not be any place to land at all."

"There's no place else to live unless they're island-dwellers. I am getting readings of large life-forms in the seas."

"Very like a whaleoid," Gross said.

"All my readings say the humans live in the mountains around the big forest. And they must live underground, because I can't see anything but huge solar collectors on the peaks."

"I see 'em. Spoils the beauty, but they have to do something for energy, don't they? They won't use nukes, they won't burn a thing. They sound like strict Church of Gaea types. The only thing that stripe of critter will disturb is rock strata. And sometimes not even that. Mach nine and dropping."

"I've found you a crashing place."

"Gee, thanks. Where?"

"On the screen."

"Okay, I need to make a right turn, don't I?"

"Twenty-three degrees, now, please."

The landing went badly. Gross made two passes over the designated landing area but found that what looked clear from space was in fact a vast muddy bog, into which the lander might have sunk without a trace. He flew around some more, using up hovering fuel.

"I can't see any place where I can set this thing down without bending a few trees. And in fact they look too big to bend."

"There isn't a clearing within a hundred kilometers."

"I'll have to poke a hole in the canopy with a grasscutter bomb."

"Oh, my, they're not going to like that one little bit."

"Got no choice, Systems. I can't take the chance of upsetting and crashing. That'll cause more damage anyway."

Gross armed the grasscutter device, let it drop, and scooted away. A bright red flower of flame blossomed in the jungle below, the concussion shaking the lander.

Gross drifted back over the target area. Below lay a nicely circular clearing, carpeted in blasted stumps. He cleared away a patch of these with the X-ray laser, using up more fuel, and then managed to set the craft down by burning the fumes that remained in the tanks.

The engines whined to a stop, and he was down. He let out a sigh of contentment.

"What an absolutely expert landing."

"What a mess you made," Systems said.

Gross looked out the viewport at the local devastation. Fallen tree trunks fanned out in concentric circles from the central blast point. "Yup. You could have given me more accurate data."

"I have no control over the resolution capability of my scanning instruments, Mr. Gross."

"Of course not. Sorry, Systems. You did the best you could."

"Thanks so much."

It was fully two standard days later before someone finally visited the ad hoc clearing: a team of men and women in uniform. Investigators. Their leader introduced herself as Ferne Mountainflower, a regulatory enforcement officer of the High Council of the Conservatorship, the chief governing body around here, it seemed.

"Ferne Mountainflower," Gross said. "Nice name."

"Thank you," Officer Mountainflower said stiffly, tall and painfully skinny in a close-fitting green uniform. "We take nature names. Your landing has precipitated an environmental crisis on this planet."

"A crisis? I did that? Little ol' me?"

She looked him up and down and did not like what she saw: a balding, burly man with a spare tire of fat at the waist and a bushy black mustache colonizing his upper lip. "The situation is not humorous, Mr. Gross. Monitoring stations on the other side of the planet have already picked up traces of the huge amounts of pollution you have injected into our atmosphere."

"Traces, eh?"

"Yes. And this local area is a nightmare. You destroyed almost half a square kilometer of rain forest."

"Jungle."

"What?"

"I prefer 'jungle.' 'Rain forest' is so . . . I don't know . . . mealy mouthed."

"The term is 'rain forest.' It will take a hundred planetary years for this wound to heal itself."

"I doubt it. While you've been taking your sweet time getting to me . . . by the way, did it ever occur to you that I might have been injured?"

"We monitored your communications. We knew you were all right."

"Thanks for making sure I had enough food and water to last while you moseyed out here. As I was saying, I've had some time to study the local flora, and these so-called trees are more on the order of leafy fungus. They'll pop back in no time. And the undergrowth is already sprouting. Look there."

Ferne Mountainflower did not look. "You are under arrest. You will have a preliminary hearing in a few days. If criminal charges are brought against you, you will be bound over for trial. If not, you will be assessed the costs of environmental clean-up."

"Nice of you to drop by. Can I stay here in the lander, or do I have to go to jail physically?"

"You can stay here. There's no place to run to, and you can't take off. Your hearing will be conducted by electronic proxy anyway. I assume you have the requisite gear aboard your ship to allow that."

"Sure do. Thanks. But I do need food and water. I've about run out."

"We've brought your emergency rations."

Gross eyed the stack of boxes marked PROCESSED QUASI-ORGANIC FOOD PRODUCT.

"Yum," Gross said.

"It will keep you alive."

"That's what you people eat usually?"

"Yes. It's good food that does not exploit any animal or plant life."

"I'm glad for that. Thank you."

"You're welcome. I hope you enjoy your stay on St. Rachel."

"Uh, Saint Rachel Carson, is it? Church of Gaea?"

"Yes. I see you're familiar with our faith."

"Run into you folks from time to time."

"You really don't have any qualms about laying waste whole planets, do you?"

"Huh? Man is the center of my universe. Man and his need to survive. Planets don't get hungry."

"You're wrong," Ferne Mountainflower stated. "Planets are alive."

"Except those that are lifeless. I prefer 'em, really. Better to start from scratch."

"Even the so-called lifeless ones. We believe that all natural things—organic or inorganic—have souls, destinies . . . in short, lives."

"Ah, rock-huggers. You're fundamentalists."

"We could be called that. The sanctity of all forms of life is an article of faith with us."

"Faith is good."

"I'm glad you agree. By the way, what was the nature of your accident?"

"Ran into something out there," Gross said.

"An asteroid?"

"Would I be standing here? No, it was some anomalous glob of junk about ten million kilometers in diameter. We hit it pretty hard. A cloud of gassy stuff. The instruments went crazy, but I couldn't make head or tail of the readings. Anyway, it blew out everything in the ship except my COI, and even it's crippled for the most part."

"No, I'm not," Systems's voice came from the comm panel.

"Yes, you are," Gross countered, turning his head. "You've been acting goofy ever since we hit that thing out there."

Ferne Mountainflower asked, "So you have no idea as to the nature of the anomaly?"

"An idea or two. But whatever it is, it's slowly intruding itself into the binary gravitational system. From what I could see it might take up an orbit around one star or the other. Maybe both."

"You don't say."

"I do. It could be a massive gas cloud of some unknown type. Might be of some concern for you."

Ferne M. smiled patronizingly. "We don't do much in the way of astronomy here."

"No, planet-huggers seldom do. I'd advise dusting off what lenses you have and taking a look out there."

"Please stop using the term 'hugger.' It's insulting."

"Sorry, didn't mean anything by it."

"I'm sure you didn't," Ferne said sardonically. "I will inform the High Council."

"You do that. Meanwhile, I'm hungry."

Gross tore open a carton and took out a ceramic container. He ripped off the foil top. Inside was green mush.

He dipped a finger into the stuff and tasted it. There was no taste. Well, there was a faint taste. It tasted like . . . mush.

He turned to Ferne Mountainflower. "I think a good Chardonnay would go with this nicely. What do you think?"

The hearing was held three days later. In the interim, Gross subsisted on the egregious green mush, judiciously rationing to himself the gallon of beer occupying one of the lander's potable tanks. The beer helped.

"We're ready for you, Mr. Gross," came Ferne Mountain-flower's voice over the headset.

"All rightie," Gross said, donning the VR gear. It was the usual helmet with goggles, its innards tuned to interface with a few implanted microcomponents inside Gross's skull. Gross disliked virtual-reality hookups, but suffered them ungladly as a part of his job.

Gross found himself sitting at a table in the middle of a circular chamber. Seated in a ring around him were about thirty people of both sexes. They all sat behind a high judicial-style bench that circled the room. Seated beside him at the table was a man dressed in the ubiquitous one-piece green suit that these people seemed to favor.

"This proceeding is hereby convened," intoned a voice that came from Gross's left. He looked up. A white-haired woman seemed to be the leader of this group. Her chair and bench were ever so slightly more elevated than those of her colleagues.

The woman kept talking, but Gross's attention was diverted to the man beside him, who leaned over and said, "I'm Glade Bower, your counsel, Mr. Gross." He reached out a hand.

"Hi, there," Gross said, shaking Bower's hand. The circuitry implanted in Gross's skull supplied him with a tactile simulation of the handshaking. The sensation was always a little odd, as there really was no actual physical contact, and the sense of physical mass and weight was only psychological. Yet, the illusion was convincing, in a vaguely dreamlike way that Gross had never really understood. Such was virtual reality.

"The facts are clear," someone else, to Gross's right, was saying. "Will the defense stipulate the facts outlined in the following summary?"

"Look at all the mischief you did," Systems's voice came into Gross's ears.

"I've been a bad boy," Gross admitted.

Words appeared in front of Gross's eyes. He read the report, nodding. Succinct, but accurate. Of course, there was the matter of interpretation:

"Did willfully and with criminal intent despoil . . . "

"Ignored all prior warnings with arrogant disdain . . . "

"Selfishly pursued his own unenlightened interests . . . "

"Established an exploitative hegemony over . . . "

"Oh, good one, that," Systems said.

"Did with imperialistic intent . . . "

Imperialistic? Well, yes, he did try to set up his own little empire out there, lording it over the indigenous gymnospores.

"Displaying an arrogant and predatory speciesism . . . "

" 'Speciesism,' " Gross scoffed. "What a hoary old chestnut. Never really established itself in the lexicon."

"Too many esses, maybe," Systems ventured.

And on and on in similar vein. Yes, it was all there. Stipulate all of that? Well, hell, sure. What did it matter, anyway?

The hearing dragged on for most of the morning. The defense had not much to offer. "Dire need," was the catchphrase. "Extreme emergency," and "he would have died, otherwise," were also paraded about while the prosecution sniped at them.

Gross lit up a cigar.

"Mr. Gross, what in the world are you doing?"

Gross puffed a few times. It was a fine cigar, cocoa brown and fat, its tobacco grown on another tropical planet from terrestrial seeds.

"He's smoking . . . tobacco!" someone gasped.

"Disgusting!"

"Phew, I can almost smell it!"

"Almost, but not quite," Gross said, "seeing as how I'm seven hundred klicks away."

"How can you do that to your body?" the white-haired Council chairbeing (whose name sounded Polynesian) asked with sincere concern for the health of a fellow human.

"Easily," said Gross.

"Smoking tobacco is not permitted on this planet. Put it out!"

"No," said George Gross.

The chairbeing stiffened. "You are prejudicing your case."

"Funny you should use that word," Gross said with a shrug. "Prejudice?"

"Yes, prejudging. The verdict is foregone, is it not?"

"Not necessarily," the chairbeing said.

Gross cocked an eyebrow at her. "Eh?"

"That you are guilty of gross criminal negligence is abundantly clear. However, under the circumstances, we might be willing to suspend the imprisonment and limit the punishment to cleanup costs, plus fines."

"Ahhhh," Gross said. "I think I see. Having a liquidity crisis, are we?"

"Please look over this list of damages and costs," the chairbeing said. "The hearing is adjourned until tomorrow."

"Quite a bill," Systems said. "If you pay it, you're broke."

"If I pay it, I'm a fool. Look at this. I'm being charged for genetic damage to a whole class of conifers a thousand kilometers away."

"All that plasma we dumped into the atmosphere," Systems said. "Nasty stuff."

"Look at this. They say I've reduced the life expectancy of a whole species of leviathan sea critters. Whaleoids."

"By a small increment, but nevertheless statistically significant."

"Sheeesh," Gross said. "Look at these administrative costs."

"Biggest item on there," Systems noted.

"What a scam. I suppose they have scientific documentation for all of this."

"I'm still downloading it, Mr. Gross. It's all supported by hard data and observation. Very objective. You have a problem with any of it?"

"Oh, I wouldn't think of impugning the integrity of their scientists," Gross said. "I'm sure everything is on the up and up."

"Oh, my," Systems clucked. "We ripped the crap out of the ozone layer. Tsk."

"Hmmm. Looks like we did. And by God, one lonely little lander did it all. But what the heck is this? . . . Jesus, Mary, and Krishna. They're charging me for any future damage when I take off!"

"Thinking ahead," Systems said. "That's a conservative estimate. If they think the landing was bad, wait till they see how we'll pollute the planet on the way up."

Gross ticked a finger against his data screen. "They have us dead to rights. I suppose we should just pony up and get the hell out."

"Except that if you pony up you will not be able to make the next installment payment on your loan. Your starship will be repossessed. I will be repossessed. Good-bye, Mr. Gross."

"Good-bye, Systems. Nice knowing you. You know what this place is?"

"What, Mr. Gross?"

"A pollution trap. Like a small-town speed trap."

"Well, we fell into it."

"That we did. We have any long-range scanning equipment up there that's working?"

"Not much. But I can bounce a simple high-frequency beam off something. Why?"

"I want you to track that cloud. Or whatever it is. I want to know where it will end up. And I want to know before the hearing reconvenes tomorrow morning."

"Tall order," said Systems. "I'm not sure I have the requisite wherewithal."

"Then cobble your where together, withal," said Gross.

"I will pay the costs and fines," Gross announced to the High Council the next day.

"A wise decision," the chairbeing said, smiling. "We will even take your personal bank draft. Of course, you will not be permitted to take off until it clears."

"Of course. But it would be simpler to deduct it from my bill when you pay me."

A puzzled silence intervened before the chairbeing said, "What did you say?"

"You will probably be needing my services as a worldscaper before long. That anomalous cloud I ran into out in space has entered your solar system and will in the not-too-distant future insinuate itself between the orbit of this planet and your sun, thereby cutting your yearly incident solar radiation just about in half."

Consternation rumbled around the great circular bench.

"Yes," Gross went on, "your planet is about to undergo a radical change in climate, with resultant violent disruptions of the planetary ecology. I'm afraid your rain forest is doomed. It will die off very quickly."

"You keep telling us about this cloud," the chairbeing said. "What is it, exactly?"

"Near as I can figure," Gross said, "it's a puff of dark matter."

"Dark matter?"

"Yes. Predicted by some cosmological theories but never observed, at least not up close. It's not matter, and it's not antimatter, and it's almost undetectable. It's the ballast of the universe, lending its gravitational energy to the task of 'closing' the universe spatially. But forget cosmology for a minute. All it amounts to is a big dark, dirty smear of stuff that's going to play hell with your sunlight. You'll have to come down from your pure solar energy–based economy—"

"We use geothermal energy, too," the chairbeing said.

"Good, but I'll bet geothermal isn't enough to make up the difference. Anyway, you are headed for a very cold planetary environment. You need some greenhouse warming."

"Greenhouse warming!" The shock was palpable.

"Yes. I realize it's an old bugbear with you people, but you'll have to face it. You need to pump billions of tons of carbon dioxide into your atmosphere. That will heat everything up nicely. Now, we can do that with nanotechnology very easily. Once I release a few of my molecular machines to do the work, they'll replicate by the trillions in your oceans and strip carbon out of seashells and fish bones and whatnot, link it with two oxygen molecules, and release the gas into the atmosphere. Now, as to food production—I think you need to start up some old-fashioned agriculture. You'll need to clear vast areas of rain forest—"

"Unthinkable!"

"But feasible," Gross said. "Again, with nanotech, I can turn that entire forest into compost in a matter of months. You'll have incredibly rich soil as a result. You can then start planting a staple crop."

"This is an outrage!" one of the Council members shouted.

"Blasphemy!"

"Sorry," Gross said, "but you people are facing a grim set of options. You will probably starve to death eventually if you don't act now."

"We wish to confer among ourselves," the chairbeing said.

Gross lit up a cigar and sat watching the High Council of the Conservatorship debate the issue in mime. It was a spirited debate, but the voices of reason seemed to prevail in the end.

"How much will your services cost us, Mr. Gross?" the chairbeing wanted to know.

"I have prepared an estimate," Gross said. "Systems, please upload."

The chairbeing's face fell. "We can't afford it," she said.

"You're broke?" Gross nodded sagely. "That's the way it is with planet-bound utopias. I've seen it over and over. High ideals, but they all operate in the red for years until they finally lurch into bankruptcy. Well, tell you what I'm going to do. I can hire myself out to you on a consulting basis, while you guys tackle the job the old-fashioned way."

"Old-fashioned way?"

"Yes. Burn the forest. That will give you enough CO_2 to fend off total freezing. I might throw in some nanotech assist, purely out of charity, to give you a proper hothouse."

"B-b-burn the rain forest?"

"Yes. I'm afraid you'll have to. Almost all of it. Though you may keep some reserve in the tropical zones. The rest of it will die anyway."

"What else needs to be done?"

"Well, your ocean ecologies are all out of whack. Those big leviathan critters are predatory. They don't eat krill, like their earthly counterparts. They prey on vertebrate sea life. As a result, you have no fish in those oceans. You could stock with terran life-forms and have a dandy fishing industry, if you kill off most of the whaleoids. Everything's out of whack. And the water's fairly frothy with plankton. Too much, producing far too much oxygen. So, you have to do two things. Depress the whaleoid population, and rip off a layer or two of ozone to kill some of the plankton. For that last job, I can give you a deal on a couple of million tons of chlorofluorocarbons."

"Oh my God," the chairbeing said.

"It goes against your religion, I know," Gross said. "But you're not the first people to have your ideals go crashing against the hard facts of reality. And that's not all you have to do. You also need . . . "

Gross and the Council struck a deal. Technicians arrived at the landing site to help get the lander in shape for takeoff. A team of technicians made preparations to rendezvous in orbit with the planeteering starship and help Gross fix it. The inhabitants hid their technological capabilities well. They had spacefaring vessels aplenty. They simply did not like to use them.

In return for such consideration, Gross would consult on the job of getting the planet into shape for the new epoch of reduced solar radiation. The charges against Gross were dropped, and the fines and assessments levied against Gross Enterprises, Inc., were forgiven. The liens were quashed.

It was the night before departure. Gross was in the cockpit of the lander, doing a last-minute check of the flight plan's orbital mechanics, when the perimeter alarm went off.

"More visitors," he muttered. "First they leave you to die, then they won't leave you alone."

He got up and went aft to the main hatch. Sending the outer door sliding back, he stepped into the airlock and hit the outer hatch's open button.

The hatch *whooshed* up and Gross found a gun barrel in his face.

"You'll never take off, planetbuster," said the young man at the other end of the gun.

"Ah, zealots," Gross said, puffing on his cigar. "Zealous for the Regulation." He peered into the darkness. "About an even apostle's dozen of you, I see."

"We won't let you destroy this planet," said a gun-toting young woman. She and her compatriots looked alike in their forest-green coveralls. Even their faces were curiously of a piece. They all appeared to be related in some way. Maybe they were.

"Your government doesn't agree," Gross said.

"We don't care what the Council says," the young man said. "They've betrayed the ideals of the Conservatorship."

"You're going to be in a lot of trouble, young man," Gross said.

"We're willing to sacrifice ourselves," the young woman informed him.

"And me, too," Gross said. "I suppose you'll have to kill me."

"No choice," said another idealistic whelp. They were indeed young, Gross noted. Average age about twenty-five.

"What's wrong with your boots, son?"

"You . . . huh?"

"Your boots. Look."

The young man lifted one foot. The sole of his boot fell off. He grabbed the heel, and it came free in his hand. He looked up fiercely. "What the hell's going on?"

"Little machines, son. My little molecular machines are at work out there, breaking down the tree stumps. You all have them all over your shoes. They will attack almost anything fibrous. When they eat through the shoes, they might start on your flesh. You'll have to run like hell away from here, shed your boots, and return home barefoot. Don't worry. The machines will disassemble themselves in a few hours. You don't have to worry about tracking them into your homes. Be sure to leave your shoes at the edge of the clearing, though. Now run along."

The others were discovering that their footwear was being eaten away with alarming speed.

"He's right! Let's get the hell out of here!"

"Let's kill him first!"

Gross said, "But then you won't know how to deal with the little machines out there that *won't* disassemble themselves."

"What?" they gasped collectively. The terror word, unspoken, hovered like a dark, menacing cloud. *Nanoweapons!* They all seemed to deflate a little, fear in their faces.

Gross continued, "A little insurance for me. You'll track the little buggers into your homes, and they'll be a nuisance, disassembling every stick and board down to its component molecules. You'll be homeless inside of a week, and then the little darlings will start in on your food supply. Unless I tell the authorities how to deactivate them."

The young man holding the gun barrel to Gross's face pulled back the firing bolt of his weapon, a fairly primitive slug-thrower. "You'll die, you bastard."

"Go home to your parents," Gross said. "You've had enough fun for one night."

Most of them could sense defeat. They lowered their weapons.

"Come on, Greentree," one of them said to the young man threatening Gross. "Forget about him."

Greentree thought about it a long time, while his intended victim regarded him impassively. Then he lowered his weapon. "You rotten, no-good bastard." He looked his adversary up and down, with no little disgust. "You fat, ugly-looking creep. You're so . . . so . . . *gross!*"

"That's the name. Now run along."

They all ran from the clearing.

Gross locked up and went to bed.

"Good thing they fell for the bluff about the nasty buggers," he said before dozing off.

"Good thing the Guild forbids nanotech weaponry," Systems commented.

"Good thing," Gross murmured.

The lander lifted off next morning without incident, spewing noxious fumes along with a thin trail of radioactive particles. The thousands of plants and animals who watched did not seem to mind in the least.

THE PERFORMANCE OF A LIFETIME

Arthur Byron Cover

Meanwhile, back in the solar system, there's trouble in the old town tonight. Leave it to the author of *Autumn Angels* and *An East Wind Coming* to focus attention on the eccentricities that make up human character. A link exists between evil and art that Cover covers all too well. Any similarities between the following proceedings and any recent high-profile criminal trials are, of course, so coincidental they're pure. ABC doesn't stand for Anybody but Clinton. It stands for a writer whose talent is so individual that he survived being workshopped at Clarion.

I don't know what I can add to the commentary about the case of *The People of Free Space v. Harry C. Barbusse* that hasn't already been said ad nauseam, so for this account I'll stick as close as egotistically possible to the facts. My regular readers will notice few observations I haven't already made for *The Hickory Ether,* the leading newsline service for the Bakuninist Habitat. I wrote many "spin" columns on the case because that particular habitat, where Barbusse had been raised, was the first to be victimized by how he put his peculiar ideas of art and rebellion into practice.

So I covered the aftereffects of the first attack and I covered all the subsequent attacks elsewhere. I covered the manhunt for the culprit and chased just as many blind leads as did the various factions of various habitat authorities, who in the early days were notorious for their staggering inability to cooperate with one another. And I was just as surprised as everyone else when Barbusse gave it all up, revealing his identity at last, and surrendered, even though from where I sat it seemed he could run the spaceways forever without a trace. I was in the courtroom for the entire trial and I witnessed the punishment. I am still in the process of covering what came next, the shocking denouement to the affair that has made the name of Barbusse synonymous with death, degradation, and betrayal.

Throughout I spoke with most of the major participants—except for the judge, of course—and snagged several exclusive interviews with the defendant that propelled *The Hickory Ether* to the lead in coverage of the affair. The visual media, of course, clamored for my sound bites. By the time it was over, my sunken beady eyes were as familiar to the general audience as was Barbusse's open, innocent face. Not that it mattered. How could I care, when my fleeting moments of fame were bought at the cost of sixteen million deaths and God knows how many survivors?

What struck me the most about Barbusse was his quiet, intense aura of normality. He was invariably courteous, even to the rudest, roughest guards, and he certainly had no compunction about laughing at a minor joke at his own expense. He was a spiritual man, too, and a staunch believer in libertarian principles—he always carried with him discs of *The Collected Remembrances of Futures Past* by the collected minds of the Dalai Lamas and *The Libertarian Ideology and the Makings of Colonial Constitutions in the Interstellar Revolutionary Era* by Russell "Roland" Kirk IV. In addition to his knowledge of the sciences—his unfortunate, tragic knowledge— he was well-versed in twentieth-century popular music and cinema, and had an intuitive grasp of the major artistic movements spanned by the more reputable habitats, as well as a working knowledge of the important political and cultural philosophers since the days of the original *Federalist Papers*. Although fond of quoting the early existentialists, such as Sartre, Blake, and Nietzsche, he always did so haltingly, as if attempting to grasp—or rethink—the implications of the concept in question anew every time he uttered it.

Physically he was a slight man, with the elongated limbs and narrow torso typical of those who've spent their formative years on the smaller habitats where the gravitational spins are weak. I have already mentioned his open, innocent face. Otherwise his features gave no hint of the strength of character (however misguided) it must have required to carry his plans to completion. His voice had an odd nasal pitch, but the power of his ideas, the clarity of their expression, and of course, the certain knowledge of his heinous deeds, forced one to take him seriously. His eyes—hard, hawk-like—suggested that for him the gap between desire and will was nonexistent. But they were a poet's eyes, and certainly did not belong to someone who surely will go down in history as a combination of Genghis Khan, Hitler, Jack the Ripper, and Benedict Arnold.

Naturally the criminal of the century inspired the trial of the century, or should I call it the circus of the century? The trial touched on but did not necessarily illuminate many social issues of the era. It seemed its every aspect—from the questionable use of the insanity defense to the proper role of art and science in a healthy society—inspired a plethora of commentary from expert and common man alike. The hyperwaves were full of the nonsense, and I say this as a man who definitely contributed his share. The entire affair, I suspect, would have been educational, a consciousness raising event of the first order, were it not for the inescapable fact of those sixteen million deaths. No living Spacer, I dare say, emerged from the litany of tragedies untouched. Certainly every living soul on the Bakuninist Habitat knows someone who perished as a result of Barbusse's lunatic theories.

Once Barbusse was in custody, every habitat who had suffered at his hands demanded the right to extradite him and try him fairly before they punished him as cruelly and inhumanely as their law permitted. The fear that Barbusse might commit suicide—or die of natural causes—before matters of jurisprudence could be worked out finally prompted all parties to compromise. Since Barbusse was in the hands of the Nuovo Monticello authorities, the trial would be held on their satellite according to the customs of their native laws, but with prosecution and defense teams drawn from legal communities throughout the entire spectrum of interstellar civilization. So if Barbusse's crimes alone hadn't been enough to warrant unprecedented interest in the proceedings, then the resulting "super team-up" of legal personalities surely would have.

The media spotlight shone like a nova blast on every participant from the day of the first press conference announcing the teams. Heading the prosecution was the ancient, frail Sidh Boumedienme, the former holy man, statesman, warrior, and philosopher most renowned in legal circles for his personal vendetta against the gangster-blackmailer Alfonso Ciccone, who'd held entire colonies hostage to his oxygen barons. (They say Sidh personally administered the lethal dosage to Ciccone.) His waning stamina aided by hormone drugs in his alfalfa soup, Sidh Boumedienme denounced the hideous crimes in poetic, unforgettable terms, anticipated every defense move admirably, and charmed every defense witness until they were off guard, then undercut their testimony with the finesse of a mongoose going after a boa. Only occasionally did the more technical presentations make him appear confused and addled, but he was fortunate in that the latest scientific advances tend to confuse most everyone these days. And of course he could always depend on the other members of his team to shore up his weaknesses.

Second-in-command was the attorney whose nickname came to be the "Speaker for the Dead," because it was her task to humanize as many victims as possible during the three weeks allotted to that portion of the people's case. This was one of many ironies in the trial, because the people's speaker had previously been famous for extracurricular activities that had more to do with the joys of life than the cold of the dead, and indeed, in order to mollify the objections of those whose societies she'd liberated against their will by convincing their courts to strike down various blue laws, she took an oath not to seduce a single man or woman for the duration. Judging from how the rapport between her and

Sidh grew through the weeks, I don't believe she kept it.

Then again, who in his right mind would expect the great, the formidable, the voluptuous, the very healthy Ju-hai Jones to refrain from embracing the viscera of life? After all, she'd once described herself as the turbulent-waters-run-deepest type, and she's spent most of her life trying to prove it. She left little to prove after this case. Her voice trembled just enough as she told the court of life after life cut short, or how colony after colony was traumatized and crippled by the great swath of death that swept through the Federation. Her wrathful indignation always lurked beneath her cool polite manner, and her compassion for the terrible suffering—even for those of the neo-Victorian societies, whom she had opposed in the past—was awe inspiring. Sidh was impressed; for her he stepped aside to allow her to summarize the people's case at the end. Ju-hai Jones's story of an alternate timeline, of the good that might have been done had but a fraction of those sixteen million lost lived their lives to fruition, instead of having their hopes and dreams cruelly snuffed out, brought virtually the entire courtroom—and the millions watching over the hyperwave—to tears.

With the rather notable exception of the defendant, who merely sat in his bulletproof Plexiglas booth and listened indifferently, as he had listened to the entire trial. Basically unmoved, he wasn't exactly stoic, for occasionally a slight smile was discernible, to the futile indignation of all who noticed.

And the judge, naturally, was unmoved as well, but I'm getting ahead of myself.

Rounding out the prosecution team was the scientific expert Titus Rasholnikov, renowned in legal circles for his uncanny ability to achieve epiphanies while under the influence of a host of psychedelic substances. Although the Jeffies officially frowned on such things, the compromise permitted the lawyers from different jurisdictions with different customs some latitude in the realm of diplomatic immunity, and so Rasholnikov functioned in court just as he did on his native satellite Ecstasy, that is, he was stoned to the max via innumerable simultaneous methods, ranging from

the sledgehammer of LSD to the more subtle, mechanistic ma-
nipulations of cyberwave implants. Perhaps it affected his performance, but if so, then a cold and sober Rasholnikov would have
possessed the most gifted mind in the history of mankind. The
blitzed Rasholnikov mind was brilliant enough. Throughout the
trial he made connections no one else could have imagined; he
pulled together the threads of Barbusse's tortured psychology with
the skill of a master novelist, demonstrating how a pair of self-
centered parents failed to note how their son dissected small animals without providing them the benefit of a painless death first.
Their parental indifference continued through Barbusse's adolescence, when the boy's artistic talents bloomed but his subject matter became ghoulish and violent, nearly all depicting the results of
harm brought to the helpless. By the time they noticed something
was dreadfully the matter with their son, it was already too late. An
unnatural attachment between art and death was formed in Barbusse's mind, and Rasholnikov connected him to several unsolved
murders during his university days. It is interesting to note, however, that in the end even Rasholnikov could not answer the question of why an artist would seek fulfillment in murdering his
potential audience. "I don't believe the defendant is bad," he said
at one point. "Just evil."

"Or perhaps he's just misunderstood," said the head of the
defense team, Lord Zachary Grynstreet, whose defense strategy involved attacking every piece of evidence presented against Barbusse to raise the possibility that he was a compulsive confessor
being framed for crimes actually committed by unknown, sinister
figures working in collusion with the authorities. Significantly,
however, Grynstreet refused to name those who had aroused his
suspicions, and he never did offer a reasonable explanation as to
why Barbusse's ship log indicated he'd visited each satellite a week
or month before a major terrorist incident.

Rotund and unctuous, his body seemingly only muscled where
it was absolutely necessary to keep it functioning, Lord Grynstreet
belonged to that class of Spacer who could not abide gravity, and

thus was forced to wear pneumatic clothing to counteract its effects in traditional artificial environments. So instead of sitting at his desk, Lord Grynstreet floated in its general vicinity, a task that doubtlessly would have been accomplished with ease had the defense team's desk not been located directly beneath an air-conditioning vent. The constant breeze made stationary floating difficult, if not impossible, and eventually the judge, noting the irritation of others, ordered Grynstreet tethered, like a zeppelin, to the floor. That more or less did the trick, though whenever Ms. Jones wanted to rattle Grynstreet, all she had to do was look in his direction and fondle her hatpin.

The number two man on the defense team was the misshapen, bitter dwarf Smiley Verboten, whose tendency to rant and rave was often rendered comical by his habit of standing on chairs or tables and waving his arms like a mad semaphore operator. He possessed some talent as an orator, but never once did he, during the trial, manage to match gesture with sentence. This type of behavior is believed to be endemic to the freakish denizens of the Lodge, and it was plain Verboten sincerely believed in his client's innocence; he pursued his half-baked conspiracy theories with a vengeance, as if passion alone would move the court to ignore an asteroid of evidence to the contrary and simply jettison the people's case. (Interestingly enough, it was rumored Verboten had obtained personality implants on the black market, augmenting his usual skills with psychic reconstructions of the great defense lawyers Clarence Darrow and F. Lee Bailey. This accusation might explain why his conduct appeared so schizophrenic on occasion, but of course it has never been proven.)

Grynstreet and Verboten got along pretty well, but they had little choice, because they could never be sure if the next sentence from the third member of the team would be helpful or disastrous for their cause. She was Mistress Prudence Khai of the Druid Habitat, a High Priestess in a cult of machine worshipers and a self-proclaimed seeker of truth who, according to her press releases, sought to sift through the deliberate lies of fiction and fantasy for the glittering generalities that were the hidden common denominator of the arts. In her view, all art forms were created equal, and if that art form happened to include the techniques of terrorism, so much the better, for it was not the purpose of the arts to heighten the awareness of the moment, to make life sweeter and more meaningful? "And what could be sweeter or more meaningful," she was fond of asking, "then the last moments of a life?" What indeed?

Whenever Mistress Khai spoke of the possibility that Barbusse was hopelessly insane, she inadvertently implied that on a deeper, truer lever, he was the sanest man Free Space had ever known. A combative sort, she normally had no qualms about debating those journalists whose negative commentaries on her ideas caught her attention. Once, however, I wrote a column postulating how disappointed she might be were her legal comrades to uncover undeniable proof that the case against Barbusse was due to mistaken identity or a false confession; then she would be unable to speak so glowingly of the nondescript little man who had peered into the abyss and confronted us all with the undeniable truth that the only purpose in life, indeed, the only salvation and the only pleasure, came from dying the good death, in as much agony as possible. Oddly, she ignored me completely, though I know the publication of the column could not have escaped the attention of her coterie of press clippers. I like to think I had struck a nerve, though of course the possibility remains that she was simply too busy to confront every journalist who wrote something she disapproved of.

Mistress Khai stood on firmer ground when she spoke of Barbusse's freedom to believe what he wished. But regardless of how philosophically credible she was at any given moment, she was at all times an imposing figure. Tall, full figured, with long, muscular limbs, she usually wore to court a semitransparent robe that offered males and open-minded females alike tantalizing glimpses of a sixty-year-old body replete with erotic potential. Her headdress, as well as her many bracelets and necklaces, contained odd-shaped parts for machines I could not recognize, though I had no problem perceiving the parts' inventive erotic imagery. Normally one did not encounter this mode of dress in a Nuovo Monticello courtroom, but again, much leeway was made to accommodate native custom. And, as some of the more exploitative journalists were fond of pointing out, had Barbusse been tried in a Druid court, his guilt or innocence would have been determined by how well (or poorly) he performed in a three-day food, drug, and sex orgy. Mistress Khai always did say the Stag God did not bless those who had taken blood not freely given.

She also proved herself the nerviest of all the lawyers in at least one respect: She was not afraid to look the judge in the eye. I dare say she was the only one in the courtroom who was not afraid. The Druids are said to believe death is but a gateway to a higher plane of awareness, and fortunate indeed are those whose consciousnesses can travel back and forth at will between the realms of the living and the dead. Surely Mistress Khai must have had a profound respect for the judge, because he was a guest in a realm she could only glimpse occasionally.

Which is to say, Judge Egmond Bysshe Disraeli was very, very dead.

He was one of the frozen, slated to be revived if there ever was a cure for the many cancers that once festered throughout his entire body, but which were now held solidly in check. Actually, if half the rumors about his confidential medical condition are true, I suspect his body is good only for compost and he will only be revived once his brain is transplanted to a mechanical body when that technology is perfected in another century or two. The notion of using a frozen judge to try the Barbusse case came about when the compromising diplomats decided that the crimes involved were so unspeakably heinous, so monstrously inhuman, that only a jurist whose connection to humanity was tenuous at best could adjudicate the case fairly. There was never any doubt that Barbusse would be punished; the diplomats' only real concern was that the trial be conducted properly so bleeding-heart historians, for whom principles were more important than people, wouldn't have anything to complain about in the future. So the selection of a famous twenty-second century jurist who even in life had dispensed justice unburdened with sympathy either for man or society was deemed perfect. Till then, many historians had wondered if society would ever see a jurist of Disraeli's like again; what a delicious irony that it turned out to be Disraeli himself.

The judge's mere presence in the courtroom infused the proceedings with a majesty that offset—though at times just barely—the circus atmosphere that sometimes pervaded the judicial process. In a word, it was awesome, simply awesome to watch every morning as the people in the courtroom rose respectfully, almost worshipfully when the bailiff wheeled Judge Disraeli to his position behind the bench. All day he looked down on us with yellow unseeing eyes, yet we the people, victimized and wrathful, remained on our best behavior, cowering like sheep in the presence of an angry deity. Perhaps we feared he would decide Barbusse's crimes weren't so bad after all, that he had committed a mere social transgression that didn't merit the involvement of the state. Rumor had it that the ability to make such a decision was a condition he had made upon learning the circumstances of his revival.

Rumor also had it that he intensely disliked his limitations of movement and perception, and that he couldn't wait to be completely dead again. If so, that was certainly understandable, for he spent his wakeful hours standing naked and upright while enmeshed in a block of methane ice. The ice at the back of his head was chipped away, a strip of frozen skin rolled back, and part of his skull cut out like a knot in a block of wood so that visual and audio input from the outside world could be transmitted to his brain via several microscopic cybernetic implants. Those portions of his brain responsible for processing information, including the areas capable of deductive reasoning and retrieving academic memory, had been carefully thawed just enough to function, but not enough to revive those areas of his brain housing personal memory. This was thought best due to fears that a frozen jurist, revived against his will for a purpose he had not consented to, would already be quite alienated from society; there was no reason to compound the risk, especially since he would be a stranger even to his descendants.

In any case, communication between the judge and his descendants—who were said to be have received some of the coveted seats for the general public, but anonymously—was unlikely, because his only communication with the outside world was achieved with the assistance of the bailiff, a telepathic empath wired with a transistor radio that received the judge's words directly from his mind; the bailiff then spoke them, exactly, to the court. Presumably his inflection was identical to how Judge Disraeli imagined it, in his frozen mind, for surely no one with human feelings, which the bailiff presumably possessed, could have spoken so coldly, so dispassionately, even while lamenting the loss of sixteen million lives. But, as the press emphasized throughout the proceedings, it was important to keep in mind at all times that Judge Disraeli's emotional being was frozen along with the rest of his body; for him the notion of sixteen million deaths was no more or less abstract or fathomable than the death of a single man.

After the trial, the judge was returned to an oblivion that is at the moment eternal, but one day may prove fleeting. Some say in anger his body should be melted down at once, that he bears his share of direct responsibility for what happened after the sentencing, but of course he had no idea what Barbusse had planned, no more than any man did. No one could have foreseen the result of what, to me, seemed like a punishment both poetic and well deserved. No single man deserves to bear the brunt of that guilt. I can only hope that Judge Disraeli is revived in a distant future when the history of these troubled times survives only as ancient legend. Then, perhaps, he shall face a destiny as free as he deserves—

—A small enough reward, for maintaining order as well as he did, better than any truly living man could have, I wager. Disraeli's unwavering, albeit unearthly, commitment to a fair trial enabled the prosecution to present the first coherent account of Barbusse's horrific career, and the defense to present the first coherent rebuttal. The full story of what came out in the trial is naturally one of the most familiar in Free Space, and has been dealt with substantially in many different venues, not only those of respectable news media, but in entertainment media including holomovies, dreampark scenarios, and in at least one fast-action scientific prose romance. Soon I'll be embarking on a book-length personal memoir on my association with the Barbusse affair, so my opinions on most topics must be reserved for that project, for which I've been paid a large advance. Consequently I won't spend a great deal of time and energy on an original approach in the following account, which I'll make as short and as painless as possible.

The Bakuninist people were infected for a week before the first symptons began to show. Suddenly large numbers of patients, weak and short of breath, were beginning to show up at the med stations. They all had cases of advanced tuberculosis, caused by a mutated, drug-resistant strain of the virus—the mother of all tuberculosis viruses, it came to be called. The Bakuninist station was quarantined and three thousand died before a cure could be found. The epidemiologists later determined the virus had been introduced artificially, via the air-recycling system.

For a change, all the diverse peoples of Free Space were united in spirit as they reeled in shock from the news. Three thousand had died as the result of a terrorist attack. The habitats' governing bodies all agreed that the parties responsible for this heinous act should be tracked down and punished. Unfortunately, the size of the terrorist cell, its group identity, and its motivation were all still unknown when Null-A was struck by a virus that was basically a form of communicable diabetes. Six hundred people developed the symptoms of severe hyperinsullinism—dizziness and convulsions, with some lapsing into comas, never to awake. Most people, myself included, then believed that two sudden appearances of mysterious plagues in two separate colonies was a coincidence rather than solely the work of terrorists; perhaps the first attack was, but surely not the second, which based on the information available at the time could be explained away as being caused by some dietary problem. Furthermore, what could possibly be the political purpose of attacking two such socially and philosophically divergent habitats? And why would the modus operandi, resulting in a totally different medical problem developing in the victims, be changed so radically between attacks?

The debate raged in all the media for about three days, then came the third plague, as certain Druids came down with virulent strains of AIDS (traced to originate in the blood supply) before a mass orgy was held in celebration of the solar solstice; several hundred were believed to have been infected during the very first week, and of course many more hundreds were infected before the epidemiologists even figured out that a terrible plague was sweeping through the station. Not only did ten thousand people die by the end of the year, but the Druids were forced to restrict their sexual practices and increase their rate of blood tests to protect themselves against future infection, severely impacting their entire culture.

For the Druids, nothing has been the same, but even while that situation was developing, other habitats were struck by severe pestilences, unique and drug-resistant forms of bronchitis, cholera, dysentery, hepatitis, mononucleosis, cancer, jaundice, gout, and many, many more. Especially hard hit was the meat-producing colony of Tombstone, where everyone had a great deal of beef in their diet; suddenly people began dying right and left from heart disease, even the children. The cause was traced to hitherto-undetected chemicals in the beef—the livestock had been infected by toxic additives to the hydroponic grain harvests of Wellville. The economies of both habitats, not to mention their populations, were devastated, and many colonies, who purchased beef and grain from Tombstone and Wellville, respectively, also reported increased incidences of deadly heart disease. The economy of Milken also took a serious dive, when most of the major players in their stockbroking industry came down with cases of Epstein-Barr that left them bedridden and, at times, too morose to live. Perhaps the most severe psychological damage in those early days of the many plagues came to the people of Gordie, the mercenary station whose macho men and butch women suddenly came down with crippling post-traumatic stress syndrome; as the Gordies were infamous for their distrust of the psychiatric profession, they refused all forms of counseling, with the result that many committed suicide or just went plain bonkers, killing friends and loved ones without warning or shooting into crowds at random, taking as many people with them as possible before they were taken out themselves, one way or the other.

That was the beginning, the first year, the year during which any feeling of security the people of Free Space might have had was demonstrated to be empirically false, the year during which every single Spacer believed that on any day he might get sick and die without warning, or worse, he might witness an unkind fate visited on his loved ones. If there was one thing the plagues proved, it was that the individuals responsible didn't care how many innocent children were victimized. Obviously they were only interested in creating as much random death and suffering as possible, and in that regard they certainly succeeded.

The plagues lasted for five and a half years. During that time the authorities of the many habitats engaged in cooperative behavior and exchange of information on an unprecedented scale, all in an effort to capture the terrorists. During that time the citizens reported all signs of suspicious behavior—no one had any scruples when it came to ratting on relatives, lovers, or friends—but all leads proved fruitless. The parties responsible were obviously quite clever—and undoubtedly self-sufficient.

There were all sorts of theories. The hyperwaves and the nets were rife with them. Anyone with half a brain—and unfortunately there were a lot more than usual, thanks to both the diseases and the emotional stress—had a theory. As time went on, some of the more implausible theories attracted followings, and many individuals adept at capitalizing on people's fears became the focus of cult followings. I confess, for a time I believed aliens bent on conquering the solar system were responsible for the many atrocities, a theory that temporarily seemed even more likely when some individuals, eventually exposed as copycat terrorists, rigged up some engines to asteroids and sent them rocketing toward preordained targets. Habitats were thrown off course, domes were shattered, many more thousands died.

And still the biological attacks continued. Toward the end the perpetrators became even more imaginative, using viral attacks or leaking strange nerve gases into colonies that affected not the bodies but the minds of those whose immune systems had thus far proven to be the strongest, or the luckiest. The Moran habitat was struck by an LSD gas that sent everyone on transcendental trips that to this day have not receded. And Valis was corrupted by a wandering virus that traveled from brain to brain, taking out pieces of one mind and scrambling them into others. That particular plague sent an unprecedented chill down the spines of every thinking citizen. It was bad enough to fear for your life every waking day without having to worry about the sanctity of your memory, too.

The law-enforcement community privately despaired at ever capturing the culprit(s). They recognized that cases like these—meaning those where the criminal(s) successfully blended in with society—were solved through a combination of hard work and luck; the hard work they had certainly provided, but where was the luck? After five years of the investigating, the scientific examining, and the trampling of citizens' inalienable rights, they should have gotten a lucky break. Yet there was no break to be had—

—Until Barbusse docked his private space vehicle at Nuovo Monticello, quietly went through customs like any other ordinary citizen, and then walked straight to the nearest constable and calmly confessed to being the heinous scumbag responsible for sixteen million deaths. Naturally the constable didn't believe him, but as there was a six-year mandatory sentence for falsely confessing to being a biological terrorist, he had a good reason for taking Barbusse in.

Then Barbusse provided the proof. As Sidh Boumedienme, Juhai Jones, and Rasholnikov so deftly presented in court, Barbusse had during his adolescence conceived the ambition of becoming a performance artist. I have already mentioned his unfortunate association of death with the arts. Because of that association, Barbusse decided to dedicate his life to practicing terrorism as an art form. He had no political agenda per se, he was merely interested in writing an epic with an ocean of blood. He decided that fictional or symbolic blood wasn't good enough; only by spilling real blood could he realize the artistic dreams he had conceived of as his destiny. Naturally fulfilling these artistic ambitions required planning and scientific genius, which he unfortunately possessed in abundance. For years he repressed his true personality, pretending to be idealistic, altruistic, almost simplistically naive, dedicated to knowledge and to freedom. After he left the Bakuninists and entered Nuovo Monticello U., society saw him as just another socially awkward, supertalented nerd with latent delusions of grandeur, that is to say, just your average potential scientist.

His status as a potential scientific great—which he established early on, thanks to the speed in which he outstripped the skills and knowledge of his professors—attracted several women (and in a few cases, men) to him, a circumstance that he took advantage of by selecting a few to become acquainted with, socially or sexually, and then ruthlessly murdering them, when time and circumstance permitted. He was not only interested in gauging his reactions to committing murder (which he had no problem with, no surprise there) but to test his skills at diverting suspicion from himself. In that regard he proved to be a quick study, and then a master. Not a single detective deduced him to be the perpetrator of any one of the ten corpses he left behind at N.M.U., although there had been a few close calls in the early days. If suspicion had come his way, then Barbusse's ambitions would have remained only dreams, and like the Marquis de Sade, he would have been forced to be content with merely writing down his most vicious fantasies. As it was, he knew he had already succeeded in becoming a master criminal; now all that remained was making his dreams a reality.

And that, unfortunately, turned out to be easy for a man of his chameleon talents. While studying for his Ph.D. at E. John Stark U. on the Dagon habitat, he adroitly assumed two personalities. By day, he was a withdrawn, antisocial dweeb, but by night he became a debonair gigolo who haunted the ritzy nightclubs in search of older men and women in need of diversion. Soon, for the first time in his life, he was raking in real credits, but not nearly enough to realize his dreams. He formed an attachment with a wealthy industrialist, and then convinced him to rewrite his will, leaving him a large stipend through which he could continue his research. Meanwhile, Barbusse's microbiological talents were proving to be more remarkable than even he had dreamed. He was growing cultures other scientists had thought impossible to grow, and he was synthesizing microbes others had yet to conceive of. And he had learned how to manufacture new strains of psychedelic drugs in his spare time. Entire counterculture movements were influenced by Barbusse's discoveries in that area, but he didn't care, all he was interested in was the money and the criminal contacts. When his wealthy industrialist friend suddenly developed a degenerative nerve disease under mysterious circumstances, Barbusse had not only signaled the beginning of his ability to kill via biological agents, he had also terminated his entire association with normal society. After collecting his inheritance, he went totally underground, harboring with drug and weapon smugglers, manufacturing new illicit substances, and hoarding his assets until the day came when he could buy his own private spaceship and equip it entirely with contraband laboratory equipment. Then it was as if he'd disappeared off the face of the solar system. Not even his criminal contacts heard of him again. Little did they realize during their association with him, they had had more reason to fear him than any lawman.

Soon afterward the "terrorist" attacks began. Barbusse lived in space, studying, experimenting, learning all he could about the habitats and thinking up what he considered to be artistically justified methods of inflicting punishment on them. Every few months he discreetly docked at a habitat for supplies, but of course, he was careful never to bring anything incriminating onto a habitat's turf, and he stayed away entirely from those who reserved the right to inspect docked vehicles at will, even though they were technically still in Free Space and were theoretically beyond the jurisdiction of any colonial authority. It was typical of Barbusse's remarkable discipline that he did not waver from this pattern of behavior, that he did not allow himself to become sloppy or grow overconfident. He kept a huge stash of gold reserve on his ship, which he used to purchase supplies, and whenever the subject of what he did for a living came up during his few terse conversations with merchants or the occasional hooker, he said he was a trader, but implied he was a smuggler and thought it would be indiscreet if he said anything more. People understood that kind of reticence, even during those times when the fear of death was thick in the air.

Clearly Barbusse could have operated for several more years if he'd maintained his high standards of avoiding suspicion and managed not to kill himself by being accidentally exposed to one of his own experimental viruses. Since his cooperation with the authorities had basically centered on revealing exactly what he had done and not on his motivations, his reasons for giving himself up remained a mystery. Even his own lawyers were forced to admit he had exhibited no signs of remorse for his deeds, and so unlike some mass murderers, had not come to the conclusion that his killing spree must be stopped. Indeed, when I interviewed Barbusse, he spoke nostalgically, almost glowingly of the days when he had been free to do as he pleased, when he had proved his worth as a performance artist for all time.

Mistress Khai, however, had hinted in a news conference that when the time came for Barbusse to speak, just before Judge Disraeli passed sentence, then the reasons for his sudden surrender would all become clear. As the defense's case had proven to be extraordinarily weak (but what had they to work with?), and as the verdict was never in doubt, the media had no choice but to pounce on the story of a potential revelation to build up audience suspense. One would think, I suppose, that the emotional satisfaction of knowing the most heinous mass murderer in history was being punished by the highest civilized standards would be sufficiently satisfying to garner ratings and generate sells, but the mere possibility of audience indifference makes editors and advertisers nervous. We reporters pushed this angle because it was the only angle we had left. Why did Barbusse do it? Why did he surrender when he could have gone on for years? Had killing lost its allure? Was he tired of being a coward? Was he hoping for some kind of redemption? The psychologists and pundits could only guess.

Finally the time came when sentence was about to be passed. Barbusse stood in prison garb and in chains before the frozen judge, whose lifeless yellow eyes nevertheless appeared to look down piteously on the craven felon before them. The judge's descendants were quite pleased: This was indeed the stern authoritarian figure whose legacy of harsh discipline had so scarred their lives to this day! Perhaps, for them, seeing the judge at work had been a cathartic experience; for the rest of us, it had been the sight of justice reaching out from beyond the grave and ensuring that Free Space would remain a decent and safe stellar environment to raise our children and to perpetuate the pursuit of happiness. How wonderful it was, for both the surviving victims and those who had lost friends and loved ones during the attacks, to finally hear Judge Disraeli say, through those eerily dispassionate tones of his ballif:

"Prisoner, do you have any words to say on your own behalf before sentence is passed?"

The silence of the next few seconds seemed eternal, and the pundits like to say all the colonies froze in their orbits before Barbusse smiled and said:

"And do what? Confess my guilt? Tell the court I feel remorse for the supposed crimes I have committed? That is impossible. I have committed no crime, I have simply lived my life as a free man, and what I have done, I have done because I am free. The press has made much of the early existentialist philosophers I have read. It doesn't really say much about a man to list what books he reads, for what counts is the lessons a man draws from them. And I have noted these proto-space-age thinkers all share a common delusion: that a good man who is truly free will wish to do only good, will in fact do only good despite appearances to the contrary. Well, those mighty philosophers were indulging in elitist juvenile wish-fulfillment. I stand before you as proof of the error of their thinking. I am a man who is free and my only desire has been to indulge in my art as I perceived it, regardless of the consequences. This I admit proudly! I know what you are about to do, all that remains is for you to decide the method. Decide! I do not fear it or you."

Judge Disraeli waited until it became clear Barbusse had finished, then said, "Are those your words to the court? Did you really mean to say you have taken over sixteen million lives merely because it was possible for you to do so?"

"Absolutely!" Barbusse replied, almost cheerfully. "Besides, think of the good I've done for the survivors! Think of how much more precious life is to them, how much more they savor every living moment. You should understand that, if nothing else, Judge, because there will come a time when you shall savor every moment as they do today."

"That is it? That is the sum total of your reasoning? You killed sixteen million people—"

"Who were as intellectually asleep as they were on the day they were born. My illustrious prosecutor here has made much of the history that might have been had my 'victims' lived. I submit to you the opposite suggestion. Now that they are gone, life continues much as it had when they'd been alive. I submit further that history will remain unchanged by their erasure from this mortal plane. From what I have seen of the people of Free Space, they remain as much asleep as always. They care much about themselves, little about others. They care much about their freedom, but they care nothing about it when their security is at stake. And if someone has to die for them to feel secure, well, that's okay with them, so long as it happens on someone else's habitat. Really, the hypocrisy of society disgusts me! What good is freedom if you do nothing with it? What good is your vaunted intellectual greatness if you conceive of no grand designs? What difference is a life, if it is lived for nothing?"

Barbusse looked around the courtroom with wild, disdainful eyes. Everyone was shocked, more chilled to the bone than the judge, I think. The depths of his pathological loathing of mankind astounded us.

"Did you think your 'performance' would make Free Space a better place?" asked Judge Disraeli, with a sarcasm that not even the level tones of his empathic bailiff could disguise.

"I knew it would make a difference," said Barbusse slyly. "Though what kind of difference, for good or for ill, was of no consequence to me."

"I think I understand," said the judge. "Now you must understand, your statement has given me no choice. I must sentence you to death."

Barbusse shrugged. Obviously he'd expected that.

"All that remains is for the court to decide an acceptable means of execution."

"That, too, doesn't matter. In the end the result will be the same."

"Not necessarily. For the survivors' sake, and for the common good, there must be a sense that justice has been done, a sense of closure."

The people gasped collectively as Barbusse closed his fist and made motions as if he were masturbating.

"Is the prisoner intimating that he has no preferences as to the means of execution?"

Barbusse laughed. "Why should I?"

"The means must be prescribed by law, a limitation the court is certain must come as a great disappointment to the people of Free Space."

"I'm so upset!"

"The court suspects you are goading us for a reason, but no matter. Unbeknownst to you, your mind has been scanned during your dreams—"

"What? That's a violation of my civil liberties!"

"Not when there is a court order permitting it. Obviously nothing less than the most complete psychological profile of the most notorious criminal in history will help prevent such human aberrations in the future!"

Barbusse's complexion turned red with rage. He shook his fist at the judge, then to the court as a whole. "You scum! You can't insult me! I am not an aberration! I am a free artist!"

"You are condemned to die by the method *legal* surveillance of your dreams indicates is the one you most fear."

Barbusse gasped. "You don't mean—"

"This court has decided that three days hence, in accordance with the deepest fears the psychologists have been able to find in the hidden recesses of your psyche, you will be jettisoned into the stratosphere above the planet Earth without benefit of a space suit or a jet pack. There you shall fall until the friction of your contact with air sets you ablaze and you burn like a tiny shooting star until there is nothing left but atoms. May whatever deity whoever might exist have mercy on whatever soul you may still possess. This court is now—"

"Wait! That's a cruel and unusual punishment!" Barbusse turned to his lawyers. "Why aren't you arguing this for me?" They only shrugged, obviously relieved that their part in this affair was almost over.

"It is an entirely legal method of execution according to the penal code of the Earheart habitat."

Mistress Khai reluctantly cleared her throat. "Your Honor, may I address the court?"

Barbusse smiled with satisfaction as the judge agreed.

"You are correct," she said, "in that the denizens of the Earheart habitat permit free fall as a method of execution, but the prisoner is always granted the option of whether or not he wants a suit, and furthermore, he is allowed to dictate the specifications of the suit, in order that he may address the issue of how long he wants to cling to life."

Barbusse turned out to have very particular ideas about what kind of suit he wanted to die in. Perhaps in retrospect it should have been obvious that he had given some conscious thought to this matter, but by then the authorities were so glad that the execution would be carried out so soon that they gave no thought to his frame of mind. In any case, Barbusse's suit was woven from plastic-asbestos threads, the most flame-resistant clothing known to the habitats and the Federation. Although the air around him might burst into flame, he would fall a great way before he himself began to burn, that is, if he burned at all.

So again, I was there. I was with a select group of reporters, authority figures, elected officials, and representatives of various victims' groups when Barbusse was suited up and pushed out the airlock of a shuttle verging on Earth's airspace. There was no ceremony involved, no last rites, no fancy speeches from the Jeffie warden or anything like that. Everybody just wanted it over with as quickly as possible; we all believed that the sooner Barbusse was gone, the sooner mankind could get back to fulfilling our destiny, whatever that was.

How wrong we were.

Like millions of others, I watched Barbusse fall on holovision via the presence of two cameras that followed him on the way down. Like those millions, I felt a grim satisfaction knowing he was plummeting his way toward the Rocky Mountains. Granted, Earth was still a quarantined planet, and certainly its civilization as it now stood had committed various atrocities against the alienable rights of man, but it was still the cradle of life, and somehow it seemed appropriate that the cruelest, most sociopathic enemy of life civilization had ever known would soon go *splat* against her surface.

Which is exactly what happened. Barbusse's suit tore like a water balloon falling from a skyscraper, and Barbusse himself burst like a jellyfish on the moment of impact. Death was instanteousness, naturally, and so, too, was the scattering of his blood cells, his skins, the tissues of his organs, and the chips of his shattered bones.

Which is evidently exactly what he had intended all along.

For Barbusse's death was truly the climax of the performance he had been giving all his life. Unbeknownst to all, and undetected by all the doctors who had examined him during his captivity, Barbusse had infected his body with a nitrogen-based virus capable of wantonly reproducing itself in thin air until it came into contact with an acceptable host. It lived in the host until the host died; and as the virus basically depleted the bloodstream of its ability to process oxygen, that tended to be only a year—which is about three months longer than Barbusse spent in captivity. Once the host died and began decaying, the virus became airborne, and used the energy it had stored to reproduce, and then to reproduce some more, until it came into contact with the next host.

Since an acceptable host was basically any form of mammal above the level of rat on the evolutionary scale, Barbusse's death acted like a poisonous dagger of death plunged straight into the heart of Earth. It was a slow death, slow to spread and slow to act, but it was death all the same.

Within four years all the protected animal life in the Yellowstone National Park was on the verge of extinction, while many human beings had already succumbed to what the people called the Blue Death.

As of this writing, Barbusse has claimed twelve million more victims, with no cure for the malady in sight. Truly, he saved his best performance for last.

THE LAST HOLOSONG OF
CHRISTOPHER LIGHTNING

Jared Lobdell

Dr. Lobdell has worked for a wide variety of magazines as both editor and writer—ranging from *National Review* and *The Agorist Quarterly* to *Extrapolation*. He is the editor of *A Tolkien Compass*, author of *Tolkien's World of the Rings*, and is currently involved in a project for Arkham House that was approved by the late August Derleth. A great admirer of the work of Cordwainer Smith, his story for *Free Space* takes off from there.

It was in the brief happy time when war was an enormous game. To be sure, people were killed, but what are people? Only fingers on the hands of robot generals. Fold your hands the way they do in church or in the old nursery rhyme. Fold your hands in the Sign of the Fish. Here's the church and here's the steeple; open the doors and where are the people? Dead, that's where. Dead in near space.

You know the story, the story of the Jeffies, gray flag, gray shades, pale shades, whiter shades of pale, not pale enough to be white and evil, not dark enough to be black and good, gray people in a gray world, a story of the twenty-first century, or was it the twenty-second? Of course, the story you know isn't true, but it's the best we have and it's famous, so we tell it.

We all know about the black flag of anarchy and the white flag of minarchy. We think we know about the gray flag of minarchy. Or Confederation. Bringing it together. Commonwealth. Confederacy. Even Confederate gray. But the Confederation came apart. The Commonwealth came apart. Everything we know about them is wrong. Everything they knew about themselves was wrong. They didn't bring it together. We can look back and know that now. But we don't.

So we tell the story. The story of Zamoyski, who came first as commander, and Zolkiewski, who came after him, and especially Christopher Lightning, who fought for them both and then fought for himself, and who broke the alliance of the gray flag and the white flag. But the stories tell us also that the alliance was never broken. Zolkiewski and Christopher Lightning broke the alliance by fighting for the gray flag against the black flag, which was what they were supposed to do, and then against the white flag, which was what they were not supposed to do. But the stories tell us also that the gray flag never fought against the white flag. The Commonwealth, the Confederacy (they called themselves after another Confederacy), they were sent to fight against the black flag, and they did.

We have the stories, some of them. We have the holosongs, some of them. But we need someone to interpret the holosongs. A dryasdust. Bone dust. Dust to dust. A robot or a person who will not let the beat of the feet and the heat of the dance and the chance enthrall him. Some things we know because we know them, and some of them are even true. The great ships of the Federation moved in their way, but they could not move at speed against the Spacers, because they could not move at speed against the worlds near a star, which is all the worlds there are but rogue worlds. The small ships of the Spacers moved in their way, but they could not move at speed between the stars: They could only move near them. How could the two meet?

Besides, the Spacers were traders. Make money, not war, was their war cry. It wasn't that they needed the people of the gray flag to fight for them—they would fight for themselves. If the Federation didn't attack them, then they would be about their business, and the business of Spacers was *business*. They sang a grand song, some said a Rand song, an invisible-hand song, everyman for himself, the devil take the hindmost, and sometimes the devil did. Or the foremost. It all depended on which devil.

The leaders of the Federation were politicians, but even so, as the years rolled by, the Federation lived. It did not live very well, and it needed the gray-flag people to fight for it, because only fools or freemen will fight for ideals when ideals are in the hands of politicians. The white-clad Bourbon in the holosong was a politician. The Hungarian and the Swede who came after him were politicians. Of course they broke the oath. What else could they do?

After a while, some of the gray-flag people didn't believe in the marketplace and they didn't believe in politicians. They made the Sign of the Fish and they spoke of community and Commonwealth. They chose their leaders for life by unanimous vote, or maybe they didn't, but there's a fragment of a song that says they did, a fragment so old that it isn't even a holosong. At least, that may be what it says, if it is not merely nonsense, for its language is full of hard words we do not know, with *z*s and *k*s and *c*s. The names of Zamoyski and Zolkiewski seem to be in that language. More than one of the languages of Old Earth made it to the stars. More than one was spoken in the Station.

We don't know how their little ships charged like cavalry of old against the Free Spacers, but they did. We don't know how they came there, when they didn't come from the Nothing-at-All, or even from the Up-and-Out. We're not even sure why they charged, why they fought for the Federation first, or why they went against it afterward.

We know the holosong made about the beginning of the breaking apart, and we see/hear Zamoyski (we think it is Zamoyski), with a great clash of chords, telling someone in a white uniform, like a Prince of the Bourbons on Old Earth, that he must swear to protect freedom, or he will not command even Zamoyski, *si non iurabis non regnabis*. If you will not swear, you will not rule.

Zamoyski is angry, but his anger does not disturb his smile nor change his voice, though the muscles in his eye sockets and his forehead show the strain. The anger is in the chords. Then he climbs into his ship, and the space cavalry follows him to a great charge. We see/hear him singing, but we cannot follow the words. They have a frayed edge, gray edge, under a grave sky. They have a strong edge, song edge, under a brave sky.

There is another holosong we have about the middle part of the business. Zamoyski is old and gray. It is Zolkiewski who climbs into his ship to lead the charge. There is a beat and a cadence, a whirl and a skirl of music. Words of bone beating on skin, given flesh and blood by the beat. We begin to learn what has happened, but we do not learn it all. There are *zaporozhe* Spacers who have joined the Boyars, the breakaway Russian Federationists at New Moscow, and now the word *zaporozhe* beats on our ears. We do not know why the Spacers are fighting for New Moscow, but we know why Zolkiewski is fighting against them all. We hear an echo of a twentieth-century song in the chords, "I will choose free will." We know that he comes out of near space into their sight at New Moscow, and we see their commander stricken, and the walls are flattened by the beat of bone on skin, and New Moscow burns. It is so hot the walls melt. Stone fire, bone fire, bonfire of rejoicing.

The oath of the man in the white uniform was not kept. That we do know. Even books—remember books?—tell us that. There is another holosong. It has no heroes. Zamoyski is caught by the dry drab enturtlement of old age and dies in bed, and Zolkiewski dies even older in the fire of battle. He is not in his ship in a battle of his choice out in near space. He is leading a battered remnant back from a campaign and is nearly home, but he is never to be home, not Manhome, not the Station, not Old Earth. We see/hear an overwhelming force strike out of the sunrise—that is how close they are to Old Earth, there is a sunrise—and the cruel horns and thrumming of ancient instruments out of Old Byzantium, Old Istanbul, are his dirge. Dirge of freedom, scourge of freedom, with him almost dies the courage of freedom. He tried to keep an oath to the oathbreakers, and was broken. But he never broke his oath, nor Zamoyski before him, or Christopher Lightning after.

The night before his last battle, Zolkiewski sent a message to his wife:

"Dear Heart, there is some kind of mutiny brewing here. A few of my pilots are plotting their own damnation by abandoning the Cause, as our former allies have abandoned it. From this betrayal I have barely restrained them. The Enemy will not negotiate and are preparing for a major battle. But do not worry. Even if I die tomorrow, I am old and but little more use to the Commonwealth. See to it that our son, heir to his father's skills, will sharpen them on the Enemy's necks; and if I die, revenge my blood. If that should happen, my dearest, I entrust you with the care and love of my children, and if it is recovered, with the burial of my body, worn out in the service of freedom and the Commonwealth. I commend myself to your prayers and urge our children always to remember the Cause. In the Sign of the Fish, yours unto death, your loving husband."

And what of Christopher Lightning? What and who is he? It is he who is striking the chords, striking the skies, striking the sky's fire, striking the sky's lyre, leading the charge in the battles the others command, leading the charge in the battles he commands, singing the death of the oathkeepers among the gray-flag people, singing the holosongs. And it is he who tells us in his last holosong—or is it not quite the last?—that the man in the white uniform, the man of the white flag, did not keep his oath, nor did the next. They did not keep their oaths to their own and certainly did not keep them to their allies.

They noted their objections, and filed the notes in File 13. They minuted their objections and classified the minutes Top Secret 25 (but there were only twenty-four levels of clearance). They issued their orders, but they were careful not to let anyone see them, lest they might be seen by spies. And with the ancient example of Nixon before them, they certainly did not record them.

We see/hear the last holosong of Christopher Lightning. The song goes *patapan, patapan, patapan,* and the heart goes *patapan, patapan, patapan,* the last great ship-charge goes sweeping, the dance goes leaping. The chance of the dance is death, and the breath of the dance is faith, but there is a cry of agony and a sky of agony, and the dance is over. The lightning strikes, the ships shrivel and go out, and the screen is blank. For a moment we think we have seen the Sign of the Fish, but we do not know when we have seen it. We do not really know if we have seen it. We do know that there is no more to see, no more to know of the story. And we know Christopher Lightning was a great commander.

"Lord Commander, what is the plan of battle?"

"We will charge in formation and drive them from near space."

"But surely they will be prepared for our charge. Always in the past that has been our plan, and they will expect it to be our plan now. With respect, sir, perhaps we should change our tactics. I believe the time is right for a different plan, and surely we have the skill to carry out a different plan."

"That is true, and the Enemy know it is true."

"Well, then?"

"Then they will expect us to change our tactics. So we will fool them by doing as we have always done. Besides, it is true that we have the skill to do something different, but there is more joy in the old. 'Change nothing old, do nothing new, and keep the taxes low.' "

"But the enemy know that saying also."

"They have heard it, but they do not know it. Do they keep the taxes low? Do they remain faithful to the old truth, to the old oath? No, they go whoring after the new. So will we not."

And they did not.

That is from what we call the last holosong of Christopher Lightning. The screen went blank when the ships flickered out and the holosong was over, so no one went on watching the screen.

Then one day a child was playing, and the officer of the day at the gravity-wave transceiver was distracted by the noisomeness of the latest piece of propaganda, and no one turned the HD player off. A strange thing happened, a change thing happened. There was a curtain call. An encore finale. Had it been there all the time?

The old twentieth-century song is in the music. We hear some of its words. "If you choose not to decide, you still have made a choice." There are other words, too, from other twentieth-century songs, but perhaps they do not matter. Perhaps the encore does not matter. Perhaps it did not happen.

But there is Christopher Lightning, on the edge of the Up-and-Out, where only the FTL ships went, not the cavalry warships of the great gray fleet of the small gray flag. We think he is at the Station, or perhaps it is a far station. We do not know why he is on the edge of the Up-and-Out. He never went into it. On that the stories and the songs, the holosongs and even the books agree. Zamoyski never went into it. Zolkiewski never went into it. Christopher Lightning never went into it. His second-in-command is speaking:

"It is not our custom, Lord Commander, to go into Far Space."

"But we can, if we must."

"It is not within our capability to go into Deep Space."

"I do not know that. I only know that we have not, and I have been told from my childhood that we cannot. My father, the Orphan Nicholas, told me that. He also told me that we might someday have to try. Perhaps this is that day."

"Why now?"

"I have had a vision. I have heard the Black of the great ships like eagles, and the Red of the blood, and the Gold of the horns. I have seen the scream of the eagles and the beat of the blood and the sound of the horns on the other side of deep space. And I know it is the Time."

He stands thirsting for justice, and hoping that justice is not merely a fancy word for revenge. We see his hands tighten, and his lips are smiling something that may be a smile. He stands re-membering those who have gone before and kept their oath to the oathbreakers. He sees in his mind, and we see/hear in the holosong, the encore, how those who fight together are a community. We catch an echo of an ancient oration we do not know, but he knew, where someone has said this, thought we do not know what else he said. Or who and when he was, or even if he was. But these are the words, these are the words of Christopher Lightning to his men, though they were another's words before:

"It is not fitting that what we have won by battle and our father's blood should become merely the source of our daily bread; it would be better to sell it and give all to the poor than to have waged war for any reason other than the fellowship of those who wage it."

We see the hands relax again, stiffen again at his side, and he steps forward, Christopher Lightning steps forward, into the gray that turns to blue, into the blue that turns to liquor, stronger than drink, wilder than music, fermented with the reds of love and death, proclaimed with the golden-noted horns. And then the black of dark. We see all the things that men have ever thought they saw, but it is we who really see them, or is it? We know that Christopher Lightning sees them, or does he? We see the phosphorescence singing and the tides in drunkspace like aurochs clawing their way out of the ocean, crossing a red sea, crossing a dead sea, crossing a sped sea, the hooves beating the reefs. We see years in the blink of an eye, and we see the eye that blinks the years, and the horizon is a great waterfall, and over it wash the bodies of the people drowned in space, in drunkspace, through archipelagoes of stars.

Christopher Lightning is talking to his second-in-command, Jan Karl. They are neither of them well pleased. Commander Lightning speaks in calm anger: "Those are my orders, sir."

"With respect, sir, you are acting like a doomed man, and you are dooming us and the Cause."

"We do what we must."

"No, sir, we do what we choose. At least I do. We have free will. At least I do."

"We have a destiny, and this is our destiny. Oh, we can try to evade it. We can compromise. We can gradually give way here and there, till we have nothing more to give. I choose not to: That is my free choice. You may do as you will, you may squirm and twist and try to make terms with evil: I will not."

"With respect, sir, I do not call it making terms with evil. I call it common sense. More than that, I call it wisdom. And 'a little bit of wisdom rules the world.' "

"You call it. You call it. No, Jan Karl, we are not doing the calling. It calls us. Freedom calls us. We can choose not to answer. We can choose not to hear. But we cannot choose whether we are called."

"Sir, are you ordering us to die for a call you hear, and we do not?"

"I give no such order. You are free born, not a slave. I am your commander, not your master. If you come with me, I command you, but I do not order you to come. If you stay behind, you may live in faithlessness and die like a cat in an alley: That is your choice."

Jan Karl turns angrily on his heel. He enters his ship, the *Zamosc,* and readies his ship for liftoff. The gray banner has turned to white and red, red cross on white field, knight field, red-cross knight, reversed field, cursed field, field of battle. The rumble of long-remembered thunder and streaks of lightning split the skies! We have seen a fleet of old gray cavalry ships, straining upon their starts. The sky clears its throat. *Pr'k.* The thunder rolls. *n-n-n-n-n-n-n-n.* Rolls away into the distance. And again and again. *Pr'k-nnnnnnnn, Pr'k-nnnnnnnn, Pr'k-nnnnnnnnn.* The ships are taking off. Far space is very far away. Deep space is impossibly far away. These are not family ships like those the Spacers sent out two centuries ago. Not one of Christopher Lightning's men will live to reach the stars if they take off. No new generations will be born on these ships. This is a charge to death. At least, that is what comes to us through the song.

One by one the ships lift off, the *Zamosc* in the van. Ship after ship takes off, with her battle thunder and flame. They are old ships, gray ships, small ships, ships that might have lifted off from

Canaveral before there was the Federation. Last of all, but gray and small no more, great and red and white in the holosong, is the *Zolkiew*, Christopher Lightning in command. He sings the sore death, the soared death, the war death that came, a game no more; sings the fought field, the shield taut and the sword bought with death; sings till the bored breath of the engines of man that has filled and battered the hard world is stilled.

The last of the thunder lingers. In formation, winking like fireflies in our mind, the cavalry ships begin their last charge, against nothing . . . through near space, into drunkspace, into Free Space that the oathbreakers never captured and the Spacers have forsaken. The fireflies wink out. We see/hear the gold and the red and the black, we know they are Christopher Lightning's colors, and we know it is gold for the past, red for the present, black for the future.

In his cabin, we see/hear that Christopher Lightning is singing, softly, through teeth almost clenched. We catch a few lines of song.

"You can choose a ready guide
In some celestial voice.
If you choose not to decide,
You still have made a choice.
You can choose from phantom fear
And kindness that can kill;
I will choose a path that's clear:
I will choose free will."

The screen darkens, then goes milky white, then blank. The music dims. There is a last skirl of something like bagpipes. There is a last beat of something like a drum. Once again, we do not quite see, but seem to have seen, the Sign of the Fish. The holosong is over.

This time there is no encore. If there ever was.

Between Shepherds and Kings

John Barnes

The man who gave us *Orbital Resonance, Mother of Storms,* and *Kaleidoscope Century* is a writer who *thinks* before he puts quill to parchment, or depresses a key on his computer. With a background as a computer-simulations expert and interests ranging from Shakespeare to semiotics, he will not let go of an idea until he has given it thorough mastication. Here he comes up with the perfect last story to *Free Space*—a Malzbergian romp through the meadows of metafiction. Oh, yeah!

> "When we are tired, we are attacked by ideas we conquered long ago."
> —*Nietzsche*

The day the invitation came for the *Free Space* anthology, Ray Terani left it on his kitchen table, where it stayed for months. That, he thinks, was his real undoing. Unfortunately it was still sitting there, unopened, this afternoon when Dafydd and Brad dropped in on him, and since he had told them before that he "loved the concept" and was "almost done" with the story, now he's out of stalling room. He'll probably have to write the sucker within the next day.

Not that having read the guidelines would make much difference. Ray is a pro, one of those guys that people call to fill out an anthology in a hurry or to whack out a cheapie novel to fill a hole in a publishing schedule. And he knows perfectly well that although world-building detail changes, all hard SF is basically the same. Memorize a dozen details and usually you're ready to go; as he sits here with the sheet in front of him and Brad trying to explain it, he's already memorized most of the details he will need.

Ray has been arguing in a quiet sort of way with Dafydd and Brad, not so much about the story that he's going to write—and he will write it, make no mistake of that, not just out of friendship or for the money, neither of which is reason enough to keep going on a story, but because he has something to say, he thinks. The argument is more about whether it's possible to write the story Ray wants to write; Ray is saying he can't figure out how, and that it's impossible to figure out how, while they're trying to prove to him that the problem can be solved and the story can be written.

Ray is only mildly handicapped by the embarrassment of being caught not having even opened the guidelines. Embarrassment rarely even slows him down. He just isn't embarrassed by the long delay he has caused by promising them a story and then not delivering, nor even by the way in which other people waiting for his story are being embarrassed by him.

Nothing, after all, could be as embarrassing as having a story in a book like this in the first place, he thinks, as Dafydd elaborates on some point or other with footnotes by Brad, *and the whole reason I want a story in it is because it's embarrassing. Because it will make all my left-wing friends go "Yuck, how could you be published in this?" And by doing that I won't feel like I've sold out intellectually to them, but since it's a very lefty idea, I won't feel like I sold out to Dafydd and Brad either. I can feel like I'm really my own person, at the center of my complex set of relationships.*

Ray prides himself on his complexity.

As Ray listens to Dafydd, he opens another beer, quietly saying to himself that he's really just having all this beer to relax his damned aching back. He spent the morning running—one way to stay off beer till afternoon, something he's been trying to do—and there must be something wrong with his running shoes because after every step after the first mile, Ray had a miserable stabbing pain in the middle of his back, right at the small, right where each little shock seemed to merge with each other shock.

Maybe the beer will even relax him enough to write his idea into a story.

Not likely though, because if it were going to help it should have already. Right now he's so relaxed he's practically comatose. The problem has been all along that the idea won't go into a story. He can feel in his bones that it won't.

While he sits there, sinking into the feeling that this job can't be done, half another beer goes down, though he notes that neither of the other guys has taken more than a sip. Well, they're talking more than he is, after all. Ray's mostly listening. Several times he has raised a point or two only to be told that the point was irrational; if he felt that way, he shouldn't.

He draws a big smiley face with his finger in the little puddle of beer on his kitchen countertop. He'll have to clean up before Leslie comes over this evening.

He starts his mental process to get the story done. He imagines space. What was called outer space till we got there. Cold, empty, lonely, vast, more clichés, and more clichés.

He visualizes the usual muscular white American man (UMWAM, he abbreviates it) posturing in front of that huge and lonely backdrop. The backdrop is *there* for the UMWAM to posture against. Sometimes the usual muscular white American men have breasts and vaginas, or dark skins, or for that matter breathe methane and live on pure thought energy, but they are still UMWAMs. They brag about achievements and all that, hey, they think the purpose of freedom is so that achievement can happen, but what they do isn't really about achievement, it's about that moment of standing against the stars.

And why do they stand against the stars? Always up close, so they won't look so tiny against all the blank that's really there. Space is 99.999 . . . percent empty, with so many nines in that last string that the last digits wouldn't be distinguishable from the error in most experiments. All that empty black indifferent clichéd void. The realer you write it the scarier it gets; mostly there's nothing at all in the universe, and the little that there is, is a thin scum sticking to the immense dark vacuum. The way a cliff without a guardrail attracts you and scares you at the same time, that void is what pulls the reader toward hard SF and what will scare him away if you're not careful.

So you stick an UMWAM between the void and the reader. You have to make that UMWAM stand close so that he subtends a lot of visual angle. Even then the lightless uncaring vacancy just kind of leaks in around the UMWAM, so you never really feel safe.

Oh, well. Ray gets up and gets another round of beers out of the fridge. He's drinking about three to Brad's two. Dafydd is sticking to Diet Coke. Have to start sobering up in about an hour; gotta be straight for Leslie. Straight and ideally hard. She's starting to suspect, a little, that maybe he isn't all that turned on by her, and he's not, and furthermore she suspects that maybe he doesn't like her much, and he doesn't, and Ray can't have that because he's convinced she needs him. He likes touching her body, but the truth is her age lines bother him, he hates all the excess makeup, the heavy tan seems weird to him, her bleached-blond hair is coarse and rough to his touch, and he wishes he could just be around her and take care of things for her, and he didn't have to listen to her or have sex with her.

Ray also prides himself on his honesty.

The next step in getting this story to be a story, Ray thinks, is to give the UMWAM a name, a job, and something that goes wrong with the job. Ray can't quite concentrate enough to do that so he tells Dafydd and Brad that they've got to hear a new CD he just got, even though he didn't think much of it, just so he can slap it on and that way they'll be quiet while he thinks.

Story must have hero. Hero must have problem. Hero must solve problem.

Problem is that for the *Free Space* anthology, the problem is supposed to be about freedom, and control, and all that, in a star-faring future.

And that's what's silly. Freedom *is* the problem. Control *is* the problem. And there will be no starfaring future.

Start again. Okay, we want hero to learn better. Heinlein said that, Brunner explained it, must be true. Only three kinds of stories, *one:* boy meets girl, *two:* brave little tailor, *three:* man who learns better. If our boy is a freedom-obsessed UMWAM With A Problem and he is introduced to a girl who has no freedom neurosis, people will just agree with the UMWAM, even if the girl wins on logic and on story outcome; no challenge to the damn stupid idea. Brave little tailor *defines* Hero With A Problem and that plotline really requires freedom; if the brave little tailor doesn't really choose to carry Sauron's Ring to the top of the glass hill where he can shoot it out with Grendel at the OK Corral, well, then why does he deserve to get to be a swan at the end? No freedom no hero. . . . So no boy meets girl and no brave little tailor.

Man who learns better it is.

Ray's pretty drunk now—one of many reasons Brad and Dafydd are his friends is that they're very tolerant of a fat balding slob whose sentences often wander far away into the ether. Nobody who wasn't could be Ray's friend. But he outlines his argument, and Brad listens, and Dafydd picks through the logic, and then Brad sums up for Dafydd, and by the time they're done, they've agreed that he should write about a man who learns better, and another beer is gone.

One of them, maybe Ray himself, suggests that the UMWAM should be from a warship, no a privateer. . . . Ray begins to giggle. He was trying to think of something innovative and here he is back with every damned cliché of historical romance. Mighty ships between the stars, so huge and mighty that they seem to challenge that vast empty dark cliché, freighters and merchantmen and battleships and a huge array of boy toys. And now *privateering?* An institution extinct on our world for generations, because it fundamentally didn't work once mass democracy and the steam engine came in, is supposed to get revived in the era of electronic democracy and FTL?

Stop giggling, Ray tells himself. The other two aren't as drunk as he is and maybe he didn't explain to them clearly enough why the privateer is such a silly idea. Maybe even if he were sober he couldn't. Maybe he isn't trying.

Nonetheless the UMWAM is a privateer, all the same. It will make the story work. When the story works the idea will get into it comfortably. Once the idea is in it comfortably, the story can get written. Better yet, once it's comfortable in there people can read the story, pretend they're thinking about the idea, and feel nice and safe, protected from the big bad idea.

So the UMWAM builds a house of bricks to keep the big bad idea away.

No. This isn't that kind of story. The mighty UMWAM and Stander Against the Stars is a privateer out there in Capitalist Space. Out robbing bad-guy spaceships. Teaching them all about freedom by taking their cargo for free and forcing their crews into freedom. Ray is having a lot of trouble feeling attracted to the UMWAM at this point, and he tries to say so, but since he started talking over the CD, so did Dafydd and Brad, and now they're all really loud, and he can't seem to form the idea he wants to say, that a privateer is the wrong hero, that at least he can start his UMWAM off in something less sleazy than being a hired gun for the state—that's the phrase, it got Dafydd nodding along—

Maybe, Ray thinks, *he could write from the viewpoint of the merchant carrying the goods?*

The phone rings. Mercifully Brad kills the CD; Ray staggers into the bedroom, through the corny little mock-Mexican archway, slipping on the cruddy hardwood floor. Gotta clean this place someday. Leslie would like that. Hell, Ray would like that. But when you get up at noon to write and knock off at six and start drinking or hanging with the guys or go out with Leslie, well, when is there time to clean? He hears his mother saying, *"So for the love of God, Ray," get a maid,"* in his mind's ear, just before he picks up the phone and discovers it's her. She stole a quarter from a nurse's purse or something and has phoned him again; she wants to ask him about something from when he was a kid, some ball game or something his dad (now six years dead) took him to, how his first wife (divorced seventeen years ago) is doing and does she know about his second (divorced five years ago), whether Ray could get some of her clothes for her from her house (sold three years ago), and all that. Finally after ten minutes he hears the nurse come up behind his mother and say that she has to get back to the area where she is allowed to be, and his mother says, "I have to go now, Ray-ee."

Ray-ee. Always cracked him up that she could make a diminutive out of that.

"Ray-ee," she says, "I haven't said this before but you know I can tell when you're drunk. And you are. And it's working hours, not drinking time at all. Ray-ee, I love you and you know you were raised better than that."

"I love you, too, Mom," he says, ashamed to say it in front of Dafydd and Brad, infuriated at himself for being ashamed. He catches them looking away, and he knows that hearing him go through this bothered them, and he knows they're still his friends and they're there with him. Suddenly he loves them very much, too, or is the love coming out of the beer bottle? Does it matter? "Bye," he adds.

"Bye, Ray-ee. Come see me," his mother says, and then the phone slams down. Probably the nurse grabbed it out of her hand and did that. Ray thinks of the novel, neglected in the next room while he talks with his friends, his third horror quickie this year and the one that will pay for taxes and Christmas. He decides that since the Mangler has to get someone in the next chapter, it will be a nurse from an old folk's home, a cruel nurse, a nurse that the Mangler will cut the breasts off of and then force them into her throat till she chokes. *Great image,* he thinks, and walks into the other room and scribbles a note to himself. His friends put up with that, too. He loves them. He really is going to write a great story for

Free Space one way or another, as a reward to them for being such great guys.

When he gets back out of his bedroom they have moved to his living room; silently Dafydd hands him the guidelines, again, and goes back to arguing some picky point with Brad. Ray can't follow the thread of what they are talking about with his head this way, so he sits down in his favorite armchair, noting that they've opened a beer and set it there for him, and thinks about the whole problem some more.

So the UMWAM works on a privateer ship. He doesn't have to be the captain or anything, it can be just his job; he can be kind of morally unaware at the beginning of the story and thus it will be easier for him to learn better. From somebody on the merchant ship they capture. The merchant whose goods the privateers are going to take—merchant? goods?

That was the question he had almost thought of before. *What* merchant? *What* goods? The only reason there could be a merchant with goods in this story is because the guidelines have been set up to create them; there's nothing less natural than a free market, so there has to be all sorts of jiggering with physics to make a free market happen as anything other than a brief historical accident. They had to come up with a magic dingus to prevent molecular-computer technology because if stuff got too abundant, capitalism would collapse—markets run on scarcity. They had to come up with FTL to get to the stars at all and then make their FTL even less plausible for there to be interstellar trade.

There's an energy associated with a body in orbit around one star, and an energy associated with a body in orbit around another star, and to get between them, there's a transition energy—the difference between the two that somehow has to be made up, out of fuel carried on the ship or some other source. That magic dingus in their FTL must be making use of at least as much energy as the transition energy (probably more, if entropy gets into it). A little doodling with plain old $E=mc^2$ shows that whatever you're shipping, it would be cheaper to stay home and transmute the same mass, by a series of nuclear fusions, out of hydrogen. With energy sources of the magnitude needed to get from star to star, why not just stay home and make the damned stuff yourself, whatever it might be?

Ray's gaze crawls down the page in front of him. No explanation offered in the guidelines. Maybe the magic wish-fulfillment dingus they've made up takes advantage of some kind of low energy of transition in some bogus other dimension between points. . . . But if the energy of transition, star to star, is so low in that dimension, wouldn't quantum effects dictate that a lot of stuff would be constantly appearing and disappearing in space, enough to be detectable?

Back out of all such considerations, as quickly as you can, if you want to write hard SF. Thinking about that kind of thing leads to noticing the puppeteer pulling the strings, seeing the man behind the curtain, noticing that the stars are tiny holes in thick black felt hanging forty feet away in a dark space. *Don't* see that. You can't write about freedom if you start noticing unfreedom, it might lead to awkward questions, and there's a story to get done.

Ray thinks, *I will get over this. I will start my story now, in my head, while my friends argue, and then when they go I will write a page or two, then shower and change for my date with Leslie.*

The privateer captures a merchant ship—no, better, a mid-twenty-first-century generation ship, a slow-moving space colony intended to get to its destination across a period of many generations. And the people on that ship stopped worrying about getting to the destination a long time ago, because living anywhere other than the ship no longer seemed attractive. It no longer seemed attractive because on the ship there is now a unique society. One without freedom or control, one that is no longer haunted by one and obsessed by the other (or vice versa).

Ray, thinking the story, there in the armchair in his living room, looks at that idea and says, *Okay, but now it has to be entertaining, and that means my UMWAM With A Problem will have to be standing somewhere physical, so that I can describe his exact experiences mo-*

ment to moment and the happy reader can hallucinate being there,
thereby ignoring more of the words and visualizing more of what the
reader wants. Well, then, let's put this UMWAM at the helm, because
surely ships have helms.

Ray pauses a long time trying to think of what controls would
be on such a helm. A steering wheel seems singularly inappropri-
ate, as does a throttle, a stick, or a tiller.

So what exactly does the control panel on a ship—that works
on a physical principle made up entirely to preserve capitalism far
beyond any point in history when it is possible for it to exist—look
like? Well, don't put him at the helm. Put him in a boarding party.

Stop giggling at FTL ships with boarding parties. The UMWAM's
in the boarding party because he's not high enough ranking to ring the
bells, he has too much experience to shovel the coal, and he doesn't have
the skill to trim the sails, okay? Ray says to himself, angry at the way
that he keeps blocking instead of flowing on this. *And give the poor*
bastard a name. He's a finagled UMWAM. Finn Agled Umwam. Finn
Agledum Wam. Finn Edumwa. Good enough. He's Finn Edumwa.

Well, great, then, so the privateer takes over this old generation
ship and sends it off on a course where a prize-claim party can pick
it up later. So Finn Edumwa is left there to force the people on the
generation ship to follow orders. Finn is now the absolute monarch
over all these people who have neither the concept of freedom nor
of control. What concept do they have instead? Wrong question.
What do non-Japanese have instead of *giri* and *gimu?* What did people fall into before romantic love? Where is your lap while you are
standing up? What is the point of this thought?

Ray sighs, thinking hard. Dafydd asks him hopefully if he has
an idea, and Ray says that he does. His idea is that tonight he will
talk with Leslie about getting her into real-estate school. Lots of
fortyish bimbos do well in real estate. Or at least lots of them are
in it. And he'll take her someplace and get her a nice dinner. He
hasn't taken her out in public in a couple of weeks and he knows
she's afraid that he doesn't want to be seen with her, when the truth
is, he doesn't want to have people realize that he no longer cares

what he's seen with. And it's not her fading tarted-up beauty, either, it's the huge gobs of random-word assemblages that pass for her conversation, the high-speed spew of self-centered psychobabble . . . all the stuff that gives away the sad fact that Ray Terani no longer listens to the women he dates, he just wants to cuddle and fuck and not be alone.

Some kind of signal passes between his friends, and Dafydd and Brad excuse themselves and head out the door, into the LA sunlight, down the peeling-painted steps to the steep little driveway and their cars. They want to leave him alone so he will be able to write his story.

Ray sits down and types eight fast paragraphs of violence, the boarding of the generation ship, the seizure and securing (good place to work in awesome details like that a generation ship would have to be kilometers long). Then he hits the point where he has Finn meeting a beautiful girl who is willing to take a job as his assistant during the long six months until the tow truck—uh, the FTL to tow the prize—arrives.

Finn is now the undisputed monarch of a generation ship with, oh, say, four thousand people on an indefinite voyage to nowhere. They don't have the idea of freedom, so they won't rebel. They don't have the idea of control, so they won't obey. They ignore him. He threatens their lives. They do what he says till his back is turned. He takes hostages. That will get the next six pages done, and with room to spare for Finn to argue with the girl and fall in love with her.

Dumb little irony. So the guy from the freedom-side ship is going to end up a tyrant. *That doesn't get me out of freedom and control, does it?* Ray thinks. It explains how freedom and control could be created in an environment without them—and thus saves Ray from describing that environment. Which was the whole point in the first place.

Maybe Finn should be converted to their way of thinking.

What was that way of thinking? Oh, yeah. The one that can't be described.

Maybe Ray is having all this trouble because Finn comes from the "freedom" side of that dichotomy.

Okay, so make him from the controlling side. Not the Federation, they're too pure a case. Let him be a—what's the silly term? A Jeffie. A New Confederate. Strange that someone would pick as an emblem for freedom a name that most of the possible readers associate with slavery (or loudly pretend that they don't associate with slavery). As if that weren't really the whole purpose anyway.

The defenders of freedom always tell you that what matters is freedom for ideas that are hated; everything else is regarded as too easy or trivial. Sort of the cold shower approach to freedom; you must have freedom so that you can listen to ideas that you don't like.

"If nobody objects," the freedom addicts say, "you don't need freedom."

But, Ray thinks—and he must remember this to annoy Dafydd with—that logically implies that if you do need freedom it's because somebody wants to do something objectionable. His fingers fly over the keys:

"This is why anyone who spends a lot of time talking about freedom—Sophocles, Socrates, Kleon, Seneca, Hobbes, Locke, Rousseau, Paine, Jefferson, Danton, Marat, Proudhon, Marx—is an obnoxious pain in the ass with no social skills. Their greatest fear is that someone might make them pay for their random assaults on people around them; they want to be free, meaning that they want it to be costless for them to annoy others. Freedom is the ability to hurt without being hurt, and as such is the ultimate free lunch."

Ray decides that's a manifesto and takes it out of the story. If you want to send a union, call a messy westerner, or something. Besides Ray's still a little too drunk to know whether or not he agrees with what he's written.

Drunk and getting horny—the creative process does that—and that's a good thing, too, because it seems to reassure Leslie if Ray sometimes makes really crude passes at her the moment she comes in the door, like it proves she's attractive rather than that he's just horny. Or maybe getting horny this way is his way of loving the poor deluded aging tart. He can't decide that either. He really isn't functioning too well mentally—might as well write, then. No need to be functional to write this stuff.

So, then, Ray will grant them that the name, the New Confederates, works for this future, because these are the new people who demand the freedom to rob and enslave whoever they can.

So if Finn is a Jeffie, a New Confederate, a freedom fraud, whatever, the question is, is he really, at his core, true to his espoused principles—or to his society's actual behavior? A nineteenth-century white plantation owner could be either really a believer in all the liberty stuff (but then why hadn't he manumitted the slaves?) or in what he was actually doing (which was more usual). So does Finn *really* believe in freedom or order? He's got to be the man who learns better, but which of the positions can learn better, better? Could a control freak learn to see reasons to just let things go by? Could a freedom addict learn to see freedom as a cause of unnecessary pain? *And could either of them learn to change into something besides each other?*

Well, now, that's what the story is about. And that's why Ray has sat here half an hour staring at the screen.

His mind drifts; idly, he strokes his half-erection. He'll do Leslie as soon as she gets here; she likes to think he likes her that much that way. He needs it anyway. And tomorrow he'll drive out and see Mom, third time this week, but it seems to cheer her so much. Tonight after he's had sex with Leslie, right there in the front hall, as fast and as hard as he can because he's scared to death that he'll start to look at her overtanned skin and cracking makeup and lose his erection, she'll smooth her dress back down and they'll go out for dinner, instead of Chinese and videos here, and he'll let her babble on about being actuated and crystals and what some producer who almost cast her said fifteen years ago. And then they'll share his bed and he'll wake up not lonely and feeling OK; tomorrow that should be good for a day without beer, and if he's sober he can go see Mom without feeling ashamed (though after his visit to her usually he'll drink and cry a while).

The thing he wants to say is, he's not choosing to do these things, these are what he is. At the end of *Barbarella,* the angel saves the bad girl as well as Barbarella, and when Barbarella complains, he explains, "An angel does not love. An angel is love." The Sufi say you can spend only what's in your purse. Ray doesn't choose, he just takes care of it, does what he can for people, even when his feelings really aren't up to it. Nor do the people he does these things for force him to do them. They don't have that much power over his life. If he dumped Leslie he'd forget her by next month; when Mom dies he'll be sad but really she was gone long ago, the wrinkled thing in perpetual care is a stray wandering whispering bag of memories from the far past. The chains that hold him are not even threads.

He is not forced, he does not choose. That's what he wanted to tell his friends, he thinks, and even though it means still being a little drunk when Leslie gets here, he goes to the fridge, opens one more beer, sits back down, and looks into the screen. It is blank, blank as the real sky, blanker than the crowded space of *Free Space*—the screen, defined as a screen, contains nothing at all, just as the universe, defined as a place for matter and energy, contains almost nothing.

Ray stares into that bottomless cliché, gaping void, blankness, and imagines a ship, immense and silent, slipping through it faster than he could see or think. Then he tries to think of a place where no one expects him to obey stern freedom, no one expects him to fit into a cold and lonely slot in an all-embracing order. He stares and stares but he just can't see it, not yet.

Free at Last

Robert Anton Wilson

There is only one Robert Anton Wilson. Coauthor with the late Robert Shea of the *Illuminatus!* books, and author of unforgettable works like *Masks of the Illuminati*, "The Schroedinger's Cat Trilogy," *The Earth Will Shake*, and *Wilhelm Reich in Hell*, Wilson is a long-time practitioner of what he preaches. The Magus Wilson doesn't want to be anyone's guru; the inner light is for you to be free. I couldn't think of anyone more appropriate to slip one last poem into this book. And let's not forget the years he spent working with his friend, the late Timothy Leary, on S.M.I.L.E. (Space Migration, Intelligence Increase, Life Extension).

Three nails and two crossed sticks,
A blood-soaked cult;
    an iron rod—
The number of a man is 666,
Ape no more
    but dancing God.

Your day is done,
    O skull beneath the skin,
Wrinkled mummy-Christ of eyeless sockets:

> Now we dare the great
>   Promethean sin
> And bring fire back to heaven
>   on our rockets.